THE BLUE MAGE

BOOK TWO OF THE **TEMPERED SOUL** SERIES

To Mike

find your magic!

J de Lancey

THE BLUE MAGE

This is a work of fiction. Names, characters, places, and incidents either are the product of the author's imagination or are used fictitiously. Any resemblance to actual persons, living or dead, events, or locales is entirely coincidental.

Cover Design: Thea Magerand
Interior Illustrations: Thea Magerand
Editing: Lesley Jones | Natalia Leigh
Book Design and Typesetting: Enchanted Ink Publishing

ISBN: 978-1-7399566-3-9 (E-book)
ISBN: 978-1-7399566-2-2 (Paperback)

Thank you for your support of the author's rights.

WWW.JODELANCEY.COM

For Dave May,

Without you there would have been no Crystal Shore,
and there certainly wouldn't have been a Blue Mage.

Thank you xxx

KILLIAN O'SHEA

'I COULD HAVE HELPED HIM, BUT I DIDN'T.'

CAPTAIN LILY ROTHBONE

'I KNOW I'M DIFFICULT, BUT THAT'S WHY YOU LOVE ME.'

SASHA

'I CAN'T KEEP RUNNING.
I KNOW WHAT I NEED,
WHAT I WANT.'

RAVEN

'YOU CAN KEEP A SECRET,
CAN'T YOU?'

TOM GAINSBOROUGH

'I'M GONNA FIND MY KINGDOM AND RULE IT LIKE I'M SUPPOSED TO.'

NEDI 'NEDGE' ORSELLI

'OH, YOU'RE A RARE ONE, EH?'

NESTA

'ONCE YOU GO IN, THERE IS NO TURNING BACK. YOU FINISH, OR YOU DIE. DO YOU UNDERSTAND?'

REN THORNCLIFFE

'HE'S THE ONLY PERSON I HAVE IN THE WORLD, AND . . . AND I'M WORRIED WE'LL BE TOO LATE.'

PROLOGUE

Sasha held a small glass jar before her. She turned it over in her hands for her entranced audience to see.

'This vessel,' she said as they gawped at the empty jar, 'contains a clear gas called nomalus.' She gave it a shake as if to prove there really was something inside and cocked her head to the right. 'If you listen carefully, you can sometimes hear it breathe.'

She grinned as she casually leant against the small wooden table behind her, which housed her tools of the trade – empty tins, empty jars, tarnished spoons, a tattered pack of cards, useless chunks of metal and pots of dyed chalk dust.

'You wouldn't believe how many people have never even heard of it.' She jumped back to sit on the table. 'A couple of nights ago, I was in this real backwater village – now, I'm talking real back of beyond, buck-toothed, bug-eyed, your mother's your brother.' She glanced at her buck-toothed, vacant-eyed crowd. 'Not like you lot here.' She swept her free hand before her. 'This is the pinnacle of sophisticated village life.'

She breathed deeply. Despite being outside and surrounded by trees, she could still smell the unwashed reek of her audience. Owls hooted from the branches above, and she cast her gaze skyward. Soft yellow light encircled a full crisp moon, and a shooting star shot across the dark sky, its silver trail melting into the night. Lucky, or unlucky? With a shrug, Sasha focused her attention back on her audience.

'They were the epitome of the brainless inbreeding villager, and their stench would put any pig to shame. I don't know if they all worked as tanners or shit-shovellers or what – I didn't stop to ask. I did my show and left. They were real dirty, filthy lumps of scum, not like you lot at all, no.' She pulled one of her knees up and eyed her audience over it. 'Anyway, I digress. The point I was trying to emphasise is they were so backward, so slow, not a single one of them had heard of nomalus gas.' Sasha huffed and pinched the bridge of her nose. 'Now to me, that really is the peak of stupidity.'

A ripple of agreement ran through her bemused crowd.

Sasha smiled. To her it was a patronising scorn-laden smile. To them it would be friendly and warm, like she was welcoming them onto her level. She practised that smile often.

'Now that we've established that you lot are not a bunch of dribbling lack-wits who wouldn't know which end of a fork to use, we can move on.' She set the jar down and peeled the lid from another before plucking out a small fragment of metal. 'As we all know, because we are a collective wealth of aptitude, nomalus on its own is completely innocuous, as harmless as a summer breeze. Yet if I add this piece of metal to the jar,' she continued, her voice growing low and mysterious, 'I will create a living storm.'

'Bullshit!' shouted a burly heckler from within the crowd, shattering the delusion of intelligence.

Sasha lifted her head and cocked an eyebrow at the man. 'No,' she said politely, 'a living storm. Watch carefully.'

She pulled a pair of dark-tinted goggles over her eyes, and before anyone else could interject, she dropped the metal into the jar with a clink. It immediately crackled with lightning. She opened her mouth for dramatic effect and wrestled with the lid as she screwed it back on. Slipping off the table, she held the jar aloft before the rows of astonished faces.

She cleared her throat. 'I give you . . . a storm in a jar!'

A gasp of disbelief ran through the crowd, lightly interspersed with nervous applause. As Sasha graciously bowed, the jar flashed brighter and shook in her hands. The tiny lightning forks inside became more violent, as though they were fighting to get out. She pulled the jar close to her chest as if she were somehow trying to contain it. She looked from the jar to her audience and just had time to flash them a meticulously crafted expression of terror before the jar exploded in a blinding-white tangle of lightning.

A great clap of thunder rolled through the clearing, followed by an ominous silence as the villagers looked at the patch of smouldering earth that had once been the travelling trickster.

'Is she dead?' squeaked a young girl.

'Won't have to pay 'er now,' grunted the earlier heckler.

'Won't you?' Sasha sat on a thick oak branch above them. The metal frames of her goggles coursed with lightning that beamed down on the crowd, eerily illuminating the clearing. This was always her favourite part of her show. 'Do you know what happened to the last village who didn't pay?'

Silence.

'The next day it was burned to cinders by a freak storm. I say freak because there wasn't any rain, only lightning. Funny, that.' She paused to allow her words to take effect. 'Children were roasted in their sleep. Grown men sobbed and screamed as their skin bubbled and cracked. Women howled in agony as their bodies disintegrated. All that remained in the morning was ash, bone and scorched earth.' Sasha covered her goggles, and she melted away into the darkness of the night.

Panicked murmurs shot through the villagers as they desperately fumbled in their pockets. When she heard the inevitable chink of coins, Sasha lit herself up again.

'Of course, that could have been mere coincidence. They were, after all, a village of shit-bathing scumbags, not like the classy types I see here.' The ghostly light emanating from her did nothing to soothe the fear she'd effortlessly sown into her crowd, and to her delight, the money piled up. 'But you wouldn't want to risk it, would you?'

Once the last of her victims had left, Sasha swung down from the tree to investigate their generosity. She pulled her goggles down and grinned as she ran her hand over the pile of cold coins. Adding that part about roasting children had certainly increased her income. She pulled her bag from under the table and set about packing away the tools of her trade.

Soon, perhaps in the next year or so, she would finally have got enough money together to leave Vermor. It would disrupt her lover's life, but they'd talked about it for hours, days and weeks, and both had drawn the same conclusion: leaving was Sasha's only option. It was the only way for her to be safe. The laws of the land wanted her dead for existing, and running and hiding all the time was exhausting. She couldn't hide who she was. Not all the time. Magic to her was as natural as breathing was to all living creatures.

Her fingers paused over one of her bottles of colourful chalk dust. It was yellow, his favourite colour. Her magic had cost her beautiful little brother his face, and maybe his life too. Guilt pulsed through her. She hadn't stayed to find out. She'd left him lying behind the barn, smouldering and screaming. That act was enough to sentence her to death. More than enough. To be a mage was an automatic death sentence in itself. She had to leave Vermor. It held too many bitter memories. Move on. Put all that behind her. The past was past, and the past was dead.

As she was stuffing the last of the coins into her bloated purse, she heard a voice.

'Impressive trick.'

Sasha turned to see the man behind her, the same man she'd caught skulking at the back of at least four of her shows. She didn't know how she'd missed him tonight; perhaps he'd learnt to be less conspicuous. Heat prickled her skin, and she reached for her necklace. Her fingers caressed the amber points of the hollow sun pendant that hung around her neck. A wash of cool swept over her, and her heart settled down.

She folded her arms. 'Ah, I see my greatest fan finally has the courage to speak to me. You might want to cover up that scar,' said Sasha, tapping her cheek. 'It makes you somewhat distinct.'

'I wonder how you do it,' the man continued, taking a step closer.

'You come and see me often enough,' replied Sasha, her back tensing. 'Surely you've figured it out by now.'

'Believe me, I've tried.'

'Then it will forever remain a mystery.' Sasha shoved her purse into her bag and put it on the table. She slipped her hand inside her cloak and dropped a small throwing knife into her palm. The metal was smooth against her rough skin.

'I've searched books, asked the right people, and as far as I'm aware, nomalus gas doesn't even exist. Care to explain that one, Sasha?'

'Number one, you need to do more research, and number two, it's rude to call me by my name without offering me yours in return.' She kept her voice calm and controlled, but inside she was screaming. There was a strong, almost definite possibility this man was a cleanser. If he was and he'd worked out her secret and tracked her down, she was in for a fight. She could just run now – there'd be no shame in that. She'd done it before. But what if this time he caught her up? She ran her thumb along her hidden blade.

'My name is Quint, and I believe I've done more than enough research on you, mage.'

'Mage!' Sasha spluttered, aghast. 'Don't insult me. Everything you see me do is sleight of hand and trickery, born from a lot of practice and extensive research, something you're clearly incapable of.'

Quint stepped into the lucid glow of the moon. The silver streaks in his dark hair gleamed in the light, and his eyes flashed with all the warmth and colour of slate. He held his arms out and flexed his palms. 'I'll give you a chance to prove yourself, Sasha,' he said, his voice flat and emotionless.

Sasha pulled up her hood. 'And I'll give you a chance to walk away, Quint.'

Quint laughed as he flicked his fingers, unleashing a flurry of ice in Sasha's direction. She dived out of the way, hitting the ground roughly and rolling to her feet as Quint's arsenal shattered on impact behind her. She stayed low, looking up through her fringe to see Quint striding towards her with a knowing smile on his face. He pulled his arm back and launched an icy spear. She dodged aside, but the spear still managed to tear her cloak and nick her shoulder. A sharp sting rushed into her wound, and she staggered back. So, this Quint was a mage – there was no doubt about it – but why was he trying to kill her? Could he be a cleanser and a mage? Was that even possible?

'Come on,' Quint spat through his teeth, 'show me what you've got.'

Sasha's fingers curled up, and her hands trembled. It had to be some form of trap. If she were to reveal what she could truly do, she'd be dead, no questions asked – shot through the head, impaled through the heart, a gory bloody mess. Or dancing a jaunty jig on the end of a rope. Quint had undoubtedly been sent by someone to eliminate her. Maybe cleansers were recruiting mages on the side these days – it'd make sense. Pay a mage to slay another, then slay that mage to double their profits.

Tiny forks of lightning flickered across her fingers. Quint's expression was painfully smug; the thick scar on his right cheek glittered with a layer of frost. His hands were before him, icicles jutting out as extensions to his fingers, water dripping from his forearms. Sasha shoved her hands under her cloak.

'I can't do anything,' she said, her hand once again grasping her knife. If she was very lucky, she could slow him down. If she was impossibly lucky, she could get away. She'd never battled another mage, and doing so without using the faintest flicker of lightning wasn't something she'd ever fantasised about. 'So, pick up all your ice and go.'

Quint shook his head and tutted. 'Do you honestly think I can let you walk away after what you've seen?'

'I think it would be wise for you to let me walk away.' She kept her tone even and her glare unwavering despite her pounding heart.

'It's a shame; you'd have fit right in.'

Sasha frowned but refused to rise to Quint's cryptic statement. She scrunched her hand up, and the lightning tingled across her skin. Quint was certainly trained in his art; there was an unnerving precision in his movements, his skill was honed almost to perfection and his confidence spilt into narcissism, but he didn't know what Sasha could do. She bit down on her tongue as Quint walked towards her, his icicle fingers melting with every step he took.

She could throw everything she had at him right now – it would knock him down at the very least – but there was something about Quint's collected manner that told her he was expecting as much. If they got into a fight, there was always the chance she'd get the Fear and be rendered unable to summon her magic. It wasn't worth the risk. She opened her hand and sent the lightning away. She'd let him pass so they could both continue with their separate lives, unscathed, unscarred and very much alive.

Quint came to a halt at Sasha's side. They stood shoulder to shoulder. His cold wet hand brushed against her hip. He leant towards her. 'I wish I were right about you,' he said in a hushed voice. 'I was convinced you were one of us. Looks like I was wrong. But now you've seen what I am, I can't let you live. Nothing against you personally – I rather like you, to be honest. But you've seen my face, you know my name. I'm somewhat distinct. You're a danger to me, so you have to die.' Quint clapped her firmly on the shoulder. 'I'm sorry, kiddo. No hard feelings, eh?' He sauntered away as if he were doing no more than crushing a tiresome insect.

Before she had time to respond, water rushed up her nose, choking her. A burning sensation ripped through her throat. Sasha tried to move, but her feet were no longer in contact with the ground. Her vision blurred and distorted. Her chest lurched as she realised she was trapped within a bubble of water. Quint was drowning her. She twisted and thrashed, but there was no way out. Death was coming for her.

Quint strolled away, his back to her; he didn't even care. He was killing her and wasn't even bothering to watch. Sasha was less than nothing to him – he'd probably forget about her by tomorrow. This irked her more than she thought it would. She wasn't going to die here like this. She balled her fists up and called her lightning to them, and they glowed and flickered. With a curl of her lip, she opened her hands and sent out a violent pulse of power. Her watery prison exploded, and she dropped to the ground, landing on her knees with a lightning-covered hand on the ground for support.

She yanked her goggles up, sprang to her feet, and dashed towards Quint with an inhuman burst of speed, lightning pulsing through her legs in flickering waves. She grabbed the watery mage around the back of the neck and slammed him face-first into the ground. With a deft flick of her wrist, she threw a bolt of energy downwards. It hit the dirt with a deafening crack and propelled her high into the air. She flipped herself over and came to the ground facing a sprawled Quint.

Sasha held her arms out and spread her fingers. Lightning coursed through them like luminous veins as she considered the man who'd just tried to murder her. Her hands shook with rage, and her face was set in a snarl. Wet hair stuck to her cheeks, and her cloak was heavy with damp.

'Get up, you bastard!' she spat at her fallen enemy.

Quint got to his feet, rubbing his neck. 'Calm down.'

'Calm down?' Sasha growled. 'You just tried to kill me!' Without a hint of warning, she threw a bolt of lightning at the ground before Quint. The earth ruptured, forcing the older mage to stagger back.

'I don't wanna fight you,' said Quint, holding his hands up in defence.

'That's too bad,' Sasha replied.

Quint summoned the ice back to his hands in the blink of an eye and launched a torrent of tiny frozen needles at Sasha. Fuelled by fury and bitter determination, Sasha vaulted high over Quint, avoiding his attack. While airborne, she threw out a long tether of lightning and used it to pull herself towards a tree. She anchored herself to the trunk with her right hand and glared down at Quint, light crawling over her skin. She raised her left arm and threw fork after fork of lightning down towards the mage. Quint leapt back, crafting a pair of icy bracers for defence as the ground split around him, spewing up clouds of dirt and clods of mud. Thunder echoed and rumbled throughout the spinney.

'Sasha!' he shouted, his voice almost smothered by the din. 'I don't want to fight!'

Sasha pulled her hand back and held it before her; the bright light that coalesced on her arm cast colossal distorted shadows about the clearing.

'Perhaps you should have thought about that before you tried to kill me,' she said.

She moved from tree to tree, raining a chaotic lightning storm down on her victim as she went. If she kept moving, this powerful enemy wouldn't sow the seeds of the Fear into her mind. She had to keep fighting. Her movements were wild, but to her annoyance, Quint dodged or deflected her blows.

She paused a moment. She had to catch her breath, but Quint didn't seem to want to let her. He hurled a giant ice spear at the tree. It neatly impaled the trunk and froze the area around it. A smaller spear was tossed towards the frozen patch, causing the tree to explode on impact.

Sasha dived from the decimated tree to another, which Quint similarly felled. It was time for her to change tactics. She cleared her head and pulled her power into her hands, using all her will to keep it there. She closed her eyes and breathed out. Everything went quiet; the crackle of lightning and the splintering of frozen wood were staunched from her mind. Her eyes flashed open, and she looked towards Quint. Shards of ice jutted from his once-smooth bracers in a complex tangle. He flicked his arm forwards, firing the shards at her. Sasha grinned and pushed herself from the tree. She wrapped her arms around her body while she was in the air, releasing the lightning and allowing it to cover her. Then she dropped to the ground. The wind thrashed her skin as she fell, burning and freezing all at once.

A powerful circular wave of lightning erupted from her as she landed. The ground around her burst open, sending up a shower of smoking dirt and burning grass. Quint's defences instantly melted, and he fell to the ground, stunned. The rippling surge of energy blasted through the trees, mercilessly setting them alight.

Sasha lifted her head to the crackling warmth of the fire and smiled to see the destruction. She made a shaky fist and commanded the surge to stop, then pulled her goggles around her neck. Her heart was thumping, and her breath was laboured. She stayed on one knee, her chest supported by her thigh. The last threads of her power sparked in her palm with a faint hum. Exhaustion seeped into every inch of her body.

'Burn yourself out?' Quint asked. To Sasha's astonishment, he got up.

'No,' she said. She pushed herself to her feet despite her nearly crippling fatigue. 'I'm just getting started.' A tiny bolt of lightning jumped between her hands as she kept her stormy unblinking gaze on him. 'Want some more?'

'I've seen enough,' Quint said, dusting down his singed jacket. 'Is it me, or is it a little too warm out here?' With a flick of his fingers, he sent a fierce blast of ice towards the flaming trees.

Within seconds, the fires were smothered. The frozen trees glistened in the moonlight like gigantic ice sculptures, chiming mellifluously amongst themselves. Sasha rolled her eyes, doing her best to look suitably unimpressed. She spread her fingers out, allowing forks of lightning to flit between them.

'Is that it?' she asked, taking a step towards Quint and squaring her shoulders. She did a quick sweep of the silver trees. Quint could have easily frozen her like that, but he hadn't. She shoved any panic she had deep down and locked eyes with the other mage. 'Do you have something else to disappoint me with? Or are you finally gonna leave?'

Quint laughed. It was a deep, harsh, grating sound that reflected off his crystal trees. 'Sasha, have you ever wanted to be free?'

'I am free.'

'No, you're not. You know what you do is forbidden. If your little facade ever came undone, you'd be put down like a mad dog by a cleanser.'

Sasha balled her fist up and threw a shaft of lightning into the ground; it reverberated through her entire body. She probably shouldn't have done it. 'No one can catch me.'

Quint smiled. 'You cut and run?'

'I do what I have to.' Sasha flexed her chest, sending spidery veins of light dashing across her body. 'Soon I'll have enough coin to leave this shit country, then I won't have to worry about cleansers or sentinels ever again. Is that free enough for you?'

'Sounds like running away to me.' Quint narrowed his eyes. 'Sasha, I'm part of a small group th—'

'Not interested. I do things on my own. My own way.'

'Don't you want to be as powerful as me?'

Sasha bristled.

'It's one thing lying to me, but don't lie to yourself, kid. I know when a mage is burnt out, and you, you can barely stand. I can see you're clinging to that last glimmer of power. You let it go and you're gone. You know it.'

'I'll let it go in your face if you don't shut it,' Sasha said.

Quint was right. If she released the last ember of power that pulsed between her fingers, unconsciousness wouldn't be far behind.

'You can't hold on to it forever,' said Quint, unfazed by Sasha's aggressive tone. 'You can feel it pulling at you. It wants to go. You want to let it go.'

'Shut up!'

'Come with me. Join us. We can make you stronger, and I promise you won't have to leave Vermor. You'll be free. Free to live here without fear. You'll be respected. But first, we need your help. And with your help, we can save all the mages in Vermor.'

'Why should I care about all the mages in Vermor? They don't care about me, I don't care about them. It's not a very complicated system.'

'I can see you're a hard sell. Let me word it another way: we have a way to channel magic directly from the Otherside, but we need your help first.'

Sasha paused and swallowed; she could taste blood. 'Directly?'

'Yes, directly. You'll be able to pull wild lightning from that wonderful world without burnout and without the risk of death. Have you ever touched your element from the Otherside?'

'Too risky.'

'Indeed it is. But it won't always be like that. Things are changing, Sasha, and they're starting with us.'

'If your group's so powerful, why do you need me?'

'We haven't got a lightning mage – you're surprisingly rare. I suppose if they're all as hot-headed as you, they burn themselves out to the brink of death.' He straightened up his burnt jacket as he spoke.

'You're recruiting me to make up the numbers, eh?'

'Not me personally. My leader asked me to find a mage like you.'

'Your leader?' Sasha's body was trembling, her muscles aching, her bones softening. A thin stream of blood oozed from the corner of her mouth. She wanted to wipe it away, but that would require movement.

'Yeah, and I think she'll like you.' He aligned his buttons. 'You in or not? I don't have all night.'

'Do I have a choice?'

'Say the word and I'll walk away. We can forget about this night. I'll even forget about killing you. How's that for a deal? You can pass out and wake up in this charred clearing and go on with your life, content with your limitations.'

Sasha looked from Quint to the icy trees, then over to the blackened remains of her possessions. Maybe she'd overdone it slightly. She glanced down at her hands and the feeble flicker that dashed across them. As much as she hated to admit it, some of what Quint had said had garnered her interest. Not saving all the mages in Vermor – definitely not that nonsense – but pulling her element from the Otherside certainly had an appeal. Elements from that world were raw, exciting and dangerous. She'd be powerful and strong, and perhaps she wouldn't have to run away after all. Working with a group bothered her though. As a rule, she worked alone, but if she didn't like this group, she could leave; she was her own person. She swallowed another metallic lump of saliva before she spoke. 'All right,' she croaked, 'you've convinced me, for now.'

'You won't regret it, kiddo.'

'You will. You'll have to carry me.' She finally released the last threads of her lightning into the ground and collapsed before the light even had a chance to fade.

CHAPTER ONE

The brilliant midday sun poured through the only crack in the curtains' defence. Its bright beam of light tore across the dishevelled living space, ignoring the piles of unwashed bowls and plates and half-drunk cups of tea as it made its way stubbornly towards the bedroom. The light dashed up the bed and settled itself over Killian's face.

He let out a miserable groan, pulled his hand out from under the warm sheets and pushed them off his body. With a grunt, he sat up and swung his legs over the side of the bed. He rested his prickly chin in his hands and breathed slowly, glancing around the room through sore dry eyes. It was a mess.

Clothes were scattered arbitrarily across the floor, empty bottles were piled up at the end of the bed and his precious swords and gun were lost amid the drifts of debris. The reek of beer and rum clung to the thick, musty air. He ran his forefinger back and forth over his bottom lip as he surveyed the carnage. This was getting out of hand.

It had been two weeks since the night he and Lily had returned from Charrington. She'd offered him a bed on her island until they could figure out what to do, but he'd declined. He'd wanted to be by himself. He couldn't face anyone, not after what had happened. So he'd shut himself away and lived off watery porridge, honey, rum and beer. It was a poor diet, but he didn't care. He was numb. Numb to every sensation. He didn't even feel human anymore.

Slowly, he got to his feet and picked his way around the mess of his bedroom, trudging through to the main room. His coat was hanging off the couch, the cuff dragging on the floor. He paused, scooped it up and placed it back on the cushions next to a pile of blood-soaked ripped bandages. A crimson-stained shirt lay close by, the shoulder rigid from dark dried blood. He turned from the grisly scene and headed towards the bathroom.

Gripping either side of the sink, he stared at his reflection. A mass of facial hair greeted him; it was getting unruly. He turned the tap, splashed his face with cold water and began to shave away the offending hairs. Deathly pale skin emerged as the hairs fell away; he half expected to see a collection of black veins pulsing beneath it. Grey circles bordered his tired eyes.

As he moved his arm, he caught sight of one of his scars – a band of ragged skin that ran from his shoulder to his elbow. He put his finger on its ravaged surface and ran it down its length. An equally thick scar ran down his right arm. Heat flared in his back, and he turned around, twisting his head so he could see the ghastly reflection. Shiny jagged skin ran from his right shoulder blade and ended on the left side of his lower back; his gaze traced it from beginning to end.

A phantom pain rippled through his leg, and he took his trousers down. Near the top of his thigh was a short thick mark, which had an identical twin on the opposite side of his leg. He shuddered as the pain of having his leg impaled momentarily flooded his senses. It didn't, however, come anywhere near to the suffering he'd endured when the Gramarye had been used against him. Never in his life had he experienced such raw, agonising pain. Every inch of his skin had been on fire, and acid-tipped needles had been pushed into his every pore. He filled the sink and listlessly set about cleaning his body with a lump of soap and a sea sponge.

To this day, he still had no idea how he'd survived; something had saved him, but what? Hours had been spent puzzling over this mystery. He knew a light had come from his body, but he didn't know how or why. He'd even tried to make it come out again himself by staring at his hand – a ridiculous notion for someone who knew nothing of the magic arts. One night he thought he saw some colourful sparks leap from his open palm, but it happened so fast, and he'd been so tired at the time – not to mention drunk – that he'd put it down to his imagination.

He rubbed the cold soapy sponge up and down his arms.

Why did Ren have to die? Why couldn't he save him? He'd promised him that he'd look after him, but he'd let him die. If Ren had stayed back like he'd said, he wouldn't be dead now. Ren's fault. But if he'd held on to him tighter, he wouldn't have wriggled free. Killian's fault. If he hadn't taught him how to steal a gun, that demon wouldn't have seen him as a threat. Killian's fault. If he'd tried to help him while he was in the grip of the demon, he could have saved him. Killian's fault. Whichever angle he looked at it, it always came back to him. He'd let him die. He'd killed him.

He worked the soap up into a lather over the rest of his body. If he'd done something, anything but stand still like a useless idiot, there was every chance that Ren would still be alive. He rubbed his foam-covered hands over his ghostly-white face. It was his fault. He'd sentenced Ren to death. Just like his mum. Just like Clem.

Killian scooped up a handful of water and washed the soap from his face. Not only was Ren dead – *my fault* – but some crazed demon was in possession of an incredibly powerful and dangerous magical artefact. *My fault again.*

With a morose sigh, he pulled the plug from the sink and watched the water drain away. He gave his body a brief rub-down with a thin towel and then tied the damp cloth around his waist. A trail of water followed him as he padded back to his bedroom.

He immediately slumped onto the bed and stared vacantly at the ceiling, his wet body slowly soaking the sheets. For a long time, he watched the dark wooden beams on their journey from one end of the room to the other. A despondent growl came from his stomach, but the thought of more watery porridge was nauseating. He needed some real food, something to make him feel almost human.

He stood up, whipped the towel from around his waist and dried himself off. He tossed the sodden towel aside and searched for some clean clothes. Miraculously, he found some. A pair of trousers and a shirt lolled forlornly out of a chest of drawers. Locating his swords was an altogether more difficult task. After excavating the entire room, he unearthed them, still in their sheaths and attached to a belt on a pair of discarded trousers. He unwound the belt and reattached it to his clean trousers.

He paced out of his room and scooped his coat up from the couch. As he shook it out, something flew from the pocket, clinking as it struck the floor. Freya's bracelet. Killian scrambled to grab it before it became lost within the detritus. The black and green gemstones sparkled as he held it up. It was a beautiful piece of jewellery, and from another world. Unique and beautiful. It could be sold for a high price, but that hadn't been Freya's intention. It wasn't his either, yet holding it caused him pain. Last time he'd held it, everything had been different – he'd been different. With a flick of his wrist, he tossed it onto the couch.

Blood surged through his body, and his heart raced as he approached the front door. A rancid sickness roiled in the pit of his stomach. He gripped the cold metal doorknob. It turned to ice in his hand, freezing him to the spot. It would be so easy to let it go, to step backwards and remain in the flat, never to look into the eyes of anyone he knew again. He took a deep breath, and without another thought, he opened the door and left.

The icy chill of the afternoon hit him. He pulled his coat close to his body and headed for the main street. It was one of those quiet days seldom seen in Brackmouth. The market wasn't on, so the streets weren't crammed with stalls and bartering customers. He drifted down the path, keeping his head down and his eyes focused on the shiny damp cobbles in case he should see anyone he knew. Seagulls shrieked overhead as if announcing his presence like a morose fanfare. They sounded even more boisterous than usual. It was as if they knew he was a killer and were doing their duty to the townsfolk of Brackmouth by warning them to stay away from him.

Despite his sluggish pace, he inevitably reached Estelle's teahouse. The desire to be with her and feel her comfort had subconsciously overridden his want for solitude. The familiar smell of warm nourishing food sailed out of the building. He put his hand on the door and hesitated momentarily before going in. He glanced around the inside, his heart thumping in his throat. A few clusters of customers were quietly drinking tea and eating, but nobody looked up. He walked up to the counter to find Estelle absent. Rose was busy washing some pans in a bowl of steaming water. She glanced up, and her pale skin flushed with a healthy pink glow.

'Hi, Killian,' she said, pulling her hands out of the water and drying them on her apron. 'What can I get you?'

'Nothing, thanks,' he said, surprised at how thin his own voice sounded. 'Stell about?'

'She's out back. Want me to get her?' She tucked a stray strand of blonde hair behind her ear as she spoke.

'Please.'

'All right,' she said as she scurried off.

Killian turned around and leant against the counter. The warmth of the crackling fireplace filled the teahouse. Orange flames licked hungrily at the flaking pieces of terracotta paint surrounding them, welcoming them into their fiery jaws with glee. The door creaked as some of the customers filed out into the street. He stared at the door. It stared back, beckoning him. Should he leave?

'Killian! Me luvver!' exclaimed Estelle so loud it made him start.

'Hey, Stell,' he said, turning around to face her once he'd recovered.

'I ain't seen you for months, me handsome,' she said, bending down and dusting the flour from her apron. 'How you been?'

'Fine.'

'Good, good, dearie. Everything go well for—' She paused to wipe her face with a cloth. 'Ren?'

'Yes.' He somehow managed to lie through the shock and pain of hearing that name when all he wanted to do was cry.

'I knew you'd help him.'

'Yep.'

'Sorry, I can't chat too long – Rose needs a break. The poor dear's been on her feet all day.'

'Uh-huh.'

Estelle put the cloth down and looked at him. As she did, her mouth dropped open.

'Killian, what happened to you?' she asked, the jovial tone gone from her voice.

'Nothing,' he mumbled.

'You're as pale as the dead and skinnier than a sapling, so don't you lie to me.'

'You're busy. I should probably go ho—'

'Nowhere.' She finished his sentence for him. 'You're going nowhere.'

'I have to . . .' His voice trailed off as his emotions threatened to overwhelm him.

'I won't hear another word.' She lifted the hatch on the counter and ushered him in. 'You know the way. Make yourself at home.'

He nodded and proceeded to the back door. It was futile to protest at her good intentions, and even if he'd wanted to, he didn't have the energy. He climbed the stairs to her flat, his feet dragging with every step. A sweet, spicy aroma wafted from her home as soon as he opened the door.

Sunny yellow drapes lined the narrow corridor that led to her sitting room. As soon as he set foot into the room, he collapsed onto her inviting deep-red couch. He had a quick glance around and spied an oil burner, the source of the scent. The room was warm and cosy; the embers of a dwindling fire flickered in the hearth. He sat up and removed his coat.

A vase of crystals rested on the dainty table in front of him. He reached forwards and picked one up. It was a small imperfect oval and was cool to the touch. He held it up to the light, which split as it hit its surface, scattering hundreds of tiny rainbows around the room. He rolled the stone between his thumb and forefinger, causing the rainbows to dart across the room like shooting stars. It didn't take long for him to lose interest and replace the stone. The soft cushions lured him backwards, and he slumped against them.

After what seemed like hours, Estelle returned. She was carrying a cake whose sweet fruity smell sought out Killian as she walked by. His stomach cried out in agony.

'With you in a jiff,' she said, glancing at him with concern in her heavily kohled eyes.

'Okay,' he murmured, half to her, half to no one.

He pushed himself up and watched Estelle as she wandered into her kitchen, but his view was blocked when she shut the door. It wasn't long before the sound of sizzling and a rich, fatty scent swamped his senses. A hollow pain lanced through his stomach, and his mouth watered. The door swung back open, and Estelle emerged carrying a steaming bacon sandwich dripping with butter.

'Here,' she said, thrusting the plate into Killian's hands. 'Eat.'

'Stell, I'm sorry,' he said, shaking his head. All his hunger abandoned him, leaving only a wretched sickness in its wake.

'Killian, please.'

'I can't.'

'For me,' she pleaded, her eyes glistening. 'I went to all that effort to make it.'

One of the few people Killian couldn't bear to upset was Estelle, so he did the dutiful thing and ate. It took him a long time to chew through the sandwich, but the salty bacon, rich butter and crispy bread tasted so good. After two weeks of living off water, porridge and alcohol, anything would taste good, but he wasn't going to voice that. As soon as he finished, she took the plate from him and replaced it with a mug of tea. She went back to the kitchen and returned with two slices of cake and a second steaming cup. She handed him the cake.

'I—'

'You can, and you will.'

He picked up the thick wedge of fruit cake and bit into it. Not a single word passed between them as they ate; Estelle wasn't even looking at him. Was she that ashamed? Did she know what a mistake, a mess, he really was? When he'd finished, he got up and put the mug and plate in the kitchen, then silently returned to the sitting room and sat down.

'Thanks.'

'You don't have to thank me,' she said. She drank the last few drops of her tea and set the cup on the delicate dark wood table. 'Killian.' She stopped and looked him up and down. 'What happened to you? You look dreadful, and I can't help you if I don't know.'

'I know . . . It's difficult.'

'Take your time, my love.'

Despair and guilt wrapped around Killian. His throat tightened, and his mouth dried up. A deep shuddering breath filled his lungs, and in a barely audible whisper, he forced seven words past his lips.

'Ren's dead, and it's all my fault.'

CHAPTER
TWO

Lily Rothbone tossed another useless book onto the desk. With a curl of her lip, she swiped up the glass of Venarian red wine. She took a long, slow sip and then glared over the top of the glass. The floor was littered with books, none of which contained any information about the Gramarye, let alone demons or whatever that thing was. It seemed Lord Aberwithe had been quite the collector of literature . . . useless literature. Over the past two weeks, she and Raven had torn apart the castle's seldom-used library in the hope that at least one of the neglected dust-covered volumes would contain some useful information. It had been a fruitless search. A waste of time. She took another sip of wine – it was bold, deep and going straight to her head – and plonked herself onto the edge of the desk.

The room was packed to the ceiling with a vast array of books, and as soon as she and Raven had disturbed the old volumes, the smell of old dust and decaying paper was rife. It was a smell she found comfort in. Back when she had a father, that scent had followed him around almost like a perfume. There had always been a book in his pocket.

Sturdy mahogany bookcases were embedded into the walls. Each case was separated by a pillar of cheap-looking marble. The designs on the stones were uneven – darker colours mixed crudely into the lighter ones. They were probably rejected pieces purchased at a low price. Above the writing desk was a small platform housing yet more books. It was supported underneath by wooden beams, and a ladder connected it with the floor. A large window in the back wall looked out into the dark rustling woods. Lily turned to look over her shoulder and gazed into the dense foliage, and her mind wandered towards Killian.

She'd not seen him since the night they'd returned from Charrington, and when she'd left him, he'd been in a bad way. She hadn't wanted to leave him alone, but he'd refused to come back to the island, and she wasn't going to stay at his place. A pirate queen like her slumming it in Brackmouth with all the ordinary folk – that wouldn't do. The weeks had dragged by like a wounded dog. Every day she'd expected him to appear on the island, but he hadn't. Every day she told herself she'd wait another day, then go and see him. But she hadn't.

The library door squeaked open, and Raven swooped in carrying a tray. Lily jumped but covered it by sliding off the desk. He walked over to the table and set down two bowls of thick steaming soup, half a loaf of bread, some butter, a plate of sliced meat and another bottle of wine. Lily seized a bowl and sank to the floor, her back resting against the desk. Raven followed suit, bringing the meat, bread and wine down with him also.

'Are we doing this all night again?' he asked.

'I don't think so,' said Lily.

'All right,' he replied as he ripped the bread and handed her a chunk.

'We've been through everything. We'll just end up going round in circles,' she added. She dipped the bread into the soup.

Raven nodded.

Lily balanced the bowl between her legs and picked up a slice of meat. She wrapped it around a hunk of bread and chewed it. 'What d'you think we should do?' she asked once she'd swallowed.

'Honestly, I don't know.'

Lily smiled. 'We're good at this, aren't we?' It felt strange to smile; she hadn't done a lot of it recently.

'The best.' He returned her smile.

They ate the rest of their meal in silence. Only when all the food was gone did Raven uncork the wine and top up their glasses. They clinked glasses, had a gulp and sighed simultaneously.

A haze of drunkenness settled peacefully over Lily, and she fully embraced it. Crushing her thoughts, worries and feelings with a fine red wine was one of the many things she was excellent at. She drained her glass and held the empty vessel aloft in Raven's direction.

A pensive look fell into his purple eyes as he poured the wine. 'Don't you think it's time you saw Killian?'

Lily took a large swig and looked to the floor, her eyes focusing on the two odd floorboards near the door. 'I was hoping he'd come here.'

'I don't think he will.'

'No.'

There was a long silence before Raven spoke again. 'You

could send someone. You don't have to go yourself, if you'd rather not.'

'I know.' Why did he have to talk about him? Why couldn't he just let her enjoy being drunk? She snatched the bottle from the floor and filled her glass up again.

'You can feel, Lily.'

She took another sip and pursed her lips. 'I know.' Then she saw *his* feet swing above the kitchen table. The rope creaked. Her heart emptied and filled back up with nothing. Darkness put its hand on her shoulder, its cool touch forever a blight on her skin. She'd long since buried her past and her feelings under rum and riches, and that was where they had to stay. The two interconnecting entities that threatened to tear her life apart. She downed the remains of her wine. 'I don't want to talk about this.'

'I understand,' said Raven. He placed a warm hand on top of hers and gave it a squeeze.

He filled their glasses and put the empty bottle to his side. 'I'm sorry, I shouldn't have pushed.'

'Don't be sorry – you're only trying to help.' She turned to her first mate and cocked an eyebrow. 'I know I'm difficult, but that's why you love me.'

'Of course.'

Lily stared into her glass of wine. Blood-red, delicious, intoxicating and soothing. She swirled it, creating a tiny whirlpool at the centre. The lush fruity waves of its scent washed over her, bringing about a certain clarity. 'I'll go and see him in a few days,' she said, her eyes still fixed on the wine.

'Good.'

Lily swigged the rest of the wine, leant back against the desk and stretched her arms above her head. She yawned deeply and let her arms drop. The world was beginning to spin with lazy, uneven revolutions. It was a bumpy ride, but she had no desire to get off it.

Raven slumped down until he was lying on the floor. He closed his eyes. Lily watched the slow and gentle rise and fall of his chest, and then she, too, slid down onto the floor, her head coming to rest on his shoulder.

Raven was her own personal calm, the safe harbour in her stormy life, and she would always love him for it. She reached her arm over his body and allowed drunken sleep to take her away.

CHAPTER THREE

Killian sat on a cushion on Estelle's window ledge and looked out over the streets of Brackmouth. The rain pounded the cobbles relentlessly, every surface shiny and slick with wet. A cluster of seagulls huddled together on the rooftop opposite. Even they seemed subdued by the torrential downpour and oppressive grey skies.

If it had been a better day, Killian may have gone outside and brushed up his sword-fighting techniques, but he wasn't going to get soaked to the skin for no good reason, even if he did need the practice. The bond he'd once had with his weapons had vanished the day Ren died. They felt heavy and lifeless now, just like him. He took a sip from his mug of tea. It was cold and weak.

Estelle's wooden wall clock chimed six o'clock, and Killian glanced over to the door. He was hoping she'd be back soon;

he needed to speak to her. The previous night had been difficult, but he'd managed to tell her everything. They'd stayed up until the early hours, Killian telling Estelle of the cornelians, the trials, the Gramarye, his desperate need to atone for the deaths of his mum and Clem and how it had all blown up in his face.

He breathed out slowly and leant back against the window. The glass was cool against the back of his head. He looked at his left hand, catching sight of something in his peripheral vision, something iridescent, and his pulse raced. Holding both hands in front of him, he critically examined them, turning them over and over, but there was nothing. He scrunched them up into tight shaking fists.

Nothing there. What am I even looking for? I'm losing it. I'm really losing it.

The door groaned open, and Estelle shuffled inside. Killian didn't know what to do with his hands. Were they glowing? Were they not glowing? Had they glowed? Was he going crazy? He stuffed them into his lap, but a quick glance downwards told him that looked odd and very unlike him. Casually, he spread them to each side. But that would put them in full view, and what if they glowed again? Had they glowed? He wrapped them around the back of his head and leant against them. Perfect. Hidden from view, and a casual attitude.

'Hey, Stell.' He hoped she hadn't noticed him rearranging his hands.

'Hello, me handsome. Sorry I ain't been back. You wouldn't believe how busy it was today.' She was carrying a large black pot. Killian sprang up from the window ledge and took it from her. 'Thank you, me luvver. Pop it in the kitchen for me, would you?'

Killian placed the heavy iron pot down on the thick wooden sideboard in the kitchen, and Estelle came in after him.

'Leftover stew. You want some?' she asked as she removed the lid, releasing its rich meaty scent.

'Please,' said Killian straight away, unable to resist the smell.

'Good, good. Sit down, and I'll bring it through.'

Killian did as she said, squeezing past her to get back to the front room. He slumped onto the couch, and his gaze strayed back to his hands. He gripped them together and watched; nothing happened. With a grunt, he let go. Estelle came back into the room with two bowls of stew and a plate of bread. She handed him a bowl and set the bread down on the delicate table. Hungrily, he dived in.

Estelle ate her way through the stew. Killian devoured his. It was heavy, meaty and tasty, warming and comforting, and packed with vegetables. With every bite, he felt like a little part of him was being rebuilt. Yet try as he might, he couldn't shake the feeling of shattered confidence, loss and failure. It would take more than decent food to rebuild that.

'That was great, Stell,' he said, dropping his spoon into the bowl with a clatter and wiping his mouth with the back of his hand.

'Good, good. Could you make some tea while I finish mine? There's something I wanna talk to you 'bout.'

Killian nodded and swept into the kitchen to put the kettle on. As he waited for it to boil, an ominous dark cloud crept around him. What could Estelle want to talk to him about? Maybe she'd realised that it was his fault Ren was dead, and she was going to chuck him out into the street where he belonged. With shaking hands, he plucked two cups from her wooden mug tree. He set them down and waited for his body to return to normal. He was being ridiculous, wasn't he?

He placed his hands on the sideboard and rapped his fingers, glaring at them. A jolt ran through his body, and his skin flashed. His mouth dropped open, and he jumped back, a trail of light following him. A ripple of nausea coursed through him when he dared to look at his hands. Shimmering iridescent light flowed over his skin; it was predominantly silver, but other colours rose to the surface – purples, blues, greens, yellows, pinks – in a constant state of flux. His breath caught in his throat as he gaped at his alien skin. Then, just as suddenly as it had arrived, the bizarre glow vanished.

Killian fell to his knees, all the strength drained from his body. What was happening to him? Using all his body had to offer, he pushed himself up. He slumped against the counter with a loud thump and gripped it with trembling hands. His body was burning, and his shirt stuck to his back with hot sweat. Closing his eyes, he tried to regain control. The kettle gurgled, and he switched his focus to that. Slowly, the shaking subsided, and he opened his eyes. With weary movements, he made the tea. He wiped his sweaty forehead with his shirtsleeve and went back out to Estelle.

'Thank you,' she said, taking the cup from him. 'You all right, my dear?' she asked, her brow furrowed.

'Fine,' he lied, sitting down in a rush so she wouldn't notice how feeble he'd become.

Estelle nodded and took a sip of her tea. She put the cup on the table and looked him up and down. 'I've been thinking 'bout what you told me all day, turning it over in my head. I don't know what you saw or what it wants with the Gramarye, but it can't be good. I think I can help, but first, I've got to come clean.' She paused. Her eyes widened, and she bit her bottom lip. After one long controlled breath, she spoke. 'I'm a mage.'

'Stell?' Killian had always suspected there was more to her than met the eye, but he'd often brushed it off as just a part of her personality and aesthetic. Being a mage put her in danger. His heart pounded. She couldn't be in danger, not her.

'I'm sorry I hid it from you. I didn't want to put you in danger. And I didn't want to upset you, be—'

'You don't have to say sorry for anything, ever.' He took a sip of tea. It was a good brew – Cylus could learn a thing or two from him. 'So, what can you do?'

'Weak hexes and enchantments. I stopped practising years ago, but I can still do some little things.'

' "Some little things," like that stone you gave me?'

'Like that.'

'I wouldn't exactly say that was "little." '

Estelle smiled, and the lines around her eyes crinkled. 'Years ago, I met a man, Ulrich. The other mages called him the warlock. He seemed to know everything – his house was full of books, even though he couldn't wield magic anymore. If there's anyone out there who knows anything about all this, it'll be him.' She picked up her teacup and stared wistfully into the dregs. She smiled wanly. 'I went to him to learn more about what I could do, but I weren't very good. It wasn't meant to be.'

'Your weak hex saved my life,' said Killian.

'That's pretty simple stuff. The right stone, the right amount of will and just enough magic pulled through from the Otherside to bring it all together. It's like making a cake that explodes.' Estelle set her teacup down. 'Ulrich will be well into his seventies by now, maybe even his eighties. With any luck, he'll still be alive.'

'It's worth a shot.'

Estelle nodded.

'That's good enough for me,' said Killian. A lightness filled his body as a tiny flame of hope burned.

'You'll have to head to Freischen. He lived in a little village called Poll – I hope he's still there.'

'I'm sure I can talk Lil into going.'

'I reckon you can. You've got a gift when it comes to talking her into somethin',' she said.

'I should have gone to see her by now. She knew Ren,' he muttered. Just saying his name dragged Killian back into the mire. 'She watched him die too and saw me . . .' He didn't even want to think about that, let alone talk about it. It only brought him pain.

'Aye, she must be hurting,' said Estelle, her tone soft. 'Killian, last night you said something. I didn't wanna ask you 'bout it at the time, you were so distressed.'

'Distressed? Me? Never.'

'Yes, you. You said you could've helped little Ren, and when that demon tried to kill you, it couldn't.' She pushed her glasses up her nose and leant towards him. 'You know why?'

Heat surged through Killian's body, and his throat dried up. He didn't want anyone to know there was the possibility that something was happening to him, something he couldn't explain or control, something that might make him dangerous to know. 'I don't know. It must have used up the Gramarye – lucky for me – and I thought I could help him because I'm an idiot.'

'You're not an idiot, me luvver. Your heart's in the right place.'

'Stell, that's a polite way of calling me an idiot.'

Estelle huffed and shook her head. 'Sometimes, lad, I wonder what you see in yourself that's so different from what everyone else does.'

Killian smiled weakly. 'What I really am.'

'I see there's no point in arguing with you over this.'

Estelle picked up their cups and her bowl and walked into the kitchen. Killian sighed and sat back. For some reason, he felt on the verge of tears. He shuddered, wiped his eyes and regained his composure to prevent their assault.

Estelle walked back into the lounge and looked at him. 'Don't know about you, but I'm shattered,' she said through a great yawn. The spidery lines around her eyes appeared deeper, and her shoulders slumped. 'I think I need an early night.'

'I'll turn in too,' said Killian. 'I'll need all my strength for the queen of the seas tomorrow.'

'You'll be fine – you've got the rare gift of pirate charming in you,' said Estelle, reaching down and patting his shoulder. 'I'll say g'night,' she added, giving him a kiss on the cheek.

'Night, Stell, and thanks.'

'No thanks needed.' She ambled into her room, closing the door behind her.

Once again, Killian was alone. He got up and walked around the room, systematically blowing out the candles and turning off the lamps. Smoke lingered in the air in wispy grey plumes, filling the room with its scent. As he sat back down, a cold chill coursed through his body, forcing him to wrap himself in a thick blanket. Eventually, he peeled his clothes off and lay back on the couch under the blanket, not daring to look at any part of his body. He rolled onto his side and watched the fire's dying embers. The deep ruby glow was a source of comfort amid the lonely gloom of the night. Footsteps echoed in the streets below; no doubt it was people staggering home from the Laughing Swan. In the distance, an owl hooted over the windswept hills of Brackmouth, the sound forlorn and haunting. Slowly, his eyelids drooped, and within minutes, sleep swept in to take him away.

CHAPTER FOUR

ESTELLE AND ROSE WERE RELAXING WITH A POT OF tea each when Killian came through the back door and walked across the kitchen. The air was loaded with the loitering scent of fatty bacon and frying eggs. He should have come to the teahouse for his breakfast rather than scraping together another awful bowl of porridge from Estelle's kitchen.

'Busy, eh, ladies?'

'Oh, the cheek of it!' exclaimed Estelle. 'I'll have you know we were run off our feet while you were happily snoozing away upstairs. This is a rare break for us. Ain't that right, Rose?'

'Yes, it is,' said Rose, nodding, her pale blue eyes intently focused on her cup.

'Yeah, yeah,' said Killian as he picked up the pot and poured himself a drink. He leant back against the counter and took a long sip. There was a cluster of old ladies chattering away to one another in one corner of the teahouse, but other than that, it was empty.

'Haven't you somewhere to be?' asked Estelle as Killian reclined.

'No rush,' he said.

'Avoiding something?'

Killian looked at her and frowned. 'Nope.'

'Why don't you tell him what you told me this morning, Rose?'

Killian looked towards Estelle's assistant. 'Tell me what?'

'I saw a man yesterday afternoon,' Rose mumbled.

'A man?'

'Yes, erm, I didn't recognise him, but he was wearing a hood and cloak. He was in the square, telling the story of a heroic man who travelled to another world. The man in his story had your name. I thought it was odd.'

'Anything else?' Killian asked.

'Erm, I was in a hurry, so I didn't stay, but I did notice a sweet smell around him. I think it was from his pipe, but I can't be sure.'

Killian grunted and put his cup down.

'Friend o' yours?' inquired Estelle.

'Yeah, sort of. I'd better get going, see what Rothbone has to say to me,' he added as he nimbly ducked under the counter.

'Good luck with that,' said Estelle.

Killian marched briskly through the streets of Brackmouth. The market was on, and the roads were heaving with people. He kept his head up and dodged out of the way of those who meandered into his path. He set his course for the quay and walked on automatic, which allowed his mind to flow.

Why was Blake coming to town spreading the word of his adventures down the Drop? Did he know what had happened to Ren? Surely he did, so why would he revere Killian as a hero? It didn't make sense. He'd killed Ren, and that was all there was to it. A fierce stabbing pain erupted in his heart, and his chest tightened in response. It was difficult to breathe.

His pace slowed until he stopped altogether and leant against the closest wall. All those feelings of guilt and despair that he'd done so well to suppress over the past two days raced back. Dizziness flooded his mind, and he couldn't think straight. He gripped the wall behind him, his fingers slipping on the smooth damp stones. He was going to faint. He lifted his head and tried to focus on something. People rushed by; their bodies merged together, creating one giant seething mass, a constant wispy stream of clothes and skin. Killian shut his eyes to blot them out, but he couldn't keep out the sound. A cacophony of voices trilled into his head, each sound like a rusty nail being forced into his skull. His knees buckled, and he sank to the ground.

He fell onto his hands and knees, hung his head and tried to steady his tremulous breathing. At least he was still conscious. He focused on his hands and nothing else while he fought to regain his breath; he was determined not to pass out in the street. The heat in his lungs lessened, and the pain in his chest faded. Using the wall, he hauled himself back to his feet. Everyone in the vicinity seemed too busy with their daily tasks to have noticed him collapse, which he was grateful for.

What was he doing? Was there any point in going to see Lily? Maybe he should crawl back to his flat and stay there – it would be safer for everyone that way. He shook his head and got back on course for the quay.

After a brief but pleasant exchange with Loris, Killian was heading towards Brackmouth Island, or was it Lily's? As he drew closer to the ominous green hump, his skin crawled and his heart rate increased. He didn't know what he'd say to her – or anyone for that matter. Hopefully she'd be in a good mood and he wouldn't be welcomed to the island by Morton again. Fighting was definitely not an option – he was surprised he even had the strength to row the boat. He frowned; he was moving fast, too fast, his oars effortlessly slicing through the waves. How was that even possible? A sick feeling built in his gut, and he looked towards his villainous hands.

They were glowing silver, pale colours shimmering within – they had the iridescence of an oyster shell. Wisps of the strange light streamed from his skin, breaking off and fading away in the sea breeze. He pulled the oars, and a rush of energy coursed through him. It was strange. He felt strong and powerful. It terrified him, and it didn't feel right.

A lone figure was striding down from the castle and towards the beach, their long black hair blowing in the wind like a warning beacon. It could be one of two people, and he didn't care which. Killian willed himself to row faster, and to his surprise, he did. With this burst of newfound strength, he was soon in the shallows. With a tremendous rush of energy, he beached the boat and jumped out into the wet sand. Pushing his damp salty hair out of his eyes, he saw Lily walking towards him, her head down against the wind. Terrified, he glanced at his hands just in time to catch the last of the silver glow fade back into him.

As soon as it vanished, he felt ridiculously weak. With legs like jelly, he staggered back and steadied himself by grabbing hold of the boat. He leant against it to keep himself from falling and breathed slowly as he tried to focus on a fixed point, anything to keep from fainting. In an attempt to appear as casual and relaxed as possible, he shoved his fingers through his belt loops. *I'm fine.*

Lily stopped in front of him, and to his surprise, she smiled. He managed to form what he hoped was a smile back.

'Good morning,' she said.

'Morning.'

'Nice of you to visit.'

'My pleasure,' he said, nodding. 'Nice of you to welcome me ashore.'

'I'm not welcoming you,' she replied.

'Oh, really?' he said, raising his eyebrows. 'Why you here, then?'

'Pirate business,' she said, placing her hands on her hips and putting her shoulders back.

'And would said pirate business involve welcoming me?'

'No.'

'Okay then, were you on your way to Bracky to see me?' he asked, hoping his playful attitude would mask his weakness. What was wrong with him?

'And why would I want to do that?'

He held her gaze for a heartbeat before giving her his best cocky grin. 'Because you miss me.'

'Oh, yes, because I miss you.' She clasped her chest with a thump. 'You're right. I was about to leave for Brackmouth to find you because I miss you. I've not been able to sleep at night because you've been so far away. Oh, how my heart aches for you, Killian.'

'I knew it,' he said with a smirk. He felt dreadful. Keeping the conversation flowing was the only thing helping him stay conscious.

'You wish it,' she sniped as she turned back to the castle. After a few steps, she spun back around. 'You coming or not?'

'No, I think I'll stay out here in the cold for a bit, then head back.'

'Suit yourself,' she said as she marched away.

Killian moved away from the boat and took a few steps. He felt so drained. Every step, every movement, was an effort. He valiantly tried to walk, but it was to no avail. He stumbled, his body became inert, and he fell to the ground. As the beach came closer, everything around him went black.

CHAPTER FIVE

SASHA SAT ALONE IN THE BASEMENT OF THE OLD farmhouse. It was cool and smelt vaguely of ale and dirt. There was no ale though. Perhaps, many years ago, the room had been used as a cellar and the only trace that remained was the smell. She ran her tongue around the inside of her mouth; she'd give anything for a beer – the rich flavour of hops, followed by a gentle wash of confidence and relaxation. She shook her head; she was letting her mind drift. Soon her watch would be over, and she could grab that much-needed refreshment from upstairs.

Pale sunlight poured in from the tiny vents on the outside wall and coalesced on the floor. Her listless gaze followed the dust motes as they twirled in the feeble light. She put her arm into the light and felt an odd kinship with it – they were both exhausted and worn out, pathetic and useless.

It had been two weeks since Quint had brought her back to this place, this derelict farmhouse hidden away within the rolling countryside. Two weeks since what little she'd owned she'd burned in a raging torrent. Two weeks since she'd reached the absolute limits of her control. She'd slept for over two days afterwards, rolling in and out of the conscious world like a wave lapping at the shore. At first, she tried to fight it, tried to remain awake, but exhaustion and sleep were her welcome friends, and she was too weak to resist them.

During this time, doubt had set in. Maybe she wasn't quite as tough as she'd thought. One fight with another mage had almost sucked the life from her. Quint had shrugged it off like it was nothing, whereas she'd hardly been able to stand. Voices had seeped down into her semi-conscious state from the others of the house. They had wanted to know why she was there; she seemed useless, she wasn't good enough for them. They had chipped away at her, adding to her feelings of inadequacy. She didn't know these people. She was an imposter.

Every now and then, a pair of kind dark brown eyes gazed down at her. Blue, green and silver light and the scent of pines on a hot summer day always accompanied the owner of the eyes, as did the return of her strength. It leeched into her body, along with the glowing colours, making her feel more alive. Then, one day, she was fully awake and able to stand. Those soulful eyes were nowhere to be found. Perhaps it was just a dream.

After she awoke, she found she couldn't summon even the tiniest fork of lightning. Attempting to do so only tired her out more. Quint had told her it would return, she just had to give it time. Kurt, however, never missed an opportunity to tell her she was worthless, that it would never return and she should leave or die.

Sasha scrunched her fists up. She hated Kurt. Of all the people in this house, he was the one who'd taken the most dislike to her. She hadn't even done anything, but maybe that was the point. The others weren't so bad. Delphina had treated her with kindness, shown her around the house and land, and made her the most delicious coffee she'd ever tasted. Dorian was somewhat indifferent to her but hadn't shown her any outward animosity, which made him okay in her book. Theo kept to himself, his expression as blank as his personality, his eyes ringed with a haunting grey. And despite how she and Quint had met, he had been good to her. He was positive her power would return. She was not so sure.

But where were those eyes? Those kind brown eyes that had watched over her. They didn't belong to anyone in the house. They couldn't have been real. That person wasn't real, but how she wished they were. There was safety and comfort there. Light and nature.

With a deep sigh, Sasha got up and wandered to the blue marble statue and the glowing green pyramid on the far side of the room. She always hated it when it was her turn to guard them. It was a thankless task, but Quint had insisted it was an incredibly important job. And at least it kept her away from Kurt. The statue was humanoid and a little taller than her. The soft flow and curves of its shape indicated that it was female, yet the detail was scant.

She placed a hand on the cold smooth surface and glanced up. The face didn't look human, not completely. It was more like a mask with large cut-out shapes for the eyes, and all that peered out was lifeless pale blue marble. The lips were in a straight line, offering no expression. As Sasha stared at it, she noticed the angle of a cheekbone. She was sure that hadn't been there the last time she'd been on guard duty. Perhaps Quint was right.

She crouched next to the green pyramid. The Gramarye, the others had called it. It truly was beautiful. An emerald light shone from it, bathing that corner of the basement in other-worldly light. Its sides curved gracefully, making it look as if it were dancing. Thin streams of coloured light shifted from within, gold, silver and sapphire. As she moved her hands towards the artefact, the colourful streams retreated to its centre and vanished. She pressed her palms against it. It was so cool and soothing. It felt like somewhere deep within, there was a great power. She stared at it, transfixed by its beauty. What was it? Where was it from? What did it mean? And why the statue?

'Your shift's over, or do you want to cuddle up with that thing?'

Sasha jumped. She let go and turned around, embarrassed that she'd been seen lost in awe at an inanimate object but relieved that it was Delphina who'd caught her. She forced out a smile. 'I was warming it up for you.'

'Thanks, very thoughtful. Here,' she added, passing Sasha a hot steaming mug.

Sasha took it gratefully and drew in a long deep breath of the bitter aroma. It wasn't a beer, but it was a close second. It smelt so good she wanted to pour it all over her body, but she managed to restrain herself and instead took a sip. It was delicious, rich, dark and warm. Her tongue curled with delight. 'Thanks.'

'You're welcome.' Delphina pushed her long black braids over her shoulder and stared at the marble statue.

'Does it look different to you?' Sasha asked.

Delphina pursed her lips. 'A little. This cheekbone here, it's standing out more. And here, above the eye, it looks like an eyebrow.'

Sasha took a step closer and squinted. 'I hadn't noticed the eyebrow.'

Delphina let out a heavy breath. 'Varo will return. She'll open up the Otherside and bring freedom to all the mages of Vermor.'

Sasha looked towards her; she was smiling and full of hope. Why did she care about all those mages? All those people she would never meet? It was a ridiculous notion. Sasha wanted her power back and to feel the Otherside flow through her, to be strong and to not live in fear ever again. The other mages, though, as far as she was concerned, were not her problem. As soon as she could channel from the Otherside, she'd leave and not look back. Take her power, leave these people and leave Vermor. The country was rotten. She didn't need it, and it certainly didn't need her. 'Quint said I'll have to speak to her, Varo, when she returns, to make me an official member of this house.'

'That's right.'

'He didn't say, but could I be thrown out if she . . . if she doesn't like me?'

'Yes, but she'll like you.' Delphina placed a firm and reassuring hand on Sasha's shoulder.

'Not if Kurt speaks for me.'

Delphina levelled her dark brown eyes with Sasha's, a ring of honey shimmering around her pupils. 'Kurt doesn't like anyone. He's difficult.'

'He especially doesn't like me.'

'I know, but try not to let it get to you. You'll get your magic back soon, and he'll leave you alone.'

Sasha nodded feebly, but she didn't believe her. She wasn't sure if she'd ever be able to pull on her element again. Maybe it was for the best after what had happened with her little brother. His face, his ruined face. All her fault, all her fault.

Melted, burnt and dripping. And what chaos would she bring if she could touch the Otherside? Perhaps she should leave before she found out. That was for the best. Run away, run away like always. No. She shuddered and shoved the thought away. Not this time. 'I should go and get some rest.'

'Drink that, have a lie-down and you'll soon be back to how you were.'

'Thanks, Del.'

With that, Sasha left the basement and padded upstairs to her room.

CHAPTER SIX

KILLIAN'S EYES FLICKERED OPEN. HE BLINKED SEVERAL times, then sat up. A heavy ache filled his weary body. He rubbed his sore muscles and glanced out of the window just in time to see the crimson sun dip below the horizon. If the sun was setting, that meant he'd been unconscious all day, maybe even longer. How pathetic. The last thing he remembered was being on the beach and trying to walk but failing miserably. With a despondent grunt, he swung his legs over the edge of the bed and placed his feet on the chilly stone floor. Resting his chin in his hands, he had a look around his surroundings.

It was the same room he'd shared with Ren all those months ago. It was a sparse affair; a small threadbare rug languished in the middle of the floor. The walls were bare stone, cold and unfriendly. He breathed out and watched his hot breath curl through the air. Between the two beds was a small rickety table. On top lay half a loaf of bread, some cheese and a candle. Its spindly legs looked ready to buckle under their tiny burden.

Killian eased himself off the bed and put on his boots. He grabbed the bread and cheese and had a bite of each. He was famished, but he wanted to hold off eating until he'd seen Lily; she might be able to offer him something better. Hanging on the back of the door and looking like a lost spectre was his coat. A dull throb pulsed through his arms and shoulders as he put it on.

He opened the door and stepped out into the corridor. All he wanted to do was find Lily or Raven without running into anyone else. Judging by the noise flowing from the door at the other end, dinner was in full swing. *Bloody Lily – if she'd passed out at mine, I'd have at least had the decency to leave her a note.*

There was only one thing for it – he'd have to find her room and hope she was in there. He'd been there once but couldn't quite remember the way. Tentatively, he reached his hand into his coat and grasped his sword hilt. Nothing happened.

He let go and wandered down the long grey stone corridor before him. The clip of his boots resonated off the thick walls. There was a loneliness to the sound. He was alone, and one was the loneliest number, after all. Collections of sunstones reclined on the window ledges and sent their peachy-pink blush tumbling out into the evening. It crawled up the walls and pooled on the floor. Setting them up in the window was a clever idea. Simple and efficient.

Artwork of all types punctuated the walls – landscape paintings, portraits of morose-looking wealthy people and even bowls of fruit. Who wanted bowls of fruit on their walls? Killian was baffled. There were masks too. Long, thin wooden ones with colourful feathers sticking out of them, small round ones encrusted with sparkling jewels and dainty elegant ones that would only cover the wearer's eyes. The castle was more like a museum than a home for a pirate crew. Lily's spoils of war had to go somewhere. At first it seemed strange to him that she'd semi-retired here on the island, but looking at her collection, there was very little to add to it. What did you do when you had everything? It was a question he'd never had the need to ponder.

A light breeze fluttered down the corridor and tousled Killian's hair. He pulled his coat closer and upped his pace from a lingering dawdle to a respectable walk. He did want to see Lily tonight, after all. After a few twists and turns, he was confronted by a spiral staircase and ascended it, knowing he was on the right path. He paused halfway up to look out of a window. The sky was streaked with deep purple clouds and was rapidly fading from blue to black as the dark of the night drew in. He reached the top and wandered to the end of the corridor until his way was barred by a thick wooden door. He cleared his throat, took a deep breath and knocked. There was no answer, so he knocked again. Still no answer.

Killian was lodged firmly at the crossroads of indecision. Should he wait outside her room or go back to his? He shook his head and rebuked both options. Traipsing all the way back to his room certainly wasn't on the cards, but equally, he wasn't going to stand outside Lily's room like some sycophantic crawler. He put his hand on the doorknob and tried to open it. It didn't budge. This, however, wasn't a problem for him. He slid down to one knee and took out his locksmith kit. Within seconds, the lock popped, and the door merrily opened for him.

He closed it and strolled into her room. An oil lamp was burning by the side of her bed, so she must have been in there recently. A comforting warmth crept through him, but he couldn't quite ascertain why, so he put it down to the red decor. He paced across the room and sat down on the end of her bed. Raven's beautiful painting hung before him. The river sparkled in the soft flickering light of the lamp, and the stars twinkled as if Raven had caught real ones and embedded them into the canvas. How could anyone compete with a man like that?

He turned to his right, and his stomach lurched. Staring back at him from within the twinkling golden frame of a free-standing mirror was his reflection. To call it ghastly was an understatement. It was pale and unhealthy, its eyes lost within a bruised shadow. Disgusted, he looked away. He tilted his head back towards the window behind him. The purple clouds had melted into thick grey sheets, and a haze-obscured moon shone dimly within the dark, its light smeared across the night sky. A handful of faint stars tried in vain to brighten the dull evening, but the spiteful clouds maliciously blocked their admirable efforts.

Killian allowed his aching body to flop back onto her bed. Grunting with satisfaction, he stretched out his legs. It was comfortable in the pirate queen's private room. He encircled his head with his arms and let his eyes close. Warm and comfortable.

'Killian! What are you doing in here?'

Lily's stern voice woke him with a start. He pushed himself up and blinked several times before the haze of black and green came into focus to reveal the pirate queen.

'Are you gonna answer me?' she said, her emerald eyes glaring at him.

'You put me up in a real shit room, so I thought I'd mosey up here to see how the other half live,' he said, his voice thick. He cleared his throat before continuing. 'It's rather nice, I must say. Warm, cosy, fully furnished – how much for the night?' he added, patting the bed.

'More than you can afford,' she grunted, removing her hat and coat and hanging them on a dark wooden hatstand.

'You're being a little presumptuous about my finances.'

'You can't afford this room,' she said, raking her fingers through her hair. The glimmer of a smirk tugged at the corner of her mouth. 'Since you're here, do you want a night-cap?'

'Sure, I won't pass on this rare spark of generosity,' he said. 'Thanks.'

'Just one,' she said, clicking her fingers, 'then you're out.'

She opened the small chest by the side of her bed and pulled out a bottle of rum and a couple of frosted tumblers. She sat next to Killian, handed him a glass and poured him a generous shot and one for herself. They clinked glasses and downed their drinks in one.

'How you feeling?' Lily asked as she automatically poured them another drink.

'Fine.' He sipped the rum thoughtfully. It was strong and spicy with a mellow vanilla aftertaste, and it warmed his chest. 'I don't know what happened earlier.'

'You've been sleeping most of the day.'

'Yeah,' he said, wincing. 'I don't know why.'

'Physical exhaustion?' she suggested.

'All I did was row over here.' He stared into his glass and swirled the rich amber liquid around, creating a vortex of alcohol, and then knocked it back. 'I'd like to think I'm fitter than that.'

She nodded, then finished her drink. 'Last one,' she said, pouring them both a third shot.

'Just one, eh?' Killian smiled. A drunken haze was already wrapping itself around his body, and it felt great. He didn't want it to ever let go.

'One, three, same thing,' she said with a careless shrug.

He took a slow sip of his shot, allowing the alcohol to burn his mouth before swallowing. 'I don't know what happened to me. It's probably best if we forget about it.'

'If that's what you want.'

'It is.'

'Then it's forgotten,' she said with a sweeping gesture.

'Good.'

'So.' She paused and downed her drink before continuing. 'Any particular reason for rowing over, or did you just feel like being social?'

'Lil, you don't have to pussyfoot around the subject. I know what you're thinking.'

'Oh, you do, do you?'

'Yeah,' he said. He gulped his rum, set the glass on the floor and then slowly wiped his top lip with his thumb. 'You want to know if I've found a way to clear up the mess I created.'

'Killian, I d—'

'Yes and no.' His voice was curt. 'Yes, because I might have found someone who can help, and no, because Ren's still dead, and nothing I can do will ever change that.'

'Killian, y—'

'I could have helped him, but I didn't.' He paused. His breath was shaking, and his vision was blurring. He couldn't break down, not now, not in front of her. It wouldn't help anyone. With a deft flick of his wrist, he wiped away the threatening tears, then ran his hand through his hair to disguise it.

'He's dead. I know it's hard, but you need to accept it. Sitting around moping about it isn't helping anyone.'

'Sometimes I dream I'm the one killing him,' he said, his voice monotone, his focus on Raven's serene painting. 'I'm stood over him and I'm just stabbing and stabbing – I can't stop. He's screaming, begging me to help, but I don't, I carry on. There's blood everywhere, it's all over me, all over the floor, all over him. There's this rasping sound, and he dies. I just stand and stare at his corpse. I can't look away, I can't even close my eyes. He stares back at me, bloody and dead. I wake up in a sweat, fall asleep, and it starts again.'

He wanted more rum. He *needed* more rum. Lily seemed to pick up on this because she reached down and filled his glass.

'It's not real,' she said, handing him the glass.

'I know, but I got him killed.' He drew a deep breath and inhaled the vapours from the rum. It was so delicious. Why couldn't he dive in and drift around in that amber comfort? That would help. That would take his cares away.

'We were both there.' Rum sloshed into Lily's glass as she spoke. 'And now we have to fix it.'

'You're right.' Killian swallowed the last of his drink, put the glass on the floor and lay back on the bed. He told Lily everything Estelle had said the night before. Every few sentences he paused to make sure he had all the details correct – he was rather drunk by now, after all. Lily listened in silence, her gaze not leaving him. As usual, her face was unreadable. How did she do that? Even after all the rum. It was impressive.

'What d'you reckon?' he asked, sitting up and leaning back on his elbows.

'I reckon it's all we've got,' she said. 'But first off, are you sure the pie-shop proprietor has all her facts straight? I don't wanna go trekking off into the wilderness for nothing.'

'Of course I am,' said Killian. 'And don't speak about her like that.'

'Like what?'

'All snobbish and superior. She has a name.'

'Okay, does *Estelle Pengelly* have her facts straight?'

'Yes, she does. And I think we can agree that my last tip worked out pretty well.'

'Except for the murderous demon we unleashed.'

Killian's heart thumped, and his chest tightened. He glanced at his glass of rum. It was empty. But he didn't need a glass; he needed a bottle. A bottle to wash away the pain, the loss and the humiliation. To drown his worthlessness in a sweet, spicy river of mind-numbing bliss.

'All right.' Lily's stern voice dredged him out of that soothing alcoholic river.

'All right?' he asked, unsure.

'We'll do it. We'll go and find this warlock, provided he's not dead already.' She wasn't looking at him.

'As simple as that?'

'We have to set things right. That thing, the Gramarye – nothing good can come of it.'

A light sensation flooded his body, and his muscles relaxed. 'No feathers or shells this time?'

Lily chuckled gently. 'I've got enough of those. You need to work on getting yourself better. Collapsing on the beach, your nightmares, the way you blame yourself. It's all connected.'

'Perhaps,' he said as he got to his feet. The rum rushed to his head, and a warm dizzy sensation settled over his body. It was not unpleasant. 'I'd best get going.'

He dusted his coat down and ran his fingers through his messy hair. Lily marched past him and opened the door.

'Killian,' she said. Her eyes looked troubled, and it seemed as if she was about to say something profound. 'Go and see Tom, Finn and Blake tomorrow. They're worried about you.' Her tone was blunt and detached.

'I will,' he said, pausing in front of her in the doorway. 'Thanks for the nightcaps.'

'Any time.'

The door shut behind him as he paced towards the spiral staircase. He was so drunk, and he needed rest. A warm bed and a good sleep. In no time at all, he was back in his room. *How did I get here so fast?* It was only when he slipped his coat off that he saw the glow fading back into his skin.

Then the fatigue hit him like a battering ram. It took all his will to stay standing, but he was determined not to spend the night on the stone floor. A muddled fog clouded his mind, and his body was perilously weak. Somehow, he made it to his bed and slumped down on the edge. He took his boots off, wriggled out of his trousers and pulled the blanket over himself. This, however, took all his remaining strength, and he passed out with his shirt half unbuttoned.

CHAPTER SEVEN

KILLIAN PACED THROUGH THE WOODS, FOLLOWING the intermittent crack of gunfire. He'd bumped into Jarran on the beach, who'd pointed out where he could find two of his three gunner friends. As he approached a clearing, he peered through the trees at Finn and Tom on the other side. The pirates were standing before a row of tatty scarecrows and filling their guns. Just seeing them forced the heavy clouds away from his heart.

Anxiety had plagued his walk from the castle. The fear of what they might think of him had almost made him retreat to Brackmouth in shame, but now, all he wanted to do was run up to them and grab them in an embrace. Hunkering down, he slunk into the undergrowth and worked his way around to them.

'You know what, Finlay,' Tom spat. 'I've had more women than you've ever had headshots.'

'More women than d'Roué?' said Finn with a grin, lining up her next shot at a scarecrow target.

'Don't jest like that, it's cruel. You know I could never be like him – the man is a god, a demon, a beast!' He paused and rubbed his stubbly beard, his peridot eyes lost in a sordid dreamworld. 'Maybe I'd be a close second though.'

'From what I've heard,' said Finn, glancing over her shoulder, 'his first mate's almost as good with the ladies as him. Come to think of it, they say his first mate is good with the men too, so you best aim a little lower.'

'All right, all right, third!'

'Really?' Finn chuckled. She fired, hitting her target full on, and its straw face caved in and smoked. 'I've heard Morton gets more action than you,' she said, turning back to Tom.

Tom folded his arms and flared his nostrils.

'Come on, it's your shot.'

'Nah, I'm done,' said Tom, sinking to the ground.

'Quittin'?'

'No, I don't think I need any more practice, that's all.'

'Looks like you need all the practice you can get,' said Killian, stepping out from the bushes.

'Killian!' gasped Tom, leaping to his feet. 'Where've you been?'

'Brackmouth.'

'Ah, come here,' said Tom, grabbing him in a tight hug. 'I tell you, it's been dull around here without you. I've missed you. I feel like I could kiss you! Don't worry, I won't, but I sort of want to. Ah, fuck it!' Tom stretched up and planted a wet kiss on Killian's cheek. 'Welcome home!'

'Thanks,' said Killian, overwhelmed by such a warm greeting. Didn't they know about Ren?

Tom grinned, let him go and pushed him away.

'Nice to see your rotten face again, you absolute shithead,' said Finn, giving him a welcoming punch to the shoulder.

'Yours too. Where's Blake? I thought you three were attached at the hip.'

'Not seen him,' said Tom, scratching his armpit.

'Me neither.' Finn's dark grey gaze was cast to the muddy ground.

'You two are pathetic liars.'

'We're not lying about anything,' Tom insisted.

'You're not answering my question either.'

'Blake's out,' said Finn.

Killian looked at Finn and cocked an eyebrow in question.

'He's busy,' she said. 'You can talk to him when he gets back.'

'I will,' said Killian.

'So, now you're here, how about a drink?' said Finn, securing her gun and pulling a roll-up from inside her coat pocket.

'Yes!' Tom beamed. 'I ain't been wasted in weeks.'

'Sounds good,' said Killian.

'I've got a bottle of the *good stuff* stashed in my room,' said Finn, slapping Killian hard on the back. 'Come on, Tom.'

Just being in the company of Tom and Finn helped Killian feel a little lighter. He was grateful for their uncanny tact around him. As they walked back to the castle together, not once did they ask how he was or what he'd been doing or mention Ren. He hadn't realised until now how much he'd missed their company.

He followed them through the cold stony corridors to Finn's room. Straight away he noticed how different the room was from his. It was warm and inviting, and the rug on the floor was dark red and thick. The furniture didn't look tired; in fact, if it could, Killian was sure it would be doing one-handed press-ups. The air smelt of tobacco with a hint of spiced rum, Finn's own brand of perfume. It was delicious.

'Nice room,' he commented. 'I almost froze to death last night.'

'You were here last night?' said Tom, frowning. 'An' you didn't come see us?'

'It was late,' lied Killian, shaking his head.

'Don't matter, you're 'ere now,' said Finn, tossing him a green bottle.

Killian had a long swig. It was good, strong and hot. It tasted similar to the brew Lily had – it must have been from the same batch. Thinking about the pirate queen brought a hollow ache to his stomach, so he took another draught to fill it. He set the bottle down and wiped his mouth. 'I wasn't at my best last night.'

'Wouldn't have mattered,' said Tom, taking a drink and sitting down on the end of Finn's bed. 'I'm used to that. I have to deal with her, remember?' He nodded towards Finn.

Killian chuckled.

'Ay!' Finn snatched the bottle from Tom.

Killian sank to the floor and leant against the wooden bed. 'He's right,' he said.

'You can shut up too,' said Finn. She gulped from the bottle.

Tom looked down at Killian and winked, causing them both to burst into fits of uncontrollable laughter. Finn snorted, but her eyes were twinkling. The rest of the afternoon breezed by. Killian found he could easily relax in their company; the rum helped too, of course. He began to wonder why he had been so nervous about meeting up with them. So far there had been no mention of Ren or demons or powerful lost artefacts. It was like everything was normal.

The afternoon seamlessly melted into the evening, and before long there was a knock at the door.

' 'S open,' drawled Finn.

A cloaked figure swept in, followed by a rush of fresh cold air.

'Nothing today,' the figure muttered as it removed its dark purple cloak. 'You know, I'm beginning to think it's a lost cause. I might give up. I'm obviously not making any progress. I'm such an idiot for thinking it'd work.'

Blake tossed the cloak to the floor and ran his fingers through his floppy dark hair. 'Pointless. I'm starving, let's get somethi—' He froze mid-sentence, finally noticing Killian sitting on the floor looking up at him.

'Evening, Blake.'

'Killian!' exclaimed Blake, his hazel eyes wide. 'When'd you get here?'

'Last night.'

'And you didn't come and see us?'

'It was late, apparently, and he didn't want to disturb us,' Tom butted in.

'So, where've you been?' Killian asked, watching Blake's expression intently.

'In town,' said Blake, picking up his discarded cloak and folding it neatly – a little too neatly. 'I needed to get some things.'

'In town? All day?'

'Yeah, all day, busy day.' He flapped the cloak open and folded it the other way, again a little too neatly.

'What'd you get?'

'I placed an order at Skevington's for some stuff – bullets, gunpowder, stuff.'

'Ah, stuff,' Killian mused, looking Blake up and down. 'I thought Finn was the master gunner?'

'I delegated,' said Finn.

'Is anyone else really hungry?' Blake asked. 'I'm really hungry. Too hungry to talk if I'm honest.'

'Uh-huh,' Finn grunted. 'Let's see what's on.'

Tom slid off the bed to his feet. 'Come on,' he said, giving Killian a nudge with his foot.

'I'm not hungry.' He yawned and stretched. 'I just wanna grab some air and go to bed.'

'Gah, you're boring,' grumbled Tom.

'You're annoying,' said Killian with a casual shrug. He looked out of the window; darkness had settled over the island. The trees wavered this way and that, harassed by the cold winds. 'Blake, toss me your cloak. It looks chilly out there.'

'It is,' said Blake, throwing the plum-coloured cloak towards him.

Killian wrapped it around himself and pulled the hood up. 'I'll see you wasters tomorrow.'

As Killian stepped outside, an icy wind whipped up the cloak, causing it to flap about him like a malcontent shadow desperately trying to sever its human bond. Grimacing, he pulled it closer to his body and made his way down to the shore. He stood a few feet from the water's edge and watched the tiny black waves as they lapped at the sand. A thin moon emerged from behind a grey cloud with a sideways grin. A few stars were scattered across the sky, but their lacklustre shimmer gave the impression that they didn't really want to be there.

He inhaled a deep breath of salty air, held it in and then blew it all from his lungs. He pulled the hood down farther, retreating into it. The depression was looming over him again. He'd felt more like his old self when he was with the others, but was that all fake? Fake happiness derived from good company and alcohol? That was entirely possible. He balled his fists up. No, he'd felt something, friendship, companionship. It wasn't all fake.

He wrapped his arms around himself and held on tight. Lowering his head, he breathed slowly, no longer feeling the cold of the wind. After a few breaths, he stared into the sea and watched the oily-looking waters on their endless cycle. The soft sighs of the waves and the gentle clatter of the shells in the backwash were a calming comfort on this inky night.

He moved his arm out from the cloak and held his hand in front of him. He turned it backwards and forwards, moving all his fingers individually. Something lurked within him, but what? Then his hand flashed, and he jumped as iridescent light pulsed over his skin. His muscles tightened, and a new strength flowed through his body – a strength he didn't think himself capable of. It was intoxicating, or was that the rum at work? The gentle pad of bare feet on the sand caught his attention, and he shoved his hand inside the cloak, out of sight.

'Raven,' he said as he turned and caught sight of the man's unmistakable purple eyes glowing in the pale moonlight.

'Killian,' he replied, his voice soft and warm.

Killian turned back around, keeping his hand covered, and looked at the small sliver of moon. He sensed Raven standing next to him. They stayed that way for some time, in silence. The waves broke on the shore with whispering moans as the treetops murmured in the wind. Killian's body relaxed; there was something about Raven's presence that made him feel at peace. He glanced at him in his peripheral vision. His long hair blew all around him, his shirt flapped in the wind, yet his mysterious ethereal eyes remained focused on the sea and the scant silver reflections dashing across its choppy surface. It was obvious he was waiting for him to speak first.

'How've you been?' Killian asked, breaking the silence, wincing internally at what he'd just said. He may as well have asked him how the weather was.

'Fine,' said Raven, his mouth curling up into a smile.

'That's good,' said Killian.

'You?'

'Same.'

'I thought so.'

Killian grunted. 'What're you doing out on a shitty night like this?'

'I could ask you the same thing.'

'I wanted some air.'

'Me too.'

There was a long pause, and the wind and waves dutifully filled the silence with their doleful lament.

'The captain tells me you have another mission for us,' said Raven.

'Something like that,' Killian replied.

'In Freischen.'

'Yup.'

'I spent some time there a few years ago.'

'Good, you'll be of some use this time,' said Killian.

'A lesser man would take offence to that,' said Raven. 'But I know I've already saved your life . . . twice.'

'You got lucky.'

Raven chuckled. 'Yes, I did.'

Killian smiled into the darkness. Raven's presence was also lifting that weight from his chest. This mysterious man, with his impossible agility and his devastatingly handsome looks, felt like the human – if he was human – equivalent of a warm blanket and a roaring fire. There was a time, not so long ago, when Killian had been deeply envious of him, but now all he wanted was to be with him, to feel that comfort roll off him, soothing his worries and fears. Did leeching off Raven's kindness and good nature make Killian a bad person? Was he using him to make himself feel better? Or did Raven genuinely care? Did he know that by just being present he helped ease the pains of others?

The first mate inhaled deeply, snapping Killian out of his thoughts. 'I'm going for a run in the woods.'

'In the dark?' Killian narrowed his eyes at the grey-smeared treetops behind the beach.

'I'll be able to see where I'm going. You can come along if you like.'

'I won't be able to see, and you know what happens when I can't see where I'm going.'

'True,' said Raven.

'Enjoy your run, you strange man,' said Killian, pulling the cloak tight against his body.

'I will.'

Killian paused and curled his fist beneath the cloak. 'Raven, I—' He stopped. He could tell him, tell him now, about the strange glow, about his feelings, about everything; he could share his burden. No, he couldn't. He screwed his fist up again; he wouldn't force his worries onto someone else. It wasn't fair. He would deal with them alone. 'Don't knock yourself out on a tree.'

'That's your area of expertise.' With that, Raven darted up the beach and leapt into the woodland beyond.

When he was out of sight, Killian pulled his hand from under the cloak. It appeared normal. *Maybe I'm going crazy.* His shoulders slumped, and he ambled back to his room.

CHAPTER EIGHT

Killian strolled the corridors of the pirate castle at a leisurely pace. He was on his way to see Lily. He knew she was in the library, but he was in no great rush to get there. The air wafting through the open windows was fresh and invigorating, pine tinged with a salty tang. Outside, the sky was clear and bright; the wind from the previous night had chased away any threatening rain clouds. Good weather for rowing back to Brackmouth. A collection of gulls chattered to one another as they glided on the air currents.

'Gulla, gulla, gulla,' Killian said to the gulls. He knew they wouldn't hear, but it was the thought that counted. Every morning his mum used to fling his bedroom window open and call the same thing to the seagulls. He hadn't said it himself in years.

After a few twists and turns, he arrived at a thick wooden door and paused to take a deep breath. Why was he so nervous? Why was he feeling so sentimental? Before he could dwell anymore, he knocked.

'Yes?' Lily's voice came through the wood. She was using her sharp, abrasive tone, and it didn't inspire much confidence in him.

He opened the door and stepped inside. Lily was sitting behind a chunky dark wooden desk, a pile of books and papers laid out in front of her. She looked up, and her stony expression softened.

'Good morning, Killian,' she said as she pushed her waves of glossy black hair over her shoulders.

'Morning,' he replied, sauntering over to her.

'I thought you'd left,' she remarked.

'I've been busy.'

'Catching up?'

'Yeah.'

He felt a little awkward standing. It was too formal, and he didn't know what to do with his hands. There didn't seem to be any other chairs available, so he pushed her papers aside and sat on the edge of the desk.

'What you looking at?' he asked, craning his neck over her books.

'The terrain in Freischen.'

He leant down for a closer look, putting his hand on the table for support. Several large and ancient-looking books were sprawled across the dark wooden table. The scent of their leather binding and dusty pages filled the air around the pirate captain. He breathed deeply. It smelt like his mother's house. He cast a quizzical eye over the open pages. Maps, landscapes and strange animals all stared back at him. A large canine creature drew his attention. It appeared to have a white blade for a tail. Its teeth were bared, hackles raised, and its spine seemed to be almost bursting through its skin.

'What's that?' he asked, tapping the picture with a finger.

'A seri-lupine,' she said, not looking up. 'Locals call them razortails. I think even you can work out why. They hunt in packs and use their tails to immobilise their prey.'

'Looks like we're in for a fun day out in the woods,' said Killian.

'If being torn apart turns you on, then yes. They aren't the only creatures over there that'll want to rip out our throats either.' She sighed and flicked through the pages of the large red leather-bound tome in front of her.

'Your throat'll be fine,' he said, glancing at her neck before averting his attention back to the beast on the page.

'It will,' she said. 'It'll be touch and go for the rest of you though.'

'Not for me,' he said, grinning. 'You're forgetting I'm a Demon's Drop survivor.'

'And how could I forget that? You dashing, fearless hero,' she said, playfully slapping him on the leg.

A delightful aroma of herbs and citrus accompanied her slap, and his heart thumped. Numbness seeped into his supporting arm, so he lifted it from the table. He flexed and stretched his fingers, then placed his hand back down on top of something warm and soft. Lily's hand was beneath his. A rush of white-hot heat crept into his tight chest. She was making him feel something, and he didn't like it. He readjusted his position and mumbled an apology.

'That's okay,' she said, sounding infuriatingly unaffected.

'So, yes, anyway,' said Killian, scrambling to regain his cool. A thick overcooked steak replaced his tongue and sizzled in his mouth. He swallowed, internally cursed his pounding heart and rolled his shoulders until they popped. 'I came to see if you knew when we're leaving?'

'In a couple of days. Seth and Morton are sorting out supplies,' she said, her eyes focused on the book, not on him. 'We're not going as far, so it won't take them long.'

'What have you told everyone?'

'The truth,' she said. 'Evil demon, nasty artefact, we need to fix it.'

'And they're fine with that?'

She looked up at him, one of her eyebrows arched. 'Killian, I know exactly what you think of me – you made that abundantly clear when we were in the temple getting that stupid artefact. But despite what you believe, I happen to like this world, as do my crew, and we don't want it destroyed by some mad shadowy thing. I have a hard time believing what happened that day myself, and I was there, but I've explained it to my crew as best I can. We need to stop it, whatever it is. I don't know what it's planning, but judging by what happened with Ren, I don't think any good can come of it. It's our fault that it has the Gramarye, and we need to take responsibility for that.'

A pang of shame at her mention of his outburst in the temple pulsed through Killian, followed by a cold lance of pain at the mention of Ren.

'You're right.'

'I know.'

'And Ren?' he asked. 'What have you told them about him?'

'That he's dead. There's nothing more to say. Finn, Tom, Blake, Raven and Seth know a little more because they knew him personally. To everyone else, he's just dead.'

Killian remained silent. Thinking about Ren still caused him so much pain. Talking about him almost broke him.

'Have you nothing better to do?' she asked, pressing her palms so firmly onto the book that the table groaned in protest.

'Yeah, I should go to Bracky, pick up some things and see a few people – Stell, Cylus.'

'Don't let me keep you.'

At this, Killian slid off the table and made his way to the door. He paused before leaving and turned back to Lily, who was busily leafing through a book. Words bubbled up in his mind. He wanted to say something – he needed to. 'Lil, I didn't mean what I said in the temple.'

She raised her head and smiled softly at him. 'Yes, you did, but it's all right.'

CHAPTER NINE

A DILAPIDATED OLD FARMHOUSE, LONG PAST ITS heyday, stood alone amongst the rolling hills of the southern and midland borders of Vermor. Overworked fields long abandoned to wild grasses surrounded it, and an empty barn slumped at the end of a driveway. A wooden wagon sat outside the barn, waiting to be of use. Two piebald horses roamed through the fields shoulder to shoulder, their antlers shorn down to gold nubs. Tired shutters adorned every window of the house, their paint partially worn off to reveal the wood underneath.

Sasha sat on the wooden steps of the porch, watching the sun dip behind the hills like a falling ruby, a glass of tepid beer in her hand. She had yet to summon any lightning. It had been so long. Every day she tried. She'd sit in her room and focus everything she had, trying to draw the element to her, but nothing. Nothing but exhaustion and failure. She felt so useless, and it didn't sit right with her.

How long before the whole house turned against her and she was kicked out, or worse?

She stood up, put the glass to her lips and took a sip. She mustn't think like that. It wouldn't help. Mental clarity and physical strength were needed if she was ever to summon again. She couldn't let the Fear get to her. Fear to a mage was like the wind to a candle. It snuffed out all ability, clouding the mind with doubts and crippling their power. As soon as it slithered into the mind, a mage would weaken. If they allowed it to take over completely, summoning any flicker of magic would be impossible, at least until they could fight the Fear.

But she could fight, and she would summon again; she was burnt out, that was all. She wasn't a husk, not yet. Soon she was going to show all the mages in this house that she was as good as, if not better than, any of them. She knocked back a deep draught of beer in silent confirmation of her vow.

A chill crept over her shoulders. She was no longer alone. Glancing to her right, she spied Quint strolling towards her, his scar glistening with ice. She couldn't quite get over how he managed to maintain it. Surely it took some level of concentration, however small, to keep the ice packed into the ditch in his face.

Quint stopped a few paces away from Sasha, lit a cigarette and took a long drag, his gaze not leaving the swaying grasses of the fields. After a few minutes of silent smoking, he spoke.

'She's on her way back.' Smoke poured from his mouth and nose.

Sasha closed the gap between them. 'You've been saying that since I woke up.'

'I know, but this time I can feel it. There's a different energy in the air. You wouldn't understand, but she's coming back.'

Sasha shrugged. She wasn't even sure who *she* was or what was so special about her. After his somewhat boisterous recruitment procedure, Quint had become rather tight-lipped about everything, promising Sasha that when *she* returned, *she* would explain everything.

Quint flipped open his cigarette case and offered her a smoke, which she gladly took. 'They say smoking ain't good for you, kiddo,' he said.

'Gotta get some joy out of life.' She popped it between her lips and allowed him to light it for her. After taking a long drag, followed by another deep swig of her beer, she spoke again. 'I've noticed a change in the statue. Every time I watch, it seems more human. Is it her?'

'Nothing gets past you, eh.'

'That's not an answer.'

Quint took a puff on his cigarette and blew the smoke across the fields in billowing waves. 'Yes, the statue is Varo. Happy now?'

'But . . . how?'

He turned to her and pulled a broken and battered pocket watch from his coat. 'So many questions. All right, I've got time.' He slipped the watch back into his pocket. 'She's strong – I've never met a mage as attuned to the Otherside as her. She used the darkness, the void, to separate her soul from her body and inhabited some old man for months and months. She sent his son on a ludicrous quest to get the Gramarye. Even I wasn't sure it'd work out, but it did.'

'That's insane.'

Quint nodded. 'And when she's back with us, we can start moving forwards, get ourselves some power and save all the mages in Vermor.'

'All the mages in Vermor,' Sasha muttered.

'You do know there're more mages in Vermor than anywhere else in the world?'

'Bullshit.'

'Language. I see you're not familiar with the concept that prohibition makes something more appealing. Imagine if cigarettes were banned, or beer; you'd want them more, you'd go to great lengths to get them – don't say you wouldn't. It works the same with mages. Over in Freischen, Venario, wherever, mages're rare. It's not illegal, so it's not dangerous, exciting or romantic. Here, however, there's a certain temptation that draws folks to the magic, a siren call. So, by helping all the mages here, you'll be helping a lot of people, kid.' Quint finished off his cigarette, stubbed out the end and flicked it away.

Sasha savoured hers a little longer, her vision growing misty as she looked out over the fields before them. Her heart thumped and her legs felt weak, but she had to say something. 'Quint, what use will I be if I can't wield anymore?'

He angled his head down towards hers and pushed his long grey-streaked hair back. 'You will.'

'Mages burn out, I know that, and I know some never get it back.' Sasha paused to take a calming swig of beer. 'What if I used everything? What if I broke after fighting you? What if it never comes back? What if I'm a husk?'

Quint gently placed his hands on her shoulders and squeezed. 'I've seen mages burn out and never come back, and I promise you, you'll get it back. You need to give it more time and worry less.'

'And if it doesn't come back?' She looked up into his dark eyes.

'Don't think about that – it'll give you the Fear.' He took a step back and flipped out his brass pocket watch once more. A small frown formed on his lips. 'I've gotta relieve

Theo. Will you be all right? I don't like leaving you distressed, kiddo.'

'I'll be fine, I've been distressed before.'

'Uh-huh. Well, you know where I am if you need me.'

The door creaked, and Quint's footsteps disappeared into the house. Sasha popped her cigarette back into her mouth, slumped forwards and rested her forearms on the rail. A cloud of smoke sailed past her vision. She'd got no-handed smoking down to a fine art, and at least she could still do that. She took a few more puffs as she listlessly watched the ever-changing sky. It shifted from yellow to orange while pink and purple clouds scattered the vista. They looked like rolling sand dunes. A mystical beach floating in the sky. There was a gentle rustle in the trees as a breeze blew in, followed by the lonely call of an owl. The horses nickered to each other. She took one last drag on her cigarette, then stubbed it out and tossed it away. She swigged the remains of her beer and went into the house.

The inside was almost as run-down as the outside. Plaster and paint peeled off the walls, the floor was of worn splintered boards and a rusted chandelier hung overhead. Wooden frames devoid of any pictures hung askew at irregular intervals. A wide hallway opened out in front of her with a staircase to the left, leading up to the many bedrooms. To the right, an arched doorway led into the main room, where she could hear some of the others playing cards. Grunts of disapproval and the sounds of coins being pushed across the table crept into the hallway.

The door leading to the basement opened, and Theo emerged. His skin was pale, and his cheekbones were high and prominent. His deep brown eyes flashed up in the direction of Sasha. Her heart pounded. His eyes, they looked so familiar. It was like she'd seen them before, someplace else. In a dream? In another life? They were devoid of feeling though. Blank and lifeless, not kind and soulful.

'Lightning,' he said. His voice was monotone and empty of emotion.

'Theo,' she replied.

He moved his head in the smallest approximation of a nod Sasha had ever seen and shuffled upstairs. His ever-present fox clipped up after him. She didn't know that much about him – in truth, she didn't know that much about any of them – but Theo seemed to keep his distance from everyone. He channelled magic through from the Otherside, Delphina had told her that, but other than that, she knew nothing. And in all honesty, she didn't really care. He was just another face she passed in a corridor, and a miserable one at that.

She walked through the arch and into the main room, the savoury meaty wafts of stew calling to her. She was hungry and liked the idea of going to bed herself. Her chest tightened when she looked at the card table. Kurt was glaring right at her from over the top of his cards.

'How's Miss Thundercrack today?' he said.

Sasha held his stare and paced up to the table. 'I'm just fine, Kurt. Thanks for asking.'

Kurt curled his lips in response and rolled his pale blue eyes at Delphina and Dorian, who were sitting opposite him. This dance had gone on between Kurt and Sasha since she'd woken up. He would ask her how she was, she would politely respond and he would sneer. It was clear that he thought little of her after the way she'd been introduced to the group, and part of her couldn't blame him for that. They were a tight-knit group of mages, each skilled in their own area. Turning up unconscious and remaining that way for several days while being touted as a new member and therefore their equal would be enough to make anyone prickly. Whereas the others seemed to have almost forgotten about her entrance, Kurt had not.

'Play your card, Kurt,' said Delphina.

'Sure.' He glared at Sasha once more before getting back to the game.

Sasha breezed past him, her head held high, and made for the pot in the kitchen. She was determined not to let him know that he'd got to her. Fresh comforting beef stew would make her feel better. She took the lid off the pan. It was empty.

'I ate yours,' Kurt said over his shoulder.

'You told me you hadn't eaten,' Delphina snapped at him.

'I lied.'

'Sasha, I'm sorry,' said Delphina.

'It's fine,' said Sasha. She reached for a chunk of hard, dry bread – it'd have to do. 'There's this.'

'Play your card, Del,' Kurt huffed, indifferent to Sasha's plight.

She couldn't stand to be in the room with him any longer, so she paced out into the corridor without so much as an arbitrary 'goodnight.' As she clomped up the stairs, something tingled in her free hand. A tiny fork of lightning was dancing on her index finger.

CHAPTER TEN

IT FELT GOOD TO BE OUT ON THE OPEN WAVES AGAIN. Or did it? Lily was sitting at her desk in her cabin, books, maps and ink spread out before her. A heavy weight pressed against her chest as she lazily flicked through the pages of a thick book. Something about the *Tempest* was different. It felt almost as if she were imprisoned on her own ship. She grabbed a mug of watered-down rum and took a swig. But how could she be trapped? She was the captain, after all; she was in charge of her own life and destiny. And yet she was responsible for all the men and women on board; they relied on her. If she wanted to run away, she couldn't.

Her gaze wandered to the pastel village in Raven's painting. It was so peaceful, idyllic and calming. Was that what she wanted? After years of sailing, pillaging and rising up the ranks, did she really want to stop and disappear? She took another swig. There was too much water mixed in her mug; it completely lacked the usual fiery kick of rum. What would she do though? Grow vines, make her own wine, bask in the sun. A tiny smile tugged at the corner of her mouth. Could she really do that? Live a calm and carefree life? After everything she'd been through and seen, it didn't seem possible. The *Tempest* creaked in answer to her thoughts, and she turned her attention back to her books. She had duties. Whatever she and Killian had released into the world had to be stopped. There was also her crew. They needed her, they relied on her. Her idle fancies had no place in her life or anyone else's.

A sharp knock rattled her cabin door.

'Come in,' she called, pushing her book to one side.

Morton Roberts swaggered in, a chilly ocean breeze accompanying him. His face was set with a hard grimace, and his leather cap glistened with raindrops.

'I need a word,' he said.

'Of course. Sit,' said Lily, indicating the chair in front of the desk. 'Drink?' she offered, shaking the rum bottle.

'Nah, I'm good,' Morton rasped as he sat down.

Lily sloshed some more rum into her mug to dilute the water. 'So, to what do I owe the pleasure?'

'Cap'n, I don't wanna be speaking outta turn, but I gotta ask, what the fuck are we doing?'

Heat rose in Lily's chest, but she shoved it away. Having an outburst of rage wouldn't help anyone. 'I thought I explained that before we left.'

'Aye – demon, artefact, that pasty lickspittle getting killed. I got all that shit.'

'And?'

'And why is that any concern of ours?'

'Morton, a demon has some incredibly powerful artefact. I saw what it could do. I saw Ren die, and it wasn't pretty. All this happened because of us.'

'So?' Morton ran his hand over his leather cap, which squeaked like a dying mouse. 'We don't need to avenge the death of that guy – he weren't one of us. He weren't nothin' if you ask me.'

Lily sighed. This was a difficult audience. 'It isn't about that. We unleashed something, and we need to set it right.'

'Why we gotta fix it? We're pirates, Cap'n – we hold allegiance to no one but ourselves. Some demon has a thing, who cares? We move on.'

'I don't think you're grasping the bigger picture.'

' 'Cos there ain't none. We've created a mess before – we never stayed behind to fix it. That ain't what we do.'

'Morton.' Lily kept her voice calm and even despite the fury gnawing at her. 'This is different from anything else. This is something that must be stopped before it gets out of hand. You didn't see what I did. The power of this thing, the determination. There's no doubt in my mind that whatever it has planned won't be good for anyone, be they an ordinary law-abiding citizen or a pirate. We started this, we gave it the Gramarye, so we must stop it. Do I make myself clear?'

Morton curled his lip. 'If it weren't for that Killian c—'

'What's done is done.'

The quartermaster breathed out through clenched teeth. 'Aye.'

'Are we in agreement?'

'Aye, Cap'n.'

The chair cheered with delight as Morton stood up. He stalked out of the cabin with heavy footsteps, closing the door behind him. Lily took a mouthful of her rummy water. She could do without her crew challenging her decisions. They hadn't seen what she had. They couldn't possibly comprehend the danger of this thing or imagine the horror she had seen. Trying to stop whatever it was was the right thing to do, the *only* thing to do. She pushed her mug away and took a deep swig from the rum bottle.

KILLIAN stood outside the mess, his legs slightly bent to help him stand in the sway of the ship. It was surprising how quickly he'd forgotten about its pitching and lurching. Nonsensical whistling punctuated with in-tune singing leaked through the thick wooden door. An ache shot through Killian's heart. Seth had been a close friend of Ren, so it was only right he paid him a visit, but guilt weighed heavy on him. Would Seth be able to forgive him for his part in Ren's death? Before he could talk himself out of it, Killian rapped on the door.

'Busy!' a voice shouted back.

Killian pressed his lips together tight and knocked on the door again.

'Didn't ya hear? I'm busy!'

He tried once more, and this time the door flung open.

'What's the matter with you? Don't ya know when someone says they're busy it me—' Seth's furrowed brow melted away as soon as he saw Killian. 'Rat killer! Killian! Crazy man! Come in! Come in!' He seized Killian by the shoulders and dragged him into the mess.

The instantly recognisable smell of rum infused with dried herbs and old wood floated into Killian's senses. He breathed deeply – it was delicious. It made him need a rum.

He really hoped Seth would take out a bottle and not put a pot of tea on instead.

'Sit down, my friend,' said Seth, indicating the rickety wooden stool at the table. 'I'll make us a fresh pot.'

Killian's heart sank as he slumped onto the stool. Though perhaps drinking rum at every opportunity wasn't such a great idea. The notched table in front of him was covered with finely chopped dried herbs and a scattering of dried mushrooms. The savoury earthy scent made his stomach growl. He glanced at Seth, who was merrily filling a pot with leaves. A scratching sound cut through the air, followed by several mews.

'Ah, Miss Rangi, you want in, eh?' Seth moved to the corner of the room and crouched down. He opened a small door, a door no human could fit through, and in stalked his cat.

Killian had heard of Rangi but had never seen her before. She was a lithe yet muscular beast with grey tabby fur and one missing ear. She strutted in like she owned the whole ship, tail high in the air. Then she paused and sniffed. A pair of large amber eyes stared at Killian. Within seconds, her pupils dilated and her back arched. Her face morphed into a terrified snarl, and she hissed and spat at him. Her fur stood on end.

'Oh, Rangi, what you doing? It's only Killian.' Seth went to put his hand on her back, but she yowled and backed away from him.

The cat growled deep in her throat, her eyes, which were now almost entirely black, not leaving Killian.

'I don't think she likes me.'

As soon as Killian spoke, Rangi ran. She bolted back through the tiny door and disappeared. Seth frowned and shut it after her.

'She ain't never done nothing like that before,' he said, going back to the pot to pour their tea. 'She's a tough cat, never seen her scared in my life. Maybe she sees you as rat-catching competition. You put her outta business, eh.' Seth chuckled to himself.

'Yeah, maybe.' Or maybe she knew what he'd done. She knew he'd had a hand in Ren's death and refused to be close to someone as worthless as him, someone who could make so many mistakes, get so many people killed. A liability.

Seth set the mugs down with a loud *thunk* and snapped Killian out of his trance. The cook popped himself down on the chair opposite, his wiry hair bobbing and the beads threaded through it clacking together.

Killian reached for his mug. It burned his fingers, but he didn't care. The tea scalded his throat, but that didn't matter.

Seth's one dark eye watched him intently. 'I know what happened.'

Killian's nose grew hot, and his stomach fell away.

'I don't think we should talk about it much,' he continued. 'Ren was a good lad, a promising chef. He helped me out a lot.' Seth's eye became glassy. 'But talkin' ain't gonna bring the little fella back. He had a good heart, and I'll miss him, but I can't even begin to understand how you must be feelin'. Cap'n told me everything, said I had a right to know since Ren was my mate.'

'She tell you I was partly to blame?" said Killian, keeping his head down.

'Nope. She said there was nothing either of you could do.'

'But I could have . . .'

'There was nothin' you could do.' Seth took a draught from his mug. 'I shoulda got us something stronger, eh?'

Killian blinked, and two hot tears streaked down his face. Then he laughed. 'Yeah, something stronger would've been nice.'

Seth reached behind and grabbed a rum bottle from the sideboard. The cork popped with a dull tone, and he poured a measure into a pair of fresh mugs.

'Thanks.' Killian took a swig. It was much better than tea, spicy and sweet, and it washed his mind in a warm haze. He took another gulp.

'I got something for you,' said Seth. He reached into the pocket of his baggy green trousers and fished out a knife. It was rather rusty and slightly blunt.

Killian took it and frowned. 'What's this for?'

Seth blinked, and a single tear seeped out of his eye. 'It was little Ren's. It's what he used down here when he helped me out.' He wiped his eye and smiled. 'It's a terrible knife, no edge, has trouble cutting butter, but Ren, he made it work. He didn't complain, not once. He never asked for another knife, nope. Just worked away with this one until he was done.'

Killian examined the knife; it was awful. Dull metal, rusted. He ran his finger along it, and it wasn't even close to sharp. It rattled too, like it was trying to escape its wooden handle. He smiled to himself as he thought of Ren painstakingly chopping everything with the worst knife in the history of the world, too polite to ask for a better one. His fingers must have ached, but he hadn't complained, he'd carried on. It made Killian ashamed of himself.

Seth interrupted his thoughts. 'Thought you should have it. A little memento of our friend Ren.'

Killian considered handing it back to Seth. He didn't deserve such a treasure, but he didn't want to upset him by refusing his gift. 'Thanks, Seth. I'll keep it with me.' He slipped it inside his coat.

'A reminder. Not that we'll ever forget him, eh?'
'Never.'
Seth raised his mug and nodded. 'To Ren.'
'To Ren,' said Killian.

CHAPTER ELEVEN

AFTER TWO MORE DAYS OF UNEVENTFUL SAILING, the *Tempest* docked in the port town of Rinden in Freischen. Raven stood at the top of the gang-plank, his keen eyes fixed on Lily as she filled out the necessary paperwork for a shrewd-looking man. There was a hive of activity at the harbour. Merchants swamped it, carrying chests and crates of various wares. The air was laden with the smell of rich spices and the underlying whiff of fish and seafood as the local fishermen brought in the day's catch. Stacks of algae-coated lobster pots took up a vast portion of the docks.

Opportunistic cats prowled between the legs of the dockworkers, looking for a tasty morsel of fish to swipe. The stone huts that lined the harbour were crawling with seagulls shrieking obnoxiously to one another. They didn't rely on stealth like the cats. Raven watched Lily follow the man into one of the huts. He rapped his fingers against his thigh as he waited.

He'd been picked for the landing party, as had Tom, Finn, Blake and Killian. The three gunners were impatiently lingering on the deck surrounded by their travelling packs, yet Killian was nowhere to be seen. The *Tempest* was to be supervised by Morton in Raven's and Lily's absence. This made him apprehensive. He knew of Morton's dislike for Killian, and his resentment had no doubt increased since this new mission had been announced. He glanced across the deck and spied the quartermaster, who was smoking with a group of crewmates and had a rare smile on his face. Perhaps he was looking forward to the responsibility.

A pair of boots clipped on wood, and Raven turned around. Lily was standing at the top of the gangplank with a document in her hand.

'We ready to go?' she asked.

'Just waiting on Killian.'

Lily rolled her eyes. 'Typical. I've gotta give this to Morton.' She flapped the piece of paper. 'Please go and drag Killian up here. I'd like to be on our way before next week.'

Raven stayed beside Lily as they walked through Rinden. He sensed his captain was hesitant about leaving her ship and wanted to be near should she need him.

Rinden was a sizeable town on the Freischen coast. It was bustling with merchants. Market stalls lined the cobbled streets, displaying wares from all around the world – wines and preserved olives from Venario, dried apricots and figs, silks, and leathers from Maldia. A tall, handsome and tanned man was selling sunstones from the island kingdom of Santonos. He'd set pieces of it into jewellery; there were sunstone necklaces, rings and earrings, and chunks of it had even been carved into animal shapes. A sunstone octopus took centre stage, its reaching tentacles pastel shades of peach and pink. Of course, it wasn't glowing, not yet. It needed to be dark for that.

Voices called over one another as patrons and merchants alike haggled with the prices. Raven caught a few suspicious glances his way. Purple eyes always got a few stares, wherever he went. His tattoo drew attention too, so he often used his hair to cover it. In the distance, the bridge over the river loomed. It was huge; two giant red-stone towers topped with turrets flanked a wide road. Beyond it lay rolling fields and dense woodland. It was all so familiar to him.

He had to say something. He opened his mouth, but the captain spoke over him.

'First stop's Morell. Should only take us the day to trek there.'

'Yes, Lily. There's something I need to tell you about Morell.'

She turned to him and arched an eyebrow. Her captain's hat was absent; instead, she'd chosen to wear a green bandana for the journey. It was more practical, after all.

'I've been there, years ago.'

They trudged on, their boots thumping on the dusty paths. The great red bridge was drawing closer. A wooden shack stood in front of it, a tollbooth.

'And?' Lily prompted.

'I used to live there until rumours spread that I was a demon.' He tapped his tattoo. 'One night the locals became hostile, and I did something stupid. I thought if they wanted a demon, I'd give them one. So, I showed them everything.'

'Oh dear,' said Lily, shaking her head, though her tone coaxed a smile out of Raven.

'It wasn't very clever of me.'

'Do you think they'll be trouble?'

Raven managed another weak smile. 'It was over fifty years ago. They might have forgotten.'

'Or be dead.'

'You have a lovely way of looking at things sometimes.'

Lily chuckled.

They reached the bridge, and Lily marched off to pay the toll. While waiting for Killian and the gunners to catch up, Raven looked up. The huge towers reached up towards the thick fluffy clouds. It was an impressive feat of engineering. A tingle buzzed through his shoulder blades, and a desire to race up those red-stone monsters flooded his mind. To feel free. To reach the clouds and glide on the wind.

'You can tell them on the way.' Lily's voice broke into Raven's fantasies and brought him tumbling back to the ground in a swirl of dirt.

'Tell us what?' asked Finn.

CHAPTER TWELVE

SASHA POURED HERSELF A MUG OF THICK DARK coffee and winced as its bitter taste coated her tongue. If Delphina had been awake, she'd have asked her to make it. No one else in the house could ever get the correct balance of beans to water. Sasha was especially bad; she kept meaning to ask Delphina what her secret was. She downed it and left the mug – heavy with unappealing grainy sludge – in the kitchen.

It was still early, but thankfully, the mornings were becoming brighter as spring chased away winter. Shafts of weak golden light fought their way through the gaps in the shutters, illuminating the front room. Dust swirled lazily within the light, twinkling gold in the sunbeams. Sasha walked through it to the hallway. The house was quiet and still. Everyone else was still sleeping. A peaceful tranquillity wrapped itself around the old building. She had grown to love these moments; she didn't have to watch what she said or attempt any idle conversation. She could be herself.

Green light seeped through the cracks in the cellar door. Nothing had happened despite Quint's faith. What if she'd somehow been duped into joining up with this gang of mages? What was she even doing there? She'd been sold a tale of freedom and power, but if anything, being trapped in this house with them made her feel even less free than before. The temptation to run and go back to her old ways crept into her mind. Another year of magic shows and she'd have the money to leave Vermor – if she didn't get caught and killed in the process. She didn't need power, and she certainly didn't need to help other mages. But that wasn't entirely true. Power would help her. Power from the Otherside could stop a whole gang of cleansers. Power like that would truly set her free. No more running. She could stay in Vermor and live her real life. She wouldn't have to uproot her lover. A life without fear could be hers. She grabbed her dull green cloak from the chipped and battered hatstand and slung it on. She pulled the hood up and marched outside to greet the cool, crisp morning.

With a quick even pace, she made her way across the fields and towards the ramshackle disused barn. She stepped inside and closed the door behind her. For the past few days, she'd been waking up early and coming to the barn to practise her skills. She was determined to return to her full power and then go beyond it. That was another of Quint's promises: that she'd exceed her limitations. However, she was yet to return to how she'd been before their fight. She balled her fists up, drew lightning into them and called to nature in her mind. Tiny forks crackled and danced across her skin. She flicked her hands open and sent the lightning racing up her arms. It tickled her gently; it felt good. She held on to it and allowed it to snake over her body. It crackled with controlled power.

She closed her eyes and let her mind seek out the one she'd left behind. It had been a series of long lonely months since she'd last tasted her kiss, felt her warm soft skin next to hers and fallen asleep in her comforting embrace. The need to be with her often took over when she was alone. She missed her mentally and physically.

Maybe she could sneak away one night, under the cover of darkness. She could travel to the south, spend a whole hour with her and be back before anyone else woke up. The lightning's crackle increased in volume and moved even more erratically over her body. Her concentration faltered as the frustration of loneliness clouded her mind. It was impossible; she'd never make it all the way there and back in time.

A pulse of anger ripped through Sasha, increasing the intensity and power of her lightning along with her thoughts. With a grunt, she stumbled and fell to one knee, her body trembling with exhaustion. She sank her teeth into her bottom lip in annoyance at how feeble she still was. The weight of her own power forced her into the ground. Her fingers dug into the dirt. She'd have to release everything soon. Stinging sweat dribbled down her brow and into her eyes as she attempted to push herself up.

She managed to get to her feet, but the strain of it left her bent double. The lightning crawled over her body like a collection of glowing spiders. It was as if it had ideas of its own. It was leeching everything she had out of her – all her strength, all her energy. Holding on and trying to control it was futile. She fell again, this time to both knees. She scrunched her eyes up and begged for the magic to leave her.

It was too much, too soon. An inferno erupted over her skin. Panic gripped her. What if this time she passed out and never woke up? No, she wouldn't let that happen, wouldn't let it get that far. She reined her spiralling mind in and focused. She couldn't let the Fear take her. Not now.

She opened her eyes, glared at the straw and dirt beneath her and whispered, 'Go.'

She clung to that word and, with all her will, forced the power away. With a tremendous rush, forked light poured from her body and into the ground beneath her – fierce, crackling, white-hot and powerful. The earth ripped up around her, showering her body with clods of warm dirt. She wanted to scream but bit into her tongue to restrain herself. Then all the sound and all the light were gone. A soft spring breeze murmured through the gap in the barn doors. The baked smell of scorched earth lingered in the air.

Unable to hold herself up any longer, Sasha collapsed to the ground with a soft grunt. For several minutes she lay face down in the dirt, her heartbeat hammering in her ears. With a great effort, she rolled herself over and laid her hands on her chest, feeling it rise and fall with her breath. It was quick and short at first, but she gradually got it under control as she opened her senses to what was around her. The gentle rasps of the wind, the mournful call of a bullfinch, the feel of the hot mud beneath her and the warm earthy smell that rose from it.

After basking in nature for a few more breaths, Sasha got to her feet and dusted herself down. She hadn't passed out, and she'd managed to send her power away. That was some degree of control. There was still a long way for her to go, but perhaps she could get there. Perhaps she wasn't a lost cause. Her fingers tightened around her amber necklace, and her heart felt hollow.

The door sighed open, and shafts of golden morning light raced into the barn. Dazzled, Sasha put her hand up to her eyes and peered through the gaps in her fingers. A dark silhouette walked in.

'Good morning, Miss Thundercrack,' the unmistakable voice of Kurt sneered.

Sasha's chest tightened. Had he followed her? Had he watched her practising? She cleared her throat and rolled her shoulders back, refusing to give him one ounce of fear to play with. 'Kurt.'

'You're up early,' he said, taking a step closer, his pale eyes locked with hers.

'Couldn't sleep.'

'Me neither.'

'How about that.'

He dragged his feet through the straw as he spoke. 'What you doing in here, then?'

Sasha glared at him, the anger already rising in her throat. 'What's it to you?'

'I like to know what everyone's up to.' Kurt grinned, which only incensed her further. 'Especially those I don't like. You were practising, weren't you?'

'It's nothing to do with you.'

'Good job I was watching you, then.'

'Leave me alone, Kurt.' She balled her fists up and turned to walk away from him, but he grabbed her arm and yanked her back.

'No,' he said.

She shook his hand off but was completely taken by surprise when he pushed her back. She tripped over her feet and landed roughly on the ground. The air rushed out of her in shock.

'You're a liability, Sasha. The others can't seem to see it, but I can. You don't belong here.' He held his hand in front of his face, his fingertips bursting into flame one at a time. 'But I'm gonna make sure the others realise.'

Sasha got to her feet, rubbing her sore hip. 'I won't fight you.'

'Won't, or can't?' Kurt cocked his head to the side. 'I'm willing to bet it's *can't*.'

Rage surged through Sasha. Who was he to judge her? He didn't know what she could do, how strong she could be. A flash of lightning sparked in her palm. It felt so good, so powerful. She levelled her gaze with his. The fire danced in his eyes; he was goading her. But she could beat him, couldn't she? She hardened her resolve.

'Come on, then,' she snarled through gritted teeth.

'At last.'

Kurt flicked his fingers and launched five tiny fireballs at Sasha. She dived out of the way, hitting the ground and rolling. She flung her hand back, smothering his flames with forks of her lightning, then sprang to her feet and faced off against him.

'Not bad,' said Kurt, 'but let's really test ya.'

His right arm became fully engulfed in flames, and he laughed. He moved towards her like he was gliding. Sasha threw fork after fork at him, but he merely swatted them away with his flaming arm as if they were no more than flies. With nothing else to do, she threw a great bolt into the ground, which propelled her upwards. She neatly flipped over his head, landing behind him. She wobbled and had to steady herself by putting a hand on the ground. There was a loud drumming in her ears: her heart. Her breathing was laboured and painful. She had to end this ridiculous fight that her stupid ego had got her into. There was no way she could win, not without being devious.

Drawing on all her concentration, she pushed a small amount of power into her feet and propelled herself forwards with incredible speed. She grabbed Kurt from behind and sank her fingers into his ribs. He gasped with pain. Summoning all she had, Sasha pushed her lightning into him through her fingertips. There was a thunderous crack followed by a low rumble, and Kurt screamed. She let go and wilted to the ground as he tumbled forwards.

Sasha stayed on her knees, her sweat-soaked hair falling in her face. She could taste blood, and her head was swimming. All she wanted to do was sleep. Maybe throw up first, but then sleep. At least she'd won though; she'd shown him who she was. A tiny smile of satisfaction forced its way onto her lips.

'Dunno what you're smiling about.'

Kurt's voice ripped through her, and her stomach dropped away. She raised her head. He was standing before her, casually brushing himself down. Five smouldering ovals smoked on either side of his ribs. The material of his waistcoat was charred, but that was all. She hadn't hurt him in the slightest. She was such a fool. As if she had the power to take him down. Her skin prickled and then turned numb.

'You're even more disappointing than I thought.'

Before she could defend herself, Kurt kicked her hard in the stomach. She gasped and fell back. Pain ripped through her. Everything hurt. She couldn't summon even a tiny flicker to defend herself. She got to her hands and knees and tried to scramble. The Fear had got her in its cruel grip, rendering her less than useless. Somewhere in the back of her mind, her little brother screamed. She blinked and saw half his face melt away before her. He wasn't there. He couldn't be. It was an accident. An accident. A dry scream lodged in her throat, and her vision misted.

'Sorry,' she croaked to a deformed ghost.

Pain exploded in her ribs as Kurt kicked her once more. It was hot and burned, and she could smell smoke. She tried to move, to do anything to get away. His warm hands grabbed her and rolled her onto her back. A flaming hand flooded her sight. She feebly tried to throw him off, to push him away, but she was done.

'The pathetic thing is, I don't even need this to fight you.' With a theatrical click of his fingers, he banished the flames.

His fist connected with her jaw, and she was swallowed by blackness.

CHAPTER THIRTEEN

THE WIND WHISTLED AROUND THE SMALL PARTY as they stood outside Morell. Killian noticed Raven retreat deeper into his hood. He felt sorry for him. What happened had been so long ago, he couldn't have predicted he'd be returning. There was no reason for him to feel bad about it.

'They're going to think you're diseased,' remarked Blake.

'Better that than realise who I am,' said Raven.

'That bad, eh?' Blake asked him.

Raven nodded beneath the hood of his deep crimson cowl.

'Don't worry about them shitheads, we'll back y'up.' Finn grinned and slapped him firmly on the back.

'Thanks,' he replied weakly. 'They don't understand; it's not their fault.'

'Aye.'

'Let's get in, sleep and get out,' said Lily. 'We can get through one night without trouble.'

Raven took the lead and marched them into the town. Killian idled long enough for everyone to move in front of him before he ambled behind them. His body was stiff, and he kept his hands by his sides, ready to reach for his swords if need be.

The houses were mostly built from heavy-looking dark stones and supported by robust wooden beams. Yellow thatched roofs perched on top. Some were plastered and whitewashed, but for the most part they were natural stone. The streets were lined with uneven chunky cobbles, which were so arbitrarily placed they looked as if they'd fallen off the houses and got lodged into the ground. Finn tripped and cursed, and Tom chuckled, but an angry threat soon silenced him. Oil lamps were placed haphazardly along the street, black paint flaking off their stands to reveal dull metal underneath. They passed a wizened man in a weather-beaten coat straining up to each lamp to light it with a long hooked flint. He paused in his work as they approached and stared at them through rheumy wrinkle-flanked eyes.

'Evenin', fella,' said Tom with a warm smile.

He grunted and nodded in response before going back to his work.

'Know him?' Tom asked Raven.

'Shh!' hissed Lily.

Raven looked at Tom. 'Sven. He's done that job all his life. I'm surprised he's still going.'

'Old man Sven,' Tom muttered.

'It's not far now,' said Raven.

They turned down another street, this one well lit. Clusters of people sauntered about on the pavements, some saying goodbye and walking in opposite ways, others debating whether to go for a drink or not. Most of them didn't even bother to look at them as they passed. Killian's stomach growled; he was looking forward to getting a decent meal and a good night's sleep. He'd been in a hammock for five nights, which, granted, didn't seem long, but he just wanted a real bed. A real bed, a hot meal and some strong alcohol – that'd do him fine. A small group of people looking to be in their late twenties strutted by, and Killian noticed their eyes fall upon Raven. He bit down on the end of his tongue.

'He better not be infected with something,' said a woman in what was little more than a whisper.

'Excuse me?' said Finn, turning around to face the woman.

'Finn!' said Lily through her teeth.

'I said I hope *that*' – she extended her fingers in Raven's direction confidently – 'isn't some diseased freak. We've had enough of them come through here.'

Raven glanced to the ground.

'Why would you think that?' Finn asked. She folded her arms and bared her teeth.

'He looks it,' mumbled a man. He reached forwards and put his hand on the woman's shoulder.

Finn opened her mouth to retort, but Lily swept in to fill her place. 'Well, he's not, so that's all sorted.' She took Finn by the arm. 'Come on.'

The group of people continued to mutter as they walked away.

'What?' whispered Finn as she fell into step with her. 'That sour-faced bitch insulted one of us.'

'So, let it be,' said Lily.

'She needs my foot up her arse,' grumbled Finn.

'Finn, we're not here to cause a scene. One night and we're gone. That's an order.'

She nodded her consent. 'Aye, Cap'n, sorry.'

'How low are we keeping this profile of ours?' asked Tom.

'Low,' said Lily.

'But what if I . . . well, ya know, hook up with a local?'

'That's not going to happen,' said Blake with a sly grin.

'Hey!' snapped Tom.

Lily sighed. 'Tom, just don't, okay?'

'But I have a tradition. A new place, a new girl. 'S what I do.'

Lily stopped walking and glared at him. 'You really are a cretin, aren't you? I don't know why I have you on my ship, let alone in this group.' She paused and ran her fingers through her hair. 'You're just gonna have to break with tradition tonight and keep yourself under control.'

'Aye, Cap'n,' he murmured.

'Good,' she said. 'I'm sure you'll find some way to entertain yourself. You're resourceful, aren't you?'

Blake glanced at Tom and smirked. 'At least you won't have to bother creating a story.'

Tom screwed his face up in response. 'I never make anything up.'

'The inn should be on the corner of this road,' said Raven.

Lily paced out in front. Killian watched her emerald coat flapping in the breeze like some furious monster of the deep. It suited her.

The scent of a rich beefy gravy mingled with one of ale in the air. It was delicious, inviting even. He breathed deeply, and his mouth watered.

His boot clipped on a cobble and echoed down the street. The soft murmur of distant voices drifted through the shadowy twilight. The smells and the sounds were all so reminiscent to him, and yet he'd never set foot in Morell before.

The air had grown chilly, so he shoved his hands into his coat pockets and followed the others at a leisurely pace. The purple of the early-evening sky contrasted beautifully with the warm orange glow of the lamplit street. It was cosy and soothing. With the exception of the group they'd passed earlier, Morell didn't seem too bad. Eventually, Killian reached the end of the road where the others were clustered outside the inn.

'That ain't a good sign,' said Finn, a smouldering roll-up hanging from her lips as she looked up at the tavern.

Attached to the side of the building was a painted sign creaking ominously in the breeze. A crude illustration of a decapitated man adorned its rough wooden surface, his long black-haired head impaled on a pike. The words *The Headless Demon* were scrawled in red paint beneath it.

'They don't like you, do they?' said Tom.

Raven shook his head. 'Not especially.'

'Come on,' said Lily. 'Let's go, have some food and get a warm place to sleep the night. I'll do all the talking,' she added.

She marched boldly into the tavern, followed by the three gunners. Raven took a deep breath and pulled the cowl closer to his face.

'It'll be okay,' said Killian, giving his shoulder a reassuring squeeze.

'Thanks,' said Raven, and they walked in together.

CHAPTER FOURTEEN

A CRACKLING FIRE BEHIND A BLACKENED METAL grill greeted Killian with a pleasant rush of warmth as he stepped into the tavern. A savoury meaty smell clung to the air, accompanied by undertones of tobacco and alcohol. A long wooden bar took up the entire left wall, behind which a sharp-faced young barman stood, gazing out the window. Rows of benches segregated by wooden screens were against the right wall, most of them filled with people who were talking, drinking and eating. Several small round tables accompanied by three-legged stools were crammed carelessly into any available floor space. The room was thick with the clamour of voices – nobody even so much as lifted their head at the arrival of the six newcomers. An empty bench lurked in the far-right corner. Lily motioned for her group to sit there while she negotiated rooms, food and drinks accompanied by Finn.

Killian sat next to Raven, who was already scrunched into the back corner; his hood remained up. It was odd to see someone as beautiful and striking as Raven attempting to make himself as small and insignificant as possible. Tom and Blake had plonked themselves down opposite and were already deep in debate over Tom's sexual conquests. Killian glanced to the bar. Lily was handing over some coins while Finn scooped up three mugs of ale and strolled over to them. She passed one to Raven, another to Blake and kept the third for herself, a wicked grin on her scarred face as she sat down.

'I can't believe you picked him over me,' Tom grumbled.

'He's first mate, Tom,' said Finn.

'I didn't mean Raven, I meant Blakey boy.'

Finn barked a laugh and started rolling a cigarette. 'You really do moan about everything, don't ya, Tom?'

'You can have mine if it makes you feel better,' said Blake, pushing the dented pewter mug towards him.

'No, it's fine.' Tom huffed and folded his arms. 'I know who the favourite is now.'

Before anyone else could speak, Lily appeared with three more mugs and set them on the table. The only free space was next to Killian, so he shuffled as close to Raven as he could. As she sat down, her thigh brushed against him. A wash of inferiority soaked through Killian as he took note of who he was sitting between. He reached for the mug and had a long deep swig. It was deep, bold and heavy, with a hint of honey on the hops, and it was very welcome.

Tom took a slurp of ale. 'What's the food?'

'Bread, cheese, beef stew,' said Lily.

'Great, I'm half starved.' Tom beamed.

Killian's stomach growled as if Tom had somehow whispered a magical incantation. He took another swig of ale to stave off the hunger. A gentle wash of calm descended upon him. The heat and comfort of the tavern mixed with alcohol-heavy ale draped itself around him. Raven's hands were wrapped around his mug; he hadn't taken a sip yet. The man must have been roasting hot with that hood up.

'Raven, why don't you take the hood off?'

A soft smile formed on the shadowed face within the hood. 'That wouldn't be wise.'

Killian looked at Lily, and she rolled her eyes. Was she inviting him to poke fun at Raven? Just as he opened his mouth to say something, the barman walked over to their table balancing six pots on one tray. He plopped the tray down and scurried off without a word.

'What'd you say to him?' Killian addressed Lily in a low voice.

'I was very pleasant.' She smirked but didn't elaborate.

Tom was the first to grab one of the pots from the middle of the table, his elbows out wide to stop anyone who might dare to come between him and his food. A suspicious look crossed his face.

'Hey,' he grumbled as everyone else took theirs, 'I thought this was supposed to come with bread and cheese. He's bloody useless.' He waved a gold-ring-covered hand in the direction of the beleaguered-looking barman. 'I might have to have words.'

'Ah, just put up with it, Tom,' said Blake.

'I don't see why I should – I paid good money for this,' he said as he removed the lid. His green eyes grew wide as he peered into his bowl. 'What is *that*?'

'Seems like you got your bread and cheese after all,' said Blake, looking into his own pot of stew.

'What? That's horrible,' said Tom as he poked the chunks of cheese-covered bread floating in the stew.

'That's how they do it over here,' said Raven. 'It's a Freischen thing.'

'So put up and eat up,' said Finn. 'It's like having a child with us.' She sighed, then took a long gulp of ale. 'I reckon I'll need another soon.'

'You take that back, Finn,' snapped Tom, pointing his spoon at her. Long tendrils of cheese dangled off it and draped themselves over the table.

Killian shovelled the stew in. He tried to catch Lily's eye a couple of times, but whatever moment they'd shared was long gone. The food was delicious though, hot, savoury and just what he needed. Ten minutes later, everyone had finished their stew and was relaxing with their drinks. Finn had been to the bar to get herself another, just like she'd said she would.

'You know,' said Tom, 'that wasn't bad.'

Blake grinned and shook his head.

'Well, you know, it was a bit different, I was being wary. Didn't want us getting poisoned or something.'

'Ooh, something different,' mocked Finn. 'Can't have that, can we?'

'Fuck you, you bastard. You know what I meant.'

Finn took a drag from her cigarette and casually blew the smoke into Tom's face.

'What's the plan for tomorrow, Lily?' asked Raven, a lock of his purple-black hair falling from inside the hood.

'Get up, early' – she glared at Killian – 'and head off to Poll.'

'It's a distance,' said Raven. 'About a week or so on foot from here.'

Lily nodded. 'I know. Scherben's on the way. We'll stop and hire some horses from there.'

'Good idea.'

'I asked in Rinden, but that scrawny mope at the docks said nowhere in town hired them. How ridiculous is that?'

The overall noise in the bar picked up. Loud distinct voices punctuated the air.

Killian looked straight ahead and spied the group from the street. 'Don't look now,' he murmured.

Finn slung a glance over her shoulder. 'Not those shits again.'

'Now, Finn,' said Lily, putting her hand on top of hers.

'I know, I know, I won't say anything. I'll keep my head down like a good girl.'

Killian pulled his legs up onto the bench and rested his chin on his knees. He subtly watched the newcomers. The man and woman who'd insulted Raven lurched towards the bar while the rest of their group, about ten others, went to sit down around a table in the centre of the tavern. They were raucous and already drunk. Pipes were stuffed with tobacco, and thick dark smoke filled the air around them.

He glanced towards the bar and couldn't help but feel sorry for the harassed barman. The man and the woman were arguing with him about the kitchens being closed. Their voices were loud and their threatening words slurred. Eventually, once the bucket of insults had run dry, they ordered drinks for their table. They turned around and leant with their backs against the bar, waiting. The man's bleary-looking eyes surveyed the room.

'Shit,' muttered Killian. 'Here we go.'

Lily grimaced. 'What d'you me—'

'Hey!' the drunken man snapped at the barman. 'What're you doing letting *that* in here?' He pointed a wobbly finger towards Raven. 'It's got some kind of disease.'

A deathly silence descended across the tavern, and everybody shifted their attention to the barman.

'N-n-no,' he stammered. 'He's a c-c-customer.'

'Oh, really?' said the man, nodding. 'Well, I think he's a rotten piece of diseased meat, and he shouldn't be in here stinking the place up. What d'you think, sweetness?'

His female companion looked up at him and swayed drunkenly, twisting a lock of blonde hair through her fingers. 'Go get him, Yann,' she drawled.

He moved away from the bar and staggered towards the table of pirates and Killian.

'If this man is disease-free,' he said, addressing the entire bar, 'then surely he can show us his face. If I am wrong, I will apologise.'

'He doesn't have to show you anything,' snarled Finn, the vein on the side of her head bulging.

'Oh, but he does. We don't want another infection around here – last one was bad enough,' said Yann, removing his hat and clasping it to his chest. 'They want to see, don't you?' he added, waving his hand around the bar.

'Yesh, we do,' said a man, standing up. He must have been in his early seventies; his skin looked coarse from working outdoors his whole life, and across his right cheek ran a thick scar.

'Thank you, Francis,' said Yann. He glared at Raven. 'Just show us your face.'

Raven got to his feet. 'Does my face mean that much to you?' he asked from within the hood.

Yann nodded. 'Get it off!'

'Very well,' said Raven. He turned to Lily. 'I'm sorry.'

He turned back to Yann and removed his hood. Yann's mouth dropped open in shock, and a gasp of surprise rippled through the silent bar.

'I-I-I'm sorry,' Yann stuttered, taking a few steps back. 'I didn't know.'

'The demon,' whispered the scarred old man. 'The demon has returned.'

'I didn't mean to hurt you,' said Raven.

'You've not aged,' said Francis, running his fingers over his wrinkled skin. 'You're the same. You *are* a demon. We were right. We were all right.'

'I'm not a demon,' said Raven.

'Your eyes, your face – you are,' the old man continued, 'and this time you will die, as will your minions.' He bent down and whispered something to a young man sitting in front of him. The youth got up and fled the bar. 'You are going to die, you filthy demon. Your tainted blood will flow through our streets, and the land will be cleansed. No more curses, no more diseases. The foul reek you left behind festered – it grew into something vile and slaughtered half of our town.'

Killian couldn't take any more. How dare these yokels speak about his friend like that.

He drained the remains of his mug and jumped onto the table. A drunken confidence washed through him as he paced up and down. 'Wait, wait, wait. What's all this about killing Raven? He's not a demon, so how about you leave him alone? And how is tainted blood supposed to cleanse anything? Surely that makes everything even more filthy and cursed, or whatever it is you folks believe. And as for us, we're not his minions; we're his friends, and we will kill for him. So back off.

'Now, we'll just sit here, quietly finishing our drinks, and then go to bed. We'll be gone in the morning, so you can deal with us for one night.'

'No,' said Yann, finding his voice. 'We won't.'

The younger men from Yann's group moved to join him. Killian sighed and walked to the end of the table, where he stood with his arms by his sides. Yann and his men glared up at him.

'You can be the first to die after we slay that disgusting demon,' said a burly man at Yann's side. He was a good foot shorter than Yann, but what he lacked in height he made up for with muscle.

'Let's not start all that demon nonsense again,' said Killian with a groan. 'Don't you know violence never solves anything?' He paused, glanced down at Finn and gave her a wink. 'Except for maybe a fight!'

With that, Killian leapt from the table and landed a punch square on Yann's jaw, causing him to fall back against the bar. The burly man swung at Killian, but he dodged out of the way, then swiftly retaliated with a powerful uppercut to the muscular man's stomach. The man fell back and crashed onto a table, which splintered and cracked under his weight. Killian jumped back, surprised. A flash of iridescence glimmered over his fingers, then was gone. Now was certainly not the time for glowing, and mercifully, that strange power seemed to agree for once. He paused and pushed his hair behind his ears.

'Right, who's next?' he asked with a cocky grin.

Yann's entire group charged at him in answer. Finn raced to Killian's side and was swiftly joined by Tom, Blake and Lily.

'I'm really gonna enjoy this,' said Finn, cracking her knuckles.

She dived into the group of men, punching, kicking and throwing them out of her way. Tom and Blake didn't need any more encouragement than that, and they launched themselves into the fray too.

'You know what, Killian?' said Lily.

'What?'

She smiled, her emerald eyes glittering. 'I think I'm gonna enjoy this too. Thanks.'

'You're welcome.'

The bar was awash with bodies, heaving, sweating, crying out. Killian waded in, keeping half an eye on the green whirlwind that was Lily's coat. He pitied the poor fool who'd try to take her on.

A punch to his gut caught his attention, and he turned and welcomed a fist to the face. His teeth sank into his tongue, filling his mouth with blood, and he fell to the floor. Darkness flooded in as bodies crowded around. He instinctively moved to run his finger along a sword hilt but stopped himself. They didn't work. They hadn't worked since—

No, don't think about it, not now. He was alone. Except he wasn't. He'd been trained by a black sentinel before his swords even had blades. Fighting was one thing he was actually good at. He could do it without cheating – Geoffrey had made sure of that.

With an obscene battle cry, Killian pushed himself off the floor and punched the jaw of the first face that invaded his vision. Burning hot adrenaline surged through his body, and a smile fixed itself to his face.

Finn had snapped off two table legs and was having the time of her life, laughing manically and beating down whoever dared to take her on. Everyone seemed to be avoiding Lily. She was standing by herself, a couple of unconscious men at her feet. Blake dived onto a table and pulled out his sword. Two men drew theirs and joined him; he beckoned them forwards before engaging them in battle. He was lithe and quick on his feet. He easily outmanoeuvred them, leaping from one table to the next, wearing them down before he swept in to disarm them.

Yann swaggered up to Killian; he was clearly back for round two. Killian sidestepped his attacker's flailing fists, grabbed him by the arm and twisted it. Yann yelped in pain. A loud thump came from behind, and Killian glanced over his shoulder. Tom was pushed up against a wall. A tall, bulky man clasped the young pirate's shoulders and pinned him there.

'Listen, I'm not a violent person,' said the man.

'Well, I am,' retorted Tom as he headbutted his adversary before he had time to reply.

Killian smirked to himself, then bundled Yann back to the floor where he belonged. The air stilled. The tavern reeked of blood, sweat and beer. Groans and gasps burbled from the bodies strewn across the floor. Reluctant fighters cowered in the corners and backed away from the doors.

Raven sidled up next to Killian, shouldering everyone's travelling packs. 'I think we may have outstayed our welcome.'

'Shit,' said Finn, throwing her table legs to the floor with a clatter. 'That's the most fun I've had in years.' She grinned, blood trickling from her lip.

'Where we gonna sleep now?' asked Tom.

'We'll find somewhere,' said Lily, stepping over one of the men at her feet to join her crew. 'We're leaving now, and we're taking our pet demon with us. I hope you enjoyed our stay as much as we did.'

Killian opened the tavern door, grateful to be getting out of there. As soon as he stepped outside, he froze. Standing in front of him were people. Hundreds of people. It must have been most of Morell's population. They were all brandishing some sort of weapon – swords, burning sticks, arrows, daggers, even a pitchfork or two. They were staring at his group with deadly intent.

'There he is,' shouted the young man who'd run from the bar earlier, 'the demon.'

'I'm not a demon,' said Raven.

'I don't think that'll get through to them,' said Killian.

'I know, and I know what I must do.'

'Kill them! Kill them all!' shouted a voice from the crowd.

'No!' shouted Raven. 'It's me you want. Take me and let them go.'

'Raven, have you lost it?' snapped Killian, grabbing him from behind and pulling him back. 'This isn't the way.'

'They'll kill you,' he said. 'If I give myself over, you'll be all right.'

'That's too bad because I'm not letting them have you.' Killian locked his arm around Raven's chest and refused to let go.

Ren struggled in Killian's grip. The white-masked face stared at him, gaping and soulless, its voice rasping and guttural. Killian's heart thundered, his eyes watered, his chest ached. Pain ripped up his spine, burning fire, acid, glass shards, poisoned needles. It hurt so much. He gritted his teeth and shoved it all back.

'I'm not letting you go, Thorny,' he whispered to Raven as he tightened his grip. As soon as the words fell from his lips, he knew his mistake. *Shit, shit, shit, shi—*

'Blake, give these kind villagers a real demon,' Lily snapped.

'Aye, Captain.'

Blake stepped forwards and lit his pipe. He took a deep inhalation and closed his eyes. After a few heartbeats, he blew the smoke out in one breath and opened his eyes. They were completely white. He moved his hands to the sky, and the smoke coalesced into deep blood red. It morphed into a huge pillar, which grew until it towered over the gathered crowd.

Blake clicked his fingers, and the pillar exploded to reveal the gigantic black-and-red demon within.

Great horns protruded from its curved skull, and a sharp hooked nose bent down towards its grinning mouth, which opened to expose rows and rows of razor-sharp teeth. It threw its muscular arms back and fanned out an enormous pair of leathery wings. A long forked tail – burning with blood-red flames – swept out from behind it. It put a massive clawed hand on the ground and leant towards the mob, its bright yellow eyes burning with malevolence. It opened its mouth again and let out a deep sickening scream.

'Let's go,' said Lily, turning to the others.

'But Blake?' said Killian. Surely she wasn't going to abandon him.

'Blake is doing his job. He'll catch us up.' Her voice was flat and emotionless. She turned to her first mate. 'You need to find us somewhere to lie low.'

Raven nodded and took the lead. He darted around the back of the tavern and down a side street, followed by Lily, Finn and Tom. Killian, however, turned back.

CHAPTER FIFTEEN

'WHAT ARE YOU STILL DOING HERE?' SAID BLAKE through a grimace.

'Defying the captain's orders,' said Killian. 'Starting a mutiny.'

Blake looked at him and smiled. He was an unnerving sight – his eyes white and pupilless. Every time he moved his mouth, the demon screamed.

'While you're here, you may as well watch this.'

The colossal demon opened its mouth wide and roared. It was a hideous noise, like thousands of distorted and tortured screams. A monstrous cacophony that ripped its way into Killian's head and lodged itself in his mind forever. Hundreds of smaller demons spewed from its gaping maw, a clawing, seething mass of red and black, each twice the size of a man. The demonic cries grew louder as the smaller ones joined in, creating a choir of chaos. The people of Morell ran in panic.

Blake dropped to one knee and raised his arms. His long fingers danced through the air, and his fresh set of spectres obeyed his every command. Some chased people down the streets, others raced along the rooftops. He clenched his fist and swept his arm behind him, which sent a group of about ten demons into the tavern behind them. Horrified cries issued from inside before the clambering bodies scrambled out of the building only to come face-to-face with the giant demon grinning at them. They scattered across the town like rabbits in a blind panic. The small demons crawled all over Morell, terrifying people and screeching in high-pitched wails.

Blake turned to Killian. 'Time to leave,' he said.

Killian nodded. He looked at the tavern's sign swinging in the wind and couldn't resist shooting it down. It fell to the cobbles with a satisfying clatter, a smoking hole in the demon's head.

'It would make a lovely souvenir,' he said as he holstered his gun.

Blake grinned and stood up, his eyes bright white. 'Let's go.'

They ran down a side street, the giant demon flying low. Its leather wings whooshed through the air, and Killian was sure he felt a breeze from it. But that wasn't possible. This demon wasn't real, was it? As if in answer to his thoughts, the great beast growled in its throat.

'He's a little off-putting,' said Killian, unnerved by their gigantic flying companion.

'He's covering us,' said Blake.

He couldn't fault that logic. The terrifying spectre would keep even the bravest villager in Morell from following them. Killian grabbed Blake's arm as the street ended abruptly and pulled him left onto a wider one. He had no idea where to go, but so long as they kept moving, ducking down streets and keeping low, they'd surely make it out. Their heels clattered on the scattered cobbles. The glowing lamps – lit earlier by old man Sven – provided some warm orange illumination in the dull misty night. Killian was grateful the old man had done his job properly.

Cries ripped through the air. Thundering boots echoed off and around the buildings. Screaming, a group of people raced towards Killian and Blake. It was an awful sound. Their faces were contorted with fear, and their eyes glistened with tears. A pack of Blake's demons swooped after them, hissing and jeering. The town was in complete bedlam.

'Do you know where we're going?' Blake asked Killian, his voice hoarse.

'Not really,' he admitted. 'We should probably head up to those woods outside town.'

'Okay.'

Killian put his head down and upped his pace; he wanted to get away from there as soon as possible. Anxiety prickled at him as he thought of the others. They'd definitely got away, but he didn't want them wasting time searching for him and Blake. The road opened out, and Blake stopped running. He leant forwards and put his hands on his knees. His breathing was heavy, and he was clearly exhausted. Above them, the giant demon hovered, the hooked tips of its great wings swishing through the air.

'You okay?' Killian asked, putting a hand on Blake's back. Heat was pouring from him.

'I'm fine,' he rasped, 'just getting some air.' He took several deep breaths, then straightened up. 'I'm fine. Let's go.'

The cries and howls grew distant as they ran through the deserted street. A startled cat dashed in front of them, arched its back and hissed at the giant demon before fleeing.

Killian pushed his sweaty hair from his eyes and looked up. The lamps were becoming scarce, the light dim. Squinting to the end of the road, he could just make out the outline of the forest-covered hills. The sparse cobbles were replaced with a dirt track. Killian stopped running and looked over his shoulder at Morell.

'Well, there's another town I can never set foot in again,' said Killian.

Blake smiled and nodded. He looked at his gigantic demon and clicked his fingers. The demon instantly lost its shape and blew away in wisps of grey smoke. The white light faded from Blake's eyes, and they returned to their usual hazel. Then his legs gave way, and he crumpled. Killian grabbed him before he hit the ground.

'So, you're not fine?' Killian asked, supporting his entire weight.

'Yeah, no,' said Blake. 'Just give me a minute, will you? It takes it out of you sometimes.'

Killian nodded, lowered him to the grassy earth and sat next to him.

Even when he was sitting down, Blake continued to lean against Killian for support, his eyes closed. 'I've never made one that huge before,' he said, 'or so intricate and elaborate.'

'It was impressive.'

'Doing the sounds,' Blake murmured. 'Doing the sounds . . . That's what drains you. Controlling all the little ones – that was hard.'

'Are they still about?'

'They went with the big one.' He opened his eyes and sat up. 'We'd best go and find the others.'

Killian stood first, then helped Blake to his feet. Blake staggered a little, so Killian put his arm around his waist and bore most of his weight on his right shoulder. 'I'll help you,' he said.

'Thanks,' said Blake. 'And thanks for coming back for me.'

'I couldn't leave you.' Killian pulled the cornelian torch from its sheath and handed it to Blake. 'Light this, maybe someone'll spot us.'

Blake took it, and once it was in his hands, it spluttered into life, igniting with green flames.

'WE should . . . go . . . back,' Tom gasped between breaths.

'Nah,' rasped Finn, leaning against a tree.

'But we've lost them both!'

'They'll be fine,' said Finn, straightening up.

'You don't know that.'

'Yeah, I do,' said Finn. 'They're big boys, and they can handle themselves.'

'But, Fi—'

'Tom,' Lily snapped, 'they're grown men. Calm down.'

'Aye, Cap'n.'

Raven stood a little way from the rest of the group. Guilt engulfed his aching chest. It was his fault Blake and Killian were out there. He should have refused to reveal his face. He should have run out into the crowd. He should have done many things, but he hadn't. Now they were two crew down. The tall trees of the thick hilltop wood rustled and quivered with the wind. But besides that, there were no other sounds. The screams and cries from Morell had faded, which meant Blake's illusion must have vanished.

Tension shot through Raven's shoulders, and he realised he was still carrying Killian's and Blake's bags. He drew in a deep breath of cool night air and wandered back to the group. Finn was smoking like she hadn't a care in the world, Lily was tapping her foot with impatience and Tom was pacing back and forth.

'I'll go out and look for them,' he said, dropping the bags to the ground.

'But, Raven, what if you get lost?' asked Tom, freezing to the spot.

With his keen night vision, Raven could see the fear in Tom's eyes – a layer of moisture glistened there.

'Raven will not get lost.' Lily spoke for him. 'Pull yourself together, Tom. Have a swig of rum and calm down.'

'Aye, Cap'n. Sorry, Cap'n.' With that, Tom set about rummaging in his bag for a flask.

Raven turned to his captain. 'I won't be long.'

'I know.'

KILLIAN gripped the torch, its strange green flames dancing in the gloom. It had already slipped from Blake's fingers several times during their amble. They'd made little progress over the dark grasslands. Blake was dragging his feet, becoming heavier by the second, and Killian was decidedly worn out too. He must have spent more energy than he'd thought during the fight, and now it was catching up with him. A smile tugged at the corners of his mouth as he remembered the look on the burly man's face when he punched him. He'd never punched someone quite like that before. It was unusual, not quite right. That power. Could it have come from the glow that lived in his body? A shiver darted across his skin. What was it? Blake grunted, snapping him back to the present.

'Oh, sorry,' Blake started. 'I was asleep, sorry.'

'It's fine,' said Killian. Relief flooded his shoulder and legs as Blake began to walk by himself. 'We'll just carry on for a little longer – reach the start of those woods over there – then we'll sleep. We can look for the others again in the morning. They won't leave without us.'

'Sounds good to me,' said Blake.

They carried on walking, the blackened woods beckoning them onwards. 'Blake,' Killian said, 'do all mages get tired like that?'

'Only if we use too much power. You see, it's linked to our physical strength and mental will . . . After a while, it starts eating away at it. The more you practise, though, the more powerful magic you can wield, and for longer. I'm getting better. If I'd tried to do what I did tonight when I was first starting out, it would've killed me.'

'Oh.'

'Why?'

'Curious,' said Killian. He allowed a few seconds of silence to fill the night air before asking his next question. 'How do you get to be a mage?'

'Lots of ways,' said Blake. He stopped walking and turned to Killian. His eyes were half closed. 'Can we sit for a minute?'

'Sure.'

Blake slumped to the cold damp grass. 'With me, it came naturally. I didn't have to force it. Others study and study at it – they dedicate their whole lives to it. Anyone can become a mage if they're willing to put in the effort when they're young. It's just some people – me included – find it easier than others. Obviously, it's not recommended in Vermor. Some can't help it though, and others, it's like a part of them. Asking them to stop would be like asking them to be someone else.'

'How old were you when you started?'

'I was late – nine or ten, I reckon. You go beyond a certain age and being a mage is impossible. It's like the doorway to magic is shut on you forever. You miss it, and it never opens again.'

'What age?' Killian asked, his skin flooding with heat.

Blake yawned. 'Sixteen, seventeen, about then. You're very interested in this.'

'Only curious. I've never known a mage,' said Killian, smoothly covering up his intentions. So that ruled out being a mage.

Blake smiled. 'This is like the reverse of when you went down the Drop. I was asking you all those questions and . . .' He yawned again, and his eyes grew glassy. 'We should probably move before I really do pass out.'

Killian stood up and put his arm around Blake to help him to walk. In his other hand he carried the torch, confident someone from their party would see the flames.

'Thanks,' Blake murmured.

'No problem,' said Killian.

A faint silvery smear stretched across the dark night sky. The moonlight, like viscous oil paint, seeped into the thick blanket of grey clouds. The stars were choked from view by the shimmering grey mountains.

Somewhere over the fields, an animal shrieked. It sounded catlike and victorious.

The wind whistled through the grasses, and a dramatic flurry of air signalled the arrival of Raven. Killian breathed a sigh of relief when he saw two eyes – glistening with a soft violet light – fixed upon him.

'Lost?' asked Raven.

'You took your time,' grumbled Killian.

'We are a bit,' said Blake, leaning against Killian.

'Come on, I'll take you to the others,' said Raven. 'Killian, I believe Lily's a little annoyed with you.'

'When is she ever pleased with me?'

'When you're stealing stuff for her,' said Blake.

'Of course,' said Killian. 'I have my uses.'

'Blake,' said Raven, turning his ethereal eyes to him. 'Thank you for what you did.'

'You'd do the same for me,' said Blake. 'We're shipmates.'

'I would,' said Raven. He looked up at the cloudy sky. 'Let's go, I'll carry you.'

Blake stumbled when Killian let go, but Raven caught him and scooped him up into his arms.

'Sorry, I'm just a little tired . . .' he mumbled, and he was gone.

'I'll wait here,' said Killian.

'Don't be silly, get on my back,' said Raven.

'Nah, I'll be a hindrance.'

'Nonsense,' said Raven.

Raven turned his broad back to him, and Killian climbed on. He snuffed out the flames of the torch and reattached it to his belt. Then they were away, tearing across the field with incredible speed. Killian gripped tight while Blake slumbered contentedly in Raven's arms. They reached the woods before long, and Raven dodged between the trees with expert precision. Killian held on, dreading the moment when he'd run up one, but it never came.

All he could see was the blackness of the night. The trees were a dark grey lurking in the black gloom, the moon a misty smudge providing no light. A biting cold wind whistled through Killian's hair and slapped his cheeks. The first mate's eyesight must have been incredible. There was something ahead. A flicker of orange. It drew closer as Raven bounded through the trees.

A clearing and a small campfire came into view as Raven slowed to an eventual stop. Around it sat Lily, Tom and Finn, their expressions impossible to read in the wavering light. Killian let go of Raven and slid to the ground. Woodsmoke coasted amongst the pine trees, and a gentle crackle wended its way through the silent night. Raven kept a firm hold of Blake. Lily stood up and went straight to the sleeping mage.

'He's all right,' Raven whispered, 'just tired.'

Lily touched Blake's pale face and moved his hair away from his eyes. 'Wrap him up well, make sure he stays warm,' she said. 'And Raven, thank you.'

Raven nodded and carried Blake away.

'Killian,' said Lily, striding over to him. 'A word.'

He readied his defence for her assault. *Here we go.*

'Thanks for helping him,' she said.

Killian was stunned. What he'd expected to be a severe tongue lashing had morphed into a compliment. He'd mutinied and got away with it. There probably wasn't a man alive who could say that. 'I couldn't leave him.'

'I know,' she said. She turned to leave but paused and looked back over her shoulder. 'We're sleeping out here tonight, so wrap up.'

With that, she walked away, leaving Killian to ponder just how much she cared.

CHAPTER SIXTEEN

Killian awoke with his face covered in pine needles. He rolled onto his back and, while brushing off the needles, stared up at the foreboding grey sky peering through the treetops. The clouds were heavy with rain. Soft mumbles moved around the campsite, indicating the others were already awake. Groaning, he sat up. His muscles ached from a night on the woodland ground. With minimal enthusiasm, he rubbed his stiff shoulders and neck.

'Oh! Look who's finally awake,' said Tom, sporting a playful grin.

'Hey, I . . .'

'Rough night,' said Blake, handing him his excuse.

'Yes, exactly. I had a rough night.' He let go of his shoulder, grabbed his brown cloth bag and rummaged around for something to eat.

Tom bounded over like a spring hare and sank to his knees next to him. No one should be that lively after a night of sleeping outside on the ground. It wasn't natural. His eyes twinkled mischievously despite his left being swollen, purple and bloated from the previous night's antics.

'I bet I'd have had a rough night if we'd stayed in Morell, if you know what I mean.' Tom winked.

'I don't even wanna think about that.' Killian looked at the chunk of bread in his hand and the cheese in the other, then shook his head. 'You really know how to ruin someone's breakfast.'

'You not want that, then?' asked Tom, reaching forwards.

Killian bit into the bread in answer. It was dry and crumbly, and he regretted taking such a big bite as it clogged up in his mouth.

'I hope you realise my track record is ruined now,' said Tom, frowning and running his fingers over his red bandana.

'My heart bleeds for you,' Killian grunted through the bread, spitting crumbs everywhere.

'I'll have to make it up in the next town.'

'Yeah,' said Blake, appearing behind Tom and nudging him in the back with his knee. 'You'll make it up all right.'

'You believe what you wanna believe, Blakey boy,' said Tom, swivelling around to fend him off. 'In the next town, we ain't sharing rooms.'

'Fine by me.' Blake took a swing at Tom and knocked him to the ground.

'You're such a bully,' muttered Tom, dusting himself off.

'You can take it.'

'I can, and I know you act like this because you're sexually frustrated. I've seen this behaviour from you a thousand times. Don't worry, Blake, you'll find someone.'

'I'm quite happy as I am, thank you,' said Blake.

'Oh, aye. A loner, eh?'

Blake shook his head and knocked Tom down again.

'How're you feeling?' Killian asked, having demolished his breakfast before Tom could put him off further. The slightly slimy cheese helped the stale bread slip down his throat.

'Fine. Really good, actually. Like normal,' said Blake.

'Good.'

'You?' Blake asked.

Killian rolled his shoulders and then ran a hand through his hair. 'All right. Just a bit stiff.'

Tom snorted and covered his mouth. Killian threw him a hard glare and curled his lip.

'Come on,' said Tom, 'you set that up yourself.'

'You have a one-track mind,' groaned Killian.

'Pfft, that's what you think,' said Tom. He straightened up and placed one hand solemnly on his heart. 'I'm a very deep person.'

Blake spat out a laugh. 'That's a first. How deep?'

'As deep as she wants,' said Tom with a sly smile.

'You're a cretin,' said Blake, and he launched another attack on his depraved fellow gunner.

Killian watched them as they play fought, rolling around in the dirt. Mud was kicked up, as were pine needles, which fell back down like hard green raindrops. Blake got the better of Tom and pinned him to the ground.

'I never knew you felt that way about me, Blake,' said Tom, struggling to free his wrists.

'In your dreams,' said Blake, releasing him and standing up.

Sniggering, Tom got to his feet and dusted his clothes off. Yawning and shaking his head, Killian stood too. He reached his arms up, stretched and let out a satisfied grunt.

'So, what's the plan, then?' he asked Blake and Tom.

'Not sure,' said Blake, shaking his head. 'You're best off speaking to the captain about that.'

'Where is she?'

'Went off with Raven an' Finn while you were snoozing,' said Tom. 'Said something about scouting the terrain and checking the map.'

Killian nodded. He contemplated looking for them, but he didn't want to end up getting lost again. Instead, he resolved to pack his things while he waited. He got down on his knees and rolled up his deep green blanket while listening to Tom chatter about the previous night's encounter.

'You were amazing though, Blake,' he said.

'I was all right,' said Blake.

'Ah, take a compliment. That demon was incredible. Even I was fooled at first.'

'It was fine, I suppose,' Blake muttered, a rose blush tinting his pale cheeks.

Just as Killian finished stuffing his coarse blanket into his bag, Lily reappeared with Raven and Finn. They made eye contact, and both looked away, Lily looking at a particularly interesting tree behind him and Killian checking his bag was correctly packed.

'Is everyone ready to move on?' she asked to the camp.

'Yeah,' said Finn, stalking over to her bag and slinging it on.

'Where we headin'?' asked Tom.

'Still Scherben – the plan hasn't changed. It's a couple of days away, so go easy on the food – it's got to last us until then. We'll be travelling through the forests – it's the fastest route – but we need to stick together. I don't want anybody getting lost. Any questions?'

'They have beds and baths in Scherben?' asked Killian.

'It's one of the largest cities in Freischen, so I should think so,' said Lily. 'Anyone else?'

She was greeted by silence.

'Okay, then. Let's press on.'

Raven leapt up and disappeared into the treetops, the dark pines swaying as he jumped from branch to branch. Lily walked after him, her bag swinging off her shoulder, followed by the others. Killian took his place at the back once more. He wished Raven hadn't gone on ahead. He wanted to talk to him, to ask him about Morell and maybe tell him about the strange thing growing – or whatever it was doing – in his body. Raven might know what it was, and even if he didn't, he'd probably be able to say something to ease his worry. He always seemed to know the right things to say and was ready to listen.

Killian sighed and looked up to the treetops. Running as free and easy as Raven would be so liberating. *I bet that would clear my head.* A pulse of intense energy rippled through his body. Iridescence flashed in his vision. *Not now.* Blood rushed from his head, and a wave of dizziness crashed over him. He placed a sweaty hand on a tree to keep himself steady. The rough gnarled bark provided him with something tangible to feel while he concentrated on his breathing. Slowly in, slowly out, in, out. *I will not pass out. I will not pass out.* Long deep breaths. The fresh air of the forests filled his lungs and his mind. Coolness and clarity. That was what he needed. Coolness and clarity. The glowing collection of colours faded back into his skin. Coolness and clar—

'Killian!' Finn's gruff voice butchered the peace of the forest. 'What the fuck are you doing?'

He thought fast. 'Nothing. Stone in my boot. It's out now.'

'Get up here! We gotta stay close.'

Killian stepped away from the tree, thankful he hadn't collapsed, and jogged to the group.

'Loiterer,' remarked Finn as he came up behind her.

Killian stayed behind everyone but made sure he kept up with them so as not to draw attention to himself. What was he? Could he be some freakish kind of mage? No, that was impossible – he was too old, the doors were closed to him. He'd seen his dark side once. Maybe it was beginning to manifest in his body. He put his hand to his chest. No, that was ridiculous. It was gone, he'd killed it. Perhaps it was whatever had happened between his body and the Gramarye. Did they now have some sort of link? Could the demon who took it find him? Its revolting guttural voice grated in his mind. Ren screamed. Ren cried. Ren begged for help. For his help. And he did nothing. His vision misted. With a shaking hand, he wiped his eyes. He put his head down and pressed on.

The dull afternoon brought rain. The canopy of trees kept them dry until the rain came down heavier. The forest floor slowly turned to mush. Finn complained the most vocally about it. Yet however much she cursed and swore at the sky, the rain still fell. It wasn't until the light began to fade, signalling the setting of the cloud-obscured sun, that the downpour started to ease off.

Raven gracefully leapt from a tree and landed in front of them. He was wetter than everyone, but it didn't seem to bother him. He pushed his dripping dark purple-hued hair back.

'There's a clearing up ahead,' he said to Lily. 'We should make camp there for the night.'

She nodded.

'I'll find some dry wood for a fire and meet you there.' With those parting words, he was racing up the nearest tree trunk.

Killian watched him disappear into the treetops, then followed the others through the woods. Time crawled by as the cold ate its way into his bones. His feet moved without him thinking, one slow trudging step after another. The night before had been exhausting, and he'd had little sleep. His mind went to steamy baths, hot stews and rich ales. A trio of warmth and comfort. It was maddening.

The rain turned to a gentle drizzle and then died off altogether. Killian ran a hand through his wet hair and tucked it behind his ears. Wind whistled high above in the trees, their branches swaying to their own woodland beat. The air was clean and crisp, like the rain had chased any dirt away. After walking for about half an hour, he reached the clearing.

A small fire, surrounded by what looked like a makeshift fence, was already blazing in the middle of the clearing. Killian dropped his bag to the ground and hung his long brown coat on the fence to dry. He tossed his blanket next to it to warm up, then sank to the forest floor. The heat of the fire slunk over him, and he breathed in deep. The woodsmoke filled his senses; it was deliciously soporific.

Raven reappeared from the darkened trees and added more bracken to the fire, then sat down himself, his beautiful eyes fixed on the dancing flames. Tom reached into his bag and pulled out a lump of dry bread and some cheese, eyeing it sadly.

'Well, this is depressing, ain't it?' he said before cramming it into his mouth.

'Just put up with it,' said Finn.

'Bread, cheese, wet,' said Tom.

'You really can be such a child at times,' said Finn, removing her own rations from her bag. 'Anyway, it ain't for long. We'll be in Scherben soon.'

Tom sighed. 'I can almost taste the beef soup-stew thing now.'

'Aye, and the rest.'

Tom's eyes glazed over as no doubt seedy fantasies of Scherben swamped his mind. Killian ate silently; he didn't feel like joining in.

'You realise we're only stopping for one night, don't you?' said Lily.

'Oh, aye, Cap'n,' replied Tom. 'All right with me.'

'It's easier for him to come up with an excuse if we only stop one night,' said Blake, elbowing Finn, who actually cracked a smile.

'You lot don't know anythin'.' Tom huffed and folded his arms.

'Clearly not,' Finn remarked.

At this, Tom launched into yet another tale of his alleged conquests, which soon had everyone – bar Killian, who was content with watching the flames – mocking him.

Blake burst into incredulous laughter. 'Every time you tell the Plyton "legend" it's different. Ten girls? Come on, Tom, even you know that's a lie.'

'It is not.'

'And they didn't pay you!' said Finn.

'They did! They told me I was the best and I deserved it.'

Killian could no longer stay quiet on the matter. He turned and looked Tom up and down. 'I'd have asked for my money back,' he said deadpan.

At this, Blake and Finn exploded into fits of laughter. Tom puffed out his chest and gave each of them a pointed glare.

'You do bring it on yourself, Tom,' said Lily, standing up.

She started making her way over to Killian. He didn't feel like talking much tonight, but maybe talking to her would help. He swivelled back around to face the roaring fire. The heat soaked into his numb skin. There was a crackle of pine needles as Lily sank down next to him. A different warmth flooded his body.

'You're quiet tonight,' she said.

'Yeah,' he said.

They remained in silence, both watching the flickering flames. Killian wanted to speak, but he didn't know what to say.

'Good talking to you,' said Lily, standing up.

'Sorry.' Killian looked up and brushed his hair from his face. 'It's just wet, awful food, no sleep.'

'Yeah, I understand, but we've got a long way ahead of us.'

'I know. I'll be all right.'

'Of course you will. You've got us.' A warm smile graced her face.

'And you've got me.'

Silence descended once more. Lily took a step backwards, like she was retreating. Killian swallowed, regretting his choice of words. What had he even meant by that? She had him? They had him?

'I'm going to bed,' said Lily. 'Raven's keeping first watch, then me, Tom, Finn, then you. I'm giving Blake the night off tonight.'

'Fine by me,' he said.

The three gunners were still laughing and joking. 'I reckon they'll be up a while longer – you should join them,' she said.

'Maybe tomorrow. I should get some rest,' he said, getting up.

Lily walked to the other side of the fire to retrieve their blankets. She tossed Killian his. 'Nice and warm. I've got a hot tip for you,' she said, pointing towards the edge of the clearing. 'The ground is dry in that corner.'

'In that case,' said Killian, wrapping the blanket around himself like a cloak, 'I'll grab my spot now.'

Killian followed Lily to the edge and made sure he was at least three feet away from her before settling down for the night. She was right, the ground was dry. It was cold and hard, but one out of three wasn't bad. He rolled himself up in the blanket and wrapped his arms around his head. Stars peered into their camp through the blankets of grey clouds. An owl hooted as something scurried through the undergrowth. He breathed out a deep sigh and closed his eyes.

'Night, Lil.'

'Goodnight, Killian.'

CHAPTER
SEVENTEEN

A DULL PAIN THROBBED IN KILLIAN'S SHOULDER as he caught sight of Scherben in the next valley. He stared down at the sprawling city, which rolled into the hills before him, knowing a real bed awaited him somewhere down there. After three nights of sleeping rough under the stars, he was certainly ready for a hot bath, a warm meal and a soft bed.

The great city was split in half by a wide river, which was covered with boats – some cargo, some pleasure. Tall narrow buildings rose up from the pavements and lined the streets. Their dark grey stones gave the whole city a blackened look, yet their structure made it reminiscent of a dense dark forest. A gigantic cathedral sprang up from the city centre. It put every building Killian had ever seen in Vermor to shame. It was a huge monstrous beast, dark and heaving. Turreted spires erupted from each corner like vicious spiked armour.

It consumed the skyline, and every other building grovelled in its shadow.

Killian knitted his hands together behind his neck and leant into them, his hair blowing all around his face in the breeze.

'Looks like a fancy place,' he said, exploring the landscape before him.

'It is,' said Raven. 'I don't remember it being this big.'

'Maybe you've shrunk since then,' said Killian.

Raven chuckled in his throat.

'Come on,' said Lily, stepping forwards, 'first things first. We find a stable and hire some horses. I'm not walking all the way to Poll. Then we'll find somewhere to stay the night.'

Killian groaned and rubbed his face. 'I'll get to have a bath.'

'Always knew you were nothin' more than a floppy-haired ponce,' said Finn, punching him in the shoulder.

'There's nothing poncy about wanting to be clean.'

Finn smirked.

'There isn't!' Killian protested.

'Woman,' grunted Finn through a cough.

Finn laughed, put her arm around Killian and followed Lily down the hill, dragging him along at her pace.

It took over an hour to traipse down to the outskirts of Scherben, where they were greeted by a stable and the pungent stench of manure.

'Reckon they'll have six?' Killian asked, looking around doubtfully.

'I can drag you behind mine if not,' said Lily.

She looked like she meant it.

There was a row of low stone buildings with soft whinnies and snorts emitting from them, as well as the whiff of hay and week-old vegetables. Next to the stables was a large barn and a pasture. Several horses were frolicking out in the grass, sunlight flashing off their silvery antlers. Killian had never ridden before, but how hard could it be? He could row a boat; surely it was almost the same, but on land, and on a creature with sharp horns and a mind of its own . . . If it cut their journey time down though, it was worth it. Probably. Lily disappeared into the barn with Raven.

Finn lit up a smoke. 'I ain't fond of horses,' she muttered. 'Flighty at the best of times.'

'Unreliable,' Tom agreed.

'I've never had much to do with them,' said Killian.

'Probably don't want much to do with you neither,' Tom retorted.

Lily and Raven emerged from the darkness of the barn, followed by a man in dirty overalls with a cigarette dangling from his lips.

'Come on, we're going to pick our steeds,' said Lily, nodding towards the pasture.

Killian winced. He'd rather walk to Poll if he was honest. Getting saddle-sore and bruised wasn't high up on his to-do list. Those antlers looked vicious too. They were a tangled collection of twisted points, each one longer than his arm. Getting injured by those wouldn't be an enjoyable experience.

The grasses of the pasture rippled in the wind, and dandelions nodded their ragged sunburst heads. The air smelt of animals and dirt; it wasn't unpleasant and was far better than low tide in Brackmouth. As Killian drew closer to the beasts, there was a distinctive shift in the atmosphere. All the horses stopped what they were doing and turned to stare at him, nostrils flared.

'What have you done to them?' Tom joked.

'Nothing,' said Killian.

He took a small step backwards. The penetrating glower of the horses didn't leave him.

'I don't like this,' said Killian, holding his hands up.

What was wrong with the horses? Did they know about the glow? A chill crept up his spine. Rangi had hated him, hissing and spitting, and cats had always been fond of him. There were the screaming seagulls in Brackmouth too. Gulls always scream and cry, but recently they'd sounded different to him. They knew. They all knew there was something wrong with him. They all knew he should have helped Ren. They knew something putrid was growing inside him, waiting to consume him and everyone he cared about. His heart drummed so hard in his chest it hurt, and he swallowed the urge to be sick.

'Killian,' Lily barked, 'they're just horses.'

One of them stomped, another whinnied, one sounded like it shrieked. Great bursts of steam plumed from their nostrils. They all glared at him. It was as if they were afraid. A large white one lowered its antlers at him, their cruel points flashing in the weak sunlight.

Killian took another step back. 'This is not normal.'

The farther back he moved, the less aggressive the horses became; however, their collective glare remained on him, unblinking. He stopped walking and looked to the rest of the crew for help. So many emotions flickered through the eyes of his companions – confusion, fear, annoyance and sympathy.

'This is *not* normal.'

The white horse stamped its hoof into the earth. The rest reared up screaming. It seemed like they were about to bolt.

The owner stepped in and cautiously approached the white one, his gaze soft. He spoke in a gentle cooing voice and rubbed its neck to calm it down. Once he'd got it under control, he turned to the group.

'He's right. This ain't normal. That fella over there' – he pointed a podgy finger at Killian – 'is cursed.'

'What a load of shit,' said Lily. 'How much do you want?'

'I don't want nothin'. I said he's cursed. Now all of you, get outta here. You ain't having my horses.'

'Fine,' Lily snapped, 'we'll take our custom elsewhere.'

After being turned away from all four stables in all four corners of Scherben, the plan changed, and Lily chose to look for an inn.

Guilt ran through Killian as he trudged through the black-cobbled streets. Because of him, they would all have to walk to Poll. He truly was a hindrance. All the stable owners had been right: he was cursed. He should have stayed in Brackmouth, out of the way. The narrow grey buildings of the city crowded around him, almost like they were agreeing with his turbulent thoughts.

Finn sidled up next to him, reeking of smoke. 'Tell you a secret, shithead. I'm glad you're cursed and damned for all eternity. I wasn't lookin' forward to planting my arse on one of those things for days. I owe you one. Tom and Blake too. They're sea lads, not horse boys.'

'Happy to help.'

Finn whistled through her teeth, then slapped him on the back; it stung.

After wandering down the long winding residential areas and side streets of Scherben, they arrived at the centre. It was alive with a pulsing hubbub. Horses and carts clopped down the wide main road, their drivers dressed in elegant suits with matching hats. A row of permanent market stalls lined the street, each one selling a different type of food from the next. There was so much more choice on offer than in Brackmouth. The air whirled with the scent of roasting meats, vegetable soups and sweet cinnamon and honey buns. Killian's stomach moaned in pain. Vendors called out into the street using all manner of seductive words to sell their products. And judging by the rapidly forming queues, it worked.

Inns, taverns and shops made up most of the city centre. Tavern doors were constantly opening and closing as patrons filed in and out. The waft of woodsmoke and sweet mulled wine billowed out into the streets.

Killian's mouth watered. He wanted food, wine, buns, a warm fire, everything. He shot an irritated glare at Lily's back. Every few inns she'd stop walking, look through the window, screw her face up and move on. This had been going on for far too long in his opinion. 'What *is* she doing?' he asked Finn.

'Being more of a dainty woman than you,' Finn whispered back.

Killian waved her insult off.

'She's tryin' to find us a fancy inn for the night.'

'Oh.'

'If you've got the coin, you may as well,' Finn continued. 'I ain't gonna complain. I wish she'd hurry up though. I wanna dump my bag and have a mosey around town.'

'Me too,' said Tom, appearing from behind. He draped his arm around Killian's shoulders. 'I can't wait to get out there,' he added, wistfully staring down the street.

'Don't bring anything back with you,' said Finn.

'Him? Bring anything back?' said Blake, falling into step with them. 'You know that's not going to happen.'

'Shut up, Blake,' grumbled Tom.

'Only saying what's true,' said Blake, giving Tom a friendly punch.

'Finn,' Tom whinged, looking to the older woman for support.

'I was humouring you,' said Finn. She started rummaging around in her coat.

'Fine,' said Tom, folding his arms. 'I'll prove you all wrong.'

Killian looked ahead, but Lily was nowhere to be seen. Raven was standing outside an inn directly opposite the imposing cathedral.

'At last,' muttered Finn. She popped a roll-up into her mouth and lit it.

'She's negotiating a price and some rooms,' said Raven as they approached.

Killian glanced at the inn. It was like most of the other buildings, tall and narrow, except its stones were carved with intricate patterns of twisting tree roots and its support beams were painted white. It seemed nice enough; he hadn't had that much experience in the finer things in life, so he didn't really have a basis for comparison. He wondered who he'd share a room with. What if he had to share with her? He'd done it before, but that had only ended in misery.

He turned around and stared up at the cathedral. He'd never seen anything as tall in his life. Its turrets stretched up towards the sky as if reaching for something just out of their grasp. A gigantic arched window flashed like a diamond as soft sunbeams fell upon it. Its frame was etched with tiny designs. He squinted, but he couldn't make them out. Killian slowly exhaled, and as he did, his body tensed.

'Impressive, isn't it?' said Raven from behind him.

'Yeah,' said Killian. 'Ever been up?'

'Yes, great view from the top. I can take you tonight if you like.'

What did he mean by that? 'No, but thanks anyway.'

'Rather climb it yourself?' Raven asked.

Killian turned and just caught Raven's grin fading away. 'I wouldn't mind,' he said, laughing to disguise his rising panic. What did he know?

'I was going to go anyway. Some company would be nice if you change your mind.'

'I'll bear that in mind.'

Lily emerged from the inn, a rare and painfully attractive smile on her face. 'All right, I've sorted us rooms for the night. Tom, Blake and Finn, you're sharing, and Killian, you're with Raven on the top floor.'

Relief washed over Killian, yet it had a bittersweet flavour to it.

'I don't know about you lot,' Lily continued, 'but I'm ready for a long hot soak and some decent food. The day is yours, so do what you want. Just remember to stock up on supplies and make sure you're in a fit state to leave first thing in the morning.'

With that, she marched back into the inn, her travelling bag swinging from her shoulder.

CHAPTER EIGHTEEN

KILLIAN'S ROOM WAS UP SIX FLIGHTS OF PAINFULLY steep stairs. Up there, the noise and aromas of the city were stifled and there was a calm tranquillity to be found. He stood on the balcony and took in the view of the cathedral with his arms resting on the black iron railing. Below, the streets were alive with people scurrying to and fro. Always going somewhere. Everybody had to be somewhere. Killian's fingers wrapped around the cold metal rail, and he gripped it tight. There was a dramatic flurry of wings as a flock of mauve pigeons swooped in from the left. They turned as if one sentient being and headed towards the cathedral.

A cool breeze filtered across the rooftops and ruffled his damp hair. The colossal cathedral filled his vision, and he slowly chewed his bottom lip as he mused over Raven's offer. Correction, Raven's ridiculous offer. How was he supposed to scale a monster building like that? He couldn't even row to Brackmouth without collapsing. Raven could carry him. That was an option. Perhaps that was what the obscenely beautiful man had in mind. No, no, that wouldn't do. Killian would only be a hindrance. And yet there was something about the way Raven had asked, almost like he knew something. Killian's stomach growled, and he turned his thoughts to the more immediate concern of food. The soft pat of bare feet on wooden floorboards caught his attention.

'We getting lunch or what?' Killian asked, stepping away from the balcony.

'Yes,' said Raven. 'I thought you'd have gone already.'

'Not without my city guide,' said Killian.

'Makes sense,' said Raven with a smile. 'It's been a while since I was here. Chances are the places I went to aren't the same anymore.' He turned his back and picked up his shirt from the bed.

Killian couldn't help but stare at his scars, two thick black lines that ran down his shoulder blades. Raven turned around to button his shirt, and Killian glanced at the floor.

'There was a place down one of the side streets near the cathedral,' said Raven, pulling his boots on. 'Decent soup and bread.'

'That'll do,' said Killian.

Luckily for Killian, who had valiantly restrained himself from buying food from the first street vendor he saw and was now so hungry he'd eat just about anything as a result, the place Raven had mentioned still existed. It was a small, stunted structure flanked by two tall, slim buildings. Four fat chimneys sat upon its rooftop, pumping out clouds of thick black smoke. It was strange to see such a squat building lost within all the slender ones. It was like it'd somehow been missed during all the city planning meetings.

Raven opened the door, and straight away, Killian was hit by the delicious smell of cooking. There was a step leading up into the building, but a low wooden-beamed doorway forced Killian and his companion to duck. It was deceptively large on the inside, probably helped by the white-painted walls, which gave it an airy feel. The restaurant was packed with people – only a few vacant tables remained – all enjoying mouth-watering plates of food while indulging in hearty conversations.

'I'll order, you find a table,' said Raven.

'Okay.'

'What d'you want?'

Killian scanned the elegantly chalked menu on the board behind the bar and mulled over the options – too many for him to decide.

'I'll take whatever the stew of the day is.' Hopefully it wouldn't be offal.

Raven nodded and stepped up to the bar to order.

Killian found an empty table near the window and swiftly claimed it. He took his coat off, hung it on the back of the chair and waited patiently for Raven. A beautiful painting of Scherben's cathedral hung on the wall to his left. Next to it was one of the city streets in the summer; the sky was a dazzling cloudless blue over a black-and-white town.

He put his hand on the table and softly drummed his fingers. All around him people were laughing, chattering, eating, slurping. They were so full of joy and completely oblivious to evil floating masks and demons. And dead friends. He paused. Some of them would have dead friends – it was unhealthy to think otherwise. People died; that was a fact of life. But the cause of death varied. He was a cause of death. A shuddering breath escaped his lips. He needed a drink, something to smooth off the painful edges. As if summoned by thought alone, a jug of frothy ale appeared in front of him.

Killian started. 'Sorry, don't know where I was,' he said.

'Neither do I,' said Raven as he removed his cloak and sat down.

Killian smiled and took a sip of his drink, then let out a sigh of satisfaction. His bones crackled and warmed, and he sank into the chair. It was exactly what he needed.

'How're you finding the trip?' Raven asked.

'It's getting better,' said Killian. 'Not sleeping in the dirt is always good.'

'It is,' Raven agreed.

'It's helping me t—' Killian began, but he stopped as their food arrived. A buxom young brunette set the food down in front of them. She smiled sweetly at Raven before hurrying back to the kitchen. Like in Morell, the stew came in a small pot with a lid, though this time the cheese-covered bread was on the side.

'Looks like you've got an admirer,' said Killian with a playful grin.

'Each to their own, I suppose,' murmured Raven.

Killian rolled his eyes and lifted the lid off the pot of stew. How could the most beautiful man he'd ever laid eyes on say something like that and mean it? He picked up a lump of the cheesy bread, dipped it in and took a bite.

'That's good,' he said once he'd swallowed his mouthful. It was rich, beefy and full of potatoes, onions and peas, with an underlying hint of red wine.

Raven followed suit.

Killian shovelled in his stew while contemplating the bar a few tables before him. It was well stocked. There were two rows of green bottles filled with wine, a shelf of rums and whiskeys, and many ales. The smell of sweet spiced wine rolled over him in waves; he'd certainly be drinking one or two of those later. Thick wooden beams ran across the ceiling. They were painted black, as was every table and chair in the building. A clatter caught Killian's attention. Raven had finished eating.

'So,' said Killian after wolfing down his last few bites and taking a swig of ale, 'has there ever been anyone special for you? I can't believe someone with your face has always been alone.'

Raven looked at him and nodded.

'There has been someone?'

Raven paused. A look of distant sadness clouded his entrancing eyes. He took a sip of his drink before answering. 'There was one.'

Raven's solemn expression made Killian regret asking the question. It wasn't his place to pry. How could he change the subject? Perhaps talk about the serving woman, or the food, drink, Lily, Ren. Anything. Why had he asked such a ridiculous question? He didn't want to know. He didn't *need* to know.

'Her name was Amaranta, and I loved her. She was from Venario, and she worked in the olive groves and vineyards – she was from a family of winemakers.' Raven paused and looked down. 'But I lost her. Since then, there has been no one else.'

'I'm sorry,' said Killian, his throat tightening.

'You have nothing to be sorry for,' said Raven.

'I shouldn't have asked about something like that. It's private.'

'It's not your fault,' said Raven, running his thumb up and down his mug. 'You didn't know.'

Before Killian could even think of something comforting to say, the brunette appeared to take away their empty bowls.

'Anything else?' she asked, all her attention on Raven.

'Two more ales please,' he said as he stood.

'I'll bring them over, sweetie,' she said, placing a hand on his shoulder.

Within seconds, she returned to the table with a slice of cake on a small wooden board and the two drinks.

'This is for you, no charge,' she said, sliding the cake in front of Raven. 'I made it myself.'

'Thank you,' said Raven.

She smiled and hurried away. The playful lilting laughter of at least three women trickled over from the bar. Killian looked at the dashing first mate and raised his eyebrows. Raven flicked his wrist at him. He picked up the dark cake and took a bite.

'It's all right,' he said. 'Try a piece.' He pushed the plate towards him.

Killian broke a piece off and ate it. It was sweet, sticky and spicy; he swallowed. 'Not bad.'

Raven left the plate in the middle of the table, and they both idly picked at it. 'We've done me, let's do you,' he said.

'What d'you mean?'

'Is there anyone for you?'

'Me? You know me,' said Killian. His tone sounded so strained and fake it was embarrassing. Heat rose to his cheeks. 'I take things as they come. If I find someone, I find someone. If not . . .' He reached for his drink and took a long gulp.

Raven smiled, put his ale to his lips, then moved it away. 'Has there ever been anyone?' he asked.

'There've been women,' said Killian, wanting nothing more than to dive into his mug of ale and sink to the bottom. 'Nothing special, a few one-night things. Don't get me wrong, they were good one-night things, some very good, but . . .' He paused and sighed. 'Nothing special. Nothing like you had. Maybe I'm not destined to be with anyone like that. Perhaps I'm not designed for love. Listen to me – I don't even know what I'm talking about.'

'Everyone has the capacity to love,' said Raven.

'I don't know.'

'I do, and you'll know what it's like when you feel it.' Raven's eyes shone with passion as he spoke. 'It feels like nothing else. You live for that person. They are your reason for existing. I could run along a thousand rooftops, leap across ravines and scale the tallest mountains, but that wouldn't even come close to the feeling of loving someone.

'When you feel it, grab on to it and hold on, because you may never get that chance again. To love and be loved is a feeling beyond all comprehension, I can promise you that. I know I'll never see Amaranta again. I'll never hold her in my arms again or kiss her, look into her eyes, feel her dark hair against my skin, but at least I had that chance. At least I had those years with her. It's better to feel love and have it taken away than never feel it at all.'

Killian was stunned by Raven's speech. He hadn't expected such raw emotion to pour from him. The first mate had always seemed so private and closed off, yet now he was opening up to him, of all people. Was he trying to tell him something? He couldn't deny that everything he'd said rang true, everything was real, but he couldn't bring himself to admit it. 'I'll take your word for it.'

'You should,' said Raven. He picked up his mug and drained it. 'Another?' he asked, a sly grin on his lips.

'Sure, why not.'

Killian eventually got what he wanted: mug after mug of warm sweet wine. And as he stumbled out of the tavern, leaning heavily on Raven for support, he smiled. His legs were like sponge and his mind hazy, yet it felt so good. Day was rapidly giving way to night, and a chill was settling into the air.

'That was more than another,' said Raven.

'At least a lot more than another,' said Killian with a drawl.

'Back to the inn?' suggested Raven.

'Yes, I need sleep.'

The city had quietened down. A calming lull hugged the buildings, soothing away the hectic stresses of the day. The street vendors were packing up for the day, and small groups of friends breezed down the streets, recounting their days to one another before heading home or to a tavern. The soft sounds of a guitar being gently plucked floated on the breeze, and as they drew closer to the cathedral, the music grew louder.

'How do you do it?' Killian asked.

'How do I do what?'

'You've drunk as much as me. But I'm staggering all over the place, words falling out my mouth like soup, and you're stone-cold sober. How can you drink that much and not be a little bit wobbly?'

'Years of practice, my friend,' said Raven with a mysterious smile.

'How many years?'

'Many.'

Killian located the source of the music as they approached the cathedral square. A man with a neatly trimmed beard and wearing a smart suit was standing in front of the gargantuan building, playing slow romantic tunes on his guitar to an audience of swaying couples. Just to his left sat an artist, her easel facing the cathedral. A small group of people were huddled around her, watching every brushstroke. She was dressed to complement the musician. Killian stopped walking and watched them entertain the passers-by beneath the pale orange glow of the street lamps.

'I like it here,' he said. 'It's not bad for a city.'

'It's better than most,' said Raven.

They crossed the square and reached their inn. Once he was back in their room, Killian immediately flopped onto his bed. It was warm and soft and welcomed him like a fluffy blanket would a kitten. He lay on his back for several minutes, the room slowly revolving around him. A calm drunken haze washed over him. Nothing could bother him now. He ran his tongue over his lips; they tasted of the spicy wine. Delicious. Raven was standing in front of the window looking out over the city.

'I wonder if everyone else is back,' Killian mused aloud as he sat up to take his boots off.

'Probably.'

Killian yawned, stretched and unbuttoned his shirt. 'I'm going to sleep.'

Raven nodded, but he didn't turn around. 'I'm going for a run.'

'A run? Now? Where?'

'Over the rooftops, up the cathedral. It's years since I've been to a city this big.'

Killian sat up straight, ceased fiddling with his shirt and rubbed his eyes. 'Isn't it dangerous?'

'How do you mean?'

'You've had a few drinks.'

Raven laughed. 'I'll be fine – I'm sober. You're not.'

Killian certainly was very drunk. The room was spinning so much that he gripped the bed to steady himself.

'Want to come along?'

'On your back?'

'Yes, it'll be an experience. The city is a different beast from up there. I'd like to share it with you.'

'I'm too sloshed for that.'

'True.' Raven removed his shirt and dropped it to the floor.

'I will when we come back through here, promise.'

'All right,' said he, turning around, 'next time.' He opened the doors and walked out onto the balcony. 'You can close these after me – I'll come back in the conventional way.'

Raven held his arms out and took a deep breath. Then they appeared again. Those same wings sprouted from his back in swirls of black-and-purple smoke. Killian blinked hard and rubbed his eyes, and when he looked back, they were still there. This time they looked different, more solid. In the past, they'd appeared spectral and had only been visible for a few moments. He blinked again. Was he seeing things? He was very drunk, after all. As he stood, the world rocked gently, and he took a step closer. No, they were definitely there. Real giant black feathery wings that glinted with a dark purple sheen. Raven looked over his shoulder and put his finger to his lips.

'You can keep a secret, can't you?' he said.

Killian nodded, unable to form any words.

'I won't be long, but don't wait up.'

With those parting words, he leapt from the balcony. Killian rushed as fast as his jelly legs would carry him to the iron railing and watched as Raven glided silently across the square like a winged phantom. He landed on the side of the cathedral, and his wings vanished. He ran straight up the side of the gigantic building – it was as incredible as it was impossible. This strange, powerful and oddly sweet man was running vertically up a building.

Once he reached the top of the spire, he paused and perched on what looked like a tree protruded from its crown. Then he dived head first off the other side of the building and disappeared from Killian's view.

CHAPTER NINETEEN

After a night of comfortable sleep and a decent breakfast, the rejuvenated party made steady progress. By mid-morning, Scherben was no longer visible, and all that lay in front of them were yet more rolling fields periodically disrupted by patches of thick dark woodland. Beyond the fields lay nothing but ominously blackened hills covered with dense shadowy pine, marking the beginning of Nocturne Forest. Seeing what lay ahead put Killian on edge; he glanced at his companions, and his body tensed.

'So, what'd you get up to last night?' asked Finn, clamping her hand onto his shoulder. The reek of tobacco emanated from her.

Killian rubbed his face to help change his expression before he spoke. There was a mild throb on the left side of his head; he'd certainly overindulged the night before, but it had been worth it. That sweet, spicy wine was something else, far heavier than the mulled they sold in Vermor. 'Not a lot. Had a few drinks, went to bed.' He glanced at Raven. 'Woke up. You?'

' 'Bout the same,' said Finn. 'Played a bit of cards.'

Tom appeared next to Finn and sighed dramatically. 'You guys really wasted your time, didn't you?'

'Tom, you were with us all night,' grumbled Finn.

'Ah,' said Tom with a seedy wink, 'I wasn't with you while you were asleep.'

Finn shook her head and let go of Killian. She scrunched her hand into a tight fist and glared at Tom. 'I tell you, Tom,' she huffed, 'if you're about to shit out one of your tales, stop now, and I won't punch your nose into the back of your skull.'

Tom chuckled, his bright eyes shifting from the left to the right. 'Ah, Finn, what tales?'

'Every word that comes out of your mouth,' murmured Blake as he sidled up next to Finn.

'That is not fair,' said Tom. 'I've said it before and I'll say it again: you two are just jealous.'

'That's exactly it,' said Blake. 'Come on, then, pray tell.'

'Well, when I got in bed, I found myself wide awake. I couldn't sleep, and listening to Finn snoring wasn't helping much, so I decided to go out for a walk – I thought it might tire me out or something. I was mooching around the city – it was dead quiet, nobody about – when I heard a scream. I ran towards it, and who should I find but that gorgeous barmaid from earlier gettin' mugged on her way home.'

'Convenient,' said Finn in a low voice.

'But true,' replied Tom. 'So, naturally, I fended off her attacker.'

'Just the one?' asked Blake.

'Yes, just the one. Look, will you just let me finish?'

'All right.'

'Right, so, yes, I fended off her attacker and thought it was only right to walk her ho—'

'Sorry,' said Blake, 'just one more thing. Does she have a name?'

'Nima,' said Tom. 'Are you done now?'

'Yes,' said Blake, 'thank you. I should be writing this evidence down.'

'I walked her home, and she was a little shaken up, as you can imagine. I got her to the door and was about to leave in a gentlemanly fashion.'

Blake sniggered.

'When she grabbed me by the shoulders and pulled me into her house. She shoved me against the wall, then started unbuttoning my shirt. I didn't know what to do – it all seemed to come outta nowhere. Before I knew it, she'd taken off my shirt and hers too. She pushed herself up against me. Ah, the feel of her body. Her skin was like silk, and her chebs were perfect, so round and firm.' He sighed, and his eyes glazed over.

'She carried on undressing me, kissing me all over, and I mean all over. I tell you, I had to do some serious restraining, I didn't want it to be over before it started, if you know what I mean. Somehow, we made it to her front room. She pushed me into a chair, took off the rest of her clothes and climbed on top of me. We had amazing sex – right there in the chair. I don't know how I did it, but I managed it *five* times before I had to leave. She didn't want me to go, but that's the way it is sometimes.'

'Utter bollocks,' grunted Finn. 'You were in bed all night, dreaming and playing with yourself.'

'I wasn't,' said Tom. 'Look at my eyes, look how tired they are.'

'He does have a point,' said Killian, giving Tom's bloodshot eyes a glance.

'Thanks,' said Tom. 'And anyway, I knew you wouldn't believe me, which is why I took this.' He delved into his coat pocket and produced a piece of silver ribbon. 'She wore this around her wrist.'

'You stole from her?' Blake frowned.

'I say it's bollocks,' said Finn, looking decidedly unimpressed.

'Finn, this is proof. Here,' said Tom, dangling the ribbon in her face, 'smell it. It still smells of her. Like a sweet strawberry patch. In fact, she tasted a little like strawberries.'

'Get off,' said Finn, swiping at the ribbon as if it were a barfly.

Tom pocketed his prize, a smug aura radiating from him.

'So,' said Blake, 'are you going to see her when we come back through Scherben?'

'Of course. I've gotta give it back to her.'

'I'll believe it when I see it.' Finn snorted and dropped her pace, taking up residence at the back of the group.

'So, do you want to know everything else?' said Tom, putting his arms around Blake and Killian and pulling them towards him.

'No thanks,' said Killian, tossing the arm off.

'Same,' added Blake, brushing away Tom's arm like it was a particularly offensive patch of dirt on his clothes.

'Suit yourselves,' said Tom, unfazed.

Killian and Blake sped up accordingly, leaving Finn to suffer Tom, and walked in comfortable silence. Raven and Lily were almost a full field in front of them; their dark silhouettes stood out vividly against the bright green of the meadow. They were walking side by side and appeared to be locked in deep conversation.

A wave of frustration crashed over Killian; he'd wanted to speak with Raven since the previous night, but he'd yet to seize the opportunity. He had questions he wanted answers to, and surely Raven wanted him to ask them. Showing him his wings last night had to be a sign that he trusted him, and he'd also opened up about some of his past. What other secrets was he keeping? He would just have to wait.

Killian sighed and took a deep breath. The air was fresh and crisp, with just a hint of moisture clinging to the breeze. A perfect natural antidote to his threatening headache.

'Want to ask me any more about mages?' asked Blake, sparking up the conversation.

'Nah, I reckon you told me everything I need to know,' said Killian, squinting up at the blue skies.

'I think I told you all I know.' He paused. 'Killian, can I show you something?'

'Sure,' replied Killian, detecting a hint of reluctance in Blake's tone.

'Don't get scared.'

'I'll try not to.'

Blake screwed his eyes tight for a second, inhaled sharply and opened them to reveal their white glow. He held his hand in front of him, palm facing up, and glared at it. Red-and-white smoke rose from his hand, and a wispy image began to appear. Killian recognised it as Freya. She was lying down and very faint, her body outlined with gossamer threads of pale white light. Blake narrowed his eyes and focused. Colour seeped into the ghostly figure. She got to her feet and moved about his palm. She stopped on the end of his finger and shook her head, and her hair exploded with a rich, glistening ruby red. She turned around to face Killian and bowed.

'You did it without—'

'The next step up.' Blake grinned, the white flashing in his eyes. He clicked his fingers, and the image vanished. 'I can only do small ones, but give me time.'

Killian smiled and nodded, and he and Blake carried on walking in silence. The rest of the day trudged by uneventfully. For hours they walked across soggy fields, the soft squish of the waterlogged mud and the rising earthy smell a far cry from the cobbled streets of Scherben. They cut through several copses in their unwavering path towards the dark forest-covered hills.

As the day wore on, the temperature steadily decreased. Killian hunched up his shoulders and wrapped his arms around his chest to keep the chill at bay. It wasn't until they arrived at the edge of the woods that he finally caught up with Raven and Lily. Lily was studying her map with the first mate, her face stern and serious. She glanced over at Killian, her emerald eyes devoid of warmth. He looked over her shoulder into the black void of the forest. Staring into the abyss was much easier than looking at her mirthless face. Tom and a more-disgruntled-than-usual Finn joined them.

'Glad you could all join us,' said Lily, her face showing no emotion. 'We're going to set up camp just inside the forest. It'll take us the best part of two days before we see anything resembling civilisation.'

Tom groaned.

Lily glared at him, her eyes reduced to aggressive slits, and her lip curled. 'To walk around would take days,' she said, her tone harsh. 'Going through is the best option.'

'Sorry, Cap'n,' Tom mumbled.

'We're all tired, cold and miserable. But we don't have any options, so let's set up camp. Raven, if you would be so kind.'

Raven nodded once and disappeared into the dense woodland.

Killian held his slowly freezing hands over the dying embers of the campfire, its deep red glow taunting him with an intense heat that would never reach him. With stiff fingers, he grabbed a stick and thrust it into the fire's dying heart. It crackled pitifully and coughed out a cloud of yellow ashes, which shone bright for half a second before turning grey and fading into the darkness. He dropped the stick and vigorously rubbed his palms together to keep his fingers from seizing up altogether. He clenched and unclenched his fists several times, then grabbed hold of his coat and pulled it tight to his body.

Scattered around him on the muddy ground were his sleeping companions; he looked at them with envy. Doing the pre-morning watch was the worst. After about four hours of sleep, he'd been roughly shaken into consciousness by a sleep-deprived Tom.

He got to his feet and paced about his sleeping friends, stopping next to Lily. How was it possible for someone so vitriolic to look so peaceful while they slept? By the dim glow of the fire and the green flame of his torch, she almost looked like a nice person. Her lips were turned up into a faint smile. Killian wondered what she was dreaming about.

He walked to the edge of their camp and looked out into the dark forest. It exuded loneliness. The dense trees blocked out most of the light the moon and the stars had to offer, making the blackness go on forever. An icy breeze forced its way through the foliage and whistled past him. Tree branches rustled disapprovingly as the wind searched for a way out.

Killian turned away from the darkness and faced the fading red light of the camp. He put his torch down, the green light extinguishing itself as soon as he released it, and closed his eyes. The world was silent, everyone was asleep and he was alone. Now was his chance to look inside himself.

He screwed his hands up and took three long deep breaths. Simultaneously, he opened his eyes and uncurled his fists. Iridescent light swam in his vision. Colours swirled over his skin like excited rainbows. He took his coat off and threw it to the ground. Shimmering tendrils of light trailed after his arms as he moved. He was covered with light. An intense strength shot through his muscles. Power hummed through his entire body. Blood pounded in his ears. He took a step back and met a tree trunk. He turned around and placed his hands on the bark. Above him, the lofty branches called to him. Could he climb it? Could he run up it? Something in his mind told him he could.

Pulling a deep breath into his lungs, he took a few steps backwards and focused on the glow. He concentrated on his feet and shifting all that wild iridescent energy into them. Power throbbed through his legs; it had to be released. Without forming any clear plan, Killian ran at the tree trunk. And then he was running up it. Each footstep sent a pulse of multicoloured light out into the woods. He was exhilarated, he was strong and powerful. Where had this come from? Why did he have it? What was it?

He was halfway up when the glow faded, taking with it the best part of his strength for payment. Lurching forwards, he gripped the trunk tight. Sweat made his palms slippery, but he somehow managed to hold on. All his body wanted to do was shut down and fall to the ground, but he was too high up. A fall now would do some serious, possibly life-changing damage.

The tree was covered with thin willowy twigs that couldn't even masquerade as branches. There was nowhere for him to pull himself up and rest. It was hopeless. If he weren't so drained, he would have a chance of climbing down, but in his current state, that was not an option. There was only one thing that could save him: Raven.

He looked over his shoulder and down into the camp. He could just make out Raven's body next to the smouldering remains of the fire. Killian laboriously moved about the trunk until he found a twig he could break off. With a satisfying snap, he ripped it from the trunk. Tensing, he looked back to Raven. If he hit anyone else, not only would he still be stuck, but his secret may be revealed, and he wasn't ready for that. How could he explain something he didn't understand himself?

He gritted his teeth and tossed the stick. For what seemed like an eternity, it floated in space before coming to land across Raven's face. The first mate leapt from the woodland ground to his feet in an instant; he crouched low, his body taut. Knowing he couldn't shout, Killian snapped off another twig and threw it. This effort glanced off the top of Raven's head. At this he looked up, his glowing eyes a welcome sight.

He walked over to the tree. 'Killian?' he whispered.

'Yes.'

'What are you doing?'

Killian paused for a long time before replying with, 'Night climbing.'

'You enjoy that. I'm going back to sleep. I'll see you when it's my turn to watch.'

'No.'

'No?' said Raven.

Killian screwed his face up. Maybe he could hold on, maybe he could climb down. In answer to his thoughts, his grip loosened. He wouldn't last another five minutes. He sighed and pressed his forehead against the trunk. 'Raven.'

'Yes?'

'Help me. I can't hold on, and I can't climb down.'

'Of course.'

He took his shirt off, and within seconds his body was flanked by two black-feathered wings. With one flap of his giant wings, he was next to Killian. 'Killian,' he murmured, 'give me your hand.'

Killian released his grip with his right hand and held it out. Raven caught it and pulled him into his arms. Raven's body was warm and safe. Killian gripped on tight, Raven's feathers brushing against the backs of his hands. He tried to make his body relax, but it refused to stop trembling. He felt like such an idiot. This was one of the most embarrassing moments of his life.

'Do you night climb often?' Raven asked as he lowered them to the ground.

'Nope,' said Killian, 'I'm not very good at it. Do you grow wings often?'

'I try not to – most people wouldn't like it,' said Raven, unfazed by Killian's direct question.

As soon as Raven landed, he released him. Killian took one step away but staggered back into him. Raven caught him under the arms and held him up. Killian's body was numb. His limbs didn't want to respond to his commands, and his legs refused to support his weight, causing him to sag against Raven. Why did he think he had a chance at controlling the glow? It had him in its grip, not the other way around.

'Killian, Killian.' Raven's voice sounded concerned. He put a hand under Killian's chin and tilted his face up. 'Are you all right?'

'Fine,' whispered Killian. But Raven was a blur through his half-closed eyes.

'What happened?' he asked.

'Night climbing,' said Killian.

'I might be able to help you.'

'I was just . . . climbing,' said Killian, letting go of Raven and stumbling towards the heart of the camp. 'That's all.'

'If you say so,' said Raven, picking his shirt up.

'I do, and I need to finish my watch . . .' The words had barely left his lips when he teetered to the side like an alcohol-marinated drunk. Raven dashed forwards and caught him again.

'No, you don't,' he said. 'I'll start mine now. You need rest.'

'I'm fine.' He was far from it.

Raven shook his head.

'I'm not fine,' admitted Killian.

'I know,' said Raven, helping him walk back to his discarded blankets. He aided his descent to the forest floor and pulled the blanket around him.

Killian rolled onto his side and propped his head up with his hand. 'Thanks,' he rasped.

'That's okay,' said Raven, taking a seat on a log behind him.

'I'll stay awake with you . . . keep you company.'

'Thank you,' said Raven. 'That'd be nice.'

' 'S what friends are for.'

He wrapped his arms around his head and stared up at the few stars privileged enough to see into their camp. Their celestial silver light melted into the dark of the night, and Killian was gone.

CHAPTER TWENTY

The second day in the Nocturne Forest blended neatly into the first. Finn grumbled, Tom attempted to lift the party's damp spirits with tales of his sexual exploits and Blake mocked him for his efforts. Raven spent most of his time in the treetops leading the way, and Killian and Lily stayed quiet.

'I've not seen many of those throat-ripping animals you were talking about,' said Killian, falling into step with Lily. Tom's legends had finally made him resort to talking to her.

'What do you mean?' she asked, not looking at him.

'Razortails.'

'They prefer the land closer to Poll.'

'Oh,' Killian mused. 'What's most likely to kill me in here, then?'

'Besides me?' she said, turning to face him.

'Yeah, besides you.' He chuckled, then glanced to the muddy track as the heat rushed into his cheeks.

'There's the noctis, a type of bat only found in here. Its wingspan is about the length of your arms. It eats whatever it can lay its claws on. It wouldn't be able to kill any of us, but a starving one or a pissed-off one could give you a nasty scratch.'

'Uh-huh.'

'Also, there're catalls, nasty things. Long, thin, spindly wildcats. By all accounts, they're vicious little fucks. Black fur, brown markings, usually lone hunters, but team up when it's required. If you see one, don't worry too much. Three or more, then run. Their claws secrete a poison – not enough to kill a man outright, but in large doses it's enough to paralyse him while he's eaten alive.'

'Delightful.'

'You did ask.'

'I suppose.'

'Don't worry though, I doubt they'll bother us. They'll be wary of such a large group. Just don't go wandering about on your own at night.'

'Okay,' said Killian. It was almost like she knew about him and the tree incident, but Raven wouldn't say anything, would he? And maybe there was a slim chance she was worried about him.

'Besides them, there's the usual poisonous insects, spiders and snakes. Stay away from anything that crawls. Fungus too, don't eat any.'

'Ah, that's too bad, I was really tempted by that pus-spewing greasy orange mushroom I saw earlier.'

'Shut it,' she said, giving him a punch on the arm.

He smiled as he rubbed his bicep. 'Good research. You know your stuff.'

'Thanks, I enjoyed it, so it wasn't hard. I wanted to make

sure we'd be all right. I don't want any—' She paused. 'I don't want anything bad happening.'

'Neither do I.'

'And it's not going to,' she added. 'This forest may be sprawling and foreign to us, but there's nothing too dangerous in here. It's only when we get into razortail territory that we'll need to step up our game – two people on night watch, that sort of thing.'

Killian nodded.

'We're safe for now,' she said, giving his shoulder a reassuring squeeze. 'They're safe,' she added, shifting her emerald gaze in the direction of the rest of the party. 'Everything will be fine.'

'I know . . . You're right.'

'I am.'

'It doesn't stop me worrying though, doubting myself,' he said in a soft voice. 'Thinking about who will die next because of me . . .'

'Nobody will die,' she said.

'It's always there, at the back of my mind. Sometimes I can hear him scream. I can't forget it.'

'I'm not asking you to forget it. But I want you to accept it. It won't go away. I know whatever I say won't change how you feel about it – the only person who can do that is you, and the only way to do that is to accept it.'

Killian put his hand to his chest, his finger ready to trace Nesta's glyph, but it wasn't there. Birds chirped in the branches above, filling the uncomfortable silence with a beautiful swinging melody. Shafts of midday sunlight broke through the canopy of dense pine trees, creating dazzling golden patches on the muddy earth. The air was chilly and fresh, filled with the scent of pine needles and sprouting vegetation. Tiny ferns poked through the forest floor, bright green and curled up tight, poised to fan out their leaves when the season asked. Killian trudged on, his boots now thick with mud and dirt. He breathed deeply and focused on the path ahead.

Lily broke the quiet of the forest. 'You went back for Blake, didn't you? You didn't have to, but you did.'

'I did that because I didn't help Ren. Doing that cleared my conscience, momentarily.'

'We both know that's not true.'

Killian sat as close to the fire as possible without igniting himself. He pulled his blanket up around his hunched shoulders and dropped his chin into his hand.

'Is it all right if I sleep now?' said Raven. 'Or are you planning more night climbing?'

Killian turned around. Raven had his hood pulled up, keeping most of his face in shadow, yet even in the dim light his eyes glowed with a soft purple.

'Go to sleep, Raven,' he said.

'As you wish,' said Raven. He leant down and gave Killian's shoulder a reassuring squeeze. 'Just in case you need me,' he added, handing him a stick.

Killian sniggered and graciously accepted the gift.

Raven grinned, then made his way to the other side of the fire. He lay down and wrapped his cloak about his body, leaving Killian alone.

Watch was always the most tedious part of the day, or night, depending on how you looked at it. Killian had grown to despise it. Everyone was sleeping peacefully, especially Finn, who'd been lucky enough to have a night off. Killian sneered into the darkness. He was always the last person Lily gave a night off to. The rotation had started again after they'd left Scherben; it was as if she'd conveniently forgotten that he was due a night off.

He glanced at her. She was lying on her side, her long black hair framing her face. The flickering fire lit up her skin, giving it a warm, inviting glow. *She's anything but warm.* Killian shuddered and pulled his coat tight beneath his blanket. Her lips moved slightly in her sleep, then parted before closing to form a soft smile. Killian shuddered again, though it wasn't from the cold. His pulse sped up, and he loosened the blanket. This wouldn't do. Having feelings like this wouldn't help. He had so many complications in his life, and how he felt about her was just another one. One he couldn't face right now. He shook his head and turned to scowl at the fire.

For over an hour, he sat feeding the insatiable fire with whatever unfortunate bracken happened to be lying at his feet. When the novelty, and the nearby sticks, eventually ran out, Killian stood. He stretched his arms and thrust his chest out to alleviate some of the tension from all the hunching. Yawning, he rubbed his eyes and picked up his torch, which came to life with its other-worldly green flames. He walked around the perimeter of their camp, partly to keep awake and partly to get some warmth back into his numb legs.

After a lap he was feeling better, more awake and alive. He pushed his way into the dense thicket that surrounded the camp, and despite what Lily had said, he went deep into the undergrowth. The others couldn't see what he was about to do.

When he was far enough away, he held his right hand in front of his face and concentrated. It began to glow;

opalescent colours swirled on his skin. He turned his hand around slowly. *How do I control you?* His thoughts were cut short by a low growl. The torch fell from his grip, the flames snuffing out instantly.

Another growl rumbled through the undergrowth. This one was closer. With a trembling hand, he reached down and gripped the torch, which sputtered into life. Dark green shadows danced around him. It was like the whole forest had come to life. Something flashed in the gloom, two bright amber lamps. Keeping his eyes fixed on the lamps, he took a step closer. He swished the flaming green stick one hundred and eighty degrees; to his left was another set of amber lamps, and to his right were two more pairs. They stalked through the shadows. Heat flooded his nose and forehead, and he lowered the torch to reveal the source of his fear: catalls, a small pack of them slinking their way towards him.

His glowing hand reached for a sword, and he held the blade in front of him, tightening his muscles. Their faces were menacing, nothing like the stray cats he sometimes fed in Brackmouth. The one to his left was the nearest; its mouth was wide open, its lips pulled back, revealing a fierce set of teeth. In the limited light of the torch, its fur looked black, bristling up on its arched back. Long thick claws extended from its paws, blackened with poison.

He focused on the glow and tried to relax. He closed his eyes, and the strange magic flowed over his body, covering his skin in a layer of humming power. Strength and energy poured through him. The magic wrapped itself around each of his muscles – it felt amazing. The gentle sound of singing crystals filled the air around him. He dropped the torch to the ground and opened his eyes.

The group of catalls stared at him. Their teeth were bared and their ears flat to their skulls. Backs were raised like a series of hairy bridges. They skulked backwards in unison. Killian could see the fear in their eyes. They were like the horses and like Rangi. They were afraid of him.

The glow pulled at him, leeching out his strength, but he had to hold on, he had to drive them away. He took a step forwards. Crystals chimed softly, coloured strands floated from his body and the catalls backed away, hissing and spitting at him. Their eyes were now black voids of dilated pupils. Then they turned and ran, fleeing into the forest to get away from the bizarre glowing man.

Killian scooped up the torch and stumbled back to the camp, the glow fading back into his body with every step he took. As he slumped next to the fire, the last of the iridescence melted into his skin. Weakness crawled over his body. Once again, using that mysterious power had completely drained him. All he did was glow, and now he was utterly useless. He looked up to the deep blue sky, and tiny pinpricks of silver stars peered back down at him. Were they really lost souls?

When it was time, he peeled off his blanket and staggered towards Lily. He paused above the sleeping pirate; she looked so comfortable, peaceful and warm. It seemed a shame to wake her. It'd only break the spell and return her to her normal vitriolic self. Killian yawned. He needed sleep. He was surprised he hadn't fallen unconscious around the campfire, given his track record with his body and the strange glow. But it wasn't like he'd done anything – he'd scared some wildcats. It was pathetic, really. He grabbed Lily's shoulder and gave her a gentle shake.

'Lil,' he whispered. 'Lil, wake up.'

'Mmm,' she murmured without opening her eyes.

'Come on,' he said, giving her another shake, 'it's time for your watch.'

'Killian,' she slurred, her eyes still closed. 'Don't go . . .'

'I'm right here.'

'I need to tell you . . . something,' she drawled.

'Okay.'

Lily fell silent; she twisted and stretched, and her eyes opened. She jumped when she saw Killian leaning over her.

'Oh, Killian,' she breathed, her voice heavy with sleep. 'I'm sure you were just in my dre—nightmare.'

'You can't get rid of me,' he said, straightening up.

'So it would seem,' she huffed. She blinked several times before sitting up. 'My watch?'

'Yup,' he said.

She held her hand out in his direction. He took it – it was so warm – and pulled her to her feet.

'Thank you.'

'Any time.'

'I could have done with more sleep,' she grumbled.

'So could I,' said Killian.

She chuckled as she bent down to pick her coat up. 'Go on, get outta here.' She gathered up her discarded blanket and tossed it to him. 'Have this, it's still warm.'

'Thanks,' he said, dropping to the earthy ground and pulling the blanket around himself. It still smelt of her, herby and fresh. He was full of her dizzying scent.

'See you in a few hours, Killian.'

'Goodnight,' he said.

Lily stalked away, doing her coat up as she went. Killian watched her go for as long as his tired eyes would allow him, his body wrapped in the warmth of hers.

CHAPTER
TWENTY-ONE

SASHA CLUTCHED HER RIBS AS SHE STUMBLED OVER the cobbles. Heavy rain lashed down, but all she could feel was the warmth of her own blood against her freezing fingers.

Ahead of her was a light, a glowing lamp swaying in the wind. A tavern sign creaked, beckoning her forwards. Lamps glowed in the windows. It looked warm and comforting in there.

She staggered towards it, her legs aching from running and her skin sore and itchy in her tight, soaking wet trousers. A great beam of bright light erupted from the tavern as the door opened.

The silhouette of a woman stood framed in the doorway. She moved towards the lamp. She was going to put out the flame, snuffing out all hope.

Sasha increased her pace. She had to get in before it

closed. Her foot slipped on the wet cobbles, and she put her arms out to keep from falling. The woman turned around. Long blonde hair swished with her movements. Pale green eyes shone with warmth beneath a thick fringe. She was so beautiful. Sasha was at a loss for words.

'Can I help you?' the woman asked.

'I . . . Yes,' Sasha managed to reply. 'Do you have a room?'

'Yes, of course.' She smiled at Sasha. 'You came at the right time – I was just closing.' She put out the lamp and opened the door once more, sending another rush of light out into the dark streets. 'Come in. I'm Ruby, I'll be your host.'

'Thank you,' Sasha rasped. 'Sasha.'

As soon as she entered the tavern, she was hit by the delicious smell of woodsmoke and ale. A warmth she'd not felt in months, perhaps years, soaked deep into her bones. Keys rattled as Ruby locked the heavy door behind them. Sasha turned to thank her once more, but Ruby's attention was on her ribs and bloody fingers.

'You're hurt.' She sounded concerned, not disgusted. She didn't know Sasha was a mage. The disgust and hate would come later, as it always did.

'A little. It's nothing. I ran into some trouble out of town.'

Ruby's warm hand took hold of Sasha's bloody one. It felt good to be held, even if it was in the most minor way possible.

'You poor woman,' said Ruby. 'I'll show you to your room and fix you a hot bath and a warm meal.'

'You don't have to,' said Sasha. This was the kindest anyone had been to her in so long. She had to fight the tears back.

'I know, but you look like you need it.' She let go of her hand and walked to the bar. 'Come on,' she said over her shoulder.

Sasha gasped and clutched her ribs, then her face. Everything hurt, everything ached. Everywhere was bruised and beaten. She glanced around the room in a frantic search for Ruby. There was no scent of her, no sense, nothing. It was a dream, or a memory, or a dream of a memory.

'You're awake,' said a soulless monotone voice.

Sasha rolled onto her side to find Theo's shadowy eyes looking at her. 'I am,' she muttered back.

'Fire left you in the barn. Air brought you to me.'

'How long was I asleep?' she asked, pushing herself up and leaning back against the wooden headboard.

'A few days.'

Her heart sank. Not again. 'You helped me?'

'I did.'

'Thanks.'

Theo stared at her, his face blank. If he weren't so soulless, he'd be handsome. Sasha cringed. She didn't have to find everyone who showed her a shred of kindness attractive.

'I'll fetch Quint.' Theo stood and glanced to the foot of Sasha's bed. 'Come on, Red.' He whistled softly.

The fox trotted out from the bottom of Sasha's bed. It fixed its amber eyes on her. Without thinking first, Sasha reached out and grabbed Theo's arm. His skin was cold, and he pulled away from her as if shocked by her touch.

'I'm sorry. Please,' she said weakly, 'stay with me a little.'

'You want me to stay?'

She nodded.

'All right, but I'll fetch you a drink first. That's what people do.'

'Don't tell the others I'm awake. I'm not ready.'

'I won't.'

He looked at the fox and clicked his fingers. The creature leapt from the floor onto Sasha's bed and curled up at her feet. Then Theo left, closing the door behind him.

Sasha pulled her blankets close and looked at the fox. It was staring back at her; it yawned once and put its head down. She wanted to run her fingers through its thick russet fur, but it had settled too far away, and movement caused her pain. A dull ache rippled through her ribs, and a deep loneliness settled on her soul. What was she doing here? What was she doing with these people? She didn't belong. Her power was non-existent once again. Nothing was going right for her. She hooked a finger through her pendant and sighed.

She should have stuck to her old plan – make enough money to leave the country, sweep Ruby off her feet, sail overseas and not stop until they reached the island kingdom of Santonos. There they could bask in peachy sunsets while Sasha let her magic run free.

There was nothing for her in Vermor except for bad memories and looking over her shoulder all the time, and she certainly had no interest in saving all the other mages of Vermor.

But that wasn't completely true; Ruby was here, and she had a life. If Sasha could channel from the Otherside without the risk of death, they could stay. No more running. Surely it was worth living and working with these mages to find out. Her power would come back. It had to. It almost had, and then Kurt had destroyed all her progress.

The door whispered open, and Theo returned holding a mug with wispy curls of steam drifting from it. A tightness gripped Sasha's chest as she looked at him, and her vision blurred. He looked so feeble and drained, and yet he'd helped her. She hadn't ever bothered to find out what magic he could pull from the Otherside – he was always so distant and quiet that talking to him hadn't seemed worth the time or the effort – but it was clear to her now that he was a healer. He had a hand in the heavens.

'I told them it was for me,' he said as he passed her the mug.

'Thank you.' She breathed in the bitter vapours of the coffee. The smell alone was enough to revitalise her. She took a sip. It was delicious, dark and smooth. Delphina must have brewed it.

Theo sat in a rickety chair next to the bed and rested his chin in his hand. His heavy eyebrows were low, and his forehead furrowed as if he was lost deep in thought. His dark gaze cast to the window.

A healer was a rare mage. Sasha had never met one before, but she knew healing required the utmost skill and concentration; what Theo did came with a cost that was written all over his face. His emotionless features, his monotone voice, his lack of desire to meet and mix with people. His existence seemed devoid of joy. Every time he used that magic to heal, he lost a little part of himself. The thought of this poor man giving a piece of himself to help her was painful. He barely knew her, and yet he'd given her something so precious. She had to do something, anything, to make his life a little more bearable.

'Where'd you get your fox from?' she asked, forcing an attempt at conversation. She had to start somewhere.

'I don't know.'

'You don't?' Sasha gritted her teeth and shuffled down the bed to be closer to the mage and his fox.

'No. It was a long time ago. He was hurt. I healed him. After that, he followed me. I don't know why.' He shrugged. 'I couldn't make him leave, so I let him follow.'

'He must like you.' She reached her hand out to stroke the fox, but it refused to come any closer.

'Maybe.'

The fox stood, stretched and moved towards Theo, proving her point.

'Did you name him Red?'

'I did.'

'Why that?' She wanted to keep the conversation flowing. It felt strangely normal.

Theo turned to her, and the faintest of smirks graced his lips. 'Look at him.' He was mocking her, but at least it was a hint of an emotion.

'I know, less of the sarcasm.' Sasha smiled. 'I was thinking of something more creative, like Ginger or Russet or Autumn – that would have been a good one.'

Theo's dark eyes filled with a deep sadness. He blinked, and it was gone. 'I don't have the capacity to think in a beautiful way. Not anymore.'

A rush of guilt washed through Sasha. 'Red's fine. I was only playing with you. I'm sorry.'

'You have nothing to be sorry for.'

Theo stood up and walked towards the window; the floorboards squeaked with each step. Red leapt down from the bed and trotted after him.

'May I?' he asked with his hand resting on the glass.

'Sure.'

He flung the window open, and a refreshing cool breeze blew in. Sasha breathed in deep, savouring the earthy and grassy scents. Her skin prickled with the cold, but she didn't care. Theo was leaning out the window, the air rippling through his dark brown hair. He shifted to the side, and she noticed his eyes were closed. The midday sun beamed down on him, giving his pallid skin a hint of colour. The light played across his face, and it almost seemed as if he were smiling. It was like she was looking back in time and seeing a tiny glimpse of who he once was. He closed the window and turned. All trace of joy was gone.

'I made you cold.'

'No, it's fine.'

He glanced to the floor, then back to her. 'I should tell Quint you're awake. He'll be worried.'

'Okay.' Sasha was starting to feel cruel about keeping Theo with her. He clearly wanted to leave and was making an excuse. Anyway, he'd already done more than enough for her. And yet there had been something magical about their brief exchange, something she couldn't quite put her finger on. She needed it to happen again. 'Theo, you'll talk to me again, won't you?'

'I . . . Yes.' He moved back towards her and rested his hand on the bedpost. Red skipped after him, his claws rattling on the wooden floorboards. 'I've spoken to you before.'

'Not like this.'

'I don't understand.'

'You told me about Red.'

'You asked.'

'I know, but we had a conversation – a real one. I'd like to do it again.'

Theo shifted, put his hand on the door handle and slowly pushed it down. 'Are you asking?'

'I am.'

'All right,' he said. He paused and pushed his windswept hair from his face. 'I'll talk to you again, Lightning.'

CHAPTER TWENTY-TWO

The small valley town of Poll came into view. It was built up around the foot of a collection of ragged hills, safe within their daunting shadows. A thin stream ran through the hills. It tumbled down various rugged waterfalls before winding through the village and snaking under a stone bridge. A great wide river coursed its way through the base of the rocky valley, welcoming the surrounding streams to become a part of it. Killian stood with his fingers through his belt loops and gazed down at the village from the crest of the hill. Finally, he'd be able to start fixing the mess he'd caused.

'So, this is the place,' he murmured.

'This better not be a waste of my time,' said Lily, turning to fire him a frosty glare.

'It won't be.' Would it? What if it was?

'If it is, I'll leave you here.'

'I can think of worse places to be left,' he said, looking back at the picturesque village in the valley.

She flapped open her discoloured, wrinkled map of the area and studied it. 'It says we should follow this road here,' she muttered and pursed her lips.

'Then we should follow the road,' said Finn, peering over her shoulder.

Lily looked towards the village. 'I can see Poll. You can see Poll. It'll be far quicker if we follow this track.'

Killian glanced at the narrow muddy track weaving its way down the hillside. He couldn't argue with her logic – Poll was beneath them, and it was the most direct route. In all honesty, he just wanted to get there and wash off the road stink.

'Aye, Cap'n,' said Finn, 'reckon you're right.'

The way to Poll was a hard-fought battle through thick berry bushes. The dirt track wound its way around them, yet Killian's coat still snagged on the clawing vegetation. Thorns scratched at the backs of his hands until he pulled them into his coat sleeves to protect them. Behind him, Tom complained of a similar series of mishaps. Finn grunted an unsympathetic response, which silenced him. Lily ploughed on ahead with a determined stomp. Leaves and thorns decorated her wavy hair like natural trinkets while weeds and stray branches caught and clung to her boots. A smile docked at Killian's lips. They were all in a similar state, but to see the captain looking like a walking hedgerow brought a certain warmth to his heart. Stumbling through the bushes had been her idea, after all.

The sloping dirt track eventually gave way to a tight set

of steep steps flanked by a high stone wall. Killian flicked a weed from his trousers and trudged down, his boots loud on the steps. A hollow growl echoed around his stomach, and his mind went straight to food, ale and wine, then a bath and a decent bed. All the good things. Lily's flora-adorned coat floated a few steps ahead of him, and once more, a smirk formed on his lips. This was all her fault. His foot jarred, and he staggered forwards as he reached the street level. He dusted his blood-smeared palms off on his coat, his skin prickling – there were definitely several thorns caught under it – and looked at Lily.

'Well, it was probably quicker,' he remarked.

'Keep your mouth shut, O'Shea,' she growled as she plucked leaves, flowers, berries and thorns from her hair and clothes.

He happily took her advice. Poll was vaguely reminiscent of Brackmouth, but without the fishy wafts and screaming seagulls. Narrow streets weaved their way around chunky rustic houses – pale grey stones were the building materials of choice around here. Dark slate roofs topped off most of the buildings, though there was the occasional yellowing thatch. A crude and uneven pathway that looked as if it had been dredged from the riverbed rolled through the quaint little town.

'Wha'd we do now?' asked Tom as he reached Killian. There was a scratch on his cheek oozing a little blood.

'Keep a low profile,' said Raven. He was unscathed and looked as dashing as ever.

'Ask in a tavern,' said Lily, taking the lead.

A deep beleaguered sigh accompanied by the smell of tobacco signalled the arrival of Finn. Blake came last, pausing to yank a thick twig from the treads in his boot.

Killian blew out a long, tired breath and followed Lily into the winding streets. The farther he went through the village, the wider the path became. The stones were pushed to the edge of the path, and flat grey slabs of rock cut through its centre, making the ground that little bit more comfortable to walk on. After days of trudging through grassy fields and loam-covered forest floors, it was odd to be walking on solid flat ground again. His feet were burning and sore. They felt like raw salted beef. He winced. Thoughts like that didn't help.

The sound of the trickling stream was constant. It was placid and soft, a welcome background noise. Tiny songbirds clustered on rooftops, preparing to roost for the night. They chattered to one another in a soulful lilt, very different to the boisterous wails of the gulls in Brackmouth.

'What d'you reckon they talk about?' Killian asked no one in particular.

Finn turned and looked at him, her dark grey eyes incredibly serious. 'Worms.'

That answer, coupled with her intense expression, made Killian burst out laughing. Finn shot him a wink and pressed on.

A few villagers wandered by, but they didn't acknowledge anyone. Perhaps people often passed through Poll.

'Excuse me,' said Lily, stopping a young man in a floppy hat.

He looked up at her from under its brim. 'Yes?' he said as he eyed the party of travellers.

'Is there an inn or a tavern near here?'

'Yes, the Old Bridge Inn,' he said, his tone indicating that he was eager to get away. 'Keep walking down here and head out of the old town. You'll come to the town square. Go right from there, then left again and down towards the new town. It's on a ridge on the border of the new and old town, where the waterfall starts and the town splits. You can't miss it.'

'Thank you,' she said, smiling sweetly. She motioned for the party to follow her.

Killian curled his lip in disgust. Sometimes she could be so polite, so manipulative, other times a raging storm full of death threats; it was hard to know who the real Lily was.

'Bit small to have a new town and an old town,' said Finn.

'As long as they've got somewhere for us to stay the night, good ale and sexy women, I couldn't give a shit,' grumbled Tom. 'I just want to get pissed and collapse in a bed with a red-hot wench.'

'It starts,' said Blake.

'How about a bit of friendly competition, Blake?' said Tom, turning round. 'You and me, see how many locals we can get?'

'I'd rather not.'

'Ah, come on. Why not?'

'It's not my thing, Tom.'

'Afraid to lose to the master?' Tom grinned.

'That's exactly it. I know I could never win against you.'

'I admire your honesty, Blakey,' said Tom. 'What about you, Finn?'

'Not interested,' Finn growled.

'Fair enough. Killian, how about you?'

'I'm your last choice? Is that it?'

Tom chuckled. 'Nah, Raven's my last choice. Look at him. Even I know I can't stack up to him.'

'And you think you can stack up to me?'

'As if you gotta ask that! How about it? You and me, we'll get ourselves wasted and wenched.'

'I don't th—'

'I'll take out the competition aspect if you want – just you and me and a couple of ladies.' He threw his arm around Killian's shoulders and pulled him close. 'Come on, Killian,' he said, upping his pace so they overtook Lily, 'how long's it been for you?'

'That's a bit personal,' said Killian, a tightness building in his chest.

'From that, I'd be guessing it's been a while, eh?'

'I'm not talking about it.'

'Come on, Killian,' Tom insisted. 'Cut loose for once. You look like you need it.'

'I don't need it.'

'Don't lie. I'll even help you find a nice lady for the night.'

'I appreciate the offer, but all I want is food, booze and bed – by myself.'

Tom sighed. 'You don't half make your life miserable.'

Killian smiled, but a deep pain wrapped itself around his soul. Having arrived at Poll and being one step closer to fixing his mistakes, his mind had started to fall back to Ren. Ren would never be able to enjoy himself and cut loose again – if he ever had. It didn't seem fair. The silly little idiot, why did he run at that demon? Killian never should have taught him how to steal his gun. If only he'd done things differently.

He traipsed across the paved town square. A giant ancient pine surrounded by a ring of benches stood proud in the centre. Several seats were occupied by townsfolk smoking, drinking and chatting as the sunset drew in, bathing everything in an orange glow. He followed the directions the local had given Lily and came to the waterfall, where he and Tom stopped to wait for the others.

Killian put his hands on the low crumbling bridge that crossed the waterfall and leant forwards to watch the tumbling waters. It was calm, the falls themselves being a gentle, smooth incline. Blackened dark grey rocks rippled beneath the surface, and shimmering patterns shifted across it.

He inhaled deeply. The air was clear, crisp and invigorating. Why was everything in his life so complicated? Why did he have to keep thinking of Ren? Why couldn't he let go? Murmuring voices floated towards him. Was that Lily? What did she want now? He blocked her out and continued to stare at the stream. The surrounding grasses, reeds and ferns nodded in appreciation.

Everything had been fine in his life before Ren had shown up. Well, almost fine, but he didn't want to dwell on his mum, Clem or his miserable directionless existence. Since meeting Ren, he'd almost died several times, been tortured by a floating mask and was partly to blame for the death of his friend. He shook his head. Now, not only did he have to set right all his wrongs, but he also had that life-sapping glow to contend with. He sighed and ran his finger along his goggles; he still liked to wear them on his head – they helped to ground him. Everything was getting on top of him again, and keeping his emotions in check was becoming increasingly difficult. There was something about this beautiful little hillside town. It was as if it was a place of hope, but if his hopes were to be dashed, what would he do?

If only there were some way to make everything right again. He put his hand to his chest. He'd gladly pierce his own heart to make everything right. No, thoughts like that weren't him. Was he losing his mind?

'Killian,' said a soft voice, cutting through his dark thoughts. 'Everyone's gone inside. Are you coming?'

Raven stood before him, yet he was blurred and distorted. Horrified, Killian wiped the tears from his eyes. 'I just need a minute.'

The enigmatic man nodded and leapt onto the bridge. A warm friendly hand squeezed Killian's shoulder, and his vision blurred once more.

By the time Killian and Raven had entered the tavern, everyone was already seated around a sturdy-looking table. Lily raised a suspicious eyebrow.

'Sorry,' said Raven, meeting her glare fearlessly. 'We got distracted by the scenery.'

'Fair enough. We've ordered food and drink.'

'Fine with me,' said Killian as he took a seat at the dark round table. He was amazed at how easily she'd swallowed Raven's lie. 'Found anything out?' he asked.

'The barmaid's never heard of him, b—'

'Great.' He clenched his fists tight beneath the table and tried to force his frown into a neutral expression.

'But,' Lily continued, 'she asked the chef, and he said he lives at the top of the old town.'

'Really?'

She sneered. 'No, I'm lying.'

Lily looked across the table at Killian, cocked her head and tossed him a sly smirk. He found himself unable to resist smiling back.

'That's good, then,' said Raven.

'Aye,' said Tom, a grin plastered to his face. 'That's not all that's good.' He subtly inclined his head back in the direction of the bar. 'You lose, Killian.'

Killian glanced over Tom's shoulder to see a red-haired barmaid. 'Well done.'

'He hasn't even spoken to her yet,' said Blake, his tone devoid of emotion. 'He wouldn't go up and order anything. Finn had to do it for him.'

'Ah, shut up, Blake. You know what I'm like around the reds,' muttered Tom.

'The same way you are around all women,' said Finn. She grabbed her tankard of ale and had a long swig.

'I don't think I need to remind you about Nima in Scherben,' Tom said through gritted teeth.

'Oh no, I remember the whole story,' said Finn. She glanced at the bar. Three steaming bowls of stew were lined up, waiting for them. 'Why don't you be a gentleman and help her carry them to the table?'

'Why don't you shut up?' Tom folded his arms tight across his chest.

'You're such an idiot, Tom,' said Blake. He stood up and sauntered over to the bar.

Tom snorted in disapproval.

'There're two spare rooms above here,' said Lily, addressing Killian.

'Wow! Does that mean I'll finally get a full night's sleep?' he asked, widening his eyes for effect.

'It does,' she replied, twisting a lock of hair around her finger. 'Tom, Blake and Finn are sharing, so I'm slumming it with you two,' she added, jabbing her fingers at him and Raven.

'That's lowering your standards,' said Killian, finding a particularly large knot in the table very interesting. The knot disappeared as Blake placed a bowl of stew down in front of him. 'Cheers.' He was grateful for the timely rescue.

Blake sat down, and Tom glared at him.

'So?' he hissed through a mouthful, firing flecks of stew over the table.

'What?' asked Blake, dipping a chunk of bread into his pot.

'She yours or what?'

'No,' said Blake. 'That wasn't my intention.'

'Pfft, you missed out,' said Tom, his frown fading.

Blake shook his head and popped his gravy-soaked bread into his mouth.

Once the food had been demolished, everyone sat back and enjoyed a second drink. Killian stretched and sighed. His stomach was full, his body was dry and the roaring fire was warming him nicely. He took a deep swig of his ale. It was tasty and was great at suppressing his emotions. He knew he'd be having another before the evening was done.

CHAPTER TWENTY-THREE

Killian and Lily stood outside a small grey stone house in the old part of Poll. The sun beat down, and a gentle morning breeze rustled the thick bushes outside the house. Killian yawned; why had she made him get up so early? There was a throb and a tightness building in his forehead. If he didn't eat something soon, he'd succumb to a hangover. Perhaps he'd drunk a bit too much last night.

'Sure this is the house?' he asked Lily with more of a drawl than he expected. He needed to get this over and done with, then eat, then go to bed to sleep off the fog.

'Yes,' she replied.

'So, do I just knock?'

'That's what most people do.'

Killian huffed as he knocked on the door. There was silence. He knocked again, and still there was no sound from inside. He folded his arms and tapped his foot, glaring at the arch-topped, splinter-riddled door.

'I think you've got the wrong place.'

'What makes you say that?' she asked, a subtle snarl colouring her tone.

He stared at the door and held out his arms.

'It's not the wrong place. I know how to follow instructions and navigate a village, thank you very much.'

'He must be dead, then,' said Killian.

'What're you talking about?' Lily sighed and leant against the stone wall of the house.

'He's old, right? If he's not answered, he must be dead in the house somewhere.'

'You've gone from wrong house, bypassed every other reason for him not answering the door, and landed straight on dead?' said Lily. 'Do you have any idea how insane that sounds?'

'I'm being realistic,' he said, putting his hand on the wooden door. 'Stell said he was old.'

'I'm sure they would have told me back at the tavern if he was dead,' said Lily.

'Uh-huh,' grunted Killian. He closed his eyes, then lurched forwards as the door opened. 'Shit!'

He stumbled up the doorstep but managed to grab the door frame to keep from falling. Sharp shards of wood pricked his fingers, and he swore again. He righted himself and pointlessly dusted down his shirt in a feeble attempt to appear dignified.

'Ulrich?' asked Lily, shoving Killian out of the way with her hip.

'Yes,' said the old man in the doorway, his voice wispy and thin, like he was fighting off an illness. 'To what do I owe such lovely company?'

'Ulrich,' said Killian, shoving Lily back. 'Do you remember a young lady called Estelle?'

'Hmm,' mused the old man, touching a dried-up lip with a bony finger. 'Estelle, you say?'

'Yeah, she was a practising mage – she stayed with you about forty years ago.'

'Estelle, Estelle,' he muttered, moving his fingers to his straggly grey hair. 'Estelle not-very-good Pengelly?'

Killian nodded, and the clouds around his heart parted slightly. 'Yeah, she wasn't, that's why she came to you.'

'Yes! I remember her. She was a terrible mage. To be honest with you, I don't think her heart was in it. Summoning from the Otherside isn't easy. How is she?'

'She's fine. She sent me to you, actually. I've got a problem, and she said you might be able to help.'

The old man frowned and looked Killian up and down slowly, critically. He opened his mouth, and a stab of paranoia pierced Killian's chest.

'You'd best come in and tell me about it,' he said, turning around and shuffling back into the house.

Killian looked at Lily, who gestured for him to follow the old man.

'Come on! Come in!' shouted Ulrich. 'You're letting in a dreadful draught.'

Lily closed the door behind them. The corridor was narrow. Killian hunched his shoulders. The stone walls were leaning in like they wanted to crush him. The floor was bare stones, and the distinct smell of chilly mould rose from them.

'Don't stand in there! Come through.'

Lily led the way down the corridor, past a battered wooden staircase that was missing several steps and looked more like a health hazard than a walkway. The cold corridor opened out into a large square room lined with bookshelves. Great moth-eaten volumes spewed from every shelf while others teetered in lofty piles on the floor. It smelt of old leather and decaying pages. Something about it reminded Killian of Cylus's place. Ulrich was on his knees attending to the purple flames of the fire, which were fading to orange. An unbidden smile formed on Killian's lips.

'Please sit,' Ulrich said, waving his hand behind him towards a rickety old bench. 'I'll get the fire going, then get us some tea.'

They sat on the narrow seat, which creaked with delight. Lily's hip pressed into Killian's.

'He's a bit strange,' Lily whispered.

'He's all right,' Killian murmured back. Would it be rude to ask for breakfast too? His stomach wept while his forehead grew even tighter. The hangover was trying to win.

'I'll be back in a minute,' said Ulrich, getting to his feet. 'Old Poppy will keep you company.' He gestured in the direction of a beautiful plump owl occupying a perch next to the window.

The owl turned its head and focused its large, perfectly round amber eyes on Lily. When it shifted its attention to Killian, something bizarre happened. Its body adjusted, and it seemed to get taller and thinner; its eyebrows curled downwards, and its eyes shrunk to tiny hostile slits. It opened its beak slightly and glared at him with malice.

He jumped to his feet. 'Did you see that?' he snapped, pointing to the sinister bird.

'Poppy doesn't like you,' said Lily, unaffected by the bird's strange behaviour.

Killian paced back and forth across the room, the owl following his every movement with its now-tiny eyes.

'Why is it doing that?' he asked. 'I don't like it.' It looked like it knew something, something deep and secret. Did it know about the glow too? And about Ren? Why did all the animals hate him? 'We should go.'

'Go?' spluttered Lily. 'This is the reason we came here.'

'So I could get stared out by a bloody bird?'

Lily slapped her forehead. 'No, so we could meet Ulrich.'

'I know, I know,' said Killian, still pacing. 'I don't like it, that's all.'

'Sit down,' Lily insisted. 'Are you hungover?'

'A little, maybe,' said Killian as he plonked down next to her. 'Yes.'

'Thought so. I can see the sweats and smell the booze.'

Killian winced. He was a sweaty paranoid mess.

'As excuses go, Killian, pretending to be afraid of a bird so you can go back to the tavern and sleep off last night's mistakes is pretty pathetic.'

Ulrich ambled into the room carrying a tinkling tray of tea and a plate piled high with glistening pastries. Killian's heart soared at the sight of them, all crispy, flaky and buttery.

'Ah, Poppy,' said the old man. 'Has someone ruffled your feathers?' He put the tray down on a table with a blue-tiled top and went over to the bird. He stroked its now-thin body. 'Now stop doing that, it's not nice.' The bird didn't move its gaze from Killian. 'Oh, come now, this young man's done nothing to upset you, you silly bird.' Poppy's beak opened wider, and the bird's eyebrows moved so close together they crossed. 'Silly, silly girl, don't do that to . . . er?'

'Killian,' he replied. 'Lily,' he added, indicating to his left.

'Mmm,' mused Ulrich, stroking the bird with one hand and his wiry mass of a beard with the other. 'I do apologise for Poppy's behaviour. She seems to have taken a dislike to you. I cannot think why. Come on, Pops, stop that now.'

The bird refused to comply with her master's requests. 'I am sorry about this, Killian. We'll take our tea outside and discuss your problem there, away from this silly disgruntled bird.' Ulrich shook his head at the furious-looking creature and picked up the tea tray again. 'Follow me.'

Needing no further encouragement to distance himself from the bird, Killian sprang to his feet and followed the old man. Lily's boots slapped on the stone floor, and her buckles jingled with annoyance.

Ulrich rocked back and brushed the crumbs from his mouth. Outside was much more habitable than inside. The three of them sat on benches on either side of a polished stone table. Overhead hung a tangled mass of grapevines where small dark fruits were just beginning to develop. A stone stairway spiralled away from the garden and up towards a door on the first floor of the house. A second stairway spiralled in the opposite direction and culminated in a gate leading out to the upper part of the village.

Killian stared blankly into his empty chipped cup as Lily explained their situation to Ulrich. Their conversation blurred past him in a stream of connected words; he didn't want to be there at all. The pastries had stymied the hangover successfully, but all the food in the world couldn't ease his growing panic.

He knew that at some point everyone would turn to him, and then what would happen? Would his secret come out? Ulrich may have looked old and haggard, but there was a wealth of knowledge hidden behind those faded eyes. Surely he'd be able to sense there was something wrong. Killian tensed. But maybe he'd be able to help him, show him how to use this strange, unusual power. Control the glow. Or at least stop it from killing him. He bit down on his lip. No, he refused to drag someone else into his mess. Whatever it was, he'd handle it alone.

'Killian!' snapped Lily, dragging him out of his thoughts. 'You did.'

He rubbed his face, then traced his goggles. 'I did what?' he asked.

Lily sighed. 'Have you been listening?'

'Yep,' he lied. It was easier that way.

'What did you do, then?'

Killian shrugged.

A tiny line appeared between Lily's eyebrows. 'You touched the Gramarye.'

'No need to get aggressive,' he said, looking her in the eye. 'I touched it. I grabbed it, and the piece of shit cut my hand.'

'Interesting,' croaked Ulrich, fixing his penetrating gaze on Killian. 'Did anyone else touch it?'

'Besides Thorn—Ren, no, just me.'

Ulrich sucked his thin lips and nodded slowly. He ran a finger through his beard. 'May I see your hands?' he asked.

Killian's stomach twisted, but he kept his expression even. 'Sure,' he replied, extending his hands across the table.

Ulrich grabbed them and turned them palm up, staring fixedly at them.

'Are you gonna tell me my fortune?' asked Killian.

'Something like that,' said the old man.

Shit.

Killian wanted to pull his hands free and run; this wasn't what he wanted. His secret was going to be revealed, and there was nothing he could do to stop it. He was powerless, completely at the mercy of this old man. *No one must know.*

'Hmm, interesting,' mused Ulrich. 'Here.' He jabbed the middle of Killian's palm, his long brittle nail pressing into the skin.

'What?' Killian asked.

'This is where it cut you.' It was more of a statement than a question.

'Yeah, there's a scar.'

'There's something here,' said Ulrich, clearly ignoring Killian's petulant tone.

'What's there?' asked Lily before Killian could toss a sarcastic retort of his own into the fray.

'I need to get my spectacles,' he said, releasing Killian's hands and hobbling towards the house. 'Don't go anywhere.'

Killian drew his hands back across the table and settled them into his lap. They were sweating, and his heart was racing. He wanted to run. His secret was going to be spewed across the table by this old man, and there was nothing he could do about it. There was a moment's silence before Lily shattered it in her usual blunt fashion.

'What was that all about?'

'What was what all about?'

'There's something off about you.'

Killian's heart sped up.

Ulrich returned wearing a pair of round glasses with thin wire frames. 'May I take your hand again?'

Killian presented his palm without protest. There was no point in resisting; he was trapped. Ulrich took his hand and glared at it, and as he stared, his glasses swirled with shades of purple. Killian felt wretched. For ten agonising minutes, Ulrich watched his palm, muttering incoherently to himself. Eventually, the old man sighed, let go of his hand and removed his glasses, which reverted to their standard translucent state. He yawned and rubbed his weary eyes with his fingers.

'There's some residual power there,' he said.

'What do you mean?' Killian asked.

'I'll need to examine you longer,' he said. 'But it seems a tiny sliver of the Gramarye resides within you. All I can think is the smallest fragment broke off into your skin when you cut yourself. I'm sure, with some more time, I'll be able to work something out. For now, it seems as if the Gramarye doesn't have its full power. Something is blocking it, but I need more time.'

'You've got it,' said Lily.

Killian was somewhat irked that Lily had answered for him, offering him up like he wasn't even a person, just an oddity to be studied. His stomach twisted. He *was* an oddity. What if old crusty Ulrich discovered something about the glow? That couldn't happen.

'Tomorrow, then?' said Ulrich, getting to his feet.

'All right,' said Killian, also standing. He made to move towards the back door, but Ulrich stopped him.

'Could you please leave that way.' He indicated the spiral stone stairway leading to a wooden gate. 'I don't want Poppy being upset again. It takes so long to calm her down.'

'Sure,' said Lily. 'Killian has that effect on most people.'

Ulrich chuckled. It was an odd crackling sound, like crisp leaves rustling in an autumn breeze.

CHAPTER TWENTY-FOUR

After returning from Ulrich's, Killian spent a few hours soaking in a bathtub, then slept off the dregs of his hangover. As the evening descended upon Poll, he made his way to the cold dusty bridge that ran over the waterfall and lay down. He wrapped his arms around his head and looked out over the darkened valley. The soft splashing of the waterfall complemented the scene. He took in a breath of the fresh mountain air; there was a sweet hint to it like it was delicately flavoured by the fruit bushes surrounding the town. The sky was fading from blue to purple as the sun slipped behind the distant mountains.

As calm and peaceful as his surroundings were, Killian couldn't help but dwell on his new set of problems. Not only did he have the mysterious glow within him, but he also had some residual power from the Gramarye. He breathed out slowly and watched the curls of breath dissolve into the oncoming night. Perhaps they were linked? His heart thumped. That had to be it. That residual power was manifesting inside him into something he couldn't control. He'd seen what the Gramarye had done to Ren, he'd felt its brutal power as it tried to kill him. Now something that vile and cruel was living inside him, sucking the life out of him.

If only he'd refused to help Ren all that time ago. His life would be infinitely easier now. But he couldn't say no; it had been his chance, his one chance at clearing his conscience. And he'd messed that up too. He looked up at the stars twinkling in the purple sky and chuckled bitterly to himself. It was either that or cry.

Footsteps tramped on the stone path behind him, rousing him from his musings. He didn't move though, even when they drew closer and stopped next to him.

'Enjoying yourself?' It was Lily.

'Always,' he murmured back.

'Here, I got you a drink,' she said, holding a pewter mug above him.

A drip of ale splashed onto his forehead. 'Thanks,' he said, sitting up.

He took the tankard from her and had a deep swig. Strong fumes coalesced at the back of his throat, and he coughed. 'That packs a punch,' he remarked, his voice gravelly. 'Are you trying to take advantage of me?'

'Raven added something extra to yours, so maybe he is.'

'He's going the right way about it,' he said, then took another swig. It tasted like something else was mixed in with the ale, a spirit or wine of some kind. It certainly wasn't pleasant – it burned.

Lily turned and leant against the bridge. 'Nice night.'

'Uh-huh,' he replied.

Silence fell comfortably between them as the sky grew darker and the stars brighter. Across the valley, the mountains loomed. The soft glow of the rising moon highlighted their lofty peaks and morphed the river into a winding silver ribbon. The tall dark trees were edged with silver starlight, and they shimmied in the breeze like a collection of carnival streamers. It was a beautiful night. Killian took another long gulp and sucked his tongue. What was that fiery flavour? And was Raven really trying to get him drunk?

He turned his attention to Lily as she downed the rest of her drink. It was impressive; he took another sip to try to catch up. Her long wavy black hair flowed like a mysterious river in the twilight. His heart thumped, so he followed her example and finished the drink. He took a deep breath and gently prodded her in the back. As she turned, he held his tankard out to her and gave her his most confident grin.

She took it from him with a playful swipe. 'Anything else?'

'Another one of those wouldn't go amiss.'

'Well, as you asked so nicely.' She bent down and picked up two more tankards from the ground. 'I hope you're ready for hangover part two tomorrow.'

Killian huffed. 'I wasn't hungover today. I was just a bit tired.'

'You keep telling yourself that.'

'I will,' he grunted, and then, to prove a point, he took a long gulp.

Lily smiled. It was a beautiful smile that touched her emerald eyes.

'How're you feeling?' she asked.

'A bit strange. The whole Gramarye residual thing is difficult to comprehend.' He shifted his attention to his drink and stared at the layer of foam swaying on the top.

'I bet.'

'It's weird to think that it left its mark on me. I don't like it – we both saw what it could do – but it's better than having nothing to go on.'

Lily nodded.

'But at the same time, I keep thinking, why wasn't I more careful? If I hadn't let it cut me . . .' He bit his bottom lip and then had a drink. A warm fog started to descend into his mind.

'At least we have a lead,' said Lily.

'Yeah.' Killian paused. 'It's a shame you didn't touch it.'

She laughed. 'Number one, do you honestly think it would have cut me? And number two, I wasn't going to touch that *thing*. To me it was a glowing green physical manifestation of your deceitful lie.'

Killian almost choked on his drink. 'Really?' he gasped amid violent coughs and bouts of laughter.

'Yes, really,' she snapped back, 'and it's not funny.'

'Sorry.' He didn't mean it.

'All that time I wasted because I was following your lies. I was a fool to believe you in the first place – temples laden with treasure left by some magical lost civilisation. What a load of shit.'

'You fell for it.'

'Perhaps,' she muttered. She drained her tankard and put it on the ground. Killian had some catching up to do.

'Perhaps?'

'I don't know.' She rested a hand on the stone wall and turned to face him. 'Maybe I wanted to believe you because I needed to get away. I was bored. I didn't know what to do with myself or my crew. Then you came along and gave me the perfect excuse to leave.'

The fog in Killian's head shifted down into his chest,

where it bloomed with warmth. 'Are you saying you didn't believe my lie anyway?'

'I did, and I didn't. I latched on to it though – it was my way out.' She sighed despondently. 'Really, I should thank you.'

'Go on, then. I'm not gonna stop you.'

She narrowed her eyes and scowled. 'No, you still lied to me.' She gave him a dig in the ribs with her elbow.

'Fair enough, I deserved that.' He drained his mug and handed it to Lily. She swiped it from his hand with a disgruntled sneer and put it with the others.

'You know, I always wondered what happened to that necklace.'

'Necklace?' she asked, frowning.

'Don't pretend you can't remember. The first thing we fought over. I always swore to myself that I'd get it back one day.'

'That hideous thing. Good luck finding it. I broke it down and sold it.'

'Shit,' he said, shaking his head. 'There goes my life's goal.'

'Stop trying to make me feel guilty.'

'Sorry.' He grinned. 'Remember when we used to thieve together?' The strong alcohol coupled with the scenery and having Lily as company was making him sentimental.

'As if I could forget.'

'I thought you'd have blanked it from your memory.'

'Believe me, I've tried.'

Killian gasped. 'I was just gonna say how much I enjoyed it . . . sometimes. You really know how to ruin a moment.'

Lily sniggered and tossed her hair over her shoulders. 'In all honesty, I wouldn't want to forget that. I need it fresh in my mind as a reminder to never do it again.'

Killian sat up and swung his legs around the wall, unintentionally brushing them against her hips. He moved his hand out to steady himself and put it down next to hers. He leant a little closer and shook his head. 'Ah, Lil, will you ever stop hurting me?'

'Not while it amuses me,' she said.

He lowered his eyes and smiled. 'So, you'll stop one day?'

She put her hand on his chin and raised his head. 'I don't think so.'

He slid off the wall and stood next to her, not taking his eyes off her the whole time. The alcohol aided him in holding her beguiling gaze. He put a hand on her hip.

'That's a shame.'

'It is?' she said as she rested a hand on his chest.

'What if this Gramarye thing is killing me?'

'Don't be silly.'

He forced a chuckle to keep the atmosphere light. 'I'm serious. What if it is and I die without giving you the chance to be nice to me?'

'That would be tragic.'

'Would it?'

'Mmm.' Her rich olive skin was tinted with a hint of rose.

'What would you do?'

'What do you mean?' she asked.

'If it was killing me and . . . I wasn't gonna be around much longer.'

'You shouldn't talk like that, Killian,' she said, pressing a warm finger to his lips.

'I know, I'm sorry.'

'But if it was . . . I suppose I'd *have* to be a little nicer to you.'

'That's good to know.' He pulled her closer, and she moved without a trace of protest.

Lily wrapped her arms around his waist and rested her head on his chest. He held her next to him. Her silky hair teased the backs of his hands. It was so smooth and soft. The herby citrus scent of her skin filled his senses. His heart thudded, and his body ached with desire.

He allowed his hands to wander up her back, tracing his fingers lightly over her spine. A sigh of contentment escaped from her, and his body flooded with warmth. She leant back against his arms to look at him. The stars sparkled in her eyes, and her lips parted. She reached her hand up and traced his jawline.

'Lil,' he whispered.

'Killian,' she breathed, moving closer. 'I—'

The silence was shattered by a loud crash, swiftly followed by raucous cheers from inside the tavern. Lily retrieved her hand and jumped backwards. Killian darted away and hunched over.

'What the fuck was that?' said Lily.

'No idea,' he said, dusting down his coat to avoid looking at her.

'I bet it's got something to do with three pissed-up pirates.'

'No doubt.'

'I should go and see what it was – don't wanna get run out of another town.'

'No,' he replied, picking up the empty mugs.

They walked to the door together and stopped inside the musty porch, Killian, Lily and their lingering awkward silence.

'I'm going up,' he eventually said, handing her the tankards.

'Okay.' They clinked in protest as she snatched them from him. She turned to the door leading to the bar.

'Lil.'

'Yes?' she asked without looking around.

The speech he'd planned in his head fragmented. Words meandered around his mind in a convoluted jumble. 'Thanks for the drinks.'

'Any time,' she said, then disappeared into the bar. A thick cloud of smoke billowed out to replace her.

Killian sighed and opened the other door. He needed to cool off; maybe some alone time in the room wasn't such a bad idea.

CHAPTER TWENTY-FIVE

Ulrich's glasses were askew and his hair a wispy mess. Great shadows of dull grey encircled his mottled red eyes. The foul odour of mouldy sweat and over-brewed coffee complemented his dishevelled appearance. He was a mess.

'Have I caught you at a bad time?' Killian asked.

'No, no, not at all.' Ulrich's voice was thick and heavy. He reached out and grabbed Killian's arm with his bony fingers, welcoming him back into his house.

Killian followed the old man down the corridor and back into his main room, but today it looked very different. Books were everywhere, strewn across the floor, the couch, the bench, covering the little blue-tiled table and a large round wooden table. The place was a complete disaster. Paper and ink were scattered everywhere, and the room reeked of alcohol, tobacco and coffee. Poppy glared at Killian from her perch, almost like she was accusing him of making the mess.

'Let's go outside, away from my grumpy owl.'

Killian gladly followed the old man out to his garden and sat back on the bench. Ulrich slumped down opposite, a smile on his thin lips.

'I've not slept,' the old man confessed.

'I can come back another time.'

Ulrich looked like he was about to expire right in front of him.

'No, no, stay. I made a breakthrough last night,' he said, removing his glasses. 'I consulted so many books – I have so many, too many. I stayed up until the birds were singing. Reading, drinking coffee, smoking. So I apologise for my current state. Anyway, I found one with a mention of your Gramarye.'

'What?'

Ulrich cleared his throat and dumped a large red-leather-bound book onto the table. He licked his fingers and leafed through the pages, stopping on one with a diagram of a prism on it. Killian's heart stopped, and his breath caught in his throat. That was it. It even had the strange symbols etched into it. The object that had caused him so much misery was staring back at him from an age-stained page.

'Look familiar?' Ulrich asked.

'Yeah,' said Killian, even though he knew the answer was written all over his face, 'that's it.'

'I read all there was on it. There's not a lot, but enough.' Ulrich closed the book with a thump, sending a cloud of dust into the biting morning air. 'I was correct though, the Gramarye is blocked from reaching its full power. It's bound shut by fifteen seals. The seals in question are souls, descendants of the race who crafted it. From what I can tell, these fifteen souls were used to lock away the Gramarye's power.'

'There were fifteen statues on the island,' mused Killian.

'That would be a connection,' said Ulrich. 'For the most part, the souls are living. The power to unlock the Gramarye is passed down through generations. Imagine the Gramarye. Now imagine it locked behind fifteen doors. Each soul is a key to a door, and the more doors are unlocked, the stronger the light of the Gramarye becomes until the final door is unlocked and it's free. It would appear that the souls bound are safeguards to prevent the power from being used. You need to discover where the remaining seals are and find some way of protecting them. And I believe you're the key to tracking them down.'

Killian stared at the warlock. 'What d'you mean?'

'A lingering presence of the Gramarye is within you. It will be pulling itself towards the seals – the artefact wants to be free again, all of it. With a bit more time, I'm sure I'll be able to work out how to use its desire to track down the seals.'

'And once I've tracked one down, what am I supposed to do?'

'Protect them,' said Ulrich simply, his faded eyes fixed intently on Killian.

'And how am I supposed to do that?' Bitter memories of Ren's death oozed into Killian's mind. 'Last time I went up against this demon, or whatever it is, it had me on my knees with a flick of the wrist. I can't fight it. I can't even protect myself against its power, let alone someone else. And if what you say is true, about the Gramarye gaining power with each broken seal, then this demon will be gaining power too. I was lucky to survive the first time.' Emotion choked him into silence.

'I'll help you as much as I can. As long as you protect at least one seal, the Gramarye will not reach its full potential.

I fear if it does, it would be catastrophic.' He stood up. 'I'll make us some tea and leave you to have a think. Then we'll see about tracking them.'

A breeze swept into Ulrich's small sunken garden, rustling the old vines above. Killian kept his eyes locked firmly on the dancing leaves. Saying how pathetic he was out loud to someone new was too much, too humiliating. He wrapped his arms around the back of his head and leant into them. At least Ulrich hadn't discovered the glow – that was one small mercy – and his skin hadn't shimmered either, which was always a worry. He could do without that secret coming out. Whatever Ulrich found out about the Gramarye and the souls, Killian would have to go along with it. He had to set right his mistake.

He wondered what the others were doing – probably having a great time. They'd be drinking, playing cards, relaxing somewhere comfortable, exploring the village, climbing the waterfall, creating illusions. Finn might even be fishing. The lucky swine.

The gentle tinkling of a tea set drew Killian's attention. He rocked his head forwards as Ulrich placed a wooden tray on the table. The old man picked up a pale blue teapot and filled their cups.

'Sugar?' Ulrich asked.

'No thanks.'

He nodded and passed him a cup. 'So?' He left the question hanging.

'I'll do whatever it takes,' said Killian, wrapping his cold hands around the warm mug.

'Good.' Ulrich smiled. 'I have a theory.' He loaded his teacup with three heaped spoons of sugar, staring into Killian's eyes as he stirred. 'You need to acknowledge the trace of the Gramarye and let it in.'

Killian gulped his tea, swallowed quickly and winced. He'd definitely burned his tongue in his haste. What if the glow surfaced? 'How do I do that?'

'That's up to you.'

'What d'you mean?'

'The trace of the Gramarye resides within you. You're the one who needs to unlock it.'

'And how do I do that?' Killian wanted to leave; this was sounding more and more like another mistake.

'Focus and concentration.'

'Not my strongest skills.'

'It is a part of you, Killian. It should be easy for you to harness that trace of power to locate one of the key souls.'

'I'm sure it will be very easy,' Killian mumbled to the table.

'All you need to do is concentrate and let it in. I'll try.'

Keeping his head down, Killian held his palms out. 'See what you can do.'

Ulrich took hold of Killian's hands and stared into them. After a few minutes, he let them go. 'I can't,' he said, his voice wheezy, 'it won't let me.'

Killian sat up and rubbed his forehead; hangover part two was creeping in just like Lily had predicted. 'What makes you think it will let me?'

'It's in you, so I assume it will let you.'

'Okay, what do I do?'

'Focus on the Gramarye, on the trace in your body. Think of the souls and allow yourself to be drawn towards them.'

Killian nodded.

He held his hands out before him, took a deep breath and blew all the air from his lungs. A cool breeze kissed his lips and whipped through his hair. His body tensed, and he closed his eyes and concentrated. He thought only of the Gramarye, picturing the strange prism in his mind.

Its green light pulsed with power as the blue mist seeped from it. The mist clouded his vision and became darker, and he felt something claw down his back. Ren screamed. A thin layer of sweat broke out along his hairline. He trembled. But he had to remain focused. He had to remain calm.

Something flickered amid the blue clouds, something bright, something blue. He reached for it, pushing through the mists, his fingers outstretched. The blue light grew brighter until finally its source was before him. A small orb of fluorescent light hovered in front of him. Gingerly, he walked towards it and held his hands above it. It throbbed with power. He moved his hands down around it, slowly bringing them together. As soon as he touched the orb, it exploded, sending out bright streaks of light in a spidery tangle. Ren was screaming again. Killian's blood was burning, his own soul trying to flee. He collapsed to the floor in agony, unable to defend himself.

He opened his eyes and fell back off the bench, hitting the ground with a thump. All his breath was knocked from his body, and he was soaked with sweat.

'What is it?' demanded Ulrich, leaning down towards him.

'I . . . I don't know,' Killian whispered between breaths. His body juddered uncontrollably. Nausea surged through him. 'There was something there, I don't know what.'

Ulrich frowned. 'Tell me what you saw.'

Killian glared at him and clenched his teeth. 'I don't know,' he said. 'I've just come out of it, give me some time.'

'Of course, of course,' muttered the old man. 'I'm sorry, new breakthroughs often get me overexcited. I'll fetch you something to calm yourself.'

'Thanks,' said Killian, getting up. His body was weak and used up. 'But I think I'll head on back now.'

'No, please,' insisted Ulrich, 'let me fetch you something to relax you.'

'Fine.' Killian slumped back onto the bench.

When Ulrich returned, he was holding a brown clay mug. He handed it to Killian, who sniffed it suspiciously. It smelt safe enough, sweet and herbal. He downed it in one and handed the cup back.

'Thanks,' he said. 'I'm still going though.'

Ulrich shook his head. 'I thought you might. I'm sorry. I didn't mean to get angry. This must be hard for you.'

'It is.'

'You'll come back tomorrow?' he asked, his eyes wide with hope.

'Of course.'

'Good, I shall look forward to it.'

Killian walked through the streets of Poll filled with a sense of relief. He was glad to be away from that house and that old bastard. Didn't he realise this was a difficult thing for him to do? The shouting and forceful attitude weren't helping at all.

He clenched his fists tight. He didn't like the old git; he made him feel more like an experiment than a person. He didn't like the way he looked at him like he knew something, and the more he wore him down, the closer he'd be to the truth.

But what if Ulrich could help him? If he knew what the glow was? No, he'd only treat him like some new discovery. He couldn't find out.

His footsteps were soft and spongy, and his body light and airy. *At least that drink seems to be working.* By the time Killian reached the bridge near the tavern, he was feeling pretty good. He paused and watched the light dance across the valley.

CHAPTER TWENTY-SIX

Tom was making his way back to the inn, his arms laden down with freshly baked bread and his bag stuffed with sliced meats and cheeses. He'd risen early to get everything ready for his perfect day. They'd been in Poll for a few days now, and it was about time he did something, anything. Killian was always ducking off to see that crusty old codger, and the captain was as elusive as ever, as was Raven. Finn spent her time chain-smoking in the bar, and he'd even caught Blake reading a book he'd found at the inn. He must have been bored. So, it was up to him, Thomas Gainsborough, to bring everyone together and lighten the mood. Well, bring his gunner brother and sister together.

The bread was still warm, and it smelt delicious. Tom's stomach growled as he marched through the streets. He made eye contact with several locals and nodded and smiled at them all. He knew they'd find him interesting to look at.

His skin tone and eye colour definitely stood out, so he didn't even attempt to hide. To his surprise, they smiled back, and some even verbally greeted him. Poll wasn't so bad.

When he reached the tavern, he went straight to the bar, knowing he'd find Finn inside lost amid a cloud of smoke. He nudged the door open with his foot, and there she was. She was so predictable. The stunning redhead was behind the bar again, but he kept his attention locked on Finn.

'Come on, Finlay,' he said in his most enthusiastic tone, 'we're going out!'

Finn turned her head, her cigarette dangling from her lips. Her eyes were marbled with red, and she didn't look impressed. 'What?' The cigarette didn't even move when she spoke. It was as if it'd become a part of her.

'I've got us breakfast – you, me, Blakey boy.'

'Come again?'

'I've go—'

The door behind Tom swung open, knocking him square in the arse. He staggered forwards yet somehow managed to keep hold of his precious cargo. A stifled giggle came from the bar, and heat burst into his cheeks. He composed himself and spun to face his assailant.

'Sorry, Tom,' grunted Blake.

'Blake! You're just who I wanted to see.'

'Uh-huh.'

Tom glanced at Blake's hand and saw the offensive book in his clutches. 'You won't be needing that old sack of words today.'

'What? Tom, it's too early for this.' Blake yawned and rubbed his eyes.

'Put that down,' said Tom, glaring at the book. 'We're going out.'

'We are?'

Tom huffed. Why was his audience being so difficult this morning? He settled the bread onto the closest table, then snatched Blake's book from his hand. He marched over to Finn's table, grabbed her arm, and dragged her up. She grunted in her throat but allowed him to move her.

'This is staying here,' he said, slamming Blake's book onto Finn's empty table. 'And *we* are going down to the river.' He scooped up his loaves of bread and opened the inn door. 'Let's go.'

'You know, Tom,' said Finn as she pulled one of the loaves of bread apart, 'this ain't bad.'

'Are you trying to say *thanks*?' Tom asked.

'I'm saying it ain't bad.'

'You're welcome,' said Tom, unable to keep the grin from his face.

He grabbed one of the loaves himself and tore off a chunk. It was fresh and springy inside, crisp and brown on the outside. He took a thick slice of ham from one of the paper bags at his feet and layered it with slices of cheese on his slab of bread. He paused to admire his handiwork, then took a bite. The meat was juicy, the cheese was creamy and the bread was like a warm fluffy cloud.

Before him, the wide, shallow river flowed over its smooth rocky bed. It rushed and churned over the worn oval rocks and filled the air with a musical tinkling. The bright morning sun dappled its surface with shifting silver discs. A brownish-green creature caught Tom's eye. At the shore hopped a tiny frog; another joined it, and another. They looked like little lost leaves. A dragonfly darted out from the grasses. Its neon-blue body looked as if it were alive with some sort of mystical energy. He kicked off his boots and dangled a toe in the cool water. It was more than cool – it was freezing, but refreshing. His gaze followed the dragonfly down the river until it became lost amid the blue skies.

Great mountains towered in the distance, hulking monsters capped with snow. He looked from the mountains to his wet feet; some of that snow was on him now. He was a part of the mountain, or was it a part of him? It didn't really matter. All that mattered was that he was creating a memory with his two closest friends in the world. He took another bite from his catastrophe of a sandwich and glanced at Finn. There was a small smile on her scarred face.

'You did good, Tom,' said Blake, coming to sit next to him on the low bank.

'Good. I just thought we needed to get out, have a break, take in the sights.'

'I thought the redhead behind the bar was the only sight you were interested in?'

Tom chuckled to himself. He really did play his sexually charged male persona incredibly well. Persona? Who was he kidding, he *was* a sexually charged male. But surely there was more to life than chebs. 'I told you before, Blakey boy, I can be quite deep when I want to be. There's more to life than a great pair of chebs.'

'What the fuck is he goin' on about?' Finn's gravelled voice cut through the peaceful valley like a rusty saw. 'He dips his toe in nature, and now he's all, "I'm cured of bein' a filthy scumbag." The first woman you see is gonna boil your blood.'

Tom turned around and looked at Finn. 'Hey, Finn, my blood ain't boiling.'

'Oh, you absolute shit!'

IT was mid-morning by the time Killian reached Ulrich's cottage. He opened the gate at the top of the stone staircase and let himself into the sunken garden. A loaf of bread, several jars of jam and honey and a block of butter were laid out on the stone table.

'Sit down, have some breakfast.' Ulrich's crispy voice filtered out from the cottage.

Killian promptly plonked himself down onto the cold stone bench. He sliced a chunk off the loaf of bread, then slathered it in thick butter and a generous dollop of blueberry jam. The berries were smaller than those found in Vermor – he took a bite – and sweeter too. The slightly mouldy taste that often accompanied blueberries was also absent. Freischen grew better fruit – definitely a reason to leave Vermor for good.

The gentle jingle of crockery signalled the arrival of Ulrich. The old man placed a wooden tray on the table between them and filled their cups. He reached for a hunk of bread, covered it in butter and slowly dripped honey over it, his eyes not leaving Killian.

'Sleep well?' Ulrich asked.

'Not exactly,' Killian replied. 'Every time I started to drift off, I saw this thing.'

'Thing?'

'Yeah, I saw it yesterday when I was trying to use the trace. A ball of light, blue and silver. I don't know.'

'It sounds connected.'

' 'S what I thought.'

'Are you ready to try using the trace again today?'

'Yeah, I wanna get this over with.'

'I understand, and I'm sorry I got overexcited yesterday.'

He waved away Ulrich's apology. 'It's fine. I suppose I'm new and fascinating.'

'That you are!'

Killian finished off his slice of bread – the jam was delicious – and turned his palm over. He ran his finger over the small scar the Gramarye had left. To think a tiny part of that thing was inside him, wanting to be whole again, killing him – it was bizarre. His heart thumped, and his skin grew warm; he had to calm down somehow, or he'd ruin everything.

He placed a finger on his chest where Nesta's glyph had once sat. He closed his eyes, blew all the air from his lungs and traced the pattern of the glyph over his skin. A wash of calm descended upon him, and his mind began to rest. Nesta's soothing voice whispered in his ear; he felt her warm strong palm press on him. Peace wrapped itself around him.

His mind went to the Gramarye, that beautiful emerald flame. The shifting greens, the gold, the silver, its beating teal heart. He opened his eyes, and it was in front of him, calling him. A sharp pain pierced his right hand. He looked at it. There was a sliver of green beneath his skin – tiny, as thin as a hair, but it was there. Light poured out of it, green fading to blue. Instead of falling, the light rose. It moved in front of him, hovering.

Ren screamed.

Killian bit down on the inside of his mouth; he had to shut that sound out.

Ren screamed again. He was calling him, begging for his help, shouting his name over and over.

Killian balled his fists up as pain threatened to rush in and overwhelm him. The trace in his palm prickled and dragged him forward. His hands rested on the sides of the ghostly

Gramarye; it was like sheets of ice, smooth, cold, cruel. He stared into its shifting surface, and a picture slowly coalesced within it.

Ren screamed.

'Stop it . . . Thorncliffe . . .' Killian whispered.

A high lonely hilltop shimmered onto its surface. A pair of metal gates with spiked rusted railings. They opened out. Dilapidated steps, crumbling edges, moss worked into the stone. Flat rocks with words inscribed on them . . . words . . . words . . . names, dates. Graves. The dead. Decay. He could smell it. Rot and mire. It wanted to pull him in. Pull him down. Drown him.

He gasped. His chest ached. It was going to rip in two.

The blue light flickered into his vision once more, pulsing with a bright silver luminescence. It moved, twirling around the gravestones, calling him – it wanted him. His hand twitched. The Gramarye wanted it. The blue light melted into the grassy ground, and he was pushed back, down the stairs and out the gates. They closed with a dull clang. He was above the hill, that high lonely hill. It was so isolated. It was forgotten. He felt its pain. He blinked, and hot tears scorched his cheeks. It was so alone.

He blinked once more, and Ulrich came into view before him, his expression confused. Killian's body was numb. What had happened? What had he seen? Was any of it real?

'I'll fix you a drink, something more than tea.' Ulrich got up and left.

Killian was nodding dumbly for some time after he left. His body shuddered. Had he left it? Exhaustion crept over him. Emotion shattered him. Ulrich returned and put a glass of clear liquid down in front of him. Killian sniffed it. It smelt like raisins and rot. He took a sip, and it burned. His lips and tongue were on fire. A wheezing cough spluttered from his throat. Then a bizarre sweetness filled his mouth. To say it was disgusting would be an understatement.

'It's grappa,' Ulrich explained. 'Think of it as extra strong wine.'

'Thanks,' gasped Killian, and he took another sip. It tasted like bitter, burning water. So, this was what had been mixed into the ale the other night. It raced through his body, warming him up and smothering his emotions. It may have tasted vile, but it had a swift way of relaxing him. 'I saw . . . some stuff.'

'Take your time.'

Killian nodded and finished off the drink. A fuzzy feeling wrapped itself around him, and he leant back into it. It was calming, soothing and numbing all at once. There was a gentle clink as Ulrich reached over to fill his glass once more. Killian put his hands on the glass and gazed at the clear drink before him.

'I saw a place,' he said once he'd composed himself.

'Yes.'

'It was . . . It was a graveyard.' Killian pulled the glass towards him. He wanted to down it all and keep drinking so the feelings would leave him completely. 'It was lonely, so lonely. I could feel its pain.' He chuckled mirthlessly to himself. 'It sounds stupid, doesn't it?'

'Not at all,' said Ulrich, his voice soft. 'Tell me what you can. Where was it? Was there anything distinct about it?'

'I've never been there before. I've never seen it. It was high up on a hilltop. It was windy and dark. It felt like the loneliest place in the world.' Killian paused and took a sip from the glass. 'It was forgotten, overgrown and falling apart. There was one thing there though, something that seemed alive. I don't know.' He ran his fingers up and down the delicate stem of the glass.

'What was it?'

Killian chewed on the inside of his lip. 'A ball of light. Bright blue, dazzling, silver trailing off it. It sank into the ground under the graves.'

'Sounds to me like an orm,' said Ulrich.

Killian blinked and rubbed his head – that grappa was getting to him. Was he on course for hangover part three? 'A what?'

'A spirit trapped in this world, one that cannot move on for whatever reason. I bet my grappa cellar that orm is your spirit, a soul that is sealing the Gramarye.'

'Great,' said Killian. He took another drink. 'If the person I need to protect is already dead, then the job's good, the Gramarye can never be unlocked.'

'If only it were so simple. If this orm is bound to the world by the Gramarye, it can be used to unlock it. Whoever has this device will be able to find it, as you have done, and will use it.'

'So, how do we protect something we can't see or touch?' He slumped across the table. 'This is making my head hurt.'

'No, that's the grappa.' Ulrich chuckled.

'That too.' Killian couldn't argue with that.

'There is a way.' Ulrich ran his fingers through his beard as he spoke, as if he was afraid to say what it was.

Killian picked up his grappa and downed it. 'I'm listening.'

CHAPTER TWENTY-SEVEN

THE SUN, A GOLDEN MEDALLION, SHONE PROUDLY in a cloudless azure sky. A soft breeze rustled the leaves in the vineyards and on the fruit bushes, which were crammed into every available space in the town, as well as on the ascending hills. Leafy shadows danced on the grey-slabbed walkways, and small birds twittered and chirped as they flitted about the vines searching for bugs. They were a riot of colour – yellow, red, blue, green, orange – and all had their best feathers on for spring. The residents of Poll ambled through the streets, some carrying baskets of fruit, others with a fresh catch of fish from the river.

Killian slunk through the small town. He was drunk. That grappa certainly was strong and had gone straight to his head. Somehow, drinking in the daytime always seemed to get him even more drunk. He frowned. Surely he wasn't turning into one of those guys who hung around the Laughing Swan in the day. He hoped not. He drew in a deep lungful of fresh air; he wasn't, he definitely wasn't. And anyway, after what he was willing to do, he deserved to be as drunk as he liked.

He reached the stone bridge near the tavern and slumped down onto it. A woman with short brown hair sitting at the other end gave him a smile, then carried on playing her guitar. The melody was soft and delicate, perfectly complementing the shimmying leaves and the gentle flow of the river.

Killian moved and stared down at the babbling stream. It was shallow and swished and tinkled over large flat stones, rolling down the hill to meet the wide river that filled the valley. He could just make out four or five figures on the low riverbank. He put a hand up to keep the sun from his eyes and squinted. It was Finn, Tom and Blake. It looked like Finn was fishing with some of the locals; that would do her some good. Tom and Blake were sprawled on the grassy bank. A dark shadowy figure that could only be Raven approached them and sat down on the bank.

He adjusted his position and focused back on the stream. He inhaled its fresh scent as it splashed over the smooth rocks. It was cool and bracing. A wave of dizziness washed over him, but there was some cold comfort to be had in it; his anxieties and fears seemed to be held at bay by the grappa. Maybe there was something to this daytime drunk stuff after all. Perhaps this was what he'd been doing wrong all his life.

A shadow joined his in the stream. He didn't move; he knew who it was. He could smell her – herbs and citrus – and his heart thumped. Had she brought that scent with her? Warmth radiated off her, or was that just him and the grappa?

'How was your morning?' she asked, breaking the quiet.

'Productive,' he replied.

Killian turned towards Lily, but there was a distinct lack of coordination in his movements. He needed some food and a sleep, then more food and another sleep.

'Killian, are you drunk?' She cocked an eyebrow. 'Again?'

He held his thumb and forefinger about an inch apart – there was no point in lying. 'A bit.'

'In the daytime too,' she said.

She shook her head, and her hair rippled like an ebony river made of silky ribbons. The midday sun soaked into her olive skin, and her emerald eyes twinkled mischievously. The grappa was really getting to him. It was certainly the grappa – he only loved her when he was drunk. She flashed him a cocky smirk, almost as if she could read his thoughts. She couldn't, could she?

'There's a bakery up the lane,' she said, pointing in its direction. 'Let's get you something to soak up whatever it is you've been drinking and chat about your productive morning.'

'Sounds good to me.'

Killian followed Lily along the smooth grey streets, his mind hazy and his movements clumsy. The delicious waft of freshly baked bread and sweet pastries hugged the breeze, and his poor abused stomach growled. Lily stopped outside a small shop, which was little more than a hole in the wall.

'What d'you want? My treat,' she said.

'Why are you being so nice to me?' Killian ventured to ask.

She leant towards him and lowered her voice. 'Because there's no one else around and you're drunk. You'll have forgotten in a few hours.' She grabbed him by the sleeve of his coat and dragged him in.

'Welcome, travellers,' said a short portly woman from behind the counter. 'Do take your time.'

So, some people in the village of Poll *were* talking about them.

The grey stone bakery was tiny but packed with produce. An arched doorway behind the shopkeeper led to the kitchens, where fires crackled and waves of dry heat rolled out. Someone was moving around back there. Beneath the glass countertop were rows and rows of pastries. Some looked like giant cowries, their mouths stuffed with purple jam and dusted with sugar; there were small heart-shaped ones drizzled with honey and large cylindrical loaves studded with dried fruits. Fresh crusty loaves hung in wire baskets behind the counter. It all smelt so sweet and inviting, Killian was overwhelmed with choice.

'I definitely want those,' he said, pointing to the jam-filled cowries. 'You pick everything else. Surprise me. I'll wait outside.' The heat of the shop was threatening to give him a premature hangover, something he could certainly do without.

Killian leant against the shop wall and waited for Lily. He could hear her chatting with the people inside and laughing occasionally. Nice, friendly Lily was out today. Eventually, she emerged with two brown paper bags full to bursting and handed one to him. It was warm and smelt so good, he dipped his hand in and pulled out a purple-jam-filled pastry.

'I hate eating and walking,' said Lily.

'All right,' Killian huffed, dropping it back into the bag.

They wandered to the town square, making a beeline for the giant pine that stood at its centre. Its branches were neatly uniform and laden with emerald needles. An inviting wooden bench circled it. As soon as Killian sat down, he grabbed the pastry and devoured it. It was sweet, flaky and moist all at the same time. The jam was blueberry and packed a tart fruity hit. It was gone within seconds, and he mercilessly chomped his way through a second one. They were so good he felt like crying. He thought he heard Lily chuckle next to him. He brushed the crumbs from his lips and turned to her. She'd pulled a chunk off one of the fruit-studded loaves and handed it to him to do the same. He ripped a piece off and put the remains in the paper bag.

'This is so good,' he said.

'Isn't it?'

He finished eating and stretched his legs out. The drunken haze faded as the food started doing its job. He wrapped his arms around the back of his head and looked up into the lofty top of the pine.

'We've gotta hide a soul in me,' he said in a breezy tone, as if it were the sort of thing he did every day. This was how he was going to play it. It worked last time, and it'd work again.

Lily stayed silent. He ventured to look at her; she was clearly listening to him while she picked at the sweet loaf.

'One of the seals is dead. Its soul is tied to the world, but if I do a bit of soul binding, it can live in me.'

Lily snorted a laugh.

'What?'

'If you "do a bit of soul binding." '

'I'm serious!'

'I know, I'm sorry.' She was smiling faintly as she spoke. 'It was the way you said it. So, you're telling me you're doing something completely ridiculous again?'

'Yep.'

'You do know soul binding is banned in most countries because it's dangerous and insane? You do know it's also rumoured to be one of the reasons my castle's previous owner went crazy? You do know that it shouldn't be messed around with?'

'I do.' Killian kept his gaze firmly fixed on the pine.

'Good, as long as we're agreed on that.'

'I know where the soul is. I could see it because of this Gramarye trace.' He paused to look at his hand. What else was it doing to him? 'Ulrich'll mark it on our map.'

'Great.'

'He's writing out the soul binding ritual too.'

'Fantastic.'

'I want you to do it,' said Killian.

'I'm sorry, what?' she asked.

He blew all the breath from his lungs and dropped his arms. He finally looked at her; her face was blank and unreadable. 'I want you to do the ritual on me. I can't do it on myself – I'll mess it up.'

'Me?' she said softly.

'Yeah, you. Ulrich said to ask someone I can trust, and even though you're . . . you, I think I can trust you.'

'Flattering.'

'You know what I—'

'I know.' She placed her hand on his arm and gave it a squeeze. 'I know what you mean.'

'So, will you?' Heat poured from her hand and into him; that fleeting bit of contact was so good.

'I don't have much of a choice, do I?'

'Nah.' Killian forced out a grin.

'Don't ask me to do anything for you again, ever. I mean it.'

CHAPTER TWENTY-EIGHT

LILY SAT IN THE BAR, CURLS OF STEAM RISING FROM her mug of sweet and spicy blueberry tea. She'd had a restless night of tossing and turning, her mind keeping her awake. At one point she'd even got out of bed completely and spent about an hour gazing at the moon, watching its silky silvery journey across the valley.

She yawned deeply and swigged her drink. The temptation to order breakfast was there, but a hollow feeling lurked in her stomach that no meal could fill. Soul binding. Of all the ridiculous things Killian would have to do, that was not one she'd have guessed at. She rested her hands on the wooden table and sighed.

Dark hexagonal stones interlinked on the floor, creating a cold and dingy atmosphere. The hearth lay devoid of fire at this time of day, which only served to back up the floor on its quest for grey misery. A wooden bar ran along the back wall, behind which a bored-looking innkeeper rested his elbow.

He didn't have the allure or charming disposition of the usual redhead – it must have been her morning off. Behind him were several bottles of the local grappa in a rusted metal wine rack. The door to the left swung open, and Lily turned, expecting to see Killian ready to go, but it was Finn.

'Mornin',' she rasped to the innkeeper, nodding once. He seemed to understand her code and poured a shot of grappa into a mug of hot tea. 'Much obliged. Mornin', Cap'n,' she added, strolling over to slump opposite Lily.

'Morning, Finn,' said Lily. She eyed her drink. 'Is that some new boozy concoction?'

Finn let out a dry chuckle. 'It spices it up a little.' She took a swig and rubbed her eyes. 'Need it to wake me up.' She took out her smoking pouch and started constructing a roll-up.

'Trouble sleeping?'

'A little, yeah.' Finn looked up and pushed her fringe out of her face. 'I got this tension keeping me awake, dunno why.'

Lily nodded and curled her fingers around her mug. 'I don't like being away from the ship this long.'

'I get yer,' agreed Finn, parking her roll-up in the corner of her mouth while she lit it. 'Lads on the *Tempest* will be fine though; we ain't bin gone that long.' She moved her hand to emphasise her point, and the smoke from her roll-up spiralled across the table. 'The lads on there are with you till the end. They ain't gonna mess up.'

'You're right.' They were loyal to her, her mini army of cut-throats. 'We should be moving on tomorrow anyway. Ulrich and Killian got onto something yesterday.'

'Oh, aye,' Finn mused.

'Details are a little hazy, but I'm gonna see the old boy today.' She wasn't sure why she didn't want to tell Finn about the soul binding, but she just couldn't. Perhaps it was a combination of it being ridiculous and her not believing it herself. Also, pirates were a superstitious lot – no doubt some genuinely believed that Lord Aberwithe had gone mad from binding the soul of his wife. She'd wait until they got to wherever this soul was hiding, then tell all.

Finn blew a small jet of smoke from her nostrils. 'We best be ready to leave in the morning?'

'Let's make it early and get outta here.' Lily smiled faintly as she spoke.

'Aye, Cap'n. An' I won't be havin' this for me breakfast tomorrow.' She tapped her mug.

Lily screwed her eyes up at the mug. 'I'm curious.'

'Be me guest,' insisted Finn, pushing the mug towards her.

Lily took a deep swig. A rush of heat coursed up her nose. Then her tongue was burning. It was like hot, bitter water. It was vile. Fiery sweet vapour coalesced at the back of her throat as she shoved the mug back across the table to her master gunner.

'That was revolting,' she exclaimed, wiping her lips with her thumb. 'The worst thing I've ever tasted.'

Finn barked a laugh. 'It's an acquired taste, Cap'n, I'll give it that.'

'A taste I don't think I'll be acquiring anytime soon.'

The door to the tavern opened, and this time Killian sauntered in.

'And 'ere comes shithead to ruin me morning,' Finn grumbled with a roll of her eyes.

'You're late,' said Lily.

'I didn't know we'd set a time,' he replied.

'Come on, let's go,' she said, ignoring him and getting up.

'I've not eaten or even had a drink,' he protested.

'Don't care, we're going.'

Lily marched out of the tavern smiling to herself as she heard Killian's boots trailing after her.

'Now, Captain Rothbone,' Ulrich addressed Lily, 'I'll show you what you need to do. It's the most important part.'

Lily nodded as Ulrich motioned for Killian to hold out his arm and turn it over.

'You need to make a cut here, on the forearm, about this long.' He drew his finger about four inches up Killian's arm. 'This is for Killian, understand?'

'Yes,' she agreed, yet there was an ache in her chest. She didn't want to hurt him. She didn't want to cut him.

'Then from here, you need to make three smaller cuts horizontally across the larger one.' He mimed the cuts as he spoke. 'The larger one, near the top, is for the spirit. The one in the middle is a little shorter and is for life and death. The third one, at the bottom, the shortest, is for the bond.'

'Straightforward,' said Lily, her eyes not leaving the skin she'd have to cut.

'He is ready for the orm, so now for the next part. You need to light a sprig of rosemary to draw the spirit to him, then you must ask the orm to cooperate. It's only a few words, and I've taken the initiative to write them down for you.' He unrolled a piece of paper covered with his spidery handwriting. He cleared his throat before speaking again. ' "Come to me, join with me, we shall live as one." However, because you're doing the ritual on his behalf, the words must be altered to "go to him, join with him, you shall live as one." ' Ulrich handed Lily the paper. 'And that's all there is to it.'

She read the words over and over again, Ulrich's spiky script crawling before her eyes. She moved her lips, muttering the words to herself. Of all the things she'd done in her life, this had to be right, it had to be flawless. With these few words, a burning herb and the cuts – Lily's stomach baulked at the thought once more – they'd be on track to setting everything right. The world would be saved from whatever was threatening its balance, and she could finally get Killian out of her life once more. Relief washed over her. He'd be gone and she could move on. Or would he? She bit down on the inside of her lip. Could she let him go wandering off with a soul in his arm?

'How dangerous is this, Ulrich?' Killian asked, his voice drawing Lily back to the present.

'You do everything right and it's not dangerous at all.'

'There're rumours about it,' Killian pressed, 'insanity, death . . . It's banned in Vermor.'

Heat surged in Lily's chest. That was not what she wanted to hear or think about.

'Mages are banned in Vermor,' said Ulrich. 'So I wouldn't take much stock in what they ban. As for over here, acts like soul binding fell out of favour over the years and became lost arts. Texts were lost, rituals were forgotten. I've spent a lifetime gathering such literature. It saddens me, but my books and knowledge are likely to die with me. I have no one to pass them to, but that's not our concern today. Should Captain Rothbone perform the ritual correctly, following my every instruction, nothing will go awry.'

'All right.'

'You do trust her?' asked Ulrich.

Killian's entrancing azure gaze fixed upon Lily. A small – and quite frankly dashing – lopsided smile graced his lips. 'Completely.'

Something raced through Lily's veins at that one word. She was used to people relying on her – she looked out for her crew, she kept them safe, she'd given them a home – but something about Killian's trust was different. It was almost as if his life was being handed to her and her alone. She would do whatever it took to protect him – for the sake of the world, obviously. If something happened to him, there was no telling what fallout would follow.

'Then you have nothing to worry about.' Ulrich smiled as he spoke and spread Lily's map across the table. 'Now, I'll show you where you'll meet your orm.'

CHAPTER TWENTY-NINE

THE STONE WAS PEELING FROM AROUND HER SKIN, the marble prison falling apart piece by piece as her strength grew.

Her limbs moved a fraction at a time; they cracked and crumbled as the stone fell away. They ached from months and months of inactivity. She started to move away from the plinth she was mounted on, taking a slow and laboured step forward. She stopped, put her hands to her face and pulled away her stone skin to get to her human self underneath it all. The marble fell away from one of her eyes as she blinked. The woman took a long breath, filling her lungs and cracking open her marble chest.

She took another step forward, then fell to her knees. She leant onto her hands, her breathing laboured as her body shook. The spell had taken its toll on her. With a growl so low it was barely audible, she balled her fists up, and her knuckles cracked through their stone barrier. Her back arched upwards like a furious cat, and a flash of light coursed through her, ripping the remains of the marble fragments from her body.

She stayed on her hands and knees, trying to catch her breath. Ripped and torn clothes hung around her, damaged in her escape from the marble prison. The dank room glowed with a fresh green light, a light that exuded power, strength and rejuvenation. She had not been in her own body for a long time, too long. It was a wonder she'd made it out of the statue and back into her flesh form. With a great effort, she crawled towards the green light, to the Gramarye. Each movement she made was more laboured than the last, her limbs trembling with exertion, sweat beading on her dust-covered forehead. She stopped next to the green prism and curled herself around it, pressing it close to her chest. It was hers. It was finally hers.

Thoughts of a sweet smiling young man healing a cut on her knee flooded into her tangled mind. Then, with a deep sigh, she slipped into unconsciousness.

CHAPTER THIRTY

IT WAS MIDDAY WHEN THE FIRST HOWL RESONATED OFF the rocky cliff faces that overshadowed the mountain path. It was swiftly followed by a much deeper one. It was difficult to tell how far away they were exactly due to the sound echoing around the thick jagged rocks, but just hearing their cry was enough to sow the seeds of fear. Killian readied his blades and mused on the glow – if only he could control it. Lily dropped her sword into her hand, Finn grabbed her gun, Blake rested his finger on his hilt and even the calm and collected Raven visibly tensed his shoulders. Only Tom remained unfazed by the threat. He critically examined his battle-ready companions.

'They're not here,' he said.

'And what do you mean by that?' asked Blake.

'The razortails, they're miles away.'

'How can you tell?' said Finn through gritted teeth.

Tom shrugged. 'A guess.'

'Idiot,' groaned Finn. 'Get your gun in your bloody hand unless you want your feet cut off.'

Tom sighed and reached for his pistol. 'This is upsetting the mood.'

As the day wore on, the path became harder to traverse. It grew steeper and the ground less stable with patches of scree littering the way. Killian's boots slipped more than once, but he managed to save himself from falling. Raven gave up on the path and took to the trees that protruded from the crags lining the way, mumbling something about scouting ahead. He leapt onto the trunk of the closest pine and raced up it, dodging the sparse branches with the elegance of a practised dancer. A fine rainfall of pine needles pattered onto Killian's head. He dusted them from his hair with his fingertips.

'All right for some,' said Tom. His foot slipped, and he bombarded Finn with a collection of rocks and stones.

'Watch it!' she seethed.

'Sorry.'

'Yeah, yeah.'

Killian marched ahead but kept behind Lily, whose emerald-green coat flapped in the fresh mountain breeze. For most of the day he'd stayed silent, apprehensive of what he might find in that lonely graveyard, his mind constantly going back to the vision he'd had. It was so cold and full of despair and isolation. Hopefully they'd be able to get in and out fast. No lingering. He really didn't want to linger there. It wasn't the place for it.

Raven swooped down from a tree just ahead of him and landed without the slightest falter. If only someone like him had got the glow and the Gramarye trace. Someone responsible. Someone strong. Killian moved to touch Nesta's glyph but had to make do with running his fingers over his goggles instead.

'Raven?' said Lily.

'I've found somewhere for us to camp, an abandoned village a short trek up the path. There's cover. We'll be safe.'

'Excellent,' said Lily, adjusting her bandana.

After another hour of walking, Killian's thighs were burning, but he kept his complaints to himself. The path widened, and the village bobbed into view. Ramshackle slate roofs splintered and jutted up into the pale grey sky, looking like collections of rotting teeth. The houses themselves were in various states of decay – two-storey grey stone heaps, some with missing walls, others with no roofs at all. They looked as if they wanted to collapse and be done with the world. Put out of their misery. But they were offered no such peace. Wild undergrowth wrapped itself around the buildings, cruelly supporting them despite their hollow protests.

Trees exploded from within houses, their roots and branches bursting through the walls and window frames. Yellowing mosses clung to whatever would have them, and vines draped down walls and across paths like lackadaisical snakes. Tiny star-shaped white-and-blue flowers speckled the landscape, their pretty heads rustling in the breeze, their presence at odds with the brutal sense of decay around them.

Dirt tracks embedded with jagged stones roughly hacked from the surrounding cliff faces lined the eerie desolate streets. Killian picked his way through the town, searching for the least run-down house to spend the night in. It wasn't ideal, but it was better than nothing. The wind groaned through the streets, lamenting and mournful, the perfect accompaniment to such a place.

Slumped across the path and slicing through a house lay the sad remains of a church tower, blocking the way up ahead. A rusted bell hung out of a darkened void in its side like the flaccid tongue of a dead dog.

Lily marched up to the collapsed tower, her shoulders square. She crouched and looked to the other side. 'Come on,' she ordered, getting down on her hands and knees and crawling through the gap between the tower and the floor.

Raven vaulted over the devastated building in a single bound, while Killian resigned himself to crawling through the dust, the other three following. The town on the other side of the tower looked the same: similar depressing grey buildings looking as though they could crumble at any minute. Vegetation holding everything together. Empty, bleak and dismal. Killian wasn't sure what he was expecting exactly. A lively town with a friendly tavern? An inn with a soft bed? Warm food and a bath?

Lily brushed the dust from her coat and turned to Raven. 'If you would?'

He nodded, and with that, he raced up the side of the nearest house and daintily bounded from one shattered rooftop to the next.

Lily leant against the trunk of a wayward pine tree. Killian squatted down and hunched over. Finn pulled her gun from her coat and fiddled idly with it, and Blake lit his pipe. Sweet smoke curled around them. Killian breathed in deep. It reminded him of simpler times with fewer dead people. The smell didn't fit with this place at all.

'Hey, Killian,' Tom said. 'Can I—'

Accustomed to that tone, Killian took his gun from its holster and tossed it to Tom.

His eyes glittered as he caught it. 'Art,' he whispered, running his finger up and down the cool barrel.

'It's a gun,' said Killian.

Tom ignored him and continued to stare in wonder, tracing his fingers over the metal vines that twisted around the weapon. 'It's beautiful. I wish I had one.'

'Well,' said Killian, looking up at Tom, 'if I die on this mission, you're welcome to it.'

Lily's boots shuffled in the dirt, and he glanced at her. She glared back at him, then lowered her head, shadows hiding her expression from him. Killian loathed that gun now. If he hadn't had it on him, Ren wouldn't have snatched it and attacked that thing. That demon. That mask. He ran his thumb along his eyebrow. But if he hadn't taught Ren how to take his gun, he wouldn't have been able to snatch it in the first place. Whose fault was it really? His or the gun? Both?

He looked at Tom, who was turning it over and over in his hands, wonder etched all over his young face. That gun was a part of Killian, but he hadn't ever used it, not properly. After Clem had died in his arms, he'd thought he wanted a better way to protect himself and others. Seeing his distress, Geoffrey Skevington had kindly given him the gun issued to him when he'd been a black sentinel. He'd taught him how to use it, how to aim. They'd practised until Killian was a crack shot, but those practice sessions and shooting of the tavern sign in Poll were the only times he'd ever fired it. To him, the gun was just death. Cold, weighted death. It didn't protect; it destroyed.

There was a rush of air as Raven landed in the middle of the path. He dusted his hands together.

'I've found a house on the edge of town.' He indicated down the street. 'It's got a roof and an upstairs. No doors or windows, but it'll do for tonight.'

'Good work, Raven,' said Lily. 'Let's set up camp and get some food on the go.'

Killian walked behind Raven as he led them through the lonely streets of the ghost town. Each house was a sad reminder that the place had once been occupied.

'I wonder where everyone went,' Killian remarked, kicking a stone, which bounced down the street and echoed off the forlorn buildings.

'Death, disease, eaten by razors,' suggested Tom.

'More like they realised they'd built their town in a ridiculous place and decided to abandon it,' said Blake.

'Not as exciting,' said Tom. 'And I thought you were the storyteller.'

'I'm being realistic,' replied Blake.

'If you say so. Whatever happened, I can't wait to leave. This place makes my skin crawl.'

Finn grinned and wrapped a muscular arm around Tom's shoulder. 'Aw, is little Tom all scared now?'

'Get off,' he snapped, tossing the arm off him. 'I'm not scared.'

'A little touchy, aren't we?'

'Look! I'm not scared, all right? So shut it.'

Finn frowned but didn't press the matter. Killian shuddered; he had to agree with Tom. This town was eerie. It radiated an aura of despair. Thick green vines were rife; they stretched over the path, dangled from rooftops and invaded any opening they could. It was as if a giant beast had been slain and its still-sentient limbs were trying to enact revenge. Raven turned again, and the outskirts of the town came into view. He stopped next to the last house on the block.

'Here,' he said. 'This is about as good as we're going to get.'

'Better than outside,' said Lily, sweeping through the open doorway and into the derelict house.

Killian followed her in. It was a mess, but he hadn't expected anything else. The blue-tiled floor had been ravaged by invading plants, wide cracks ran up the plastered walls and the wooden staircase was partially collapsed. Thick grey cobwebs swung down from the ceiling like jellyfish tentacles, and a layer of dust smothered absolutely everything. It reeked of decay and damp, earthy and rotten. A ruined table lay slumped across the middle of the floor, its legs spread out in a most undignified way. The back wall housed a fireplace, foaming at the mouth with stones, old wood, plants and general filth.

'This place is perfect,' Killian gushed. 'When can we move in?'

Lily curled her lip. 'It has a roof,' she said. 'That's more than we're used to.'

'And an upstairs,' added Raven, bounding up the wrecked staircase. 'The floor's better up here,' he called down, 'plant free.'

'Fine,' said Lily, folding her arms. 'We'll sleep upstairs, two people can watch downstairs. We'll take shifts.' She paused and glanced at the party. 'Killian and Blake, Tom and Raven, then Finn and me. Any questions?'

Silence.

'Good,' she said, her face softening. 'Tom, Killian, get some firewood and head back to that stream we saw and fill these up.' She held out some empty waterskins.

'Aye, Cap'n.' Tom saluted.

Using every fibre in his body, Killian managed to resist the urge to grimace. He snatched the skins from her, smiled and promptly followed Tom outside.

CHAPTER THIRTY-ONE

It was only after Killian had disappeared from view that Tom started to regret his decision for them to part ways. The sun was sinking, and the darkness was sneaking in. His back prickled, and he slipped his gun into his palm; he felt safer that way. There was a crunch, and he whirled around, gun pointed, but there was nothing there. He hated feeling like this. Fear wasn't something he was supposed to have anymore; it should have been beaten out of him long ago. He sighed. He wasn't afraid, and he'd prove to Finn he wasn't. He was walking around razortail territory alone, which proved just how much of a man he was. A snap reverberated about the woods, and his body instantly stiffened. He wished Killian were there.

He tightened his grip on his gun – his palm now slippery and moist – and pressed deeper into the undergrowth. All he had to do was find some nice dry kindling. Get out, get back, and brag to Finn about going it alone in such dangerous countryside. Maybe he'd elaborate about seeing a razortail. Maybe he'd say he killed one. He ran his tongue along his teeth. As long as they didn't think he was a coward anymore. He frowned bitterly. What Finn had said had really got under his skin. It was already festering like a boil.

He tossed his bag to the ground and filled it with any twigs and bracken he could find. He sighed as the initial fear of the forest wore off and the reconnaissance became dull. There was a sharp snap, and he froze. Another snap broke through the silence. His body grew rigid, and his lungs turned to lead.

Behind him lurked a sound that chilled his blood. Low breathing, rasping, guttural, not human. Panic charged through his body, and his heart stopped. Sweat trickled down his cheeks like tears. He drew in a slow deep breath and turned around.

A pair of glowing yellow eyes stared back at him. The creature's back curled up high, its spine almost bursting through its skin. Its lips peeled back to reveal two rows of vicious-looking teeth, brown and matted with filth. A razor-sharp bone tail was raised behind it, slicing through the air with short aggressive movements. It growled at him, its eyes burning with hunger. For Tom, all sound faded away and was replaced with a high-pitched whine.

The razortail crawled towards him, its belly dragging along the ground. It snarled, and a thick stream of brown saliva dripped from its mouth. Tom swallowed – he had to regain control over himself. He shook his head to dislodge the ringing. The sounds of the woodland rushed him – snarls, chattering birds, falling leaves and insects humming. The world was alive. His hands came alive too, and before he had time to think about it, he'd shot the creature in front of him. It barely had time to yelp as the bullet ripped a hole in its skull. It flopped down in the dirt, dead.

Tom took a shaky step back, sweat pouring from him. He ran his palm over his head and blew out a long breath as he stared at the dead beast. He'd killed one, and he was still alive! His sigh of relief caught in his throat as another pair of yellow eyes emerged from the woods. Panicking, he fumbled for his shots to refill his gun but dropped them on the ground. The creature's snarls were joined by those of another, and another. A whole pack of yellow-eyed monsters sloped out from behind the bushes. The razortails barked and howled to one another, hackles raised, bloodstained tails pointed, dark fur matted with filth, ready to chase their prey. Tom's breath stuck in his throat. Somehow, he managed to turn his trembling body around and run. He was going to die.

'Killian!' he screamed as he ran, his vision misted by tears. 'Killian, help me! Please!'

TOM'S pleading screams cut through the dense woodland and straight to Killian like an arrow. He ran as fast as he could in the direction of the cries, his legs pumping like pistons as he tore through the forest, spraying clouds of pine needles and mud in his wake. Another cry thundered through the air. He gritted his teeth and pushed harder. Sweat cascaded down his face and stung his eyes. His shirt stuck to his chest, and his trousers clung to his legs. The full waterskins slapped against his thighs, adding an unnecessary hindrance to his running. With a flick of his wrist, he detached them. They thudded to the ground, sagging forward. He clenched his fists and thought of the glow, trying to focus on that dormant power as he ran.

Come on, work! Just this once, do what I say! He glanced at his hands. Nothing. *You piece of shit!*

'Killian! Help me!'

He put his head down and pushed forward, ignoring his tired legs and focusing on Tom's direction. A surge of power rippled through his body, and he gasped. A faint iridescent glow danced in his peripheral vision. He sped up.

TOM was tiring fast. He opened his mouth to plead for help once more, but no words came, only a strangled rasp. Behind him, the creatures snapped their powerful jaws and howled to one another. They were mocking him – they could easily catch him now and rip him to pieces, but they wanted to enjoy the chase. His lungs burned – every breath was like he was swallowing a mouthful of pepper – and his legs were becoming unstable.

There was nothing but a collection of twisted trees and a wall of high grey rock in front of him. Of all the places he could have run to in the whole damn forest, he'd run to a dead end. He stopped and pressed his back against the barrier of rock. If he weren't so exhausted and if his muscles hadn't turned to sludge, he'd have been able to climb to safety. But not today.

He pulled his sword from its scabbard and held it out in front of him pathetically as the pack of razortails slunk towards him. The blade slipped from his sweaty hand and fell to the ground. He was useless with a blade anyway. Tears trickled down his face as he cursed himself for not practising. Finn was right. Why was she always right? The creatures howled to one another once more and moved closer, their tails cutting through the air with a swish.

Tom tensed, ready to have his throat ripped out, and then Killian was there. He leapt down from the rock face and landed between him and the creatures. Was he shining?

'Get down,' he said, pushing him back.

Tom nodded – his teeth were chattering far too much for him to even contemplate forming a sentence. He lowered himself to the muddy ground and hunched up, unable to take his eyes from his shimmering companion.

Killian stepped towards the razors with a confident swagger and unsheathed his swords. His body was covered with a strange glow. Tom had never seen anything like it in his life before. Silvery light flowed over him with waves of other colours rippling through it. Pink, purple, green, blue, yellow. He looked like a diamond. Two large ghostly horns protruded from his forehead, which curled back and around like those of a ram.

The razor at the front of the pack growled. Saliva dripped from its gums. It howled and charged. Killian remained still until the beast was almost upon him, then neatly sidestepped and tore his sword through the creature's thick muscular neck. Its body fell limp, and its head rolled to the ground. Tom's heart pounded in his ears as he looked at the severed head. Blank dead eyes gazed back at nothing.

Snarling, the rest of the pack darted towards Killian. He vaulted over the four beasts, the shine trailing behind him like spiderwebs. He turned himself over in mid-air, landing behind them. There was a hum of energy as he dashed forward and slew two of the razors, followed by the sound of crystal shattering. They fell to the ground without so much as a yelp. The remaining two set their eyes on Tom and raced towards him.

Tom's heart leapt into his throat. With any luck, he'd throw it up and die before they had the chance to tear him to pieces. Was that a less painful death? He'd find out soon.

A crackle of energy ripped through the air, and Killian landed between him and the creatures. He slashed the one closest to him across the throat, sending a shower of blood onto the forest floor. It gurgled a yelp and slumped to the ground. He then plunged his left sword into the heart of the other as it sprang at him. It squealed in agony before falling silent, crimson pumping all over the pine needles.

Killian sighed deeply and dropped his swords. The shimmering light faded from him, his horns vanished and he crumpled to the ground with a heavy thud. Tom stared at his body. What had happened? What should he do? Was he a demon? There were horns. He'd seen horns! His breath burst from his lips in juddering gasps. All around him lay the slain corpses of the razortails, blood and death everywhere. And there lay Killian, motionless in the dirt.

Gingerly, Tom got to his feet and walked over to his friend. He stooped down and put a hand on his shoulder. He was still breathing, so he was alive, but his eyes were closed. What was that shimmer? Had he really been glowing? Surely not. Tom shuffled away from Killian and rocked back on his heels.

Was he a mage of some kind? He frowned. Tom had never seen a mage like that before – that glow, that shimmer, those horns. It was as incredible as it was terrifying. There was something strange going on. How long had Killian been able to do that? Whatever *that* was.

A buzzard shrieked from above, and Tom started. They had to get out of there and back to the others. Despite his rising fear, Tom reached out his hand and shook Killian.

'Killian, Killian,' he said through his teeth. 'Wake up.'

He didn't stir. His breathing was heavy and his body limp. Tom gripped him tighter and shook him again, saying his name over and over. A soft groan came from his fallen friend.

Tom's hope rose. 'Killian, get up.'

Killian's eyelids fluttered open. He looked confused and exhausted. 'Are you . . . okay?' he asked, his voice faint.

'Yeah, yeah,' said Tom, 'I'm fine. What about you? What *was* that?'

Killian pushed himself up and supported his body with the backs of his arms. 'I don't know.'

'It was weird. You shimmered, like a diamond or something, and killed them all. And then you just, I don't know, collapsed. Are *you* okay?' Tom edged a bit closer to Killian, wondering whether he should help him to his feet.

'I just need a few minutes. It drains me of everything, but I'll be all right. I think you should have this,' he added, taking his gun from its holster and holding it out to Tom.

'Your gun?' asked Tom.

'It's better with you,' Killian replied.

'Don't you need it?'

'I don't think so,' said Killian weakly. His eyes closed as he spoke. 'We can go soon, just need a rest.'

'I'll stay right here.' He crammed Killian's gun into his belt. He'd wanted that gun for so long, but now he had it, it felt strange, almost like Killian was saying bye to him. No, he wasn't. Tom was just reading into things too much, as usual.

'Thanks, Tom.' Killian sank back to the ground. 'Can you do me a favour?'

'Anything. You saved my life and gave me your gun. I owe you thousands of favours.'

A tired smile graced Killian's face. 'Don't tell anyone I glow. I need to figure it out myself.'

'Sure.'

CHAPTER
THIRTY-TWO

THE EARLY SPRINGTIME SUN SHONE OVER THE ragged fields. Sasha paced across them with a steaming mug of coffee in her hand. She stopped at the fence that bordered the land of the broken-down farmhouse, put a foot on the first rung and looked out. Delphina, Kurt and Dorian had been tasked with fetching supplies from Morford – the next town along – and she eagerly awaited their return. They were rapidly running out of food and anything to drink that wasn't water.

She was beginning to wonder if she'd made the right decision in following Quint. Except for the appearance of the Gramarye and the slowly shifting features of the statue, nothing had happened since she'd arrived. She'd been fed all the promises of power and freedom but had yet to see any of it. In fact, she felt worse off. At least when she was on her own, she was free and had a plan – it wasn't a great plan, but it was hers, and it would have worked. There had been occasions when she'd had to cut and run, but at least she could go wherever she wanted. Now she was trapped in this run-down house, waiting for something that might never happen. If she left, she was sure they'd hunt her down. A rook let out a raspy caw from a nearby sycamore tree. She turned to the ebony bird and nodded. It knew. She downed her coffee and walked back to the house.

Theo was leaning against the porch when she arrived. His eyes were as blank and expressionless as ever. Despite his promise to talk to her, they'd not had a conversation since the morning he'd helped her. Perhaps healing her had taken even more from him than she realised. Guilt prickled through her. If only there were a way for her to give it back to him.

'Morning, Theo,' she said.

'Lightning,' he replied with barely a nod.

Red looked up at her, yawned, then curled around Theo's feet and put his head down. A waft of coffee from Theo's cup caught on the breeze and roamed over to Sasha. It was grotesquely pungent.

'Can you make that any stronger?' she asked, giving him a wry smile.

'It's how I drink it.'

Sasha curled her lip. 'Rather you than me.'

'It's the only way I can taste it.'

'What d'you mean?' She took a cigarette from her trouser pocket and lit it up. She kept her eyes focused on the shimmying grasses and curls of smoke rather than him.

'I . . . It doesn't matter.'

Sasha turned back to him and blew a plume of smoke from the corner of her mouth. 'It does.'

'In what way?' He took a swig.

'I might make it for you one day – I don't wanna do it wrong.' She gave him a playful wink.

A shadow of pain swept across Theo's eyes. It was as if he was trying to smile, trying to acknowledge her joke and accept some kindness, but for some reason, he couldn't.

'Strong is fine.'

'Okay, I'll remember that.' She leant over the porch rail and took another drag from her cigarette. 'It's nice we're talking again.'

'Did we stop?'

'No, we just haven't since you helped me.' Sasha's body twitched as her mind quickly recapped her beating at the hands of Kurt to her. If it hadn't been for Delphina and Theo, how much worse would she be now? And if it hadn't been for her, what would Theo be like now? She was just one of the string of people in his life who'd taken a piece of him and given nothing in return. Everyone took from him, and no one ever gave back.

'You're right, I'm sorry.' Theo's dark gaze was locked on the wooden porch.

'You don't have to be sorry.' Sasha turned back to him and touched his arm. He pulled away like she was on fire. 'I'm sorry.'

'No, I ca—' He fell silent. He looked beyond Sasha as if he were seeing through her to somewhere else. Perhaps he was looking into the world he drew his debilitating magic from. 'Some things are impossible for me. I'm less than most people.'

'You're not.'

Theo quietly drank his coffee, not giving Sasha's words a flick of acknowledgement. The wind buffeted his tatty brown waistcoat, but he didn't appear bothered.

Sasha turned away, stubbed out her cigarette and looked out over the field again. A cart pulled by two horses was making its way up the driveway. Delphina was at the reins, and

Dorian sat next to her while Kurt stayed in the back. They came to a halt outside the house. Delphina leapt down and set about securing the horses to the fence. Sasha ambled over to them and helped unload the back of the cart.

'Any trouble?' she asked as she lowered a sack of potatoes to the ground.

'A few people stared at Del,' said Dorian over his shoulder.

'A few people always stare at Del,' said Delphina as she went to the back of the cart. Her deep brown skin made it apparent that she wasn't of Vermorian descent, and she was often the source of stares, particularly in smaller, more isolated towns. 'It's nothing unusual. Here, allow me,' she said to Sasha, giving her a gentle nudge out of the way with her hip.

Delphina spread her arms out as the wind swirled around her. She began to rise off the ground, her long black braids whirling about her like streamers. She extended her hands towards the produce in the back of the cart, and that floated too. Like a gull in the breeze, she glided back, bringing all the items with her and away from the cart. Little by little, she lowered them and herself to the ground.

As soon as she touched the ground, the wind vanished. She pushed her hair out of her face and turned her dark eyes to Sasha. 'It makes it easier for everyone,' she rasped.

Sasha nodded, taken aback by Delphina's display of power and control. She was a tall, lean woman, tight strong muscle packed to an athletic frame, so an imposing figure even without her sharp and controlled mastery of the air. Despite this, though, her breathing was heavy and laboured, so it had taken something out of her. Sasha was about to offer her a smoke and a sit-down when the front door to the house burst open with a splintering crack and Quint raced out.

'She's back!'

'Varo,' said Delphina.

'I need help getting her upstairs. Sasha, with me. Theo, she'll need your help.' He ducked back into the house.

Sasha's heart broke as she watched Theo obediently nod. Didn't anyone care? She walked back to the house and went inside with him.

'Theo,' she whispered to the mage. She wanted to grab his arm again but held back, given how well it'd gone down the last time they touched.

'Don't,' he murmured.

Quint's voice carried from the cellar steps. 'Sasha, down here, kiddo. I would have asked Dorian,' he explained as she followed him, 'but he can be rough at times, and this is a delicate situation.'

'I understand.'

The green throb of the strange prism pulsed up the steps, yet it seemed to be muted, almost as if a cloth had been dropped on it, smothering its vibrant colour. When she reached the basement, she saw the reason. Curled up around the artefact lay a woman; she wasn't moving, but her chest was rising and falling. The statue was no longer on the plinth.

'Is she . . . ?' She turned to Quint.

'Yes, now help me get her upstairs.' He squatted next to the unconscious woman.

Quint took great care in prising the woman away from the artefact she desperately clung to, and together, they lifted her up. Dust and fragments of marble tumbled from her body, clothes and hair as she was moved. Her warm body slumped against Sasha's.

Her heart was beating its steady rhythm against Sasha's ribs, and her breathing was deep and heavy. She was alive. Alive, after being encased within a layer of marble. It defied logic.

They carried her out of the basement and up the stairs to the bedroom, where Theo was already waiting. Their movements were slow and gentle so as not to hurt or wake her. Together, they eased her onto a bed. Sasha was transfixed by the woman. Her dark hair glistened with a deep blue sheen – no doubt remnants of her marble prison. Sasha pushed it away from her face, expecting blue dust to cover her hands, but it remained on Varo as if it was part of her now. Her lips were pale blue, and patches of aquamarine marbled the skin on her face and neck. It streaked over her collarbone and looked to continue beneath her ragged clothes.

Sasha found herself wondering what the woman's eyes were like, what her voice was like, how she moved. Feeling unnerved by this, she backed away.

'Draw the curtains,' said Quint as he knelt at the end of the bed and unlaced her boots.

Sasha nodded. A pang of relief shot through her chest; moving away from this enigmatic person seemed like the best thing to do.

'She'll come back to us,' said Quint, pulling the covers over the woman. He looked over his shoulder. 'Theo, you know what to do.'

'Yes.'

Sasha watched, mesmerised, as Theo crossed the room and stood over Varo. His palms shimmered with white light, waves of blue and green rippling through it. His face glowed in the hue of his magic, and a tiny distant smile formed on his lips. A deep sadness grasped at Sasha, and in that moment, Theo looked at her. His eyes were full of emotions – kindness, love and self-sacrifice. Was that who he really was? Then it was gone, and he turned back to his patient.

'Come,' said Quint, putting his hand on Sasha's shoulder and pulling her back. 'We need to leave him to do his job.'

She reluctantly followed Quint. A soft pitiful whine rang down the corridor. Red was hunkered on the floor. His head was down, but his eyes were visible. They were shining with moisture and full of distress. A tight pain spread over Sasha's chest. She needed a beer.

CHAPTER THIRTY-THREE

'No one goes up there. Not anymore,' said a middle-aged man with tired grey eyes.

Lily looked towards the lofty and isolated graveyard perched on the hill and the overgrown track leading the way. Brambles, grasses, weeds and twisted trees ripped up and abused the pathway. They were just another obstacle in her way. The wind flapped her coat; even that was irritating.

The small village of Appsen was nestled within the shadow of the hill. It was like a place that time had forgotten. The houses were very basic squat cylinders with thick thatched roofs. Muddy paths ran through the settlement, connecting the houses. Lily had noticed a tavern and a village shop – they'd be useful for the way back. No inn though. It was as if it didn't ever have visitors. Though given the way the villagers had acted towards her and her crew, she wasn't surprised. It seemed like everyone wanted them to leave. Outsiders were not welcome or wanted.

The outskirts were used for farmland, some cattle, some crops. It was self-sufficient. No one had any need to leave. Perhaps no one ever did. That would explain why they were so cagey. The skies rolled with thick grey clouds, the sun choked from view.

'Why not?' Lily asked.

This was becoming tedious now. So far, the villagers had either ignored them or told them exactly the same thing about the graveyard. The man chewed the inside of his cheek as he regarded her. That was tedious too.

'It's far,' he said. 'And something ain't right up there. Folks have heard voices, scratching, hissing. Demons. It ain't right. The dead ain't worth the risk. We still remember 'em from down here.'

'What d'you mean?' Killian butted in.

Lily's nostrils flared, but she kept herself from saying anything.

'What I said. It's not right up there. Demons or something.' He glanced at Finn's scarred face and took a step back. 'I told you enough.'

He thrust out his hand. Lily dropped a gold coin into it, and he was gone.

'Wha' d'we do?' asked Tom, frowning up at the graveyard.

'What d'you think?' said Lily.

Before the young gunner could answer, Lily had turned around and set off up the path, knowing the others would follow her.

It was dusk when Lily caught sight of a rusted gate. It was torn apart and twisted out of shape by ravaging undergrowth. Vicious spikes of metal curled outwards like gnashing teeth desperately snapping at the invading vines and ivy.

It was a monster, defeated by nature.

High stone walls led up to a flight of steps that coiled away into darkness. Despair loomed from the dark maw, and the wind whistled out between its teeth. It flittered through Lily's hair, nudging her backwards, whispering to her not to enter. No good could come of this place.

'Right,' she said, 'let's get this over with.'

'All right,' said Finn. 'But first can you tell me what we're doin'?' She lit a roll-up and took a drag.

'You tell them,' Lily said to Killian.

'We're gonna hide a soul in me,' he said in a nauseatingly cheery voice.

'What?' spat Finn.

'We need to hide a soul to stop the Gramarye being unlocked.'

'Ain't that dangerous?' asked Tom, drumming his fingers on Killian's gun. 'Soul binding's banned. It turns you mad.'

'Not if it's done right,' said Killian, his voice calm and even. 'Lily's doing it on me, so you've nothing to worry about.'

'I ain't worried about you,' said Tom.

'Then why are you asking about the dangers?' said Blake.

'No reason.' Tom pouted and folded his arms.

Killian chuckled. 'Tom, you really do care.'

Having heard enough of this light-hearted banter, Lily stepped through the gate, its broken metal teeth snatching at her heels, and stalked away up the spiralling moss-covered steps. To hear them idly chattering in that way made her seethe. The thought of performing the ritual on Killian weighed heavily on her shoulders, and they were making jokes about it. She wanted to punch someone – or something.

As she clomped up the ruined steps, her eyes clouded over. She paused to rub at them with her sleeve and leant against the wall. The voices of the others grew – they were laughing, actually laughing. Heat smothered her face, and her stomach twisted. She slipped her hand under her coat and ran her finger over a dagger that hung from her belt. Soon she'd be using it to carve Killian's arm. She didn't want to cut him, didn't want to hurt him, not like this. Her fingers traced the length of the dagger and curled around the blade. The sharpness of the blade would have easily cut anyone else's skin, and yet she felt nothing. It had to be done, whatever way she looked at it, and she must shoulder the responsibility. Still gripping the blade, she pushed off the wall and continued up the steps.

The staircase curled once more and then opened out to a long, narrow brick corridor. The walls leant in, suffocating her. It was as if they wanted to absorb her and make her a part of this place forever. There was a rank taste to the air, like decay and rot, bitter and rancid. She picked up her pace; she had to get out of this oppressive passageway.

Weak shafts of grey light dragged themselves into the end of the corridor, and Lily stepped out into an old courtyard. Half-dead trees hung dismally in clusters in the hard earth. Before her rose a great arch: the entrance to the graveyard. Weeds and mosses wrapped themselves around it while dust-filled spiderwebs rippled in the breeze at its apex. She placed her hand on the weather-beaten arch and peered through.

There were rows and rows of mausoleums, each sealed with a gate. Some were plain, others had elaborate designs etched into their brickwork. Statues adorned the tops of several – there were trees with faces carved into their trunks, as well as horned demons and kneeling women, all staring up towards the grey sky with blank expressions. What was it even for? This place was abandoned and forgotten, and yet it seemed to relish visitors. Branches and vines grabbed at her with every step she took. It wanted her to stay. It wanted them all to stay. It desired someone new, someone fresh.

Beyond the elaborate tombs lay a walled pathway. Long rectangular plaques were placed at regular intervals in the walls – barely legible names and dates etched into them – behind which forgotten bones crumbled to dust. What a waste. The narrow walkway, flanked by winding walls filled with bodies, snaked its way around this strange lair of the dead. Lily took a step inside. To her right and towering above was a small ruined castle. Great swathes of ivy covered much of its brickwork, its strong grasp weakening the already-defeated building.

An icy sensation prowled her spine. The place unnerved her. It was a forgotten city of the dead. No good could come of it. Perhaps those villagers were right. She had half a mind to leave. She turned on her heel as the rest of the party emerged.

'Cap'n,' Tom whined as he got closer, 'are you really gonna let him do this?'

'It's out of my hands, Tom,' she said, keeping her tone as blasé as possible.

'But—'

Lily glared, but Killian grabbed him by the shoulder.

'I suggest we get some rest and do this thing in the morning, when we're fresh,' she said once her group had assembled around her. She pointed towards the sorry excuse for a castle lurking above. 'We'll sleep there. It's high and relatively well protected. I doubt we'll need a watch tonight.'

Without another word, she ducked down the dead-lined corridor and pressed on in the direction of the castle.

AFTER navigating several ramshackle spiral stairways, which looked like they were held together more by the moss than the mortar, and wandering down narrow cobweb-covered causeways, Killian reached the top of the castle ruins. Before him lay a tangled patch of grass and weeds and a haphazard collection of crumbling headstones. A chill ran across his neck, and he looked down. He didn't want to dwell on it too much, but there were bodies somehow lodged in the roof of the castle. They were a part of the building. It didn't feel right. Nothing here felt right. Everything was off. The air, the trees, the grass, the buildings. Everything.

In the left corner was a small shadowy collection of steps no doubt leading down to some other crypt. Killian was surrounded by death, and it did nothing to ease his apprehension of the task ahead. But for his own sake as much as the others', he put on a brave face.

'And what a delightful spot you've found us, Lil,' he said.

She curled her lip in response and scanned their surroundings. 'It's safe enough. We'll eat before it's dark. No fire tonight, it's disrespectful.'

There was a small circular patch of grass at the centre that didn't appear to have been used as a burial site. Killian removed his kit and wrapped himself in a blanket. The winds were cold and biting being so high up. They howled and moaned, the perfect sound for the city of the dead. Some rations were tossed into the middle by Finn: smoked meats, hard cheese, dried fruit and crusty bread. Killian grimaced as he dragged his teeth through the chewy meat; what he wouldn't give for a hot meal.

'Any idea how we find this lost soul, then?' asked Finn.

'I can find it,' said Killian. He'd had enough of trying to eat. 'Easy.'

'Go on, then,' said Tom.

'I will in the morning. It's pretty taxing on the body, you know,' replied Killian, leaning back on his arms and gazing up at the moody grey sky.

'Here,' said Tom, tossing a hand of cards onto Killian's stomach. 'I'm gonna beat you down this time all right. I think I've got you all worked out.'

Killian scooped up the cards with one hand and propped himself up on the other. 'Nah, I'm good, thanks,' he said, throwing them back to Tom, who fumbled to catch them.

'What's the matter?' Tom frowned. 'Scared you'll lose?'

'Yeah, something like that.'

RAVEN crouched on one of the corners of the tumbledown castle, surveying the village of Appsen far below. Dim orange light flickered around the small thatch-roofed houses. He couldn't blame them for abandoning the graveyard. It was ridiculous to have it all the way up the hillside just so the dead could be closer to some god or other. If they knew the truth, it would never have been built in the first place.

A strong breeze blew his hood back, and his hair billowed out. He put his elbow on his knee and rested his chin on his fist. Something about this place, besides the hundreds of rotten bodies, put him on edge. Behind him, Tom's swearing, Killian's cocky retorts and Finn's and Blake's sniggering were riding the wind. Fog clouded his vision, and for the first time in many years, he felt fear. He cursed himself under his breath. He should have left before he became too attached. That was what he'd always done, run before he was forced away from those he cared about. He knew that was too painful. He was an idiot. Why hadn't he left? He slowly trailed his finger over his tattoo; it was too late now, far too late.

'Raven.' Lily came to stand next to him.

'Lily.'

They stayed silent, both peering down at the flickering torches of the village far below. Lily dug her fingers into a patch of moss and idly scraped it from the surface, flicking clumps over the edge and into the darkness below.

'Careful with that,' said Raven, 'it could be all that's holding this ruin together.'

This coaxed a tiny smile from her, but she continued with her digging. 'So be it.'

The moss tumbled down, bouncing off the castle walls before being swallowed up by the gloom. He knew she was thinking the same dark thoughts as him – he could always tell. He rested his chin on his fist again. Would he be of any use to her? He'd always been able to comfort her before, help her when emotions clouded her judgement, but this time it was different. They each may have harboured different feelings for Killian, but that didn't stop them feeling the same creeping darkness about his fate. Besides Lily, he was Raven's only other true friend. For years he'd tried to keep his distance with people, even with the crew, but with Killian, it was different. With him, he felt something he'd not felt since Amaranta. He closed his eyes and made a silent pact. If all went well, he'd tell Killian the truth about who he was.

'Raven,' Lily muttered. 'Are we doing the right thing?'

He winced but didn't show it; he had to stay strong for her. 'I believe it's the only option.'

'Mmm.'

He reached down and took her hand in his. 'Don't worry, everything will be fine.'

CHAPTER THIRTY-FOUR

A HIGH-PITCHED SCREAM PIERCED KILLIAN'S DREAM, and he awoke with a deep gasping breath. He sat straight up, bringing the blankets around him. It was still dark, yet something was creating a faint glow.

Close to the place he'd dismissed as a crypt, something was pulsing with a pale white light. His companions were still slumbering. Perhaps only he had heard the scream. He put his boots on and stumbled off in the direction of the light.

He rubbed the crusty sleep from his eyes as he walked, his mind hazy and dizzy and his body a little unresponsive. Several subsided graves caught his feet, tripping him up. Some had sunk so far into the ground that the bodies beneath must have been hanging through the ceiling in some areas of the castle. Killian shuddered. Death was surrounding him too much lately.

A weightlessness descended over his body. Was he still dreaming? He looked back towards the camp but couldn't see his own sleeping body, though he wasn't sure what seeing that would prove.

He reached the steps at the far wall, crouched and peered down. Ten or so crumbling steps led down to what looked like a tomb, the pale light illuminating the flat gravestones on the walls below. The hair on the back of his neck stood on end. Was he really going to go down? He had another glance over his shoulder before treading towards the light.

The room smelt damp and musty, like a forgotten church. Slimy moss lined the cracks in the floor, which, to his horror, was made up of plaques. The flat stones also adorned the ceiling and were covered with black mould – they were all around the room. He was surrounded by bodies; his throat swelled, and his heart burned. He wanted to get out and run to the others. But what he wanted to do and what he actually did were rarely the same thing. The far wall glowed brighter than anywhere else in the room. Despite his every nerve ending screaming for him to leave and run, he walked towards the glow.

As he drew closer, the light coalesced to form an orb of blue light. He stepped closer, and it hovered in front of him. He reached forward and put his hands on either side of it. It vibrated, sending waves of energy into his palms, then shot off to the right, illuminating another stairwell and disappearing down it. Killian followed. What else could he do?

Down he went, the ball of light leading the way. More and more steps loomed towards him in what seemed like a never-ending spiral. When he reached the bottom, he was confronted by a long, narrow corridor. He pushed his way down, past ancient spiderwebs and slimy mould. It eventually took him outside.

In front of him lay another castle wall. It was covered with ivy and lichen, and there was no door. The ball of light tore to the left, and he rushed after it. He raced through a patch of moonlit wild grass and dodged the hulking tree that sprang up in the middle, vaulting over its gargantuan roots. He came to a skidding halt as the ground dropped away. The orb dashed somewhere beneath him.

'Shit!' he hissed through gritted teeth.

He was standing on the top of a grass-covered wall. It looked easy enough to climb down, but did he really need to climb it? He tensed his body, summoning the glow back to his skin. It took a few minutes, but soon that jolt of power coursed through his body and the strange iridescent energy flowed over his skin. Crystals shattered, and he sprang down, landing heavily. His knees buckled, and he toppled forwards.

'I need practice,' he muttered as he got up, dusting the moss from his coat.

Weakness seeped into his muscles, and he slumped to the ground. The glow was draining him rapidly. He had to banish it before it knocked him unconscious.

'Go away, go away,' he whispered.

Iridescence danced defiantly in his vision. He dug his hands into the cool, refreshing earth and willed the glow to leave him. It had to go, it had to leave him. His body was floating, his head swimming. Why had he summoned it in the first place? What a pointless thing to do. He should have climbed down.

'Please . . . leave . . .'

A summer breeze rustled the grasses and ruffled his hair, and the glow faded back into his skin. He crumpled up, gasping, delighting in the feel of the damp grasses on his sweat-soaked body. Gradually, his strength crawled back into his muscles. The glow had come so close to rendering him unconscious again, and this time it'd come on scarily fast. Killian needed to work with it more before using it for meaningless tasks. Perhaps it was punishing him.

Before him was another wall, a small section covered with black metal bars at the centre. He hauled himself to his feet and staggered over. He gripped a cold rough bar and peered in. A long rectangular room was illuminated by the glow of the blue orb. The walls were dark and looked to be embedded with yet more eerie graves, their surfaces blackened with age and decay. Vines shimmered blue in the light as they hung limp from the ceiling, exhausted after years of battling their way through the ground only to be confronted by a mausoleum. An ominous damp and musty smell radiated from the tomb.

The blue orb floated around inside, swaying from one side to the other like a disheartened pendulum. It came to a halt at the back of the room, hovering over a shadowy rectangular stone dais. Killian watched and waited, but the orb moved no more. Deep down he knew he'd found what he was looking for, but he had to be sure.

He closed his eyes, tightened his grip on the bars and focused on the image of the Gramarye. The sinister blue mist clouded his vision, wrapping itself around him. He tensed, and the blue orb flickered into the whirls of mist. He reached his hands forwards and held them either side of it. It didn't move, it didn't explode. He opened his eyes and stared into the tomb.

'Stay,' he said to the orb, holding his hand out. 'I'm coming back.'

CHAPTER THIRTY-FIVE

'I've found it.'

Killian's thick voice broke through Lily's slumber. She sat up and rubbed her face with the heels of her hands. The dawn was just coming up, bathing the top of the ruin in a weak yellow light. After several blinks and a long squint, she could focus on him. He was about two feet away, crouched down and hunched over. One hand gripped his knee, and the other was massaging his temple.

'Have you slept?' she said through a wide yawn. 'You look worse than usual.'

His lips twitched into a smile. 'Worried about me?'

'Nope.' With that, she hauled herself up in pursuit of something to eat.

She located the bag of rations and pulled out a hunk of dry bread and a wedge of cheese. The cheese was hard but strong. The pungent flavour went right up her nose, and her eyes watered.

She knocked the crumbs from her lips and addressed the other four. 'Wake up, you lazy bastards!'

There was some grunting and mumbling as they stirred.

She glanced towards Killian and tossed him a sizeable lump of bread. He caught it with one hand. 'You look like you need something,' she said.

'Thanks.'

'Ah, what?' groused a half-asleep Tom. 'No meat. Ugh, fruit—'

'Deal with it.' Finn huffed, sitting up and rubbing her head. 'It ain't poison.'

'May as well be,' Tom muttered, eyeing a dried piece of apple with suspicion.

'Anyway, Killian,' said Lily, ignoring her disgruntled crew member. 'You were saying?'

'I found what we're looking for.'

Tom spun around to face him. 'Killian, you look like shit this morning.'

'Cheers,' he replied. He ran his finger along his bottom lip before continuing. 'I got woken up by a light last night. It was moving around, so I followed it. It led me underneath here, to . . . I don't know. It must be a secret place or something. It's waiting for me.'

Dull grey haunted the skin beneath his brilliant blue eyes; he looked dreadful, but there was nothing Lily could do about that. 'Right then,' she said, getting up and brushing the crumbs from her lap. 'Let's go and cut you up.'

'I can't wait,' Killian drawled.

Lily fumbled under her coat until she found her dagger. As she closed her fingers around it, her stomach lurched. The metal was cold against her skin. Like a corpse. Like death. Soon it would be warm and covered in his blood. She gritted her teeth and pushed her thoughts to the back of her mind.

'Lead the way,' she said, pointing the blade at him with a dramatic flourish.

Tom grumbled about his poor breakfast as he rose, but Finn swore him into silence. Killian grabbed the stick he'd brought back from the Demon's Drop, and it crackled to life with green flames. He gestured for them to follow as he walked away.

After much moaning from Tom, countered by threats from Finn, the party emerged from a web-lined corridor into the bizarre hidden courtyard. Killian snuffed out the flames and stuffed the stick into his belt.

'It's only a little farther,' he said over his shoulder.

Lily blinked – this place was amazing. A hidden courtyard in a forgotten part of the castle, only accessible by pathways through dilapidated tombs. The morning sun shone golden light down on the grass, and the dewdrops sparkled like crystals. Colourful flowers spotted the surface, pinks, blues and yellows stretching up for a taste of sweet sunlight. Drafts of a delicate floral scent mingled with the fresh aroma of the grasses and dew. White-and-purple butterflies flitted around her feet, dancing from one flower to the next. Small patches of lichen scattered the castle walls, but they were mostly covered in deep green ivy. It crawled up, working its way into the surface, clinging on like a desperate lover. Thick green vines draped themselves over the brickwork, then cascaded down like an emerald waterfall. The centrepiece of this secret garden was indubitably the giant oak tree. Its curled branches twisted out in all directions and were adorned with a thick canopy of orange, gold, red and yellow leaves, which didn't make any sense; autumn was still months away. Its thick roots were partially raised from the earth, like it could stand up on them at any given moment and walk away. A little way ahead, Killian had stopped walking and was crouched down. By the time she and the others caught up with him, he was standing again.

'It's down here,' he said, indicating over a ledge.

Lily peered down. 'You climbed down here last night?' she asked.

Killian nodded. 'Doubting my skills yet again.'

'Of course. Let's go, then,' she said. 'Raven?'

Once they'd all been carried safely down, Killian marched towards a mausoleum locked with metal bars. Lily gazed back up the wall. It was a long way to the top. Much to her annoyance, she was impressed that Killian had climbed it. Of course, it was a stupid thing to do, especially alone at night, but that wasn't really the point, was it?

'Told you,' she heard him say softly.

She caught up and peered through the bars. A blue orb of light was glowing above a raised platform. Sickness stabbed at her stomach, and her eyes welled up. She muttered something about dust under her breath and wiped away the threatening tears with her sleeve. With deliberate slowness, she pulled the dagger from her belt and waved it at Killian.

'You ready?' she asked.

He knelt at the barred gate and caressed the lock. Within a few seconds, the gate groaned open. He took his coat off and dumped it into the damp grass, dropping his swords and stick on top too.

'Oh, wait.' He riffled around in his coat until he produced a worn, blunt knife. 'Raven,' he said, 'please look after this.'

The first mate took it with a puzzled look, then tucked it into his belt.

'Close the door,' Lily said to Raven, then followed Killian inside.

The room was lit by a faint blue glow. Everything was so ancient and decayed it was almost impossible to tell a grave plaque from an ordinary brick. Limp vines hung from the ceiling and dragged through Lily's hair. She batted them away with annoyance.

She approached the dais, which was swimming with silver-blue light. It was an unremarkable object, a long rectangular chunk of aged marble. The edges bore a twisted pattern that glistened in the glow of the orb, but besides that, it was rather ordinary.

Killian slouched onto it and gripped the sides. 'Ready to do this?' he asked, glancing up at Lily through his eyelashes.

'I'm doing the easy part,' she replied.

'I suppose.' He rolled his shirt sleeve up, then lay down.

'Do you think it knows?' Lily said, motioning towards the orb with her head.

'I don't know, it seems that way,' he said. 'Maybe it'll be easier than we thought.'

'Maybe. Give me your arm.'

Killian held it out.

She looked at him and took a few deep breaths, then took his hand in hers and squeezed it tight. 'Ready?'

'Always.'

She turned his arm over and sliced into his skin, making a cut half the length of his forearm. Blood bubbled up and trickled over her hands, dripping onto the floor.

'Ow,' he said, throwing her a warm lopsided smirk.

'Sorry.'

'Had worse.'

Lily tensed and moved the dagger back towards his skin. With swift and decisive motions, she made the next three cuts, all within an inch of one another, the top one three inches long, the middle two, and the final one just an inch across. The blood was flowing fast now, and the splats it made as it hit the stone floor turned her stomach. The dagger slid from her hand and clattered to the floor.

She took the rosemary from her pocket and lit it. Smoke curled through the air as she swept the lit sprig around. Its herbal scent was welcoming and helped beat away the overbearing must and dirt. As soon as the atmosphere was heavy with its smell, she dropped it and stamped out the flames. Now for the final part.

'Go to him. Join with him. You shall live as one.'

The blue light flickered like a candle and glided towards Killian's bleeding arm.

'It's working,' she whispered.

'I knew you could do it.' He smiled at her through the haze of the blue glow.

Then time seemed to slow down. There was a hissing sound. It grew louder, like it was coming from all the walls, seething and angry. Lily tried to turn around, but it was difficult to move. It was like she was stuck in honey. A deep red orb erupted from one of the blackened plaques, dashing straight towards Killian's arm. By the time Lily could shield him, it was too late. The red orb dived into the cut at the same time as the blue one. Killian's arms flew up, his back arched, and he sank back onto the marble. Everything was silent.

'Killian?' His body wasn't moving, and his eyes were closed. 'Killian, are you all right? Talk to me.'

There was no response. She put her hand on his; it was wet with sticky blood. Grimacing, she summoned the courage to look at his arm. It wasn't bleeding anymore. Instead, the mark she'd etched into his skin was beaming with a deep red light.

'Killian,' she said, urgency taking hold of her. 'Get up. We need to leave.'

Killian jerked his hand away from hers and slowly sat up. He turned his head in her direction, his eyes still closed. Lily's stomach dropped into the abyss. Her legs became weak, and she stumbled as she took a step backwards.

'Mine!' Killian snarled, gripping his chest with clawed-up hands.

Lily's breath caught in her throat, and her body trembled. He opened his eyes. Gone was the sparkling blue, the cloudless sky. All that glared back at her was baleful fiery red.

'Ah!' he roared. 'Flesh!'

He leapt from the dais, glaring from her to the bloody dagger to his arm and back to her again.

'I see I have you to thank.' His voice was deep and distorted. This wasn't Killian. 'Let me show you my gratitude!'

Before she could move, Killian leapt towards her. His outstretched hands grabbed her throat, and he shoved her into the wall. She struggled against his grip, but it was iron. The life was being squeezed out of her. Grey mist poured into her vision as her lungs burned. He let go with one hand and punched her across the face. For the first time in years, Lily felt pure pain. It erupted in her cheek and spread out over her face.

She coughed and spluttered as she tried to force ragged breaths into her lungs. A cruel grin taunted her, and her abdomen exploded with pain. Before she could cry out, she was punched again, and her body smashed against the wall. She slid down to her knees and gripped her stomach. Her vision blurred. It hurt, it hurt so much. A long trail of blood oozed from her mouth and dribbled onto the floor. Killian grabbed her by the shoulders and wrenched her to her feet.

She staggered back and tried to focus on him, but her vision was swimming. He hurled her against the wall, knocking the remaining breath from her lungs.

'You set me free,' he said. 'I'm free, I'm . . . I'm . . .' His voice faded, and he reeled back to slump to the floor.

Lily stared at him, too terrified to move. With a groan, he got to his knees and looked up at her, his eyes blue again.

'Killian!'

His body was shaking. Pain was etched all over him. 'Lil, I can't control it.' His voice was faint.

Lily swept down towards him and grabbed him by his biceps.

'Lil . . .' he whispered. 'Something's wrong. Something's there that shouldn't be.' Screaming in pain, he toppled onto her chest. 'I can't stop it . . . It wants me. It wants me dead.' He managed to pull himself back and stared into her eyes. 'Help me.'

Blue eyes closed, and his head hung forward. A maniacal grin crawled its way onto his face, and his eyes flashed open to reveal scorching red. Thinking fast, Lily punched him to the floor, then dealt him a powerful kick to the stomach.

He gasped and wheezed, clutching his body and glaring at her from under limp strands of sweat-soaked chestnut hair. Blood seeped from the corner of his mouth.

'I'm gonna get you outta him!' she growled, kicking him again for good measure before running to the door.

Raven yanked it open, and Lily raced through. He slammed the blackened iron gate shut with a deafening clang and dropped the lock. The strength left Lily's legs, and she collapsed to the cold dewy grass.

'It's wrong, it's wrong, it's all wrong,' she muttered.

A snarl lured her attention back to the mausoleum. The red-eyed Killian was clawing at the gate, his face contorted with rage and hatred. Blake and Finn stared in silence. Tom had crumpled to the grass and turned away.

'Let me out!' Killian screamed. 'Let. Me. Out.'

Lily got to her feet and marched up to the furious snapping monstrosity. Blood-covered hands gripped the bars, the skin from his knuckles smeared off. She moved her face as close to the bars as she could. 'You're staying in there,' she said. 'And when I get back, you're coming out of that body.'

Killian grinned back at her, seemingly unaffected. 'Not if I kill *him* first.'

Furious, Lily reached through the bars and grabbed him by his shirt, pulling him close. 'I pity you. You should have picked a weaker man to possess.'

'What would you know about that? I think he's perfect. Absolutely perfect.' He wriggled from her grip and stalked back into the darkness of the tomb.

Demonic laughter emanated from the crypt, echoing around the stunned party, who remained motionless on the grass. Lily clung to the bars – they were all that kept her standing – and stared into the gloom. His shadowy outline was sitting cross-legged on the dais. Blazing-red eyes sliced through the dark, highlighting his sinister grin in the fiery light. He was mocking her. She screwed her bloody hands up in frustration – she wasn't going to let him win.

'Lily?' said Raven, placing a gentle hand on her coiled shoulder.

'We have to save him,' she said, not taking her gaze away from the glowering shadow.

'We will,' said Raven.

'I know,' she replied. She let go of the bars and turned towards him. 'We will.'

Raven nodded.

Lily stepped away from the tomb and paced over to Tom. He was hunched up in the grasses, his head down.

'Tom,' said Lily. She squatted down next to him and forced a smile onto her aching face. 'It's going to be all right, don't worry.'

'I'm not worried,' he replied, squinting as he looked at her. 'You're hurt.'

He was right, she was hurt, but how? She tenderly touched her swollen skin. 'It's not bad. Come on.' She stood up, pulling him to his feet with her.

'What'll we do?' Tom asked, bending down to dust off his knees as he spoke. 'We can't just leave him like that. It is still him, isn't it?'

'It is,' said Lily.

'So,' grunted Finn, walking over to them but not taking her eyes off the two distant red fireballs. 'What was that?'

'Something. I don't know. I couldn't stop it.' She tensed her fist to keep from breaking down. 'It took him.'

'But we can free him, can't we?' asked Tom, his eyes hopeful. 'He's not gonna be like that forever, is he?'

'No, no, of course not,' said Lily, trying her best to sound confident. 'We're gonna save him. We'll split up.' She paused and glanced at Raven. 'Raven will stay here and keep an eye on him. The rest of us are going back to see Ulrich. He told us of the ritual; he'll know how to undo it. Poll's only a few days away, less if we get a step on.' She looked in at the red eyes. They were moving closer. 'The sooner we get going, the sooner we have him back.'

'You think you're getting him back,' Killian snarled through the bars.

Lily glared at him, then turned her back. 'We'll leave all our rations with Raven. We'll have to go without. We can stock up down in Appsen.'

'He's mine,' said Killian. 'This is all mine. I can feel him fading.'

Lily's body shook with rage. 'I'm getting him back,' she said, spinning to face him.

'You're not,' he said with a grin. 'It's only a matter of time before—' He stopped, the words getting lodged in his throat. 'Stop it!' he screamed, grabbing his chest with one hand and his forehead with the other. 'Stop it. Stop!' he cried out, sliding down the bars to the floor.

Lily dashed towards his fallen body. She dropped to her knees and slipped her arm through the bars, giving his shoulder a shake.

'Killian, Killian,' she whispered, 'is it you?'

He lifted himself to his knees and pressed his hand against the bar. He opened his eyes – they were blue, sparkling azure blue.

'Lil,' he croaked, stretching his fingers through the bars. She took them in her hand and squeezed tight; his blood smeared all over her skin, but she didn't care. His body shuddered. 'Lil,' he said again, then swallowed. 'It's a good job you got the chance . . . to be nice to me.'

'But I didn't,' she said. It took all her will to fight back the tears.

A heavy breath tumbled past his lips, and he managed to form his crooked smile. 'You've been . . . nice enough, for you.'

She cursed herself for feeling heat rise to her cheeks. 'Stop talking like that.'

'Like what?' His hand slipped out of her grasp and hung limp at his side. Blood trickled from his knuckles, and tears sprang up in his eyes. 'Like what?'

'Like it's the end.'

'But it doesn't look . . . too good . . . does it?'

'It doesn't look too bad either.'

Killian winced. His body became rigid as he fended off an attack from the unseen force. He put one hand on the floor and pulled his knee up to rest his chest against it. 'It hurts,' he said weakly. 'It's fighting me, Lil.' He grabbed a bar to steady himself. 'I can't keep it back. It's so strong . . . I'm so tired.'

Lily seized his hand, her fingers slipping on the blood. 'You just have to hold on for a few days, only a few days, then I'll make everything better. I promise.'

Killian's arm trembled under the strain.

'Now, I want you to make a promise,' she ordered. She reached through the bars and grabbed his arms to help him stay upright. 'I want you to promise me that you'll hold on until I get back. Five days maximum, and I'll be back to fix you. Don't give in. Fight, please, Killian.'

His breathing was heavy; his shirt was soaked with sweat, clinging to his body. 'Don't . . . leave me,' he said, his voice growing fainter.

'Raven's staying.'

'Good,' he murmured. 'Not that I can't . . . handle this by myself.'

'Of course. You went down the Drop. This is nothing.'

'You're right.'

The bar slipped from his sweaty palm, and he sank to the floor. He grabbed hold of his body and groaned in pain, twisting about on the floor, gasping, his eyes shut tight.

'Killian, come back, please.'

His back arched up, and he cried out again. He rolled onto his side, and his eyes fluttered open; they were faded, like the sparkle had been turned off. For a moment, he lay still and just breathed.

'I can't promise,' he said, his voice scarcely audible. 'I can't fight all the time.' To back up his claims, his body bent, and he cried out. 'But I'll try not to fade away. I'll try to do that.'

'You never promise me anything.'

'I'm sorry,' he whispered. His body gave one last shudder, and he closed his eyes.

CHAPTER THIRTY-SIX

VARO STUMBLED OVER HER LACES AND FELL, HER knee smashing on a rock as she rolled to the ground. She turned onto her back, clutching her injured leg in pain as blood poured between her fingers. A shadow fell over her. Looking up, she saw him. Long dark brown hair blowing on the breeze, a warm scattering of freckles over his nose and cheeks. He smiled at her.

'Let me see, Frannie,' he said, reaching a hand down, a gentle green glowing on his fingertips.

'You know that's not my name.'

The young man sighed and rolled his eyes. 'All right, let me see, Varo.'

She moved her hand away from the wound, like she always did. He crouched lower and pressed his hand to her injury. His skin was soft, cool and soothing.

'Take a deep breath, warrior queen,' he said, his whole

arm now glowing green, the light of which pooled in his deep brown eyes, 'and count to five for me.'

Varo took a long juddering breath. 'One, two, three . . . four . . . five . . .'

VARO woke with such a deep gasp that Sasha jumped back, her heart leaping to her throat. She turned from the window. Varo wilted back into the bed, her chest rising and falling rapidly. Inwardly, Sasha cursed herself for being the one unfortunate enough to be in the room with her when she woke up.

'Can I help?' she asked as she approached her.

Varo's eyes were open. One was a deep brown, the other completely blue and swirled with white. Maybe it was a side effect from being encased in marble for so long. She blinked several times, but only the brown eye closed. A tiny line formed between her dark eyebrows.

'I don't know you,' she said, her voice thick.

'No.' Sasha took a wary step back. Despite the obviously weakened state Varo was in, there was a distinct threat of power about her. She didn't particularly want to see what a woman who could encase herself in marble and leave her own body could do if she was pushed or detected a threat. 'I'll get Qu—'

'No.' Varo eased herself up to sitting. She turned her head towards the open door and flicked her wrist, closing it with a gentle breeze. 'I want to know who you are. I don't want someone to tell me.'

Sasha's tongue morphed into a giant uncooked steak. It didn't want to work or move. She tried to swallow, but her throat was dry. A jug of water sat beside the bed, and she nodded towards it. 'May I?'

'Be my guest.'

Sasha poured herself a glass and took a long gulp. It was still cool from the chunks of ice Quint had formed in it earlier. She took another swig, then sat down in a creaky wooden chair.

Varo looked her up and down, and Sasha shuddered beneath the power of her gaze. Her marbled eye stared on, devoid of life or emotion, but the brown one was deep, stormy and full of power and intensity. High cheekbones were framed neatly by her feathery shoulder-length dark hair, which still retained an inky blue glow from the marble.

'I'm Varo,' she said, some of the heaviness having left her voice.

'Sasha,' she replied, offering her hand.

'Well, this is a good start,' Varo said as she shook her hand. 'Why are you here?'

'Quint asked me to join you.'

'I worked that much out, but I want to know about you. What can you do?'

'Lightning.'

Varo nodded. 'Rare.'

'So I'm told.'

'Show me.'

Sasha's face grew hot, and her nose fizzed. She was about to reveal herself as a failure already. 'I can't,' she said, lowering her gaze to the floor.

'Burnt out?'

'Yeah,' said Sasha. 'I was good, I had control. The night I met Quint, I lost it. I got angry, and I used myself up. It's still there though, I promise.' She looked towards the marble-patched mage.

'Don't look so frightened,' said Varo, a smile forming on her blue lips. 'I understand. Things like this happen to us.'

'You're not going to throw me out?'

Varo chuckled. 'Of course not. Your lightning will come back to you; you're not a husk yet. Now tell me, Sasha, what made you join us?'

'Nothing, not really.'

'And you expect me to believe that?'

'I don't know what to say,' Sasha admitted.

'The truth will be fine,' said Varo. Her voice was powerful yet warm. There was a hypnotic quality to it. 'I need to be able to trust you, Sasha. You must understand that.'

'You trust Kurt?' she asked.

'With my life. You, I wouldn't trust you to pour me a glass of water. You see my predicament?'

In immediate defiance, Sasha reached for the jug and poured her a glass of water. She offered it to Varo with a wry smirk.

'All right, maybe you can do that,' said Varo, taking the glass with an amused smile.

'I want to be free,' Sasha said in a low voice. 'I cut and run all the time – it's tiring. I was saving up to pay for passage on a ship and move to Santonos, but why should I? Vermor is my home; I should be able to live here without fear. Quint mentioned magic from the Otherside would be mine if I joined – I could wield it without the fear of death, or even burnout. I'll be honest. That does have an appeal.'

'And helping other mages of Vermor?'

There was no point in lying. 'I didn't care at first, but I'm warming to the idea.'

White light danced across Varo's marble eye. 'Have you ever killed anyone?'

Sasha's heart skipped a beat, and a tightness rushed to the

bridge of her nose. Was this some sort of test? If it was, what would be the right answer? Varo's gaze did not leave her; it wasn't demanding or intimidating, it was more like she was asking her to share. There was kindness and understanding in her one brown eye.

'No,' Sasha said. 'Cleansers have chased me before, but I always get away.'

'Until the time comes when you don't.'

Sasha nodded and swigged down some of her water. She was unsure as to whether she was answering her questions correctly or not.

'Sasha.'

Varo had sat up in the bed and let the sheet fall away. A loose deep red vest covered her chest, and her right arm was bound tightly in a leather bandage. Blue-and-green swirly patches littered her body. There was something utterly beautiful about it, about Varo. Strength, beauty and pain all merged together in this woman. Varo said Sasha's name again, breaking her trance. For a fleeting moment, she considered running out of the room. Instead, she blinked and regained her composure.

'Yes, sorry.'

'Do you have any family?'

'No, we severed ties after . . .' She paused as a swell of emotion rose inside her. 'After my accident. I—'

'You don't have to tell me.'

The heat drained from her, and she shook her head. The accident was not something she ever wanted to talk about. 'I have a lover. I miss her.'

'Then you should visit her.'

'I was under the impression that I was here for . . . some length of time.'

'Sasha, you're not trapped here, nor are you obligated to stay. I want people here who want to be here.'

'But when Quint recruited me, he . . .' Sasha's voice trailed off. She didn't want to get Quint in trouble.

'He can be heavy-handed at times, but don't worry or dwell on that. If missing your partner is making you hurt, go and see her, heal that hurt. That will make you stronger. Perhaps it will speed up your recovery.' She reached over and placed a cold hand on Sasha's forearm. 'Kindness and love always help with recovery. If you have someone who offers you that, you need to see her.'

'Thank you.'

'I'm not a monster, far from it.' She turned her head and stared out the window as she spoke. 'I know what losing someone you love feels like, and I know what it's like to have no one. You have someone – you need to embrace that. You may leave and visit her, but I will expect something from you when you return.'

Sasha put her glass down. 'That sounds fair.'

'You say that now, but you don't know what it will be.' She turned back to face Sasha and opened the door with another neat flick of her wrist. 'If you decide not to return to us, that's your choice. We won't hunt you down – that's not our way. I want freedom, and trapping someone here goes against everything I'm fighting for. How far away does she live?'

'She's in Brackmouth, about a day in a carriage.'

'Brackmouth, very interesting. Take a few days' leave. Go anytime, but tell Quint before you do. I'm tired. I need to rest now,' she added, nodding towards the door.

Sasha stood. 'Thanks for understanding.' With that, she scuttled out of the room, her mind a mixed tangle of emotions. Varo wasn't at all like she'd expected her to be. She was reasonable and seemed like she genuinely cared. Sasha wasn't trapped either; she could leave if she wanted to. That was something to ponder on her journey.

A slight spring crept into her step as her mind went to Ruby. Whatever she decided, she'd get to spend a few nights with her. That would be enough to see her through anything.

CHAPTER THIRTY-SEVEN

After two days of brisk marching and one night of very little sleep, Poll sketched itself into view. Its thick stone houses packed together tightly around the foot of the hills were a welcome sight, the churning waters of the river a beautiful sound. Hope swelled up inside Lily. She'd managed to slice down their journey time. If all went well, they'd be leaving Ulrich's within the hour and making their way back to Killian and Raven.

Her cheek throbbed as she paced through the tranquil streets. Killian had hurt her – badly. An ugly purple bruise covered her stomach, and her left eye had been swollen shut for at least a day. How had this happened? How could he hurt her? It wasn't right. No, he couldn't hurt her. It was that thing, the thing that now lived inside him. That was logical. That was it. Killian couldn't hurt her himself; that was an utterly ridiculous notion. That monstrous spirit was the problem.

Lily gave Ulrich's door three sharp knocks. Once again, there was a delay in him answering the call. Her stomach sank. What if this time he really was dead? What would she do? How would she save Killian? She glanced at Blake and caught his hazel gaze. He was a mage – couldn't he do something? Didn't he know something? Blake looked to the ground as if he knew what she was thinking. Lily snarled and hammered the door again, this time with more aggression.

After what seemed like hours, the door squeaked open to reveal Ulrich's wizened face. 'The lovely lady pirate,' he said in his dry voice. 'And to what do I owe the pleasure . . . again?' He glanced over her shoulder at the small entourage behind her, and his neck twitched. 'Some of your crew?'

'Yes, some of my best,' she replied. 'I need your help. Can we come in?'

The old man cast his eyes over the three unfamiliar faces before nodding. 'Please,' he said, stepping back into the house.

She followed him into his sitting room, her crew close behind.

'Have a seat,' he said, indicating the bench.

Lily nodded to her crew, and they sat. She remained standing, one hand on her cocked hip. The small blue-tiled table had a steaming teapot resting on it with a chipped mug next to it. Books were crammed into every available space. Some were strewn across the floor, others piled high; it seemed the old man hadn't cleaned up since her last visit. The back door was yawning open, letting in a fresh breeze from the hillside.

'Allow me to fetch you a chair,' offered Ulrich.

'No, I'll stand,' she said. Something about his overly hospitable behaviour put her on edge. She glanced at the owl who'd taken such a dislike to Killian. It observed the three pirates on the bench and remained fluffy, fat and wide-eyed.

'You don't mind if I sit, do you? My old bones like to complain when I stand too much,' Ulrich said.

'By all means,' said Lily, smiling as sweetly as she could, her back tensing.

Ulrich lowered himself onto his threadbare couch and grunted with satisfaction. 'That's better. Now, my dear, what can I do for you?'

'Something went wrong.'

'Really?' asked Ulrich, his faded eyes growing wide.

'Yes,' she said, moving her hands behind her back and gripping her fingers. 'We managed to hide the soul in him, but something else joined it.'

'Somethin' bad,' Tom chipped in.

Ulrich rubbed his beard, and his eyes flashed with interest. He sucked on his teeth. 'Any more details?'

'It was red, a glowing red ball. It came from nowhere. The cut in his arm, it's red. So are his eyes.' She paused to regain her composure. 'He's not himself anymore – not all the time. We've got him locked up.'

'He's picked up an enlii,' said Ulrich, his fingers twisting faster through his wiry beard.

'A what?'

'There are two things a spirit can do when the body dies: one is to accept death and move on, the other is to tether itself to the world. Those that remain come in two types: the enlii and the orm.

'The orm, like the one you were seeking, are benevolent beings, devoid of true thought and feeling. In essence, they are a flicker of energy. These are tied to the world by powers beyond their control. Your spirit is bound to the Gramarye as a seal, so its essence cannot leave this world. Others are bound by the love of another. Soul binding was born of grief-stricken lovers unable to let go. They'd bind their lover's energy to them until they too die, and both are set free. Rather tragic.

'The enlii are different. The enlii are those who choose to stay behind in the hope that one day they can have a body again. They skulk around graveyards close to their own remains, waiting for an opportunity. The years are never kind to the enlii. The longer they wait, the more embittered they become, the more desperate, violent and selfish. Back when soul binding was common, people were occasionally infected by enlii. They were driven mad until they either gave up and let it take over or took their own lives. This was one of the many reasons it fell out of favour.'

Red-hot anger raced through Lily. She gripped her fingers tighter and tried to remain calm. 'Why didn't you warn us about this?' she asked, fighting to keep the tremble from her voice.

'You didn't ask,' replied the old man.

Lily burst into fits of hysterical laughter. 'I didn't ask?' she gasped between sniggers. 'I didn't ask.'

Ulrich put his hands on his knees and smiled at her. 'You didn't.'

She stopped laughing and glared at the man. 'No, I didn't,' she said, her voice as cold and sharp as a slice of ice. She leant down towards the warlock, her hair tumbling over her shoulders like an inky waterfall. 'So, I'm asking now. How do we get that *thing* out of him?'

'My dear,' said Ulrich, drawing himself upright, 'it would be better for everyone if he was forgotten about and left locked away wherever you have him.'

'What?' It took every fibre of her will to keep from punching the old man.

'Hiding the seal in his body was an excellent idea – it will now be extremely difficult for whatever, or whoever, has this Gramarye to remove it from him. And when he dies, the soul will go with him. Now, with an enlii inside him too, I imagine it'll make it impossible for anyone to locate him. The fractured personalities of those three life forces will cause so much confusion – as I'm sure you've already seen – that it's unlikely whether even this Gramarye could track them down. It may not seem it now, but it's worked out much better this way.'

'So,' said Lily, softening her voice, 'you're saying the best thing to do is leave him there?'

Ulrich nodded. 'Yes. Think about it – his sacrifice could prevent a greater calamity.'

'I see. What will happen to him?'

'Most people last four or five days before they're lost forever and the enlii has control. If you keep him locked away, he'll eventually starve to death, and the orm will die with him.'

'When you sent us away, exactly how aware were you that something like this might happen?'

'Very. There're so many tales about that place, the only real explanation would be an enlii in the grounds,' the old man admitted. 'But as I said, this is the best-possible outcome.'

'Indeed,' she said, wrapping her hair around her fingers, anything to keep herself from punching his jaw off. 'And was there a way to prevent this?'

Ulrich narrowed his eyes and remained silent.

A swell of heat burned away Lily's stomach. That reaction was all she needed to see. She felt like crying and screaming simultaneously – the old man had used Killian as a pawn. He knew this was a possibility, and he'd deliberately not told them.

Lily turned to her scarred master gunner. 'Finn, rip the bookshelf apart. Bring me anything related to soul binding.'

'Aye,' she grunted, then set to work ripping books off the shelves and flicking through them in a most disrespectful manner. 'You can help too,' she said over her shoulder to Tom and Blake.

'Wh-what are you doing?' said Ulrich.

'Finding evidence,' said Lily, sitting down on the edge of Ulrich's table.

Ulrich's eyes flashed to the group of pirates ransacking his collection of tomes. Books were scattered through the air, pages fluttering. The smell of leather and dust swamped the room. Poppy watched on, unfazed.

'Of what?' he asked.

'Your deception, then I'll pass my sentence. I'm fair and believe in democracy, after all. Finn, burn the ones with no use.'

'Aye, Cap'n.'

'No, no, don't, please!' Ulrich pleaded. 'Those texts, some are ancient – they must be preserved.'

Lily gave him an indifferent shrug. 'Keep looking and burning, guys.'

'No, please!' Ulrich fell to his knees, his shrivelled old eyes brimming with tears. 'Please don't, I'll . . . I left it out.'

Lily slid off the table, grabbed Ulrich by his shoulder and dragged him to his feet. She glared at him and pulled her lips back over her teeth. 'Left *what* out?'

'The enlii, I didn't tell you about them because I was . . .' He paused and lowered his head. Lily dug her nails into his shoulder. 'I was hoping he'd catch one. I was hoping that cursed place had one.'

It took all of her will not to crush his shoulder into meaty dust, but she needed him. She drew in a deep calming breath to placate the rage within.

'As I said, sacrificing that one man to prevent a greater calamity is the sensible thing to do.' He straightened up and looked Lily in the eye. 'I could have given you some herbs to keep the enlii at bay, but I didn't.' He curled up his lip and sneered. 'I *wanted* this to happen.'

It was too much for Lily. Maybe Raven could have kept his cool in a moment like this, but she certainly couldn't. She grabbed Ulrich around the throat and lifted him off the floor. 'Finn!' she snarled through gritted teeth. 'Burn something, anything! Wait! Anything but the bird.'

'Cap'n, as if I'd do that.' She grabbed a book she'd already discarded and lit the corner of it.

'Now, Ulrich, you are going to help us,' Lily said calmly as the old man wriggled and choked before her. 'You are going to help us get that thing out of him.'

She released him, and he dropped to the cold stone floor like a sack of potatoes. He rolled onto his back, his chest heaving as he fought to get air into his lungs. Lily stepped over him and crouched down, pressing a knee into his chest.

'Is there a way to save him?'

Ulrich remained silent.

She pressed down hard. 'I could crack your chest, and you know it. Now, tell me.'

'Yes,' he wheezed. 'But it's insane . . . I won't—'

She reached behind her for the teapot and tipped the scalding contents all over Ulrich's string-bean arm. The old man hissed through his uneven teeth as if he was afraid to cry. Lily tossed the teapot over her shoulder without a care, shattering it. Moving on, she grabbed his hand and snapped a finger. It cracked like a winter twig. A silent scream tumbled out of his mouth as he stared in shock at his limp swinging finger.

'I can do them all. I can do your toes too. I can pull out your fingernails. I can take your eyes. It'll take a while, but I've got time.'

'If I weren't a burnt-out husk, I'd kill you,' Ulrich drawled. 'And all your crew. I could pull fire from the Otherside. Dark, twisted fire. It was so beautiful. You wouldn't stand a chance, you evil bitch.'

She snapped another finger, and he cried out, so she broke another. 'Could, would, can't.' She reached for his thumb. 'I'll ask for your help one more time.' She applied pressure to his thumb until tears sprang into his eyes.

'All right! Stop! Please! I'll . . . I'll help,' Ulrich gurgled, thick yellow drool oozing from his mouth.

'Good. I knew you'd make the right choice.' She considered snapping his thumb but thought better of it – he might need it, after all – and stood up.

Ulrich staggered to his feet and collapsed back into a chair, staring in horror at his ruined digits. Three fingers dangled and swung in all directions, a broken, twisted mess. Tears streamed down his face, getting lost in the deep ruts of his skin. Lily didn't care for his pain; in fact, looking at him only made her want to break more of his fingers.

The three gunners paused in their ransacking of his collection of magical tomes. Finn lit a cigarette with the corner of her burning book, then smothered out the flames with her coat.

'Are you done looking at your fingers?' Lily spat.

The old man gave a meek nod.

'What do we need to do?' she asked.

He coughed and wiped the saliva from his mouth with his one good hand. 'There's a potion that was used,' he croaked. 'It has to be put in his eyes when the enlii is in control.'

'I can do that,' she said. 'Get on it, old man. I wanna be gone by tomorrow.'

'I can't make it,' he rasped.

'What d'you mean?' she asked, narrowing her eyes to deadly slits.

'There's an ingredient, but it's impossible to get it.'

'What is it?'

'A marine plant. It only grows on the seabed. You can comb the beaches of Freischen in the hope that one has washed up, but you don't have time.'

'Describe what I'm looking for.' She folded her arms.

'You can't search all the beaches f—'

'Tell me what this thing looks like. I won't ask again.'

'As long as you haven't burned it, I can show you,' he said, easing himself up and shuffling to a bookcase.

He ran his good fingers over several dust-covered volumes, paused on one and plucked it from the shelf. He waddled back to his chair and flopped down. There were gasps and groans as he leafed through the book with his one good hand, accompanied by the soft patter of his tears hitting the pages. Tears of regret, no doubt.

As Lily watched him feebly work his way through the book, she felt a desire to slam it shut on his hand, then punch him in the jaw and pull out some of his teeth. Give him something to really cry about. Viscous green mucus dripped from his nose and mixed with the foul drool that pooled on his ragged shirt. Disgusting cretin.

'Here,' he said, inclining his head towards an image.

Lily leant down and peered at the plant in question. It was long, thin and wavy, with teardrop shapes hanging from its branches. She scanned the description – blue body with silver buds. She frowned as she stared at it. It looked so insignificant. She balled her fists up in irritation. If only she could beat the enlii out of Killian; that would be easy.

'I need the buds,' mumbled Ulrich.

Lily nodded. 'May I have the page?'

'Yes.'

Lily smiled and took great pleasure in tearing the page from his obviously ancient book.

'Is this all you need?' she asked.

'That's all. I have the rest here.'

'Right,' she said. 'Finn, Tom, you two are to stay here and assis—keep an eye on dear old Ulrich, make sure he doesn't try to run away.' She turned to Blake. 'You're with me. We've a long way to go and not much time.'

CHAPTER THIRTY-EIGHT

CRIMSON FLAMES IGNITED THE HORIZON AS the garnet sun fell. Burnt orange faded into a washed-out yellow before shifting to myriad shades of green, through which the first evening stars shone like delicate ice crystals. The wooden panels of the veranda creaked and groaned as Sasha wandered along them. She took a sip from her mug and hung her arms over the railing.

She was waiting for Theo. She wanted to speak to him about her plan to visit Brackmouth. After the evening meal, he'd been summoned upstairs by Quint and Varo. The blue-marbled mage still hadn't recovered from her ordeal and needed Theo's help. A shudder vibrated down Sasha's spine. They had to stop using him and let nature heal her. How much more could he take? Part of her was anxious about leaving him, but she had to see Ruby again. It had been so long. She ran her finger over the intricate flames of her amber necklace. Too long. And she could stay. Stay with Ruby forever. But in order to live that life without fear she would need the power of the Otherside, and the thought of leaving the group and abandoning Theo didn't feel right. Not anymore.

The door scraped open, and a blast of light shot across the porch. The sound of heavy footsteps followed. Leather boots scraped on wooden planks as if the wearer could barely lift their feet. A body thumped against the porch rail. Sasha couldn't bring herself to look.

'Do you have one of those for me?' Theo's voice was flat.

'I do actually.' Sasha stooped down and grabbed the vessel she'd filled for him some time ago. 'It's not very good.'

'I doubt I can tell the difference.'

She handed him the mug of tepid beer and was horrified by what she saw. His skin was deathly pale, unhealthy. He'd only been gone an hour, but he looked so much worse than before. Dark circles ringed his eyes, the whites of which were mottled with red.

'Thanks,' he said.

A thin stream of blood oozed from the corner of his mouth.

'Theo, you're . . .' Sasha moved to wipe the blood from his face, but he flinched, spilling beer over his already-tatty shirt. She put her hand on his shoulder and looked into his eyes as she wiped the blood away with her thumb. 'You're bleeding.'

He looked to the floorboards. 'I'm sorry,' he murmured.

'No, don't be, it's not your fault. Couldn't you taste it?'

'No.' He pushed his hair back and took a swig. 'I don't taste much of anything. It's another thing that makes me less of a person.' He eyed the mug. 'This could be water, coffee, poison, blood – I wouldn't know.'

'But why?'

'It takes everything from me. It started off as little by little, then it got more. I can't taste, I can't feel, I don't know what happiness feels like, or sadness. I'm a shell around nothing.'

'So stop.'

'I can't. I have to keep going. They promised me . . .' He took another drink.

The wind rustled in the grasses around them, and a barn owl shrieked into the twilight; its ghostly white form lurked over the fields like a silent spectre. Small mammals scuttled and scampered beneath the porch. The air was fresh and pure, with a hint of mossy earth. It was invigorating. Sasha couldn't imagine not enjoying it, not feeling it, not feeling anything. She had another drink and let the beer coat her tongue. No taste either – what sort of world was this man living in?

'Theo—'

'Shh.' He glanced to the left, indicating they should walk along the porch.

Sasha allowed him to lead her off the porch and out into the field. The two piebald horses watched them as they paced through the grasses, plumes of steam bursting from their nostrils. The tragic lumpy remains of their antlers soaked up the setting sun and took on an amber sheen. When the two mages were a good distance away from the house, Theo spoke.

'By the time I met Water and Leader, I was too far gone. I'd used my power to heal too much.'

A dull pain pressed against Sasha's chest. A power, a magic, so beautiful and yet so cursed.

'There was no way back for me. I was – I am – empty.'

'But you—'

'No.' Even though he cut her off, his voice was soft. 'I am. They promised me I could be whole if I joined them.'

'But they're killing you. Even I can see that – you must too.' A rush of white-hot anger burst through Sasha. Her arm prickled like her lightning was returning. She lifted her hand. Thin, tiny forks flickered over her skin. Then it was gone, almost as if it were embarrassed to be seen with her. 'I'm going to Brackmouth in a few days; you should leave too. Come with me and vanish, don't ever come back here.'

'Lightning, you know what the Gramarye is, don't you?'

'The green thing.' Sasha didn't really care. Getting Theo somewhere safe before he was used to death was more important.

'It's a link to the Otherside.' He turned his hands over, palms facing the darkening sky. They shimmered silver, blue and green. Sasha looked at his face; that spark had returned to his eyes again. It was those eyes. The eyes she saw when she was drifting in and out of consciousness all those weeks ago. He wasn't a dream. The smallest of smiles tugged at the corner of his mouth, and there was such emotion within it. It was as if in that fleeting moment, he could feel something. 'The world where this comes from – Varo said there's a way to open up a path leading there with it, a path over the veins that connect everything. The Gramarye was locked away for hundreds, thousands of years. Its link between our worlds was too close, and that made it dangerous. But if that link can be made again, to the Otherside, if I can get there, I can be whole. I can be human again.'

Theo's eyes were glistening, his lip trembling. He curled his hands into fists and banished the shimmering glow. No sooner had it gone than his face became set in stone once more.

'I have to try, I have to keep going. It's the only chance I have.'

Sasha's eyes prickled with burning tears.

'There's nothing else for me.' The moon had risen while they'd been talking, and it bathed his worn face in its pale glow.

He was so broken, so ruined. She'd taken from him twice. The red in his eyes, his deathly pale skin, his frail body – she was partly to blame for all that. In that moment, her mind was made up. Her life and happiness could wait. 'I'll help you.'

'Lightning, I—'

'No, let someone help you for once. I don't know how, but I will, I promise. You've saved me twice, so I owe you.' She moved to put her hands on his shoulders, but he took a step back and away from her touch. 'Just promise me you'll look after yourself while I'm away. I can't help a corpse.'

CHAPTER THIRTY-NINE

RAVEN HUNCHED UP ON ONE OF THE DESPONDENT castle's battlements and gazed across the graveyard. Headstones protruded out of the long willowy grass like broken teeth. It had been several days since the others had left. The creeping sensation that something had gone wrong wrapped itself around him. Going to look for them was out of the question – he couldn't abandon Killian. He felt bad enough that he'd come up to the castle for a few hours, but he needed some time to think, to reflect and to work out how to keep his rapidly declining friend from yielding to insanity and the monster that lurked within.

His stomach growled. Their rations were running low; soon he'd have to venture down into Appsen to get supplies. He'd not eaten a thing since Lily had left. Eating wasn't something he really needed to do. Hunger was an illusion brought on by his semi-mortality, but what a painful illusion it was. He'd been trying to feed Killian all they had during the moments he was in control. It was obvious that the demon within him was trying to weaken him by starving him.

Raven leapt from his post and landed upon a gravestone without faltering and headed back to the tomb, dreading what he'd find on his return.

Killian was as Raven had left him, sitting cross-legged on the dais, holding out his arms, flexing and relaxing his muscles, a look of confusion and fury on his face, his red eyes flaming. With a gut-wrenching scream, he thumped the platform. His head pricked up, and he glared fiercely at Raven. Snarling, he leapt down and sprinted towards the bars. He seized hold of the black metal and growled. Spit oozed from his lips in a long vile string.

'Why do you keep hurting him?' asked Raven, catching sight of his bleeding knuckles.

'What's it to you?'

'I care about him.' Raven sank to the ground.

'That's a shame.' Killian grinned and then lapped the blood from his hands. 'I'm not giving him up. He's perfect.'

'He's all right.'

Killian crouched, catlike, and continued to lick the blood. 'You don't know, do you?' he drawled between slurps.

'Know what?'

He burst into fits of foul laughter. 'I can't believe that I know and you don't!'

'Know what?' Raven asked again. His patience was wearing thin.

'This body!' Killian snarled, rocking onto his toes. 'It's full of power, so much power. So much. It's intoxicating.'

'What power?'

'I don't know. He was your friend, you shou—'

'*Is*,' said Raven.

'Huh?'

'He *is* my friend.'

Killian laughed again. 'Believe what you want. But sooner or later there'll be a time when he's not coming back, and this will be mine.' He ran his fingers over his body, grinning. 'To do what I please with. All this power will be mine.'

'Show me,' said Raven, getting to his feet. He'd had enough of playing games.

'Show you what?' Killian sneered.

'This power.'

'I can't . . . yet.' He faced his jailer and glowered with his blood-red eyes. 'But when I work it out, you're the first person I'll try it on.' He spat on the floor and wiped his mouth with the back of his bloody hand, streaking his lips and jaw with crimson. 'I'll have you begging for mercy, then I'll see you dead.' He cocked his head to one side and smirked.

'I'd like to see you try,' said Raven, his muscles tensing.

'Maybe one d— No!' Killian snapped, wrapping his arms around his chest. 'Go away! Go away! This isn't yours, not any—' His voice trailed off as he collapsed to the floor in a cloud of ancient dust. He screamed, and his body convulsed, and then he fell silent and still.

Killian was curled tight in a tremulous ball in the dirt. His knees were pulled into his chest, his trembling fingers locked around them. Raven reached through the bars towards his friend and laid his hand on his sweat-soaked back.

'Killian, it's okay,' he said.

Killian remained on the ground, wheezing, his back and shoulders jerking with each gasping breath. It was as if everything had been ripped out of him and all that remained was a broken shell.

'Killian,' said Raven, giving his shoulder a gentle squeeze.

Killian whimpered and pushed himself onto his knees. His face was shining with sweat and covered with smears of blood. With his eyes still closed, he groaned. The groans turned to cries, which in turn morphed into screams of agony. He grabbed the back of his head, clawing at his skull with bent fingers. The horrific cries shot through Raven and lodged in his chest. He had to do something, had to help him.

'Killian,' he said, grabbing his friend's head and tilting it up. 'Look at me, look at me.'

Killian's eyes were still shut tight. Limp strands of damp hair clung to his cheeks.

'It hurts, it hurts, it's burning me!'

'Let it go, Killian,' said Raven. 'It's gone. Open your eyes and look at me.'

His eyes fluttered open.

Raven wanted to cry when he saw the azure amid the bloodshot whites. His friend was back.

'Raven,' he croaked.

'Don't talk, just drink,' said Raven, thrusting a waterskin into the tomb.

The monster had denied Killian food and water the whole time it had been in control in a malicious effort to push him to the brink faster. Killian drank deeply. Water splurged from the side of his mouth and ran down his neck. Once he'd drained the skin, he looked at Raven and pushed his sweat-slicked hair out of his face.

'Hello,' he said, offering a weak smile.

Raven let out a deep sigh as the tension left his back. 'I thought I'd lost you,' he said, sinking back down to his knees.

Killian slumped back against the wall and drew his knees to his chest. 'You're not that lucky.'

'Give me your hands.'

Killian dangled his arms limply through the bars.

'Nasty,' said Raven, hissing through his teeth. Killian's knuckles were a bloody, bruised mess and swollen to twice their usual size.

'Can you stop him from doing shit like that to me, please?' muttered Killian.

'He doesn't exactly listen to reason. Hang on.' Raven fumbled through the brown cloth bag full of potions Lily had left him. The small glass bottles clinked together, and the coloured liquids sloshed inside them. A rainbow of concoctions.

'You want the blue,' said Killian.

'Dark blue?'

'Other will do.'

'Ah, here.' Raven held the bottle up to the sun and removed the stopper. A tart whiff sprang out.

Killian held his hand out, wincing in anticipation. Raven poured a small amount of liquid onto the wound.

Killian cried out in pain. 'Shit! That hurts, that really, really fucking hurts.' The blue potion mixed with the blood on the back of his hand and turned into a murky purple sludge.

Raven took a cloth from the bag and wiped away the purple ooze. He grabbed a bandage and wrapped it tight around Killian's hand. 'Done.'

Killian pulled his hand back through the bars and stared at it. 'Hurt more than last time.'

'Maybe that's because it was Lily who did it before,' said Raven, rummaging in another bag.

'What's that supposed to mean?' Killian huffed.

'Nothing,' said Raven, smiling to himself. He stuffed some dry bread and a hard lump of cheese through the bars. 'Eat this while you can.'

Killian took it gratefully and demolished it within seconds.

'There's not much left,' said Raven. 'I'll have to visit the village and buy some more.'

Killian chewed his lip, and his eyes glistened. 'Okay.' His voice hitched as he spoke.

Raven nodded and sat back, resting on the backs of his arms. He blew all the breath from his lungs and tried to relax. Killian was still alive, and that was all that mattered.

'Raven?'

'Mmm?' Raven turned towards him.

'Am I gonna die?'

Raven darted back towards the bars. He wanted to open them, to grab and hold his friend, but it was too risky. 'No,' he said, shaking his head. 'They'll be back soon, and everything will be fine.'

'I feel like I'm dying. It hurts all over. I'm fighting all the time, and I don't know how much longer I can hold on.' His voice trailed off, and his breathing became heavy and laboured.

'Don't talk like that.'

'It's so hard. I feel weaker all the time.'

'Look, Killian, don't talk, and don't think like that. Just try . . . try to hold on.'

Killian leant his head back and stared up at the rocky ceiling of his prison cell. He sighed deeply. 'Raven, there's something I've gotta tell you. My secret. I should've told you already. I should've told someone.'

'Don't feel like you have to,' Raven said.

'I do,' Killian murmured. 'I've got some sort of power, like a mage, but I've never practised before in my life. It's not elemental, it—' He screwed his body up and tensed. The demon was trying to take control again. 'Raven! Help me!' he cried out, his back arching. He thrust his hand through the bars and into the grass, his fingers searching for something. 'Please! Don't let it take me!'

Raven grabbed his sweaty hand in a firm grip.

'Killian,' he said, his voice gentle and calm despite the panic eating away at him. 'Killian, look at me, look at me, don't close your eyes.'

Killian hissed and snorted. He kicked his feet into the ground and screamed. Raven let go of his hand and reached through the bars to grab his shoulders. He yanked Killian close, holding him against the icy metal as he thrashed about.

'Killian, relax. That pain, it's nothing – ignore it,' said Raven.

'Nothing,' Killian whispered, his body slowing in its convulsions. 'It's nothing.'

'That's right.'

Killian reached his arms between the bars and gripped Raven's back, his fingers digging in painfully. 'Nothing, nothing, nothing,' he repeated.

The air around them stilled, and all Raven could hear was Killian's shuddering breaths. He held him tight. The cold bars pressed into his body, but he didn't care. He would hold on for as long as Killian needed.

Gradually, Killian's breathing slowed, and he let go. He slumped against the moss-covered wall, his shirt plastered to his body with sweat.

'I did it,' he whispered.

'You did.'

Killian wiped his wet forehead with his sleeve. 'Raven, I need to show you something.'

'Rest.'

'No, I'll pass out soon anyway,' Killian gasped between breaths. 'Watch.'

Killian closed his eyes, and an iridescent glow flooded his skin. Raven blinked and rubbed his eyes; what was he seeing? Pink, yellow, green, blue and purple all wrapped within a silvery glow swirled over Killian's skin. It was like a soap bubble. As he laboriously got to his feet, trails of this strange light hung from him like tentacles. With the sound of a shattering crystal, giant horns appeared. Raven stood up and took a step backwards. The great ghostly ridged horns curled around Killian's face. They, too, shimmered with the other-worldly glow.

'I would jump for you and get stuck in a tree again, but that's a little hard to do in here,' Killian said, his voice faint.

'I knew you were hiding something, but I didn't expect this. Why didn't you tell anyone?' asked Raven.

'I don't know what it is. It's something to do with the Gramarye, and it's killing me. I don't wanna be a hindrance,' Killian said. He staggered forwards, putting a glowing hand on the bars to steady himself. Wisps of coloured light broke from his skin and faded away like the morning dew. 'And I'm scared. I'm scared that I'll fail.'

'What do you mean?'

'Either this is killing me, or I'm meant to be able to use it to help protect something. But I can't use it. It drains the life out of me.' He slumped to the floor. The swirling colours faded back into his skin and his ghostly horns vanished. 'Raven, if he works out how to use it, you have to kill him.'

'Killian, you c—'

'No, whatever it is, it's powerful. If he masters it while he's in control, you have to kill him. If not, he'll escape with it. That can't happen. So please, kill us.'

Raven stared at Killian. Why had he stayed with the crew? He should have left like he always did. No deep attachments. Not again, never again. Killian wilted onto his side, his eyes shut, his breathing deep and even.

'Promise me . . . Promise me that you'll kill us.'

'I don't—'

'Please, I don't want to cause any more grief. It'll be better for everyone this way.'

'I won't kill you. And if it comes to it, I'll fight him myself until you come back.'

The corners of Killian's mouth twitched up into a weak smile, and a tear seeped from his closed eye. He opened his mouth to say something, but unconsciousness beat him to it.

CHAPTER FORTY

LILY AND BLAKE THUNDERED THROUGH NOCTURNE Forest. Animals and pine needles alike scattered out of their way. Their stolen horses grunted beneath them, steam erupting from their nostrils in great gasping plumes. Lily dug her heels in, driving her steed faster. Her mind was ticking over how long they'd been. She frowned. It would take a few more days to get back to the ship, plus about a week to get back to the graveyard, then there was finding the damn plant. Killian had only been given four or five days before the madness was irreversible.

For the hundredth time, she cursed Ulrich's name; the old bastard had known all along. How could he have been so cruel? Why hadn't he warned them? But if he had, she doubted it would have stopped Killian. Her hands screwed up in rage. She lowered her head and kicked her horse harder. Why did he always have to be so impulsive? It was ridiculous. Always putting himself in danger – it made her so mad. Why could he not see? Her vision blurred. She tried to trick her mind into thinking that it was the wind, but she knew that wasn't the case. He was such a noble cock. She ground her teeth. If only he could see what he was really like, maybe then he'd be able to forgive himself for Ren and stop doing ridiculous things.

She glanced at her ring. Dark greens, bright greens, sea greens and dull greens all swirled together beneath the glass of the moon. She shuddered as she remembered that helpless feeling of drowning so long ago. Lily's knuckles went white as she gripped the horse's reins. She could still hear their voices in her head, taunting her and laughing, feel their hands on the small of her back as she was pushed into the lake within the Cerulean Caves.

It had been impossible for her to fight against the currents, and she was swept away through a network of underwater tunnels. When her body was finally released, she opened her eyes to an underwater cavern and floundered hopelessly, dizziness trying to overcome her. There was no point in attempting to escape. All her life she'd been alone, and she was destined to die that way.

A radiant blue light filled her vision. No, it wasn't blue, it was green. Or was it turquoise? Aqua? Cyan? It was a colour she'd never seen before. It was pure, it was ocean, it was life. Something took her hand and slipped the moon ring onto her finger, and she could breathe. She floated, exhausted from fear and panic. The glowing blue light moved about her. It didn't seem to have any set form. Its back end morphed from that of a fish to legs and back again. Sometimes it had arms and hands, other times claws and pincers. What she assumed was its face had no set features apart from its eyes, which swirled with every shade of green imaginable.

'What are you?' she asked.

'The spirit of the ocean, its soul. Many call me the Big Blue.' The voice went directly into her head, musical and calming.

'What have you done?' she asked, looking at the ring.

'Saved your life and granted you a great power.'

'Why?'

'You fell in.'

A simple answer. Lily watched the Big Blue and wondered whether she was still drowning and if this was one final trick being played on her. The spirit moved one crab-like claw towards her, and she backed away. The claw morphed into a hand, and sitting within the palm was a spindle shell. It was completely white, and the end looked to be fashioned into a mouthpiece. The spirit thrust it closer to her, and she gingerly took the offered shell.

'You will see me once more. It is for you to decide when. Blow into the shell, and I will come. I will obey you and only you. I can touch you and only you. Only you may travel within my soul. We are tied now.' The Big Blue's voice bubbled into her brain. 'Choose the time wisely.'

'But I don't understand.'

'You are alive – the ring has made it so. It has given you great power. You will no longer feel the physical pain of this world, and you will be exceptionally strong – but this strength, unlike your protection, will deplete as you use it. Pay attention to the colours within the ring – the more you use your enhanced strength, the more the ring will wane from green to grey. When it becomes grey, your strength will abandon you, and you must take the ring off or it will drain your life to replace its own. With the ring removed, you will once again feel pain. A new moon will return its power, so keep watch of the skies. Now go and make your way in this life. Give yourself a good life. You are my gift to the world.'

A numbness crept over Lily. She was a gift to the world? It felt wrong.

'Come.' The Big Blue gripped her hand and pulled her forwards.

She was surrounded by bright blue light. She blinked, and she was moving at a phenomenal speed through the caves. The Big Blue twisted and turned down various tunnels until they came out into the open sea. The spirit carried Lily to the shore and released her onto the beach, then disappeared beneath the waves. She crawled up the sand and sat back, holding her hand out and admiring the shimmering ring. It was the most beautiful thing she'd ever owned.

She rolled back her shirtsleeve and dug her nails into her arm as hard as she could. She felt nothing. She let go, and there was nothing there, not even a dent. She clutched the spindle shell to her chest, then slipped it into her pocket.

The sky shifted to a dark blue and was peppered with silver stars. A shooting star dashed across, yet she felt no need to make a wish.

She had lain back in the sand and smiled. The smiling had quickly turned to laughter. And for the first time in her miserable life, she had laughed herself to sleep.

'What did you say?' asked Blake, angling his horse towards her.

Lily snapped back to reality. 'Nothing, sorry, I was . . .'

He helped her out. 'Thinking aloud.'

'Yeah, something like that.' She looked ahead. The trees were thinning. 'We're almost clear of this bloody forest – we should easily make Scherben by nightfall.' She turned to her gunner mage and smiled. 'How does the sound of a hot meal and a warm bed grab you?'

'Like nothing that's ever grabbed me before.'

CHAPTER
FORTY-ONE

KILLIAN SAT WITH HIS CHEEK PRESSED AGAINST THE cold moss-covered wall and stared out at the garden beyond his prison. With the rations exhausted, Raven had left for the village below to buy something to keep him alive. He grabbed a waterskin and took a deep swig. Somehow, he'd managed to stay in control of his body for a few days, but he felt his strength fading with every minute, and with Raven gone, it was even more of a strain. He wiped his mouth with his shirt sleeve and set the water down. Crusty scabs flanked by violet bruises covered his knuckles. The monster inside was determined to hurt him. As he gazed longingly through the bars at the swishing emerald grasses and wild flowers, his body became rigid. He needed Raven back. The demon was trying to mount an attack.

He thrust one hand through the bars and dug it into the grass, fingers grasping at the cool mud. The other clutched his chest in an attempt to placate his burning heart. Hot sweat poured down his face, stinging his eyes and the cuts on his lips. The now-all-too-familiar pain of the rotten spirit bubbled up through his body. His heart raced, and his breath became short and quick. The first bolt of pain ripped through him. It hurt. It hurt so much. It was like his blood had turned to lava and was scorching a path of agony through his body. He tilted his head back and cried out. Before he had a chance to recover, more pain lanced through him. His back arched, and he screamed, his eyes filling with water.

He blinked away the tears and sweat and tried to focus on something. There was a crack in the ceiling. Growling in his throat, he stared at that crack and the moss that had gathered around it. The whole left side of his face bloomed with agony. It felt like his cheekbone was slipping underneath his eye. He dug his fingernails into his chest and tore clumps of grass and earth from the garden with his other hand, but he did not take his eyes away from that crack.

He took a deep breath and held it, then blew it all out. He repeated this several times, counting with each breath. Slowly, he regained control over his breathing, yet still he didn't take his eyes from the crack. It ran across the breadth of his tomb, widening in the middle. Thin plants crawled out of the wider parts and peered down at him. They were probably sneering with haughty disgust at how pathetic he was. Killian curled his lip at them and swore. They could sneer all they wanted. They weren't having to deal with this.

What was he thinking? Sneering plants? He was losing his mind.

He loosened his grip on the grass and let go of his body. Five thin crescents welled up with blood on his chest. He put his hands on the floor and eased himself up. The spirit seemed to have backed off. He leant against the stone wall and breathed out a great sigh of relief; he'd survived another battle. A cool breeze whistled in from the garden, and he sucked it all into his lungs. Where was Raven? He needed him.

Heat raced through his body, and he stumbled forward. It was attacking again. His body convulsed, and he groaned. He tried to roll over; he had to see that crack. If he could focus on that, he'd be all right. He kicked at the floor uselessly with his heels and pushed himself up with trembling arms. Pain coursed through him, binding itself to him and refusing to let go. His arms gave way, and he fell, twisting with agony.

'Stop it!' he cried out.

In answer, the pain grew more intense. A vile hissing noise and the rumbling of deep distant laughter filled his head. He reached forward with bent claw-like hands, trying to seize hold of the bars, hoping that clinging to something solid would help him stay in control. The bars were dancing and waving at him from the other side of the world. Gathering the last ounce of strength he had, he dragged himself towards the door. Pain was all over him; his skin was burning, his eyes bursting open, forced out of his skull by his cheekbone. Even his scalp hurt when his hair moved. Crawling along the floor was like a form of self-inflicted torture.

'Killian!'

A voice cut through the din. Was it real? Was he hearing things? He lifted his head and saw a dark shape framed by a pair of even darker wings crouching by the door. Its hand was reaching through towards him.

'Killian!'

He lifted his arm and feebly stretched for the offered hand. His vision was a distorted mess. He swiped for the hand and missed. It took everything he had to lift his arm and try again. This time the dark shape grabbed him; it clung on tight and dragged him towards it. Killian's body fell limp as he was pulled towards the light down a long endless corridor. Everything about him wobbled, everything was soft. He tried to lift his head to see the crack. That would help, that would keep him there. The crack and those sneering plants would save him. Another hand gripped him tightly on the shoulder and pulled him up to his knees. He lolled forward, his chest pressing against the bars. The cool, clarifying bars. He wanted to melt through them. Fall apart and make all the pain stop.

'Killian, stay with me.'

That voice again, he knew that voice. He reached for it. It lingered in front of him in a cloud of black and purple hues. If he could anchor himself to the voice, he'd be all right. His fingers moved through the smoke, but he couldn't grip it. There was nothing solid. He cried out, and his body refused to move anymore.

The black-and-purple shade didn't let go; it held him tight. 'Come on, Killian, be all right,' he whispered.

Slowly, Killian lifted his head, and his eyes peeled open. A comforting yet devastatingly handsome face filled his vision. 'Thank you, Raven.'

CHAPTER FORTY-TWO

The sun was slowly setting, casting beams of rich orange and red onto the windows of the town of Rinden. It was a welcome sight. Lily was sweat covered and exhausted; Blake looked even more so. His hair was stuck to his forehead in a damp, greasy sheet. They'd barely slept as they'd hurried back to their docked ship – any lost time and they could lose Killian forever.

'After I've got what we need,' said Lily as they paced through the town, their steeds' hooves clip-clopping on the cobbles, 'we'll stay a night and leave first thing in the morning. I don't know about you, but I need a bath and a hot meal.'

Blake nodded and then ventured to speak. 'Tell me if I'm asking too much, but how are you going to get this plant?'

'I have an old contact that spends a lot of time in the oceans.'

Blake chuckled. 'Now I have more questions.'

Lily smiled. 'I'll show you. You deserve to see. Maybe you'll get some inspiration for a story.'

'Captain, you don't have to share your secrets with me, I'm ju—'

'Just one of my most trusted crew members. I know.'

Blake's pale skin flushed scarlet.

Lily scanned the streets until she spied an inn with a stable. The building was painted white and adorned with blackened beams, and a wooden sign hung on a post outside. She took her coat off, pulled a pair of goggles from the inside pocket, and then handed it to Blake.

'There're some coins in the pocket. Go in and book us a couple of rooms for the night. Leave my coat in my room – it'll only get in my way. Book the beasts in too,' she added, nodding at their road-worn horses and wondering if they'd be able to manage the return journey.

Blake nodded and ducked inside while Lily waited outside.

She watched the town as it drifted by. People rushed about with places to be, urgent looks etched into their faces. Some sauntered, and others were blind drunk, their slurring voices filtering through the air. Colonies of boisterous gulls gathered on the sloping slate rooftops and squawked. A flicker of a smile dashed across her lips. It didn't matter where in the world she went, the seabirds were always aggressive and dominant, their cries easily carrying above those of the townsfolk. They knew what they wanted and how to get it. What a charmed life they must lead.

The inn door squeaked, and Blake stepped back into the street, followed by a young boy of about fifteen.

'Done,' he said, brushing his dark hair from his eyes. He took the horses' reins from Lily and passed them to the young man, then pressed a coin into his palm.

'Let's get to the docks,' said Lily.

As they walked towards the sea down the narrow streets of Rinden, Lily gave Blake a rough idea of her plan. A pang of shame struck her as she spoke.

'I need to sneak onto the ship and get something from my cabin. I'll meet up with you afterwards.'

'Aye, Captain.'

She sighed. 'Am I a bad captain?'

'Of course not,' said Blake. 'Why?'

'I'm sneaking on board my own ship.'

'Sometimes avoiding explaining something that doesn't make sense is for the best. Take it from someone who knows,' he replied. 'And we need to do this, or who knows what will happen.'

'What if Ulrich's right? What if it's best to leave Killian locked away?' A pain lanced through her chest as she spoke. 'Isn't that for the best?'

'I don't know.' Blake chewed his lip and glanced up at a cluster of chattering gulls. 'But I doubt he'd leave any of us like that. Maybe leaving him would guarantee success, but if we get him out, we can keep on fighting. I don't think I could live with myself if I left him like that.'

The pungent reek of salt-and-seaweed-infused nets filled the air, signalling their arrival at the docks. Lily eyed the moored ships bobbing gently on the lapping waves. The *Tempest* – her ship, her kingdom – stood tall and majestic amongst them. Her stomach twisted. She knew exactly how to sneak on board and had always had a planned route should the need arise, though in her mind, she'd always been sneaking on board to heroically save her crew, not to creep past them. She glanced to the left at the miles of rock pools set beneath craggy cliff faces; she wouldn't be seen there.

'Blake, I want you to meet me over there.' She motioned to the dark sea-worn cliffs. 'Wait for me, and take these.' She slipped her boots off.

'Aye, Captain, and good luck.'

Lily scanned the dock once more. It was lined with makeshift market stalls cobbled together with wood and stained cloth. Baskets of fresh fish, crabs, lobsters and mussels were displayed on each one, guarded by a fisherman or woman attempting to sell their goods before the end of the day. As a result, the docks were busy, which was perfect for what she had in mind. Stray cats and dogs bounded up and down the cobbles. Some begged for scraps while others tried their best to steal what they could.

Shouts of 'Lobster! Crab! Lamprey!' boomed around the docks.

Lily hurried along the flat grey-stone path, weaving in and out of the workers, shoppers and whiskered opportunists. When she reached a break in the stalls, she approached the edge of the docks. The *Tempest* was moored a few ships away. She glanced around to make sure no one was looking in her direction, set her goggles over her eyes and dived into the harbour.

The salty sea was cool and welcoming after her sweaty ride through the countryside. She remained underwater as she swam towards the ship; surfacing would only risk being seen. Despite the churned murk of the harbour water, she picked out the *Tempest* with ease among the other docked ships.

She swam around to the stern and grabbed the wood to the left of the rudder. Her muscles tensed, and she hauled herself out of the sea. She yanked her goggles down around her neck, gripped the wood tightly and began to climb. It was slippery and difficult to find handholds, and her body still ached from her fight with Killian. Damn that stupid enlii. The journey had exhausted her too, and climbing up the stern dripping wet wasn't a leisure activity.

A cold wind blew in from the sea; she shivered and paused. Her fingers were numb. She edged her hand down to her mouth and blew a blast of hot breath onto it to try and waken it. Any normal person would be in a lot of pain from the cold, probably with splitting knuckles, so she should count herself lucky. Though, sometimes, feeling temperatures could be incredibly bothersome. It wasn't that it hurt her – it just made her uncomfortable.

She pressed her head against the weather-worn wood and closed her eyes. For a brief moment, her grimace melted into a smirk as a memory drifted back – glowing lights in the black starlit sea, a half-naked Killian with a blanket. Sometimes being cold did have its advantages. Her grin faded as she recalled the last time she'd seen him. If she didn't hurry, she'd lose him forever.

She wriggled life back into her fingers and carried on climbing. It was hard going, but she was almost there. She gritted her teeth as she negotiated the platform that jutted out below her cabin. With trembling muscles, she pulled herself up and over it. She could have used her ring to give herself a boost of enhanced strength, but she didn't want to risk it. Not yet. She may need that strength in the future, and the thought of her ring fading to grey scared her. She'd never fully drained it before, and now was not the time to be vulnerable – though it seemed she was vulnerable to people possessed by an enlii. How annoying.

She stood on the ledge, back to the ship, catching her breath while staring down at the oily-looking waters lapping at the hull. She turned around, stretched her arms up and reached for the ledge above. With a final strain of muscles, she pulled herself up and onto the window ledge outside her cabin.

With one hand she clung to the frame, and with the other she reached for her belt and unsheathed a dagger. There was still dry blood on it. Killian's blood. She flattened herself against the glass and worked the blade in between the frame and the wood, sliding it up and down, searching out the hidden latch. There was a click, and the window swung open. Lily tumbled through onto her bed.

For a heartbeat, she lay still and soaked up the ambience of her beloved cabin, then slid off the bed to her bare feet. She padded across the room to a set of drawers and opened the bottom one. A fake panel lay in the bottom of the drawer. She removed it to reveal the oaken box with the octopus carved on the lid. Inside was the spindle shell. She took it from its green-velvet bed and snapped the box shut.

It was strange being in her cabin. Everything felt so distant and yet so familiar. Her captain's hat dangled from her hatstand, the emerald-green feather winking at her in the low light. Raven's beautiful painting of the pastel village beckoned her to it. It wanted her to dive into it and never return, to find peace, tranquillity and happiness. Books, maps, writing paper, make-up, wine bottles, rum bottles, silky bedsheets – it was all hers, and yet there was something different about the room. It felt off, as if she didn't belong there anymore.

Before she could think any more absurd thoughts, she scurried back to the window and climbed onto the ledge. Once outside, she pulled the window shut and used her dagger to drop the hidden latch. She put her goggles back on and dived into the sea, keeping beneath the waves as she swam from the ship.

Guilt rippled through her as she moved through the water. She'd deceived her loyal crew. What was becoming of her? And what were those disgusting feelings the cabin was dredging out of her? She didn't belong? Utter nonsense. It was all Killian's fault; if he hadn't got himself into this situation, she wouldn't be feeling like this. Though, if he hadn't done what he'd done, the world would probably be in considerable danger. However, she could just leave him there, locked in his tomb, and as Ulrich had said, the world would almost be guaranteed safety. He'd eventually die, and the orm would go with him.

But she couldn't leave him. Why couldn't she leave him? It would make everything much simpler. The world would be protected, and she could go about her life without him. Surely that was her dream: a life without Killian and all the irritating things that came with him. All those confusing thoughts would be gone, and she could bask in the glory of knowing she'd helped to save the world from . . . something. An evil porcelain mask. A murderous porcelain mask. Something dark and foreboding that haunted her dreams.

She surfaced in the shadows of the cliffs, well away from the docks. Squinting at the shore, she spied Blake sitting on a dark seaweed-covered rock, smoking his pipe. Perhaps he'd catch some shrimp while he waited. Lily gripped the opalescent shell tight and dived beneath the waves once more.

She swam down about fifteen feet before she put the shell to her lips and blew. There was no sound, so she blew again. Still nothing. Her chest tightened, and a sickness built in her throat. It wasn't working. Nothing was coming. Her hands floated limp at her sides; her body was numb. She'd failed him. Killian was lost. She was freezing cold, soaking wet and utterly exhausted, and it was all for nothing.

Then the water began to glow with a bright turquoise. Shafts of silver shimmered through the currents. Her heart pounded, and her spirits lifted. Green, blue, cyan, azure, jade, emerald – they all mixed together and surrounded her. The Big Blue was coming, just like the ocean spirit had promised her.

CHAPTER FORTY-THREE

KILLIAN REACHED THROUGH THE BARS AND GRABBED the offered food, his heart pounding and his arms trembling. He couldn't cram it into his mouth fast enough. Thick pastry split open and filled his mouth with cheese and some kind of smoked meat. He didn't care what it was. It was food, and that was all that mattered. It was such a relief to eat again.

'Enjoying that?' asked Raven.

Killian wiped the crumbs from his mouth with greasy fingers. 'This is the best thing I've ever eaten.'

It didn't take him long to consume everything – it was like he inhaled the food. He sighed and leant back against the wall. An icy gust blew in through the bars, and he shuddered. A cold night was on the way.

'Here.' Raven pushed his cloak through the bars.

'Won't you be cold?' asked Killian as he reluctantly took it.

Raven shook his head. 'I have other ways of keeping warm.'

He stood up and removed his shirt. His ludicrous body and gorgeously tanned skin still drove a spike of envy through Killian's chest. With a rush of air, two huge purple-black wings appeared. Raven sat down cross-legged and wrapped his feathery wings about his body. His purple eyes shimmered in the oncoming dusk.

'I don't think I'll ever get used to that,' said Killian, pulling up the hood of the cloak.

'You're one to talk.'

'A little bit of glowing is nothing compared to those,' said Killian, jutting his chin out in Raven's general direction.

'If you say so.'

A comfortable silence fell between them. Raven looked snug all wrapped up in his wings, and Killian was cosy in the cloak. The evening sky was cloudless and littered with faint stars. Only a precious few had the opportunity to peer down between the castle walls and into the strange hidden courtyard. Half a silver moon shone amongst the stars, casting ghostly shadows all around.

Killian closed his eyes; it was so quiet, so peaceful. Insects rustled in the undergrowth, and far below in Appsen, owls hooted. Raven's cloak smelt like him, like a crackling campfire on a cloudless night, somehow both woody and fresh. He wrapped his arms about his head. If only he weren't locked in a mausoleum. If only he weren't possessed by something intent on taking over his body. If only he didn't feel like he was dying, this place wouldn't be so bad. A sharp bolt of pain raced up his spine; he tensed and grunted in his throat but remained in control. The demon was resting, gathering strength for its next big push.

'You all right?' Raven asked.

'Fine,' Killian lied, 'twitch in my spine.'

Raven nodded and regarded Killian through soft eyes. 'Would you like to know about me?'

Killian was taken aback. The mysterious man was offering up his secrets. It would certainly help him to keep his mind off the monster within him. 'Oh, so now I'm dying, you finally decide to tell me about your sordid past.'

Raven smiled and edged towards the gate. 'I know it hurts you, Killian. I know you're terrified, and I can't promise everything will be all right, but I am here for you.'

'Thank you,' Killian croaked. He pulled his knees close to his chest and wrapped his arms around them.

'The closest comparison I can use to what I am, or was, are the sun messengers I've read about in the texts of Santonos. These benevolent winged beings are said to have descended from the sky to bring the people of the kingdom good news and comfort to ease their suffering. My kind also came from the sky, and we have wings, but that is where our similarities end. I used to kill your kind to keep the world in order. Disease, natural disasters, even the act of tripping and breaking your neck could be attributed to us. Of course, not all death was our doing – humans find many ways to cut their lives short.' Raven paused, his purple eyes focusing on the grass. 'My brothers and sisters took great pleasure in destroying lives. They enjoyed watching the carnage and despair. I, however, saw something different. I began to watch the people. They seemed to find such meaning in life, in one another, in nature. Everything was fleeting, and yet they made it count – or at least tried to. It made me feel so alone. I was jealous of you, with your lives, dreams and hopes. I wanted what you had.

'One day I saw a woman. She was a beautiful Venarian. Hair like midnight, eyes the colour of honey. Every day she worked in her family's vineyards and olive groves. I couldn't help myself – I had to come down and see her properly. For days I watched her. She'd hum and sing while she worked. It was the most beautiful sound I'd ever heard. Swinging, lilting, full of joy. During the hottest part of the day, she'd sit under the fluttering vines and draw. Sometimes she'd look right at me and smile even though she couldn't see me. It was strange.

'Every day I returned to her. I was fascinated. I couldn't stop myself. One particularly hot and dusty day, she slipped on the smooth rock of the terrace. Without even thinking about it, I manifested myself and caught her. I remember she gave a tiny scream of surprise, and I set her on her feet and vanished as quickly as I could. My body tingled all over as I made my way back home. I'd never felt like that before.

'I returned to her the following day. She got her sketchpad out again during her midday break, and to my surprise, she started drawing me into her landscape. A new feeling surged through my body. It's hard to describe, but I suppose it was joy. For the first time, someone wanted me. She smiled as she drew, and occasionally she talked to me. I didn't know what to do; I was too nervous to appear again.

'Every day she'd call out to me, always with a smile, and told me not to be afraid of her. After a week, I couldn't take it anymore. I wanted her – I needed her. While she was adding the final touches to her drawing, I made myself visible. She was so absorbed with finishing it she didn't even notice me, but when she did, she jumped and dropped her pad. She didn't speak for a few minutes. Her breathing was off, but I managed to calm her down. We sat in the olive groves and talked. It's still one of the best days of my life.' He cast his gaze to the stars. 'I was so happy, Amaranta.'

He paused and drew his finger over his eyes. 'She didn't believe me when I told her what I was – I left out the horrible parts – yet she was playful about it. She made me prove it, so I showed her my wings. I won't go into detail over what else happened that afternoon – I'm not Tom. As the evening drew in, I knew I had to go, but I promised her I'd return.

'As soon as I arrived back home, I was immediately set upon by my siblings. They'd been spying on me, and I'd broken a rule. I panicked. I thought they were going to kill her. I tried to throw them off, but four on one is never good odds, and they beat me down.

'I came to in a dark cell. As soon as my eyes opened, I was hauled to my feet and dragged away. I was brought out before our master, our father, Doradi. He'd already decided my fate; there was no point in even arguing.' Raven stopped.

'Raven?' said Killian. It was clearly a painful experience to talk about, and he just wanted to break out of his prison and give the beautiful man a hug.

'I'm sorry,' he said, shaking his head. 'To think it still affects me all these years later. He had my wings ripped from my back. My tattoo, which marked me as one of them, was blackened. I endured days of savage beatings. There were times when I wanted to die, but the thought of Amaranta kept me going. When they grew tired of their torture, I was brought before Doradi again, and he told me my eternal fate.

'I had upset the balance between the humans and us by revealing our existence, and as a result, the world was now under my protection and mine alone. Doradi and my brothers and sisters were leaving to find a new untouched world to watch over and manipulate. I was to be left behind with my ruined world. From then on, every death, disease and disaster would be my fault. Doradi granted me immortality. I was to live among the humans as a mortal but remain immortal. Everyone I'd ever meet would die, yet I'd be doomed to live. As a parting gift, he ordered my siblings to leave Amaranta alive for me.'

Killian was almost too afraid to ask, but his curiosity won over. 'Did you go back to her?'

'I did, and I fell in love. The tattoo didn't bother her; she told me she liked it – the blackened brand of a disgrace. She gave me the name I use today, telling me it suited me better. A new name for a new life. My wings returned – I found I could summon them at will. And for five years everything was well. We worked on the farm and drank wine in the balmy summer evenings. When we were sure nobody was about, I'd take her flying.' His eyes glazed over, and he smiled. 'I'd get her as close to the ocean waves as possible. Sometimes I'd dunk her in – she always pretended to be furious, but I knew she wasn't. There were times when we'd sit amongst the olive groves all night, talking until the stars faded and the sun came up.

'Then she got sick, and there was nothing I could do. She died at forty-two, taking my secret with her. After she was gone, I lived in Venario for some years, moving from place to place. She always dreamed of living in this little village called Magniroa. She didn't make it, but I did. She would have liked it there.'

'Raven, I'm sorry,' said Killian.

'You've nothing to be sorry for. I would rather have had those five years with Amaranta than nothing at all. It took me a long time to realise that. Her death still hurts, but at least we had a chance.' Raven rubbed his eyes. 'Don't you think I'm a monster?'

Killian sat up straight. 'Why would I think that?'

'I was responsible for deaths, I killed your kind for hundreds of years, I upset the balance, I've got these!' he said, seizing his wings, his eyes shimmering.

Killian shook his head. 'Raven, you did the world a favour. Without you upsetting the balance, they'd still be here, watching us, meddling, picking and choosing if we lived or died to suit them. The lives you saved by falling in love make up for those you took. And as for your wings, if I'm truthful, I'm jealous of them.'

Raven let go of his wings and looked to the grass beneath him. Killian grabbed the bars and pulled himself towards him.

'You're *not* a monster,' he said.

'I . . .' Raven paused and shuddered. 'Thank you.'

CHAPTER
FORTY-FOUR

IT HAD BEEN A LONG RIDE FROM MORFORD – THE closest town to Varo's hideout – to Brackmouth, but Sasha hadn't ridden alone. For most of the journey, a well-to-do-looking family of five had stared at her, apart from the baby; the baby had screamed constantly. They'd left her in peace at Charrington, and she'd travelled the rest of the way on her own.

She alighted from the carriage in Brackmouth's town square and paid the driver. Night had already descended upon the small fishing town, thick and dark. The cobbled streets glowed orange with the light of the oil lamps that adorned various buildings around the town. She stood still, listening to clip of the horse's hooves and the creaky roll of the wheels as the carriage melted away into the darkness. A shudder ran up her arms, and she pulled her cloak closer. But she wasn't cold. She was nervous. It had been such a long time since she'd last seen Ruby. What if she didn't want her anymore? What if she turned her away?

She ambled about the town, too self-conscious to walk into the Laughing Swan straight away. She had to build up to that. A handful of late-roosting gulls swooped onto a nearby rooftop and cackled at her. Without a true purpose – other than avoidance – she wandered the streets and veered off through the network of fishermen's houses. The scent of salt and seaweed grew the farther in she went. Perhaps she should go to the river that split the town in half and sit and look at it. Maybe sleep next to it, then deliver Varo's letter – she was tempted to read it but had managed to resist the urge – first thing in the morning and return to the others.

She balled her fists up; she was being pathetic. Varo had allowed her to leave, to visit Ruby; she shouldn't squander the opportunity. Her mind fell to Theo; she hoped he was all right. She owed it to him to make the most of her trip. She turned around and walked back in the direction of the Laughing Swan.

It didn't take her long to locate the tavern. The welcoming warm orange glow lit it up like a beacon in the gloomy night. Light dappled the cobbles surrounding it and beckoned her in. She put her hand on the thick wooden door and pushed it open. Instantly, the smell of woodsmoke, tobacco and beer hit her. It was comforting and nostalgic. She glanced about the tavern. Soft murmurs swam in the air. There were three separate groups playing cards but no one else other than that. It was late, after all, and a quiet night. She looked to the bar to see a flash of flowing blonde hair disappear though a doorway.

With no real plan formed, Sasha approached the bar and sat in one of the tall chairs. It was hard and wobbled slightly, but she didn't care. A thick-set barmaid with deep brown eyes approached her.

'What can I get you?' she asked.

'A beer's fine,' said Sasha. She took off her dull green travelling cloak and hung it on the back of her chair. Underneath, she was wearing her favourite brown leather doublet. It hugged the curves of her body, cutting her a slim yet shapely figure.

'Sure,' the woman replied. 'We're closing soon, so you best drink fast, me luvver.'

A groan rose from one of the card tables, followed by the scraping of chairs.

'You need to do something about this guy, Brinni,' one of the card players called over. 'He's a cheat!'

'Barrington,' said Brinni in a firm-yet-friendly tone.

'Hey,' a different voice shouted back, 'I don't cheat, I'm just good. If you wanna talk about cheating, maybe you should talk to O'Shea.'

'Oi! Killian ain't here to defend himself, so I'll have less of that,' said Brinni.

'Yeah, yeah.'

Sasha looked over her shoulder. The group of men were throwing on their coats.

'Done for the evening?' Brinni asked.

'Yeah, thanks. Probably see ya tomorrow.'

'Of course you'll see me tomorrow,' said Brinni with a broad toothy grin as she stepped out from behind the bar. 'You guys can't keep away.'

Sasha made a start on her beer. It tasted good, but it was lacking something. Her gaze focused on the door where she'd seen the blonde hair vanish. Her chest ached. Perhaps her doublet was too tight?

One by one, the other card tables emptied, and the players stumbled off into the night. A gust of cold air blew in as each of the players left. The bar grew quieter. No more mumbles. No more whispers.

Sasha supped at her beer in the hope that if she left the tiniest amount in her mug, she wouldn't be kicked out and into the night. Where was Ruby? Why had she gone? She took another sip. Footsteps approached her, and a shadow fell over the notched bar in front of her.

'It's closing time, me handsome,' said Brinni.

Sasha glanced around the tavern. She was indeed the only one left. Sleeping by the river it was, then. She was so foolish. Why did she think she could waltz back into Ruby's life after all this time like nothing had happened, like she hadn't been away for months? She ran a finger sadly around the flamed edge of her necklace. Tomorrow she'd throw it into the sea and move on. A door creaked.

'It's okay, Brinni. You can finish. I'll clean up after this one.'

Sasha's body surged with joy at the sound of that voice – sweet with just a playful hint of sarcasm. She couldn't bring herself to look up, so she stared into her beer mug.

'If you're sure, Rubes,' said Brinni.

There was no reply, but judging by the sound of Brinni's footsteps, there had been a nod. Sasha drank, not lifting her head. She was so nervous. Were her trousers too tight? As with her doublet, she'd worn her favourite figure-hugging pair of leather trousers because she knew exactly how they made her arse look.

'Night, Ruby,' she heard Brinni say.

The door opened and then closed. A key turned. A lock dropped. Then silence. Sasha downed the remains of her drink. She was such an idiot. Taking a deep breath, she slid off the chair and turned to face Ruby.

Ruby was standing a few feet in front of her. Her arms were folded, and her face was stern. Long blonde hair flowed down her body, begging for Sasha's hands to get lost in it. A disc of amber glistened around her neck – she still wore it. Pale green eyes stared at Sasha from under a thick fringe; they were hurt, and she was ashamed.

'Ruby, I can explain. I—'

'Don't . . . Don't say anything yet.'

Ruby closed the gap between them in a few strides. She put her hands on Sasha's hips and pushed her back against the bar. She leant close, her lips parted slightly, and she kissed her. It was a kiss full of longing and passion. Sasha put her arms around Ruby's back, pulling her as close as she could, kissing her back.

Heat surged through Sasha as Ruby moved her hands up her body. Cord strained against leather – her doublet being unlaced. Within moments it was undone, and Ruby was pulling it open. The beautiful landlady trailed kisses down her neck and over her bare chest. She was so tender and sensual. This was not at all what she'd expected.

'Ru—'

'Shh,' Ruby cooed as she moved her smooth hand into Sasha's trousers. 'Just feel what you missed.' The warmth of her breath teased Sasha's skin.

Sasha gasped and gripped the bar to keep steady. She gazed at the ceiling and willingly allowed her lover to take her somewhere warm, safe and pleasurable.

CHAPTER FORTY-FIVE

SHIMMERING AZURE LIGHT ENGULFED LILY ROTH-bone. Or was it turquoise? Blue, green or sapphire? It was *that* colour, the one she'd not seen since her early teenage years. The colour that didn't belong to anyone or anything. It was the colour of life, of a spirit, of her saviour. It swirled around her, turning her body about in the water until she had no idea what direction she was facing. Up was down, down was up, left and right had no meaning. She clutched the spindle shell tight in her fist, unsure if she should blow it again. At last, the light began to settle.

It condensed in front of her into the form of a naked humanoid. Bright turquoise skin pocked with patches of twinkling green and silver scales wrapped around the spirit's body. Lean, defined muscles shimmered beneath that skin. A broad chest tapered down into dramatic sumptuous curves at the waist and hips. Long powerful legs seamlessly blended into elegant silver-lined flippers. Thick strips of silver-blue kelp-like hair billowed over a wide pair of shoulders and reached out towards her on the current. A pair of metallic-blue lips turned up into a smile. Large eyes devoid of pupils swirled with shades of green and glowed with an intense power.

Lily couldn't help but marvel at the great spirit, transfixed by every inch of the beautiful body before her. She couldn't remember the Big Blue looking this incredible, but their last meeting had been a long time ago.

'Liliana Maggiore, my gift to the world, we meet again,' the spirit said in a soft and musical voice like a gentle current.

'Hello, Blue,' she said, 'and it's Lily Rothbone now.' Somehow, her words travelled through the waves.

'Rothbone,' the Big Blue repeated, a touch of abhorrence colouring that mystical tone. 'Maggiore was such a beautiful name.' Ethereal green eyes looked her up and down. 'No matter the name, I see you have grown into a fine woman.'

'You look better than the last time we met too.'

'I am whatever I want to be.' The spirit slowly swam towards her and took her hands. Intricately patterned emerald fins adorned the backs of the Big Blue's arms, waving in the currents like seaweed. 'Now tell me, Lily, why have you summoned me?'

'I need your help,' she said, not taking her eyes from the entrancing face that filled her vision. 'A friend of mine's in trouble, and I need your help to save him. He doesn't have much time.'

'You want my help to save another?' The being's voice was captivating. It was like the whole ocean was whispering to her.

'Yes,' she said. Her skin prickled, and her pulse raced.

'You know you may never summon me again.'

'Yes.' She nodded as best she could while underwater, her hair swirling around her like a cloud of ink.

'And yet you use your one request to save another?'

'Yes.'

'Then it would seem that I gave the world a true gift.'

'There are plenty who would dispute that,' she said.

'Let them.' The Big Blue pulled her forwards, then let go. She floated about a foot away from the magnificent ocean spirit's body. 'How may I assist you?' Long flat hair swept across Lily's cheeks.

'I need a plant that grows somewhere in the oceans to help me free my friend.'

The Big Blue's eyes narrowed as the spirit listened to her describe the plant. Once she'd finished, the being swam up and above her. A great blue shadow towered over Lily.

'Lie flat, facing the seabed.'

Lily did as she was told – it was strange for her to be taking orders for once. The Big Blue's arms wrapped around her waist. Rubbery green fins brushed against her stomach; it was an odd sensation but not unpleasant.

'You're coming with me,' the voice of the oceans murmured. 'Put your hands on my arms.'

As soon as Lily gripped on, the being kicked with a mighty pair of legs. Powerful flippers effortlessly propelled them forwards.

They raced through the water, passing all manner of sea creatures. Massive sharks floated by, too stunned by their speed to even attempt a snap. They passed a pod of gigantic whales, whose sleepy eyes were unable to focus on the illuminated blur that was Lily and the Big Blue. Lily's eyes, however, were open wide, absorbing everything. A longworm came into view, a great flat sea beast easily the length of her ship, its back covered with a brown shell and coated in algae and barnacles. She knew these innocuous creatures favoured the waters of Venario, often loitering in the harbours, so they'd travelled far in the space of no time at all.

They tore through a wandering shoal of jellyfish, whose transparent forms were touched with a faint shade of purple, their long tentacles glowing white. Despite their deadly tendency, they were beautiful.

As they burst free of the jellies, the Big Blue changed direction sharply, powering them upwards. They erupted from the sea, and Lily cried with delight as she stared at the choppy waves below. Then they plunged down, going deeper and deeper. Flashing neon lights twinkled and scattered as they swam through them, filling the water with thousands of tiny blue and green stars. Lily smiled sadly, and her chest tightened.

'What is the matter?' asked the Big Blue, levelling them off.

'Nothing. Those lights reminded me of something, that's all. It's nothing.'

'It didn't feel like nothing.'

'What d'you mean?'

'Your heart skipped – I felt it,' the oceans murmured back.

'Oh.'

They swam on through the darkened depths. Lily couldn't tell just how deep they were, but almost every creature they passed glowed. Fish pulsed with lines of rainbow-coloured neon lights, and jellyfish drifted on the currents, glowing with purple-and-blue light. Gigantic squid appeared from the darkness, great monstrous things with golden eyes as big as Lily's head and beaks twice the size of that.

After a few minutes of silence, she spoke. 'I was hurt a few days ago.'

'How so?' the Big Blue asked.

'I was punched, and I felt it. I've felt pain before, but not since I used to . . .' Shame silenced her.

'Since you used to what?'

'I used to fight for money. Sometimes I'd slip the ring on and off to make it seem realistic. But one day I came up against a man who could hurt me. He drew blood even when I had the ring on. That man's my first mate now, and he's not what you'd call normal.'

'Is he from this world?'

'No.' She felt a pang of guilt for blurting out Raven's secret so freely, but in her defence, she doubted the Big Blue would tell anyone.

'And this other person who hurt you, are they from this world?'

'Yes, he is.'

The spirit abruptly stopped swimming and sank down to face her. 'The ring should always protect you physically, unless you've used all its strength.'

'And if I did that, I'd have to take it off or it would drain me of my life. I've never used it all – I'm too scared.'

'Show it to me.'

Lily held her hand out, and the being ran a huge webbed finger gently across the surface of the ring, examining its craftsmanship. Blue-green fingers closed around it, and a pulse of energy passed between Lily and the sea spirit. The Big Blue gripped her shoulders and stared at her, green eyes swirling with compassion.

'The ring won't protect you against those from another world. It is attuned to the nature and balance of this one. Who attacked you? Who hurt you?'

'It was my friend, the one I'm trying to save.'

The Big Blue frowned. 'I don't understand.'

'It was him, but it wasn't. It was his body, but not his mind.'

'And he pulls no magic from the Otherside?'

'No, he can't wield it,' she said.

'Has he ever hurt you before?'

'No, never.' But there was that one time in her cabin when he returned from the Drop. He'd squeezed her hip, and it had hurt, hadn't it? No, it couldn't have. It was all in her mind.

The Big Blue nodded, and the being's long hair wriggled like streamers in the breeze.

'Surely it was the enlii,' she said. 'The dead spirit inside him. The thing I'm trying to save him from. That's what hurt me, not him.'

'No, the dead cannot hurt you, Lily, unless they control a human who can.'

'Are you saying Killian can hurt me?'

'It would appear so.'

'How?'

'I don't know.' Swirling other-worldly eyes gazed at her. 'But if he cares about you as much as you obviously care about him, I'm sure he won't use your weakness against you.'

Killian, my weakness. Perfect, typical and painfully true.

'Are you ready to continue?'

She nodded, and with that, her waist was grabbed and they moved again. Lily remained silent. Why of all the people in the world was Killian one of the few who could hurt her? True, he was a pain in the arse, but he always had been. The first time she'd laid her eyes on him, she knew he was trouble. Maybe she should have let him take the bullet instead. Life would definitely be a lot less complicated now. For one thing, she wouldn't be somewhere deep in the ocean.

And the Gramarye would still be locked away from the prying claws of evil porcelain-faced demons.

She smiled thinly to herself; she knew she could never have done that. As well as seeing trouble, she'd also seen something else that night, something that would explain why she kept a single ruby from the necklace they had fought over in her bedside drawer in the hope that one day he'd climb through the window to get it. She screwed her face up; every time she thought of that ruby, she felt pathetic. She closed her eyes and could see it sitting in her drawer, waiting for him. What was her problem? Surely, she didn't. No, she didn't. She hated him, everything about him – his attitude, his remarks, the way he looked at her, the way he carried himself, the feel of his skin, his ridiculously blue eyes, his lips . . . She hated it! All of it. She tensed. Why him? Of all people, why did he have to be her weakness?

It wasn't just that though. She knew all too well what happened if you let love into your life. You became weak. You committed foolish acts, like her father did. Loneliness crushed you twice as hard. You ruined your own life, as well as the lives of those around you. She was already committing a foolish act right now, and she didn't even love Killian. She didn't, she couldn't. It would be her downfall. It was in her blood.

The Big Blue dived down again. Sharp rocks were outlined in the haunting glow of the being's body. They swam around them, going deeper, twisting and turning in the dark waters, until they stopped. The spirit pulled Lily up to a standing position and took her hands. She looked down. Just below her feet was a vast reef. Jagged deep-sea corals glimmered within the green-blue light of the Big Blue. Great clams yawned open, giving Lily a clear view of the inside of their purple mouths.

The Big Blue's legs moved as if walking through the water. An encouraging arm wrapped around Lily's waist and prompted her to do the same. Before long they were both strolling through the water above great swathes of coral. The silvery tentacles of gigantic anemones swayed and shimmied. A cluster of about forty yellow-and-white-striped garden eels wriggled and nodded in the deep-water currents. They dived into the sands simultaneously when Lily's shadow was cast over them.

'We're almost there, Miss Maggiore.'

'I'm Rothbone now,' she replied.

'I prefer Maggiore. Why did you change it?'

'It didn't suit the person I became. It was a part of my past that I had to shed.'

'And what sort of person did you become?'

'A ransacking, murderous bitch of a pirate,' she said bluntly.

'Thank you for being honest.'

'You knew?' she asked.

'I live in the oceans, and you spent a number of years on them.'

'You saw me?' she muttered, slowing in her water walking.

'On some occasions.'

'Why didn't you take the ring off me?'

'Because you are my gift to the world.'

'You're a strange ocean spirit. I've done some evil things. The first thing I did after you gave me the ring was go back to the orphanage and scare Carrow and Nisa half to death. After that, I collected debts for gangsters and lowlifes. I beat people bloody and fought in the streets. Then I decided to return to the sea – it was the place of my rebirth, after all. I built my way up to pirate-queen status. You have to shed a lot of blood to reach that.'

'And your point is?' asked the Big Blue.

'I've been a horrible person. I don't deserve this power.'

'What are you doing now?'

'I don't understand.'

'Tell me what you're doing. Why you're here, with me.'

'Because . . .' She sighed. The being's kelp-like hair skimmed the backs of her arms; it was so smooth and soothing. 'Because I want to save Killian. He means something to me – I don't know what – and I can't bear the thought of him suffering.' She paused and pulled her body back against the Big Blue's. 'That's the main reason. Also, there's the small matter that the world may be in danger. Once I free him, I'll help him protect the . . .' Her voice trailed off. She felt stupid and sick, like at any moment she'd break.

'You see,' said the Big Blue, 'you did deserve it. You'll always be Liliana Maggiore to me, always. I saw something in that poor vulnerable young girl. She was my gift. And I fell in love with the pirate Rothbone. I could still see Maggiore, but she was a woman, a beautiful, strong woman.' The spirit's voice dropped and became pained and low. 'I both yearned and feared the day when you'd finally summon me. I knew I would be able to speak with you again, yet once that time was over, never again.'

'Blue,' she whispered and turned around.

Shimmering muscular arms wrapped around her and held her tight. Lily clung on. This ocean spirit had saved her and deserved her love. But as much as she wanted to give it, she couldn't.

It was the Big Blue who broke the embrace. 'We must find your plant, Miss Maggiore. Time is your enemy,' the spirit murmured, taking her by the hand once more.

CHAPTER FORTY-SIX

'TOM!' SNAPPED FINN. 'WHAT'RE YA DOING TO THAT bloody bird?'

Tom jumped at Finn's bark, his hands still on either side of the soft sleek owl. 'I'm stroking her thin.'

'She don't like it,' she grunted back.

'Yes, you do, don't you, Pops?' Tom stared into the owl's large amber eyes. 'You love it, you love it. You love strokes from old Tommy.' As if in answer, the bird gently nibbled his hand. 'See, she does, Finlay.'

'Pah, if you say so.'

'I do. Don't I?' he added, giving the bird another tickle under the chin before leaving her alone.

Finn was sprawled on the depressed-looking couch constructing a roll-up, her dark eyes intently focused on the tobacco and papers. It was at times like this Tom wished he smoked too, just for something to do. He'd tried it once, but it made his throat feel like overcooked meat, so he didn't try again. Leave the smoking to the experts, like Finn and Blake. He glanced over at the warlock. The old man had been completely silent throughout his pirate occupation. All he did was sit at the round wooden table near the archway that led to the kitchen and read his books. Occasionally, he'd get up and examine whatever it was that he kept in all those jars and bottles in the cupboard. Tom almost felt sorry for him, with his broken hand a limp tangled mess. But then he'd remember Killian, and all sympathy would go out the window.

He frowned. Would Killian ever be the same again? Whatever 'the same again' was for Killian these days. Tom had seen him glow; he'd seen horns – great big ram horns cut from ghostly diamonds. And the way he'd moved hadn't seemed human at all. It wasn't a trick of Tom's panicked and stressed mind. Something was wrong with him, something more than just the enlii. Maybe it was for the best if he stayed locked away.

Tom bit down on his lip. What was he even thinking? Killian was his friend. He'd saved his life. He should want him to be free, both physically and mentally.

'What's with that face?' Finn's voice broke into his thoughts.

'What face?' asked Tom, a little startled.

'Your face. You looked like you were thinkin'.' Finn parked the completed cigarette in the corner of her mouth. 'I don't like it when you think too much – it's always disgusting.'

'Not always.' Tom chuckled. 'I'm actually a very deep person.'

'Oh, aye?'

'Aye,' Tom insisted. 'We got any of them pastry things left? I'm starving.'

'Go look in the kitchen. I ain't ya mum.'

Tom ambled to the kitchen.

'While you're in there, I wouldn't mind a tea an' something to eat myself.'

'Sure, Mum,' he called. A faint growl seeped into the kitchen, and Tom grinned to himself.

He grabbed the matches from the grey-stone worktop and lit the stove, then filled a copper pan with water and set it over the heat. As he waited for it to boil, he picked up a pastry and stared out the window over the warlock's sunken garden. Small yellow-and-green birds flitted about amongst the flowers and bushes, chirping to one another. He took a bite. It tasted divine. It was a tragedy Seth couldn't whip up something like them. The pastry was crisp and fell away in buttery flakes. The jam at the centre was both sweet and tangy.

Tom stared into the window and caught himself looking back. Finn certainly wasn't his mum, but who was? The sad truth was that he didn't know and never would. All he knew of his past was that he was born somewhere other than Vermor and a merchant stole him from his mum, his true mum, as a treasure for his wife. He grew up in Ridley with them, but they weren't his family, they weren't his parents. When he discovered he was no more than an art piece for a rich couple to display to their friends, he ran away. He covered his face in that woman's thick pale make-up to hide his dark skin from anyone who might be looking for him, and he didn't look back.

Who was his dad? Where was his mum? What country was he from? Who was he really? He didn't know. He didn't even know what his real name was. Thomas Gainsborough was an amalgamation of two names from two separate gravestones.

He had a deep sigh and reached for a second pastry. It was just as tasty.

It was Finn who'd found him, after he'd spent the night weeping in the graveyard. She must have known who he was, she must have seen the reward available for his safe return. But she didn't give him up; she took him to Lily and made sure he became a member of the crew. She taught him everything she knew about guns.

'Tom!' Finn growled from the other room. 'You best not be eating everything in there.'

He quickly swallowed. 'No.'

'Liar! It's your turn to stock up anyway. I went last time.'

'Get me a tea, Tom,' grumbled Tom as he shoved a handful of crispy leaves into a bowl and poured the hot water over them. Making a pair of brews was tedious without a teapot; it was such a shame that the captain had smashed Ulrich's perfectly fine one. He glared at the leaves as they twirled through the water, slowly turning it a golden-brown colour, then reached for the strainer. Tea sloshed over the worktop as he slopped it into the mugs. It splashed onto the back of his hand, and he swore under his breath. Tedious. That's what it was, tedious.

'Get me some food, Tom. Go to the shop, Tom.' Balancing the pastries and mugs on a tray, he waddled into the sitting room. 'Anything else you want, Miss Finn?'

Finn frowned, her mousy eyebrows almost meeting in the middle. 'I seem to recall I did all of that yesterday.'

Begrudgingly, Tom put the tray down on the low tiled table in front of Finn. 'All right, maybe you did,' he muttered from the side of his mouth. 'I just forgot is all,' he added with a shrug.

'You always forget those days,' she said, reaching for a sweet treat.

'I should write it down,' said Tom as he flopped next to her on the couch. 'A rota, that'd be good.'

Finn chuckled as if the thought of Tom doing anything like that was incredibly amusing.

Tom grabbed a mug of tea. 'Finn, do you ever think about your mum and dad?'

Finn turned to him, pastry flakes on her lips, her face twisted into a scowl. 'No.'

'Sorry, silly question,' said Tom. He swigged his tea. It was too hot and burned his throat. 'I sometimes think about mine, and I don't even know 'em. My real parents, that is.'

'Mine were bastards, but at least I knew 'em.' Finn wiped her mouth with the back of her hand and pushed her fringe from her eyes.

'I know nothing. Mine could be a king and a queen – I could be a lost prince with a claim to a far-off kingdom. Imagine that, Finn – me, King Tom. I'd make you a lord or something, don't you worry about that.'

Finn laughed. 'Don't ya think they'd look for you if you were a lost prince?'

'Of course not, because then I wouldn't be lost,' said Tom; he was on to something here. 'A lost prince must find his own way back home and claim his kingdom using the strength and determination he's built up along the way. As soon as all this shit with Killian is over, I'm gonna find my kingdom and rule it like I'm supposed to.'

Finn slapped her forehead. 'So, what you're sayin' is, you're too good for us?'

Tom almost spat out his tea. He swallowed, then followed it up with a coughing fit. 'What do you mean?' he wheezed out.

'You wanna go off to the land of La and sit your arse on a throne, no shits given for the rest of us. For me, for Blake, for the cap'n.' She lowered her eyes. 'I suppose I can see your point. Who could ever take the place of the family you know nothin' about?'

'Wait, are you saying *you're* my family?' Tom slammed his mug down onto the table as a swell of joy rushed through his body.

'Did I say that?' asked Finn.

'No, but almost.'

Finn folded her arms and huffed with indifference.

'You did!' Tom pounced on Finn and gave her a tight hug. 'You're my family! My real family,' he gushed, making sure his sentiment was as mawkish as possible.

'Get off, get off,' said Finn, pushing him back and re-adjusting her hair. 'Maybe. You're like an annoying little brother, not that I know what one of those is like.'

'Probably like me,' said Tom, flashing her his most charming grin.

'Probably.'

'You know, maybe I'll give up on this forgotten prince lark and stick around to annoy you.'

'Oh, lucky me,' Finn groaned.

CHAPTER FORTY-SEVEN

With one hand gripping the plant and the other holding on to the Big Blue's arm, Lily was powered through the water at a great speed. Fish, algae and jellies all whipped by her vision in a neon blur, illuminating the darkness of the ocean briefly before fading into the black.

She glanced at the Big Blue's strong muscled arm and longed to look at the sea spirit's face, but at the speed they were travelling, it was impossible. They hadn't spoken since she'd retrieved the plant. The silence that hung between them was painful. She wanted to say something, but she couldn't summon the right words. What exactly do you say to an all-powerful water spirit who's just confessed to loving you? If she didn't say something soon, they'd be back, and she'd never get to see this wonderful being again.

'Blue?' she said, finally cutting through the silence.

'Yes, Lily?' a voice sang to her in all the currents.

'After today I won't see you again.'

'No, you won't.'

'There's no chance, no way we can meet again?'

'I'm sorry.'

Kelp-like hair tickled her back, and she tightened her grip on the spirit's arm. 'That's not fair,' she mumbled. 'Why does it have to be like that?'

'It is the way. I have given you a gift, I have answered your call. There can be no more contact between our two worlds.'

'Who made up these stupid rules?' she snapped.

'I did,' the Big Blue said.

'What?'

'I created the ring, and I found the shell. I enchanted them both with the essence of the oceans and my soul. You cannot see me again.'

'But what will happen if I do?'

'I will die, and the ring will cease to obey you.'

'What! Why would you do that?'

'It was a precaution. I didn't want to become a slave to the human with the shell. I never imagined that someone like you would be the one I gave it to. When I saw you drowning, I knew I had to save you, and I knew I had the power to do so. I saw something in you, and I didn't have the chance to remove my enchantment. I knew it would come back to haunt me.'

'Blue,' she said, shaking her head. 'Thank you.'

'I'll never regret saving you.'

Lily relaxed into the strong grip of the Big Blue's arms, and before long they arrived where she'd used the shell. Strong blue-green arms released her into the waters, and she floated before the ocean dweller. She took a moment to drink in the beautiful majesty of the great spirit of the sea.

'This is where we say goodbye,' the Big Blue said.

'It is.' She swam into the spirit's arms and squeezed tight. She stretched up and kissed a shimmering blue cheek. The Big Blue's skin was smooth and cool, and it glowed softly at the touch of her lips.

'I will miss you, Liliana Maggiore.'

Lily looked up into the eyes of the ocean being. Every shade of green imaginable was swirling in them. 'I'll miss you, Blue,' she said. 'I always thought if things ever got too bad, at least I had that one chance to call you . . . and now, I'm alone.'

'Lily, you're not alone. I won't be around for you, but others will. All you must do is let them.'

She plucked the shell from her belt and held it out. 'Please take it.'

'I cannot.'

'In that case.' Lily took the pure-white cone in her hands and crushed it. Its sparkling shattered remains sailed off in the undersea currents.

'Please will you promise me one thing?' the water spirit asked.

'Anything.'

'When the time is right, become Liliana Maggiore again.'

Lily nodded, her eyes threatening tears. 'I promise.'

'Thank you,' murmured the Big Blue.

She wrapped her arms around the great water spirit one last time.

'Can I ask you for one more favour?' she asked.

'Of course.'

'One of my crew travelled a long way with me. He's on the shore. Will you show yourself to him?'

'It would be my pleasure. I'll make it extra dramatic.'

Beneath them, the ocean surged with power, and frothing white water shot up and billowed over them. Something solid formed under Lily's feet, pushing her and the Big Blue up. They broke the surface, and she clung to the Big Blue, looking down. A great foaming column of water was, to her amazement, lifting them out of the ocean. It sparkled with blue light and flecks of silver and green.

She spied Blake sitting at the edge of a rock pool, and his eyes grew wide. The column of surging water moved towards the shore with both Lily and the Big Blue atop it. When they were close enough, the spirit's gentle webbed hands pressed into her back, encouraging her to step out onto the rocks and go back to her life. She reached back and ran her hand along the fins of the ocean being's arm, then took a step forward onto dry land.

Lily turned around. Her eyes became lost in the beauty of the great spirit of the sea. Turquoise, azure, emerald and jade all shimmered over smooth skin. The silvery patches of scales flashed golden in the final rays of the setting sun. Long green hair cascaded over broad muscular shoulders. Blue lips formed a sad smile. The Big Blue nodded once and leapt backwards into a graceful dive and was gone.

Lily's legs wobbled, and she stumbled to her knees. With a grunt, she yanked her goggles down around her neck and breathed slowly. She put a hand on the cold, hard rocks in front of her and gazed at the silver-blue plant. She clutched it so tightly it hummed against her fingers. She'd done it; she was going to save him, though it had cost her the Big Blue. A shudder coursed through her spine, and she slipped the plant into her pocket. Her skin was icy, her hair was a cold, wet curtain draped over her back and she was exhausted. Bone tired. It had been a long time since she'd felt so drained, emotionally and physically. All she wanted to do was get back to Poll as fast as she could, but she knew even she needed some rest.

Something soft and warm wrapped around her shoulders. She sat up and leant back against it.

'You look like you need it,' said Blake.

She pulled Blake's cloak close to her body and gingerly stood to face him.

'Thank you.' Her body wouldn't stop trembling.

She took a step towards him and stumbled. The gunner caught her and supported her with his shoulder. Lily grasped his arm. All her energy was drained.

'I'll help you, Captain.'

'Thanks. Let's get back to the inn. I need a long soak and a longer drink.'

'Me too.' Blake paused a moment. 'Captain, what was that?'

'A friend.' Her eyes burned with tears. 'A good friend. I'll tell you over dinner.'

'I've never seen anything more beautiful in my life.'

Lily smiled and turned to look back out to the sea; she took in a deep lungful of salty air. 'Don't ever forget,' she murmured.

CHAPTER
FORTY-EIGHT

THE BOISTEROUS CRIES OF A ROWDY FLOCK OF gulls roused Sasha from her slumber. She rolled onto her side and opened her eyes. Ruby had gone. She sat up and pulled the brown woollen blanket close to her naked body. It still smelt of her lover, a sweet vanilla-and-cinnamon perfume she cherished.

Ruby's bed was beneath a wide lead-lined window. A lone seagull perched on the other side, staring in at Sasha with its beady red eyes. It cocked its head, squawked once, then flew away to join its gang on the rooftop over the road. The walls of the room were of flat grey rock, common in most homes in Brackmouth. Adorning the wall was one of Ruby's paintings – a depiction of Brackmouth Beach on a sunny day, the sea a deep turquoise with white-tipped waves. In the distance loomed an island, a great mass of green. Ruby had told her of Lily Rothbone, a pirate queen who lived on the island with her crew. She was the reason

Brackmouth was the safest town on the coast; no one would ever dare raid it with such a fierce guardian watching over. The locals loved her, and she returned that love with her own brand of protection. Sasha decided that she'd like to meet this pirate queen one day.

A small desk stood opposite the bed, three books resting on top of it, their spines and pages bent from excessive reading. Sasha read the titles: *The Warrior Queen of Santonos*, *The Hermit of Hare Hill* and *The Secret Life of the Ocean Dragons*. She wasn't much of a reader herself, but she knew it was one of Ruby's passions. Perhaps she should buy her a new book.

Sasha put her hands behind her and stretched out her back, groaning with satisfaction. The previous night had been incredible. Ruby had shown her what she'd missed with every part of her body. She'd lost count of how many times her body had arced with pleasure. She'd almost been spent by the time they made it up to the bedroom. But Ruby had wanted to keep going, and as exhausted as she was, Sasha had desired the same.

Her body ached, but it was a good ache, one that made her feel whole. Despite this, apprehension gnawed at her. They hadn't got around to talking about anything last night. What would she say? She didn't want to hurt Ruby. Beautiful, kind, sensual Ruby.

The door gently swung open, and Ruby entered the room. She was carrying two steaming mugs and was wrapped up in Sasha's travelling cloak. It didn't look like she was wearing anything else. The cloak wasn't covering her all that well either. Her left leg was exposed all the way up to her hip, as was her right shoulder.

'Do you like what you see?' she asked, pouting her lips at Sasha.

'Very much.' Sasha's heart was pounding, but was it desire or fear?

Ruby sat on the edge of the bed and smiled. 'Good, I like a mug of tea too.'

Sasha took the offered mug. 'Thanks, but that's not what I meant.'

'Wasn't it?' Ruby said. She looked at Sasha over the top of her mug, her jade eyes flashing with faux innocence. With a sly grin, she took her mug with both hands, allowing the cloak to fall away and expose the top half of her body.

Sasha took a swig of the tea, but she could hardly taste it. She was too busy drinking in Ruby. Golden sunbeams fell on her body, highlighting her like a glowing goddess. She was all sumptuous smooth curves going in and out in all the right places. Her long blonde hair fell over her shoulders in sleek waves. It parted at her chest, giving Sasha a view of her full round breasts. Her circular amber pendant lay between them like a miniature sun. She wanted her again – the heat was building in her groin.

Ruby drank her tea like it was all that mattered to her, her pink lips kissing the mug with each sip. Every movement she made felt like a deliberate seduction. As much as Sasha wanted to take her, kiss her all over and make her cry with joy, they had to talk.

'You were going to say something to me last night. You were going to explain.'

Ruby put her mug on the floor and crawled towards Sasha. She sat back on her heels and remained tantalisingly out of reach. Perhaps that was for the best.

'Yeah, I—'

'You're going to break my heart, aren't you?' Ruby's pale gaze went to the window.

'No, Ruby, I'm not,' Sasha replied. 'I wanna be honest with you.'

'Go on.' Her voice was flat; it reminded Sasha of Theo.

'I met a group who can help people like me. They're mages. They have a way to help me be free. I've just got to work with them for a bit, that's all.'

'How will they help you be free?'

'I can't say, exactly.' Sasha felt utterly foolish saying those words. 'They have something though, something powerful.' She paused. She didn't want to tell Ruby too much about the Gramarye in case it got her or Theo into some sort of trouble. 'Something that can help,' she added, inwardly wincing at how vague she was being.

'What is it?'

'I can't say.'

'Can't or won't?'

'Can't, Ruby. I'd never keep anything from you, I promise. I just know it can help me. No more running, no more looking over my shoulder.'

'I can keep you safe.' Ruby turned from the window to Sasha, her gorgeous face full of determination and love.

'I know you can, but what life is it for me? Hiding all the time, unable to use the thing that makes me feel whole.'

'Isn't that me?'

'You're not a thing – you're my lover. This is different. Just think, we could stay here. No running off to Santonos or Freischen or Venario or whatever country doesn't want to kill me for existing.'

'We could stay here?'

'Yes, we could, I promise. You won't have to give up your life, your town, the things that make you *you*.' Sasha inched towards Ruby. She reached forward and ran her fingers over the smooth pendant around her neck. 'You still wear this.'

'Of course I do – it's a piece of you.' Ruby's eyes were glistening. She grabbed hold of the flaming ring around Sasha's neck. 'And you still wear yours.'

Sasha nodded. Her skin tingled as Ruby's fingertips graced it.

'I'm your sun,' said Ruby, clicking her necklace into the gap at the centre of Sasha's. 'And you're my flame.'

'Forever,' said Sasha, looking at the newly formed amber sun between them. 'I promise.'

The two women remained half naked and connected by the amber sun. Outside, the early-morning sky darkened, snuffing out the golden light. Rain fell, pattering against the windows. Shadows draped themselves over Ruby's perfect body. Sasha's lips throbbed, and her chest ached. She reached forward and rested her hand on the curve of Ruby's waist. A low gasp of desire escaped her lover's mouth. Eyes filled with wanting gazed at Sasha. Ruby's warm hand took Sasha's and guided it up her body to her chest.

'How long will you be gone?' Ruby broke the necklaces back into two separate pieces with her free hand.

'I don't know,' Sasha murmured. She took Ruby's chin in her other hand and ran her thumb along her bottom lip. 'As long as it takes.'

Ruby kissed Sasha's thumb, sending waves of longing through her body.

'I'm scared,' said Ruby. 'How well do you know this group?'

'Well enough. We've the same goals, freedom for mages. I know you don't really understand what it's like. But running all the time and denying what you are is exhausting. I just want to be me, but if I am me right now, I get hunted down and killed.'

Ruby took Sasha's hand in hers and kissed her palm, then her wrist, slowly trailing up her forearm. She stopped at the elbow and looked up. 'I don't understand what it's like, you're right, but I do know I want you to be safe.'

She pulled the blanket away from Sasha and carried on kissing up her arm until she got to her neck, where she moved to her lips. Ruby kissed her softly, slowly. A rush of pleasure coursed through Sasha as Ruby's tongue brushed against hers. She moved her hand to cup Ruby's breast, then lowered her head so she could kiss it – soft, gentle kisses at first – then slowly, sultrily, she ran her tongue along it. A moan of pleasure came from her partner. That sound alone was almost enough to take Sasha to the brink of ecstasy herself, but somehow, she held back. This was Ruby's time. With the greatest of care, she pressed her teeth in, nipping at her flushed skin in a way she knew would peak her arousal.

'Do whatever it takes,' Ruby said, her voice peppered with groans. 'As long as you come back to me.'

'I'll always come back to you.'

Sasha used her body to push Ruby down onto the pillows. She climbed on top of her and slipped her hand between her thighs to finally give her release.

CHAPTER FORTY-NINE

Killian awoke with a start. His body burned all over with intense pain. He leapt to his feet and lumbered over to the bars, snatching them in his sweaty palms. Tears filled his eyes, blurring his vision, and he cried out. This was it, the day he was going to lose. His head drooped forward, and the metal slipped from his grasp.

'Killian! Hold on!'

The voice was muffled and distorted. He lifted his head and opened his eyes. A purple-and-black shape floated about before him, yet he saw no clear lines; it looked like a shadow melting into the moonlight. He moved a trembling hand and shoved it through the bars. The shape appeared to touch it, but he felt nothing – nothing but pain. He hung his head, trying to focus on his hand.

'Look at me. Look at me.'

The voice was growing faint. He tried to move, tried to obey it, but he couldn't. His eyes closed. Something cold grabbed him on either side of his jaw and jerked his head up.

'Open your eyes, Killian. Look at me!'

He forced them open, but all that lay before him was a seething dark mass, two piercing purple lights glowing from inside the smoky void. What was it? It seemed to know him.

'Killian, stay with me.'

'I . . . can't,' he croaked.

'You can.'

Something touched his shoulders. It was a firm reassuring grip, icy cold against the burning heat in his body. He was lifted up. His legs wobbled against the strain, and he fell against the bars. His prison bars. Sweat covered him, and his thin white shirt plastered itself to his body like a second layer of skin. The pain grew more intense; it was so raw, travelling right down into his bones. He thrashed and groaned. It felt like his spine was bursting through his back.

'Don't let it take you.'

'I can't fight it,' he rasped, his mouth dry. 'I can't. It hurts.'

'Don't give up.'

He pushed against the bars and staggered backwards, freeing himself from the cold grip on his shoulders. He slumped against the wall but somehow remained on his feet. Hands clawed against the wall, his fingers curling into the gaps between the stones, scrabbling for something to hold on to. The shape was still at the gate and calling him. He tried to move. He wanted to go towards it. Why had he pushed himself away?

He moved one foot, then stumbled and went crashing to the floor, his teeth sinking into his lip. The rank taste of blood filled his mouth, and he tried to spit it out. The voice whispered to him, beckoning him back to the light. He turned his head towards it, but it was so quiet now, he couldn't even make out individual words anymore. Sweat poured from his trembling body, splattering on the stones. Blood trickled from his lip and dripped to the sweat below. Each drip sent a ripple of agony through his body.

He could no longer hear the voice, but he sensed it was still there; he could feel it. He raised one arm and held it out in the direction of the foggy black silhouette. Could it save him? He tried to move his legs, but they were unresponsive. Pain rushed at him again, and he collapsed to the floor screaming.

There was a hissing noise in his head, and he couldn't switch it off. It was growing louder and louder. It was consuming him whole. He rolled to his side, digging his nails into his chest. The pain, the sounds – it was too much. He couldn't take it. The fight had left him, and his strength had gone. He'd lost.

CHAPTER FIFTY

LILY'S MOUNT SNORTED AND SWEATED BENEATH HER, yet still she dug her heels in, driving it on. She and Blake had travelled swiftly over the past few days with very little rest and had made good time as a result, even if it was at the detriment of their and the horses' health. One more day at their current rate and they'd be in Poll. All she could think of was getting back to help Killian. Would they be too late? Would his mind be gone forever? The dense forest surrounding her answered with its gloomy sorrow. No light pierced the thick canopy above. All around her was suffocating darkness. A bad sign.

Within half a second, everything turned upside down. Lily was hurtling through the air, cold wind lashing at her cheeks. Her horse crashed to the ground, screaming amid a cloud of leaves and dirt. The muddy earth came up to smack her in the chin, and she rolled onto her side, paralysed with shock. Blake tumbled from his horse, his eyes white. A sickening crunch resounded through the forest as his body smashed into the ground. Shaking herself down, Lily staggered to her feet and dashed to her fallen gunner. There was a clatter of panicked hooves as their horses vanished into the undergrowth.

'How bad is it?' she asked.

'Bad,' he rasped, clutching his side.

She grabbed his hip and ran her hands over his body. He screamed in agony. 'Shit, sorry.'

'Whatever you have, hand it over now,' said a voice from behind. 'We're already pissed off those horses bolted, so don't provoke us.'

Lily turned to see their attacker. Before her stood a man in a dull green shirt and trousers, both cut to fit his body, hugging every muscle. A pair of mask-covered icy-blue eyes flashed within the shadow of a broad leather hat. A wide mouth gave her a lopsided smirk. It looked like the sort of mouth that had told some eloquent lies in its time. He twisted a silver necklace around his finger as he regarded her.

Lily stood tall, put her hands on her hips and glared at him. 'Who are you?' she demanded.

Her blunt question seemed to throw the man off-balance. He pushed his hat back and ran a glove-clad hand through his short blond beard. 'I ask the questions around here,' he snapped back.

'I'm not in the mood, nor do I have the time for dicking about with some ponce from the forests.' She bent down and helped Blake to his feet. 'You've caused us a great inconvenience. You're lucky I've not already ripped your throat out and left you hanging by it.'

The man's mouth dropped open. Clearly, he wasn't used to being spoken to like that. Lily turned to leave, Blake leaning against her, wheezing in pain, but two other masked men emerged from the undergrowth, blocking their escape.

The first had wavy shoulder-length black hair and deeply tanned skin. He had a strikingly handsome face, complemented by his unusual eyes: one green, the other brown. The second man's face faded into insignificance when compared to the other. Both wore dull greens and browns – the perfect attire for robbing those who travelled through the woods.

'Please don't leave,' said the one with the hat. 'We hardly know each other.'

'Get out of our way, or I'll kill you,' she snarled.

'Hear that, Leif?' He addressed the handsome one. 'If you let her go, she won't kill you.'

Leif smiled and bowed. 'Off you go,' he said in a charming musical voice.

Lily took a step forward, and Blake grabbed her arm. 'Careful, I think they're mages.'

'There's no *think* about it,' said the handsome one.

'Ooh, what will she do?' said the one with the hat.

'If you don't shut up, I'll—'

'What? What will you do?' he asked, a smug grin plastered on his face.

Lily didn't know the answer to that. She couldn't risk Blake getting hurt again – he was in bad-enough shape as it was. If only she knew what type of mage this man was. If he pulled magic from this world, she'd be fine. If it was from the Otherside – given what the Big Blue had said – there would be a problem. She laid Blake down to keep him from harm's way and tucked the precious plant under his arm.

'Keep this safe,' she whispered. Then she turned to the one in the hat and pointed her finger at him. 'I'll fight you.'

'What? Are you crazy? You do know I'm a man and a mage, and you're a woman.'

'Yes, yes and yes.'

'I don't fight women,' he said, puffing out his chest.

She clenched her fists and bent her knees. 'But you're fine with slinging them from horses?'

'I see you have an answer for everything,' he snapped, throwing his hat off with an unnecessary flourish. He lifted his mask and pushed it onto his head to keep his floppy hair from his eyes. He brought his hands down across his chest, creating an X of fire that hovered in front of him for a few seconds before fading out of existence. 'You don't know what you're getting yourself into, *woman*. I'll say it once more – give us everything you have, and I'll let you and your man go.'

Heat bloomed in Lily's chest, and she shook her head. His magic was fire and posed no threat to her. She would destroy this pathetic man for slowing her down.

'Very well,' he said, loosening the buttons on his doublet. 'Just so you know, the man who's going to kill you is called Raynn.'

'Captain Rothbone.' She took off her coat and dropped it to the grass.

A nervous glance passed between Raynn's two companions, but he didn't seem to notice it. Instead, he bowed and ended the pleasantries with a toss of a dagger. Lily put her arm up. The dagger ripped her sleeve and clattered to the ground. She rolled up the sleeves of her shirt, making sure Raynn could see he'd done her no damage. The mage took a tentative step backwards. Seizing her chance, Lily darted towards him. She cracked him hard in the jaw, knocking him to the ground. Once again, she held off from using her ring. She had no idea what state Killian would be in when she got back – she might need its power.

Raynn sputtered out a thick lump of blood and spit. Lily kicked him hard in the side, knocking him onto his back. He put his hand up to shield his eyes as she loomed over him.

'Well, Raynn,' she said, leaning down towards him. 'You can either stay down or get up – it's your choice.'

Raynn thrust his hands forward and released fire into her chest. The force of the blow knocked her back, and her shirt ignited. She dived to the ground, rolling to suffocate the flames. Raynn was back on his feet by the time she got up. Lily glanced at her shirt. There was a gaping black hole in the middle. She ground her teeth. She'd take his shirt as a replacement.

'What's the matter?' asked Raynn, holding his flaming fists before him. 'Am I too *hot* for you?'

Lily's rage boiled over; her entire body was coated in burning-hot fury. Who was this man? This utterly ridiculous man? He'd thrown her from her horse. He'd almost snapped Blake in two. And he was delaying her return to Killian. This rancid little man could cost Blake his legs, Killian his life and her – what would he cost her? A lot.

She crouched down and dashed forward. They became locked in hand-to-hand combat. Raynn seemed to be focused on keeping his hands alight, leaving him open to many of Lily's attacks. She forced him back, jabbing at his ribs and hips. A flaming fist roared towards her, but she dodged aside and grabbed his arm. She sidestepped behind him, yanking his arm upwards. He gasped and cried out. She let go and booted him hard in the back.

He fell forwards but managed to bring his hands out in time to save himself. He planted them in the mud and neatly flipped himself over and onto his feet. Without turning around, he thrust his fists behind him and released the fire. Lily dived to the ground as two roaring fireballs ripped past her head. She scrambled to her feet, dusting down her shirt, and glared at Raynn, who swivelled on his heel to face off. Despite the fact he was grinning, Lily could tell by his slumped stance that he was exhausting himself.

'Ready to give up?' he asked.

'No.'

'Very well,' muttered Raynn.

He let out a deep roar, and his body was alight. Flames licked him all over. He glowered at Lily with wild eyes. Tiny fireballs rolled from his body and ignited the patches of grass beneath him. Lily looked at Blake; he was lying on the ground a few feet away from the flaming mage. She had to draw Raynn away from him before her gunner's broken body was burned to a crisp. She leapt back, turned and shot into the undergrowth. Raynn followed. They raced through the woodland. Lily rushed around trees, bounded over rocks and dodged the roots bursting through the forest floor. She was painfully aware of her ever-maddening pursuer. Great streaks of flame careered past her. Balls of fire smashed at her feet. The forest crackled and popped all around her. Though his fire couldn't hurt her, it didn't stop her feeling the heat and force of it. Sweat poured from her every pore.

A great crack echoed all around her. The mage was soaring through the air, covered in flames. He was a seething orange-red mass of flickering heat. There was something beautiful about the raw power of it. He landed a few feet in front of her, and she skidded to a halt. Raynn was gasping and wheezing. His skin was pale, and his limbs trembled beneath the thin layer of flame that encased them.

'This is where it ends,' he gasped.

A great sheet of fire roared towards her. Lily threw herself to the ground, covering her head with her hands. The heat was intense – it was like she was being boiled alive in her own sweat. Any longer and the rest of her clothes would catch fire, and that wouldn't do. But, as swiftly as the heat came, it disappeared. She pushed herself up and looked over her shoulder, expecting to see a blazing forest, yet the trees were unscathed. Raynn was sagging forwards, resting his weight on a bent knee. He looked completely spent.

Lily swaggered over to him. 'Give up?'

'You've not won yet,' he panted, holding up a dagger.

He pounced at Lily, thrusting his dagger at her. The blade struck her ribs but didn't so much as scratch her. Lily looked into Raynn's eyes, which now seemed so feeble and lifeless. She could slit his pale throat and shower herself in his blood for delaying her journey. Or break his legs and get some revenge for Blake. But what would that achieve? A dead mage in the woods and some minor bit of satisfaction for her? It hardly seemed worth it, and perhaps this man and his crew could be useful to her. She was the executioner, and his fate was decided. She wrapped her hand around his blade, yanked it from his slippery palm and tucked it into her own belt.

'Nice blade,' she said to his stunned face. 'It's mine now. I'll be taking your shirt too.'

'But it was expensive . . .' murmured Raynn as he collapsed into her arms.

CHAPTER
FIFTY-ONE

RAYNN'S BODY SLUMPED ACROSS LILY'S SHOULDER, his limp arm slapping her on the back as she walked. The wind whistled through the hole in her shirt, and she regretted not swapping it for his straight away. The plan was to dump the unconscious leader at the feet of the other thieves, save Blake and steal a shirt. Easy, swift and efficient. Picking up and carrying the ridiculous mage had drained the smallest amount of green from her ring, but she couldn't leave him in the dirt – he might be useful. It was only a tiny amount anyway. Hardly noticeable. A soft groan came from behind, and the arm stopped slapping her.

'Why didn't you take my shirt and leave me?' he whined into her ear.

'Good morning,' she said.

'Morning!' he spluttered. 'How long was I out? Where are you taking me, woman?'

'A couple of minutes, and I'm taking you back to your crew.'

He blew out a long breath. 'Don't say things like that. I thought I'd lost another day.'

'I'll say whatever I want.'

The mage huffed. 'You haven't answered my question,' said Raynn. 'Why didn't you leave me behind?'

'You might be useful. I don't break stuff if it has a use.'

Ulrich's shattered teapot sprang into Lily's mind; she hoped Tom and Finn were getting on all right without it. Smirking, she pushed her way through the last of the undergrowth. Twigs snapped beneath her boots, and Blake and the two other mages turned around.

'What did I tell you?' said the plain-looking one, getting up.

Leif shook his head and followed him.

Lily slid Raynn off her back. His legs wobbled as he touched the ground, and he grabbed her to steady himself.

'Right,' snapped the plain one, 'what needs doing?'

'Nothing,' said Raynn. 'I burned out a little, that's all.' He sounded ashamed.

'Again!' exclaimed Leif. 'Not that I'm surprised. No self-control.' He glanced at Lily and rolled his eyes like he was forced to deal with this sort of thing on a daily basis.

'I've just got a few bruises, Arow,' said Raynn, brushing the fussing man away from him. 'It's not worth it.'

Arow nodded.

'It's getting late,' said Raynn to Lily, his hand on her shoulder for support. 'You and your man should stay with us tonight. Arow can heal his injury.'

He was right – the night was drawing in, bringing a cool breeze with it. As much as Lily wanted to leave immediately, if Arow could help Blake, they had to stay. Her gunner was in a bad way. While the others had stood, he'd remained on the ground, clutching his hip and trying to disguise his obvious pain.

'You got in my way, Raynn,' she snarled. 'I should snap you like a twig.'

'You can if you want.'

'I have someone depending on me, a friend. If he suffers because of you, there won't be enough of you left to feed a dog.' Her heart pounded, and her skin grew hot.

'I'm sorry, Captain Rothbone. I'm sorry.'

Leif's mismatched eyes widened with shock. 'Could you say that again please? I don't think she heard you. I don't think *I* heard you.'

Raynn swallowed and stared into Lily's eyes. 'I'm sorry. I'm really sorry. Really sorry.'

'All right, stop licking my boots – it's pathetic. If we leave first thing, we can make up for some lost time, though we don't have our horses.'

'If I had horses, I would gladly give them to you, but I don't. I can provide you with somewhere warm and safe for the night. Also, Leif is an excellent cook.'

'That'll have to do,' said Lily. She turned and looked Leif up and down. 'You best be fucking good.'

The three mages led Lily and Blake through the forest at a leisurely pace. Blake gripped Lily's shoulder for support, his limp heavy.

'It hurt?' asked Arow, sidling up next to him.

'Yeah,' replied Blake. 'A lot.'

'No promises I can fix you. I don't like helping,' he said. 'It's bad for me.'

'Thanks, I think.'

Lily glanced at Arow. He was a strange one. Gruff, with an almost bitter edge to his tone, and yet he was the one who could help Blake. A healer. Raynn controlled fire. So, what was Leif's speciality? Assuming they were all mages, that was. She trudged through the forest following her guides until they came to a dense patch of trees, bushes and scrubs. It was so thick, all light seemed to be absorbed into it. She frowned and reached for her sword.

'We don't need that, miss,' said Leif.

Leif stood in front of the thick vegetation and tensed his arms. His hair whipped up around him and his shirt blew about wildly. He held his hands forward, and as he moved them apart, a pathway formed through the undergrowth. Strong gusts of wind held back the thorn-laden branches, bent thick trunks and created a roaring tunnel of air. Arow sauntered up to the wind tunnel, stepped in and was blown off his feet, down the path, out of sight. Raynn followed suit.

'Go on,' said Leif, nodding towards Blake and Lily.

Lily stared down the path. Everything was held back and out the way by the force of Leif's air. There was no twisting and bending of branches like in a storm; instead, everything was pushed aside, creating a neat walkway leading to what looked like a cluster of tents.

'You two first,' said Leif, grinning. 'I've got to close it up behind us.'

Lily stepped into the path of Leif's magic and was swept off her feet. She hurtled between the bending trees and yielding bushes, their thorns not even getting close enough to snag her clothes. Leif was a talented man. As she got towards the end, she slowed, the winds allowing her to right her body so she could land on her feet. She looked around to see Blake racing down the tunnel. She reached out her arms and grabbed him, helping him to his feet.

'Thanks, Captain,' he said, leaning on her.

Leif sailed down the tunnel, clearly showing off. Lily didn't want to look, but she couldn't help herself. He drifted on his back, his arms around his head, the forest closing behind him. Everything creaked and groaned as branches and trunks rearranged themselves. As he got to the end, he slowed until he was barely moving, just hovering on the breeze. With a smirk, he clicked his fingers, and the air rushed up his back, pushing him onto his feet. He dusted his hands together and gave the closed-up forest a quick glance over his shoulder.

Lily diverted her gaze from him and looked about the clearing. A ring of trees, bushes and other dense, impenetrable vegetation encircled a great patch of grass spotted with wild flowers. Above was a view of the dark cloud-covered sky. A window to the outside world. Their base of operations was impressive. It was secluded and nigh on impossible to penetrate unless you knew Leif.

There was a flap of cloth, and a woman emerged from one of the three dull green tents at the centre of the camp. She pushed back the hood of a cosy-looking black cowl. Like Leif, she had olive skin. Her dark hair was cut short, her cheekbones high and her jaw strong.

'Visitors?' she asked, her dark brown eyes glaring at Lily and Blake with suspicion.

'Yes,' replied Raynn.

The new thief raised her arms in question.

'Oh, sorry,' said Raynn, flustered. 'Captain Rothbone and, er . . .'

'Blake,' said Leif.

'Yes, yes, of course,' murmured Raynn like he already knew but it had slipped his mind. 'Captain Rothbone, Blake, this is Nedge. She pulls through from the Otherside, talks to the void. Dark magic, nasty dark magic,' he added. With a flick of his doublet tails, he marched towards the stone circle that stood in front of the tents. He crouched next to it and closed his eyes.

Nedge strode up to Lily and Blake, the suspicion in her eyes now replaced with glittering wonder. 'Are you *the* Captain Lily Rothbone?' she asked as she shook her hand.

'Yes,' she said, 'and Blake here is the only mage in my demon crew.'

Nedge chuckled and shifted her attention to Blake. 'What d'you mage?' she asked, taking his hand.

'Illusions,' said Blake. 'I create art out of smoke.'

'Oh, you're a rare one, eh? You can show us some later,' said Nedge. She turned to Leif and nodded her head in the direction of Raynn. 'What's with him?'

'He got beat down by the lovely Captain Lily Rothbone,' said Leif. 'And he burned himself out . . . again.'

Nedge smiled incredulously and shook her head. 'Will that mope ever learn?'

A deep rumble thundered through the camp, followed by a sharp crackle. Everyone turned to see Raynn squatting by a fire in the stone circle. He swiped off his hat – the crow feather that adorned it fluttered – and tossed it onto the grass.

'Shit, I'm surprised he could do that,' said Leif.

'That's it,' shouted Raynn to the others. 'I've done my part.' He lay down and stretched himself out like a cat before the hearth.

Leif wrinkled his nose. 'And I suppose that means I'd better do my part.' He turned to Lily and Blake. 'Make yourselves at home.' He paused, glanced at Lily's burnt shirt and without hesitation removed his. He was slim yet muscular; his body tapered down to his hips, every inch of his torso tight and toned. He held the shirt out for her. 'Take it, I've got another somewhere.'

'Much appreciated,' she said, swiping it and doing her best to maintain eye contact rather than gawp at his body.

He smiled at her and vanished into a tent. Raynn appeared to mutter something to him as he went by, but she didn't catch it.

CHAPTER FIFTY-TWO

Lily sat in the grass with Blake, Arow and Nedge. They were a little way from the crackling fire, but the heat of it played over her skin delightfully. She pulled Leif's shirt close to her body. It was far too big for her, but at least it didn't have a huge hole in the front of it. An owl screeched, dived from one of the tall trees and circled the camp. It soared overhead like a great white ghost before rising above the treeline and melting into the oncoming night.

'Give me a look,' said Arow to Blake.

The gunner lifted his shirt to reveal the gigantic ugly bruise that covered his hip. It reached up to his ribs and littered them with purple blotches. His skin had blackened dramatically in a very short space of time. Arow laid his hand on it, and he winced.

'Sorry,' he muttered.

'That's all right,' said Blake through his teeth.

Arow clapped his hands. 'I can sort it.'

'Not a great idea,' said Nedge.

'Why?' asked Lily.

'Arow has a problem.'

'I do not,' he spat back.

'Point proven,' said Nedge. She turned her attention to Lily. 'Arow can heal people, which is absolutely lovely. Fractures, cuts, most poisonings, broken bits – fixed.' She clicked her fingers. 'But the more Arow uses his gift, the nastier he becomes.'

'I am *not* nasty,' Arow protested.

'Shut it,' said Nedge. She reached forward and gave Lily's hand a squeeze. 'He can be a right piece of shit sometimes.'

'Ne—'

The female mage glared over her shoulder at Arow. A faint wisp of deep purple smoke puffed from her shoulders and faded into the night. It seemed to be enough to silence him.

'I've seen him refuse to help people,' she continued. 'The scum's done that to us before. But he can't help it, so maybe *scum's* a bit strong. Being a moody shit is better than the other way you folks go, eh, Arow?' She jutted her chin in his direction. 'Emotionless zombie or eternally pissed off? What a choice.'

Arow looked at her and sighed, then turned to Blake. 'Well, today I'm having a good day, so make the most of it.' Green, blue and silver light pulsed in his palms. A faint scent accompanied it, like crisp leaves on an autumn morning. 'This may hurt a little.'

Before anyone had a chance to stop him, Arow pressed his hands onto Blake's injured hip. Blake gritted his teeth, sucking air through them as the strange light poured into his skin. Bones ground and crunched – it was an awful sound, scraping and hissing – as everything reset. Tears brimmed in his eyes. He blinked, and they rolled down his cheeks. His lips trembled, and he looked as if he was about to scream, but then Arow stopped, and the light and colours evaporated into thin air.

'All done,' he said, sitting back. He shot Nedge a fiery glare.

'Thanks.' Blake looked down at his hip. It was still bruised but appeared markedly less so. Gingerly, he touched the spot. 'It doesn't hurt so much.'

'That's how it works,' said Arow.

'So, Blake,' said Nedge. 'You're a mage, huh?'

'Yes,' he replied.

'And Captain Rothbone—'

'Call me Lily.'

Nedge grinned. 'Lily, are you still based in Vermor?'

'Yes,' she answered slowly. It felt like a trick question.

'How's that for you, then?' said Nedge, flipping her attention back to Blake.

'I don't know what you mean,' said Blake.

'Living in Vermor, the shithole country that bans and murders mages.'

He chewed his lip and then sighed. 'To be honest, I've not thought about it much since I joined the captain's crew. But before then . . .' He shook his head.

'We only hear talk an' scraps from folks who've never even been. Rumours and shit,' she added most eloquently.

Blake tucked a messy lock of dark hair behind his ear and took out his pipe. He filled it with tobacco and lit it. The hazel in his eyes faded to a ghostly white, and his pupils were swallowed up by its brilliance. Nedge rubbed her hands together. She looked like the cat who'd got the cream, the mouse and the fireplace.

He took a long deep drag from his pipe, held it in for a moment, then blew it all out in one long breath. He held his hands up and clicked his fingers. Great rolling fields appeared all around the gathered group. A small town sprang up in the centre of the image. He drew his fingers over the hovering settlement and painted a snaking river through the town. He flicked his wrists, and the town suddenly surrounded them. Nedge's eyes widened as she looked around. Thatched houses lined the dirt-track streets, and people wandered up and down.

Some of the people were normal, average folk, others were flamed-up fire mages. Lightning mages raced through the scene at an alarming rate. Nedge jumped as one ran right through her. Lily smiled to herself, feeling a certain pride at Blake's talent.

'Years ago,' Blake began, 'and I mean hundreds of years ago, it was all right to be a mage in Vermor. Those who wanted to practise did, and those who didn't didn't. Anyone could be a mage if they tried, and everyone knew that. And everything was fine . . . until it wasn't.'

He took another puff on his pipe and blew away the image of the town, replacing it with a series of portraits of kings and queens, one after another, each looking noble, each holding their palm out with some type of magic dancing within it – fire, wind, dark and light from the Otherside. Blake clapped his hands, and the kings and queens whirled together and blurred out of existence. He lifted his hands and ran them through the smoke, creating a great turreted castle that floated in the air. The castle swept closer to the three spectators until it enveloped them in its smoky walls.

Courtiers bustled up and down a long, wide corridor in a frantic hurry. A red carpet rolled out, leading up to a gigantic wooden door that was carved with designs of ivy and chunky roses. Blake cleared his throat and snapped his fingers again, and the door opened. The carpet led up to a glittering throne, sparkling with gold and glowing with encrusted gems. Sitting atop the throne was a stern-looking man wearing a crown. His eyes were dark and lined with wrinkles, and he glared at the door, a sceptre in his hand.

'King Androw couldn't summon a flicker of magic. As a youth, he drank a lot and spent most of his time at parties with the rich and fashionable.' A dark tone coloured Blake's voice as he said those words. 'He visited brothels – never the same woman twice – gambled and forgot to bother with magic. By the time Androw was in his twenties, he was panicking. He couldn't summon anything. It was too late for him. That door in life where you can learn to harness an element or something from the Otherside had been slammed in his face.

'He couldn't wield however hard he tried, and that wasn't good. It would make people think he was weak. Enemies would come thick and fast if he didn't do something about his problem. So, with his trusted advisors, he hatched a devious plan. A new religion was just what he needed. He sent his cohorts to every church in the country with the order to bribe or maim. As it turned out, most orators were willing to take a dirty backhander rather than lose a limb or three.

'Ionism spread through Vermor like a rash, telling tales of a mysterious unwielding martyr called Andle.'

Nedge huffed and rolled her eyes. 'That name sounds awfully familiar.'

'I know,' Blake agreed. 'Magic was evil and those who controlled it damned. It was preached in every church, on every street corner. It was so simple and so effective. Then the culls began. Mages were already diminishing in number due to the rapid spread of hate, but those who didn't give up their art were hunted down by the cleansers.'

Four people clad in shimmering white armour, each with a red plume on his or her helmet, rode into the middle of the group. Their horses reared up. A lightning mage lumbered by carrying an unconscious woman. His pace was sluggish and laboured; he was almost burnt out. The cleansers laughed and gave chase; they ran him into the ground. He collapsed to his knees, trying to defend the woman as they beat him to death.

'Cleansers were rewarded well for a kill, so recruiting more was easy. It wasn't long before mages seemed to die out. No one wanted to be that rotting corpse hanging at the town's entrance. Cleansers are still all over Vermor – they're bounty hunters for hire. They don't dress in that silly white armour anymore, which makes sense. These days you never know if you're standing next to a perfectly innocent person or an unscrupulous mage killer.' Blake clicked his fingers, and his images melted away, revealing the gloom of the forest once more.

Arow frowned. 'Aren't there texts from before this Androw muddied everything, proving it's all lies?'

'There probably were,' said Blake. 'But all it takes is a few bonfires to completely erase history.'

'No offence,' said Nedge, 'but your country's shit.'

'None taken. I'd probably be dead myself if I weren't with Captain Rothbone.'

Nedge looked at Lily and smiled. 'You're all right, Captain Rothbone.'

'I know,' said Lily, flicking her hair over her shoulder.

Nedge chuckled.

'Oi!' shouted Leif from over by the campfire. 'Is anyone gonna eat tonight, or was I slaving away over this for nothing?'

CHAPTER FIFTY-THREE

THE SUN WAS SETTING AS SASHA TRUDGED DOWN the long winding dirt road that led to the farmhouse. There was a hollow ache in her chest. She'd left Ruby that morning, promising her she'd return and they could live their lives together. It was what she wanted more than anything, but was it even possible?

Her thoughts turned to Theo, and her stomach dropped away. Would he have deteriorated further in her absence? Would the others have used him even more? She'd only been gone a few days, but he wasn't looking great last time she saw him. Part of her knew that he was the main reason she'd returned. She had to help him. She'd promised she would. Someone had to.

As much as she tried to hide it and shove it away, she had a frustrating habit of trying to help the most broken of people. She'd once given all her money from one of her shows to an old man just so he could find a bed for a few days and get a hot meal or two. It would get her into trouble one day; perhaps this was the time. Theo would be her undoing. But she couldn't leave him, she just couldn't. He'd saved her twice. She owed him. And perhaps there were other Theos out there who needed saving. All the mages in Vermor, they needed help too.

Golden light glinted off the windows of the farmhouse as it welcomed her down the path. Long grasses rustled in the evening breeze, and a cluster of unruly sparrows chirped in a nearby tree. The air was clear and crisp, a stark contrast to the air in Brackmouth, which always had the underlying tang of fish, salt and seaweed.

Sasha's feet ached. They were sore and dry, raw and painful. A bath would be nice, a long warm bath to soak off all the dirt and sweat of the roads. It was too much to ask that a certain beautiful, sweet and understanding woman would sponge her down. A low groan escaped her lips. Thoughts like that were not going to help her.

As she approached the porch, the front door sailed open, and Quint strolled out, a cigarette firmly clamped between his teeth.

'You're back, kiddo,' he said, giving Sasha a once-over with his slate glare.

'Well noticed,' she said, stepping up onto the squeaking wooden planks. 'You got a spare one of those? I'm out.'

'Sure.' Quint took a cigarette from inside his battered duster coat. 'I already told ya, they ain't good for ya.'

'Yeah, yeah.' Sasha popped it into her mouth. 'Light?'

Quint huffed, struck a match and lit her cigarette.

She took a deep inhale, then slowly blew out a long plume of smoke. It tasted good. Deliciously bitter.

'You have a good break?' Quint asked.

'Yeah, thanks. It was good to see her.' She tapped the ash from her cigarette over the rail. 'I delivered that letter for Varo too. Got this in return.'

She handed Quint a slightly squashed rolled-up piece of parchment. The desire to read it while she was travelling back had been maddening, but she'd managed to resist. Some things weren't for her eyes.

'Good, good.' Quint tucked the mysterious letter inside his coat.

'He was a weird old codger.'

'I've heard he's eccentric – I reckon that's the word Varo used.'

Sasha nodded. 'He reeked of whiskey and mushrooms.'

Quint chuckled. 'What a delightful perfume.'

'Anyway, I feel better now, more focused. I know what I want.'

'What's that?'

'To be free and to live with Ruby without looking over my shoulder all the time. I want to live in Brackmouth with her and have a quiet, easy life, not run away to another country. So, I guess I'm all in with you folks.' She took another drag. It felt good to say it, to give voice to her dreams and desires. 'Did I miss anything while I was gone?'

'A little. Varo's up and about. Things'll start moving forward.'

'Really?'

Quint nodded. 'She wants a meeting with us all together. Tomorrow at sundown, in the barn.'

'Okay.' Sasha's skin tingled. Something was finally happening.

Quint took a few more drags on his cigarette before stubbing it out and tossing it away. He glanced at Sasha, then said in a voice that indicated it was more of an afterthought, 'Theo almost died on us.'

'What?'

Quint sighed and rubbed the bridge of his nose. 'We pushed him too far healing Varo. It weren't pretty. I didn't know what to do – who heals a healer, eh?' He sounded embarrassed and ashamed. Perhaps it wasn't an afterthought; maybe he didn't want to say it at all.

'How is he now?' she asked. She tried not to sound too concerned, and yet all she wanted to do was find him and see for herself.

'Alive, breathing, resting.' Quint shook his head.

An awkward silence settled over the two of them. How could they be so reckless with his life? Sasha furiously puffed on her cigarette – she wanted it gone. Having a bath was now the last thing on her mind.

Quint stepped off the porch and with his back to her said, 'It was an accident.'

'I know.' Sasha extinguished her smoke, shouldered her bag and went inside the house. She stopped by the kitchen and was relieved to find the coffee pot bubbling away. Delphina and Kurt were sitting at the far end of the room playing cards. Dorian looked to be asleep on the couch, a purple blanket covering his face.

'Hey, Sasha.' Delphina looked up.

Kurt remained quiet.

'Hey,' Sasha replied. 'Can I pour a cup?'

'Go ahead,' said Delphina with a lazy wave of her hand. 'I ruined it anyway. Made it too strong.'

At this, Sasha grabbed two mugs and filled them with the thick black liquid. 'Thanks,' she said as she left the room. She was pleasantly surprised that Kurt hadn't spat barbs at her this time.

She ascended the decaying wooden stairs two at a time, briefly stopping by her room to drop off her bag, then made her way to Theo's. The floorboards creaked in protest at her every step, and the air was thick with dust. She stood outside his door, the two steaming mugs in her hands. After taking a deep breath, she opened the door.

The sunset had lost its golden shimmer and was now shifting into beautiful shades of peach and pink. The light poured in through the window, giving everything a rosy tint. Theo's silhouette was stooped at the window; even his dark shadow looked frail and used. His shoulders were sagging and his legs bent. Sasha closed the door with her foot. Red looked up at her from the bed, but Theo didn't move. The fox yawned and went back to sleep. She swallowed a thick lump in her throat and crossed the room. A deep feeling of guilt and blame gnawed at her. If she hadn't swanned off to see Ruby, he might not be in this sorry state.

'I've got you a drink,' Sasha said, her voice hitching slightly.

Theo turned to her. His face was worn and tired. Grey rings circled his eyes, and his cheekbones were more prominent than before. His dark hair was a matted mess. Didn't anyone care about him? His pale skin, however, soaked up the dying rays of the sun and glowed with a healthy radiance.

'Lightning,' he said, his thick eyebrows knitting together, 'why are you here?'

'Please take this.' Sasha shoved the mug into his hand. She moved to stand next to him and focused her gaze out the window to avoid looking at him. The lump was returning to her throat, and her eyes stung. She blinked, and warm tears streaked down her cheeks.

'You got this for me,' said Theo in a flat voice. She heard

him take a sip. 'You were gone for a few days. Did you have a nice trip?'

Sasha chewed on the inside of her lip and sniffed. 'Yes, thank you.'

'Brackmouth, a long way.'

She wiped her damp face with her palm and took a swig of coffee to steady herself. It really was strong. 'Yeah, it's quite a jaunt. My feet are killing me. I need a soak in the bath.'

The room shifted to a different colour. The peachy sunset was beaten into submission by silver, blue, and green glows. Sasha turned, and to her horror, she saw the colours were in Theo's hand.

'I can take away the ache. Blisters, sores. If you take your boots off and sit down, I—'

'No, Theo, I don't need it.'

She moved to touch his arm, and he darted back as if mere human contact would cause him pain. He staggered back, fell onto one knee and hung his head. The colours remained in his palm, swirling. A shimmering gateway to another world. His breathing grew heavy, and it was accompanied by a sound of soft dripping.

'Let it go, Theo.' Sasha approached him as she spoke.

'But I can help you,' he whispered.

She crouched down to his level and picked up his mug, which he must have placed on the floor before trying to heal her. The man took better care of a mug than he did of himself. Sasha's heart broke all over again.

'Here,' she said, offering him the drink.

He lifted his head. A thin stream of blood was oozing from the side of his mouth. His dark brown eyes were so soulful and compassionate. Green-and-blue light pooled on his skin.

‘I can help,’ he murmured.

‘It’s fine.’ Sasha flashed what she hoped was a comforting smile. ‘I promise, I’m fine. Just let it go, and we’ll have our drinks together.’

Theo nodded and closed his eyes. His face was serene and at peace. The light faded, giving Sasha a glimpse of how handsome he really was. The sunset flooded back into the room, and his face grew worn once more. He opened his eyes and took the mug from Sasha.

‘Thank you, Lightning.’

‘It’s okay. You have blood coming from your . . .’ She tapped her lip.

‘Sorry,’ he said, wiping it away.

‘Quint told me what happened to you.’ She reached for her own mug as she spoke. ‘You need to be careful and take it easier.’

‘You’re the only one allowed to burn out around here – I know that.’

Something strange happened. Sasha looked at Theo, and there was a tiny smile on his lips and a gleam in his eyes. Warmth swelled in her chest. He was making a joke. He was showing some emotion, mentally and physically.

She curled her lip and rolled her eyes. ‘Don’t rub it in.’

‘Someone had to take your place while you were gone, Sa—Lightning.’

‘Don’t do it again.’

‘I’ll try not to.’ He blinked, and the faint smile was gone. Once more, he was a blank slate. He took a long swig of his drink.

‘I mean it, Theo. You need to be careful.’

Theo pressed his lips to the mug and looked at her over the top of it. His eyes were full of confusion. ‘It doesn’t matter what happens to me.’

Sasha's throat grew tight, and her chest throbbed with a dull ache. How could he say something like that? Did he not care about himself at all? He'd lost *that* much of himself.

'Yes, it does.'

'I suppose I'm needed to help others.'

'No, not that.' Sasha moved towards him, and he flinched. 'I want you to be okay.'

'But . . . why?'

'I don't know. I care about you for some reason.'

'I don't understand. I'm barely human.' He glanced into his mug. 'I can't even taste this. I can't feel anything.'

'That doesn't make you less human. You're more human than most people I know.'

'I doubt it,' he whispered.

They sat together in silence, drinking their coffee. The room grew dark around them as the last of the sun's light was devoured by the oncoming night. Deep blues and greys took over from the cheerful oranges and pinks. A silvery light shimmered through the window. Sasha looked over her shoulder to see a ghostly quarter moon peering in. It looked so wise. That moon must have stared down at many other scenes like this one. It would know what to do and what to say to this poor broken man.

The sound of claws rattling on the floorboards broke the quiet. Red had leapt down from the bed. He trotted over to Theo, rubbed his snout against his leg and then curled up next to his side. Theo ran a hand through his fur, stopping to tickle him behind the ears. Sasha swigged the remains of her coffee. It was cold. Disgusting.

'I promised I'd help you, and I will. I'll do whatever it takes to get you to the Otherside.' She held her hand out towards Red, who sniffed her, then licked her palm. 'I know what sort of person you are and what sort of person you were. I can tell. Sometimes I can see it – I know that sounds ridiculous – but with some people I can just tell. You've been used, Theo, time and time again.' She desperately wanted to touch him, to hold him and show how much she cared and that he was safe with her, but she knew he'd shy away. Theo would touch others to heal them, but no one could touch him. 'I won't use you – I'll help you. I am going to fix you, and I am going to save you.'

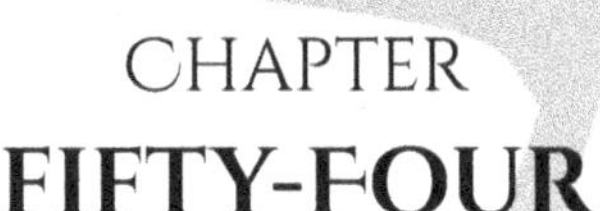

CHAPTER FIFTY-FOUR

Lily finished her bowl of spicy stew and set it down.

'Looks like I won't have to murder you, Leif,' she said, rocking back on her elbows.

'Thank you,' said Leif, leaning back next to her.

The flickering flames highlighted his muscles – not that they needed flattering lighting to look good. Twilight played across his handsome face. He was rather beautiful, and his body was incredible. Lily almost bit her tongue. What was she thinking? She couldn't let her mind get distracted by that. She was on an important mission to save the world and someone who may or may not mean anything to her, someone she could maybe let in without the fear of what might happen in the future. It had been a while, though, since she'd last been with a man. Even Raphael, that preening piece of sea scum, had noticed. How long had it been?

No, don't think about it.

'Cold?' she asked. 'You can have your shirt back.' Maybe her mind would stop wandering if he covered up.

'I'm fine. It looks better on you anyway,' he said with a sly smile.

Lily politely returned the smile and glanced at the others. Raynn had fallen asleep as soon as he'd finished eating. Blake, Nedge and Arow were sitting in a cluster on the other side of the camp, chattering away to one another, probably about mage stuff. They may as well have been a million miles away as far as she was concerned. So she was stuck on her own with a devilishly attractive man, who seemed to be coming on to her. Great.

Leif leant his head back and looked up through the circular window in the trees. The clouds had shifted, revealing a scattering of stars. 'What's it like on your ship?' he asked, as if trying to make idle conversation.

'Undulating,' she replied.

'But you must have seen some places.'

'Yes, that's what ships are for, going places.'

Leif glanced at her. 'What a fascinating conversation, Captain Lily Rothbone. I should be writing this down.'

He was so attractive. Why didn't she just take him now? 'Isn't it funny that a bunch of forest fawns like you know about me. I must have done some good things. Or some very bad things.'

Leif rolled onto his side, propping his head up with one hand. 'We only live in the woods for a few months a year.' He paused and shook his head, smiling. '*Fawns.*'

'What do you do the rest of the time?' she asked, turning to face him.

His heterochromatic eyes were looking right at her, his free hand twisting a silver pendant between his fingers. Damn, he was very attractive. The fire crackled, and the treetops sighed gently. A faraway fox called out, and clusters of insects trilled all around them. Green-and-yellow fireflies flickered in and out of the bushes that lined the camp. Smoke danced on the breeze, a warm familiar scent amid this strange new place.

'We spend everything we make in the woods,' he said. 'A few months robbing in the woods pays for living the high life the rest of the year in Scherben. A lot of travellers come this way – it's the most direct route from Scherben to Bramon. We easily make enough coin.'

'And what high life do you live?' she asked.

'Drinking, gambling, smoking and sex. We eat the finest foods, drink crates of the finest wines and women and men clamour for our attention. And then there's the clothes, but that's more Raynn's area of expertise. The first thing he does when we get back to Scherben is buy a whole rack of new clothes. He picks my stuff out for me because I'm too busy.' A devious grin flashed across the mage's face. 'I'm not into clothes. I find my other pursuits much more interesting.'

'I see,' she said, arching an eyebrow.

He glanced down to his chest for a second and smiled. 'Cooking can be sweaty work.' He winked.

'I wouldn't know – I have people to do that for me.'

'The advantages of being a pirate queen, eh?' Leif idly traced a finger though the cut of his muscles.

Lily wished she could take her eyes off him, but she couldn't. Her heart thumped in her ears, and her body ached. She wanted to touch him, wanted to climb on top of him, but damn it, something was stopping her. It wasn't her fear of what could happen or her need for control. It was something else, something she didn't want to acknowledge.

'Something wrong?'

'No,' she said, getting to her feet. 'Just restless.' She had to get away from him.

Leif joined her. 'Me too. Shall we take a walk?'

'Around the camp?'

Leif smiled and shook his head. He seized her shoulders and pulled her against him. Before she could get out a word of protest, they were in the air. A rush of wind ripped all around her, propelling them high above the circle of trees.

'Don't let go now,' he said.

Lily grabbed his waist and held on tight. Far below, the campfire flickered. Blake, Nedge and Arow were shadowy smears in the grass. The high cold wind whistled through her hair, and a giddy weightless sensation encompassed her body as her feet dangled down into dark nothingness. Dangling feet. Swinging forwards and backwards. Her stomach coiled, and she dug her fingers into the mage.

'Ouch,' he said, but there was a playful lilt to his tone.

The air rippling through Lily's hair gradually became gentler as they floated to the ground. The trees once again grew tall around her, their dark shapes welcoming her in. The mossy ground came up to meet her feet as they landed on the other side of the camp. Leif released her shoulders, and she took a step back. Even in the dim gloom of the forest, she could make out his cocky smile and the sparkling whites of his eyes.

'A little warning next time,' she scolded.

'Where's the fun in that?' He grinned, interlocking her arm with his.

Lily allowed him to lead her around the forest; there was no harm in that. His skin was warm next to hers. Patches of silver moonlight highlighted the ground sporadically. The air was clear and cool to the skin but not uncomfortably so. Tree branches rustled in the breeze, murmuring the secrets of nature to one another. The ground was soft with a carpet of pine needles and moss, which filled the forest with their fresh earthy aroma. In a nearby bush, a spider was intently remaking its web in a pool of starlight. Silvery threads formed intricate patterns as the creature worked tirelessly. It scuttled backwards and forwards, up and down, laying thread after thread.

'So, Rothbone,' said Leif, shattering the stillness of the night. 'It's not a very Venarian surname.'

'Who says I'm from Venario?'

'The Venarian in me,' he replied.

'Close. I'm half. My mother was, my father wasn't.'

'That makes two of us, then.' His tone was deep and husky, and it brought a fire to her chest. He slipped an arm about her waist and pulled her close.

She twisted to face him. 'Were you born there?'

'Yeah,' he said, moving closer to her. 'Hot, sunny, passionate Venario. Mum was from the Causters, Dad Venarian. Put those two beautiful races together and you get?' He left the question hanging.

'I have no idea.' She wasn't going to play his games or stoke his ego. 'Why d'you slum it here?' She untangled his arm from around her.

'I travelled a little, hooked up with Raynn and he talked me into this business.'

Lily chuckled. 'Business!'

'Thieving is a very lucrative business.'

'Can't argue with that.'

Leif's muscular arm wound its way around Lily's waist again. She wanted to flick him away again, but it felt so good to be held. So warm and safe. She turned to him, and he slipped his hands onto her hips. A dizzying rush coursed through her as he leant down and kissed her on the forehead.

'You're so beautiful . . . Would you . . . ?' he whispered as he squeezed himself against her.

She knew the answer should have been yes. A year ago, it would have been a solid, irrevocable yes. She would have thrown him to the ground, ripped off the remains of his clothes and fucked him until they were both too exhausted to carry on, but now . . . something was different. Just being alone with him in the forest made her feel guilty. It was ludicrous. But she did, and she couldn't stop those feelings. They were flooding her mind. But why?

Damn Killian! Damn him to the bottom of all the oceans! Tie a weight to him and toss him down a blue hole. Get him gone.

'Leif,' she murmured, 'I can't.' Her voice tapered off. She was a fool.

Leif sighed. 'I should have known you were just a tease.'

Lily's shoulders stiffened at the accusation. 'I am not a tease.'

He put his hand on her chin and tilted her head up. 'You've been leading me on all night.'

'I certainly have not!' she said. She snatched his shoulders – he winced – and glared at his almost-perfect face. 'You're the one standing around half naked, not me!'

He merely smirked at her aggression. 'You could be half naked too. Though it would be best if we were both fully naked – it works better that way.' He winked his green eye.

'I should take your face off,' she snarled.

He tested her. 'Go on, then.'

'Believe me, I would, but you'd probably get a kick out of it. You seem the type.'

'I'm hurt.' He frowned and widened his eyes, which only made his face infuriatingly appealing.

Lily looked away so as not to be accidentally seduced by him. 'Take me back to the others now, you sleazy scumbag.'

'Oh, come on, Lily, don't be like that. We were getting on so well.' He was smiling again.

She dug her fingers into his shoulders and briefly toyed with the idea of kneeing him in the cock. Instead, she pushed him away, breaking his grip. She folded her arms over her chest. 'Take me back, Leif,' she said. 'I don't want to fuck you.'

He put his hand to his chest and looked saddened. 'Lily,' he said, 'I don't want to fuck you.' He took a tentative step towards her, holding his hands out at his sides, leaving his body open. 'I want to make love to you. Fucking is what I do with the ladies of Scherben. With you it will be different. It will be my whole body and soul. You've enraptured me with your passion, fire and beauty – to only fuck would be doing you a great injustice.' He took another step closer and risked putting his hands on her shoulders. 'I want to feel you, all of you.' He ran a hand down her back, and she shivered at his touch, much to her annoyance. 'I want to give you pleasure.' He lowered his voice to a husky whisper. 'I want you to feel my love, my passion, my burning soul.'

'Sorry to disappoint, but I don't want to. Take me back now and I won't hurt you,' she said.

Leif heaved a great sigh. 'I'm sorry this is the way it's gotta be. But if you're in love with someone else, I shouldn't be standing here confusing you.'

'What?' she snapped. 'I am *not* in love with anyone.'

Leif leant forward, his eyes twinkling. 'Of course you are – that's the only reason you'd deny me.'

'I could prefer women. I could be celibate. Maybe I just don't find you attractive, you egotistical bastard. I've met some men in my life, but you must be the most conceited, arrogant shit of them all. Please tell me, do women actually fall for that "make love" dross?'

'I've never said it to anyone else but you.'

'How much of an idiot do you take me for?'

Leif shook his head, conceding defeat. 'Come on, I'll take you back,' he said as he pulled her close.

'Finally,' she grunted, refusing to allow his tone to lure her in.

'You have no idea what you've just missed,' he murmured in her ear.

'You unbelievable narcissistic cock!' she yelled as they soared into the sky.

CHAPTER FIFTY-FIVE

Lily woke with a start and sat bolt upright, her heart pounding. Her sudden movement roused Leif, who'd managed to sleep next to her in the slightly overcrowded tent despite her obvious attempts to get away from him. He blinked and sat up.

'What's wrong?' he asked, scratching his chest.

'We have got to go.' The words tumbled from her mouth. She turned to Blake and gave him a rough shake. 'Blake, get up. We're leaving.'

Blake grunted, twisted under the covers and came to. 'Captain?' he drawled. 'What's happening?'

'We're going.' She got to her feet and buttoned up Leif's shirt.

Blake nodded and, as if he were running on automatic, got to his feet.

Lily pushed back the canvas door and filled her lungs with the fresh morning air. The scent of the dewy grass and damp moss awakened her sleep-dulled senses. Golden sunlight poured into the clearing through its round window, turning every bead of moisture into a tiny glowing sun. She buttoned her coat over her shirt as she waited for Blake. He soon emerged from the tent flap, squinting into the light and rubbing the back of his neck. The commotion she'd caused had stirred the others, and they, too, emerged, half dressed, from the other tents.

She marched up to the gang of bandits. 'You almost broke one of my best gunners in half, but you fixed him, and your hospitality didn't go unnoticed. We're allies now.' She held her hand out to Raynn.

'I can't believe I'm out in the daylight without doing my hair,' he said as he took the offered hand. A small smile cracked across his face. 'Yes, Captain Rothbone, allies. We've never had allies before.' His voice trailed off, and he flicked a hand through his messy blond hair. 'I hope you make it to your friend in time.'

'I will.'

Lily noticed Leif's eyes were cast to the ground. He couldn't meet her gaze. How pathetic. She opened her mouth to say something as Arow barged him aside. Leif staggered but said nothing.

'Here,' said Arow, shoving a thick chunk of seeded bread into her hands, 'for the journey.'

'Thanks.' She tossed the food to Blake, who stuffed it into his bag. 'Right, which way to Poll? It's disorientating in here.'

Raynn rubbed his beard and pursed his lips. He pointed. 'That way. Keep going, and you'll be there by tomorrow evening if you hurry.'

Lily's heart sank. She tried to disguise it, but it was impossible. It felt like such a long way, and they'd lost a lot of precious time. If only they hadn't lost their horses. If only Killian hadn't been possessed. If only the Gramarye were still locked away. But there was no point in dwelling on the ifs. All she could do was move forward.

'I'm sorry,' said Raynn for what seemed like the fiftieth time in the past twelve hours.

'We'll make it.'

Lily and Raynn marched towards the thick wall of trees. Blake followed, walking alongside Arow and Nedge.

'If they ever try to do you in back in Vermor, just come here,' said Nedge. 'Bandit, pirate, same thing. I don't give a shit.'

'Thanks.'

Leif was still hanging back and squinting up into the thick canopy of the trees that surrounded them. He was dragging his bare feet, which shone with damp from the wet grass. He put his fingers on his cheekbone and made slow circular movements. What was he doing? The strange man. Lily was about to shout 'bye' to him in her most sarcastic and abrasive tone, the one she reserved for only the most special of occasions, when he finally looked at her. He dropped his hand and strode towards her, his eyes set with hard determination.

'You need to get to Poll fast, right?' he said.

'Yes.'

'I can get you there fast.' His lips twitched into a weak smile.

Lily cocked her head to the side, and Raynn's brow furrowed.

'I can ride the wind. I'll get the three of us there like that.' He clicked his fingers.

'All the way to Poll?' asked Lily, her tone laced with scepticism. 'That sounds a little—'

'Yup, all the way. Don't worry, I won't hang around like some worthless dross. I'll drop you off and come right back here.'

'You're insane,' said Nedge with a nervous laugh. 'How you gonna do that with three people?'

'I can pull from the Otherside,' said Leif. 'It's easy.'

'It's dangerous and you know it,' said Nedge, a hint of desperation in her tone. 'Those elements aren't the same. They suck you dry fast, an—'

'Nedge, I know, and I've been practising.'

'She's right though, it's dangerous,' said Raynn, who was still trying to tidy his hair. 'What if you become a husk, or worse? Don't be selfish, you idiot.'

Leif dismissed Raynn. 'I'm not about to take mage advice from you, lord of the burnout. And how, exactly, is helping other people being selfish?'

'It could kill you,' Arow grunted, 'and I ain't healing you.'

'And I told you all I've been practising.' Leif grinned with pure confidence. 'Arow, you will heal me – I know you will,' he added.

'I don't care how much you've practised,' said Nedge, 'idiot.' She huffed and folded her arms.

Leif sighed. 'To be honest, I don't care what any of you say.' He winked at Lily. He pulled a pair of goggles from his pocket and set them over his eyes. 'I'm a scumbag and I know it, so let me be a good guy for once.'

Before anyone could move or speak, the air began to whip up around him; his trousers rippled, and his hair flapped. Colours flashed within the winds – dark purples, pinks and blues. It sounded different, deeper, more rumbling, like it was full of devastating power. He lifted his hands and cut a pathway through the trees. They instantly yielded to his command.

'You're insane!' Raynn shouted over the turbulent winds.

'I hate you!' Nedge added.

Leif responded with a wild grin. 'Okay,' he said, shifting his attention to Lily and Blake, 'come here.' He reached his hand out and beckoned them.

'Come on,' said Lily, grabbing Blake, who looked awestruck.

Lily edged towards Leif, the wind buffeting her clothes and her eyes streaming. She took another step and was lifted off the ground to join him in the swirling colour-speckled winds. Floating within the winds was an odd sensation. It had seemed so loud and violent from the outside, but inside there was a gentle calm. The air was cool and refreshing, like a tall glass of icy water on a hot summer day.

'Come closer,' said Leif, the hint of a tremor in his tone.

'I'm not falling for that cheap trick,' Lily bit back, her ebony hair billowing out around her.

'No cheap tricks.' Leif chuckled. 'It makes it easier for me if you're closer. Blake too.'

He held his hands out. Lily pushed towards him like she was swimming in the air and grabbed on.

'Great,' Leif puffed.

His muscles were quivering under the strain.

'Are you sure?' Lily left the question hanging.

'It's nothing, really,' he said, his voice strained. 'Before we go, just in case, Li—Captain Rothbone . . . I'm sorry about last night.'

She smiled at him; it was impossible to pretend to be angry. 'I know.'

He laughed, the mirth touching his eyes. 'Let's go.'

With an intense rush of wind, they were off. They were through the circle of trees in a matter of seconds and racing through the forest, everything merging into a luscious verdant blur. They erupted from the woodland and raced across meadows studded with wild flowers of all colours. Cattle paused to look up in wonder at the ball of colour-dashed wind housing three figures, and crows cawed aggressively as their airspace was invaded.

Lily pressed her hand on the pocket that contained the plant. Soon everything would be better, and all this would be worth it.

CHAPTER
FIFTY-SIX

Tom traced his fingers over Poppy's left wing and then her right, her feathers smooth as silk against his sea-worn skin. The bird stared at him, her round amber eyes unblinking. This had become their morning ritual, and Tom was sure she loved it as much as he did. Not that he could tell – she never gave much away. A mystery woman.

'I'm gonna miss you, Mrs Pops,' he said to her. 'I think you'll miss me too, eh?' He stroked her again, and much to his delight, Poppy gently nibbled his finger. 'Daw, you will, won't you?'

'Mornin', Tom,' Finn drawled as she sloped into the lounge. 'What're you doing?'

'Talking to my mate,' he replied. 'You?'

'Making some tea,' she said through a yawn, 'and breakfast. Want anything?'

Tom turned to her. 'Aye, whatever you're having.'

She nodded and looked at Ulrich, who was sitting slumped over the table surrounded by books and glass bottles containing liquids of various colours. 'Want anything?'

The old man creaked his head up. 'Some tea and bread please,' he said in a scratchy voice.

'Almost done?' she asked, motioning towards the bottles.

'I just need the ingredient from your captain.'

'Oh, Ulrich,' said Tom, one hand still on the owl, 'if only you'd told us about all this evil-spirit shit first, we could have avoided this nasty situation.'

Ulrich huffed and glared at the piles of books before him.

'He's right, you know,' said Finn. 'I don't like keeping an old geezer like you under house arrest, but after what you did to Killian, you fucking deserve it.' She screwed her fist up and pounded the table, and the glass bottles wobbled and clinked. 'And you knew about it all along. Didn't you feel guilty when you were working with him? Didn't ya think about tellin' him of the dangers?'

Ulrich calmly removed his spectacles and placed them on the gnarled table. 'No, I didn't. If his loss meant a safer world, I was willing to deceive him.'

Finn glared at him and shook her head. 'You're lucky we need you alive.' With that, she stomped to the kitchen.

'Don't you be scared of old Finn,' said Tom to the owl. 'She's only like that to people who deserve it.' He tickled her chin, and she hooted back.

The sound of Finn aggressively making breakfast filtered into the sitting room. She really was livid. Plates and pots smashed and crunched. Cutlery rattled, and the pirate swore. Tom glanced over his shoulder at the old man. His face was drawn and his beard wispy; he seemed to have aged about ten years in the past few days. His broken hand had blackened, and he hadn't moved it in days. Had he known about Killian? Had he known about the glow and the horns? It was possible. A fizzing sensation ran up Tom's nose, and his forehead grew hot. Was that why Ulrich hadn't said anything? Because Killian *was* the real danger? He could ask him, but no, no, that would betray Killian's trust, and he couldn't do that. But what if Killian was dangerous? The man had grown horns and glowed like a star. There was something not right about him.

Finn clomped back into the room and slammed three cups of tea onto the round wooden table. She tossed Ulrich a hunk of bread, which he dropped in his lap.

'Thank you,' he said.

'She doesn't need your thanks,' snapped Tom as he grabbed his mug.

Finn chuckled and wandered back to the kitchen. 'You know you've done something genuinely wrong if you've got Tom pissed off at you. It takes a lot to make him hate someone.'

Tom slurped his tea and glared at the old man. 'Too right.' Even if Killian was dangerous, he was still his friend, and this old codger had no right to do what he did.

There was a frantic hammering on the door. Tom jumped and almost slopped his tea onto his shirt.

'Finn! Tom!' It sounded like Blake.

Tom thumped his mug down and raced to the door. He yanked it open to reveal Lily and Blake looking very dishevelled. The captain's hair was all over the place, a wild tangle. Blake's was always a bit messy, so he didn't look much different in that sense, but his clothes looked like they'd seen better days – creased, battered and with some buttons hanging off. The captain was wearing a shirt that wasn't hers too; it was far too big for her.

'You're back,' he exclaimed, deciding against poking fun at their appearance.

'Is that a touch of disbelief I detect in your tone, Tom?' said Lily as she swept into the house, her green coat flapping behind her.

'No, I knew you could do it,' he said.

'Is that bacon?' asked Blake, hurrying after her.

Lily marched into the main room and instantly sought out Ulrich. 'Well, well, old man, you have been busy,' she said, eyeing all the various potions, spilt bottles of powder, burnt-down candles and small black pots.

'Cap'n!' yelled Finn, leaping from the kitchen. 'Did you get it? Want some breakfast?' She held out a crusty roll filled with warm smoked meats and dripping with butter.

'Thank you,' she said, taking the offered food. 'Finn, cooking?' She cocked an eyebrow.

'We got a rota,' said Finn.

Lily bit into the roll and chewed. 'I'm impressed. And yes, I got it.'

'Impossible,' grunted Ulrich.

She put the food on the little table and delved into her coat to produce the plant. It was a spindly thing with silvery lumps growing on it. It looked like common seaweed to Tom, but silver. The magic, or whatever was in it, must've been in the silver.

Ulrich's mouth dropped open. He tried to close it, but it was like he'd lost control of his own jaw. 'How did you get that?'

'A friend owed me a favour.' She stepped up to Ulrich and placed the plant on the table before him. She leant down and grabbed hold of his shoulder, her fingers tensing as she pressed them into his flesh. 'You best get brewing the rest of that antidote, and then we'll be on our way.'

'You'll leave?' he asked. 'You won't kill me?'

'Not all of us.' She smiled at him sweetly. 'Just in case you do decide to deceive me again, I'll be leaving Finn and Tom here to keep an eye on you.' She turned around and looked at Tom.

'Aye, Cap'n,' he said.

'Aye! Don't forget, Tom, you're on kitchen duty tomorrow,' Finn barked from the other room.

Lily yawned. Her eyes were bloodshot and had deep lines beneath them. The bruise on her cheek had faded though; Tom could barely see it. She looked tired. He'd never seen his captain look so exhausted and worn down. It frightened him a little.

'I'm taking a nap,' she announced. 'Wake me up when it's ready.'

'CAP'N, Cap'n.'

Someone was shaking her arm. It sounded like Tom. It seemed like she'd only just collapsed onto the couch and closed her eyes. Surely she was entitled to a few more minutes of rest.

'Cap'n, wake up, you wanna see this.'

With a grunt and a yawn, Lily pushed herself up. It took her a moment to get her bearings. She'd travelled a lot during the past few days – and in some unusual ways. Her body still felt as if it didn't belong to her, thanks to Leif and his unorthodox method of transport. Her limbs were heavy, but her head was light. She wanted to close her eyes again.

'He's done,' Tom said.

At this, she sprang to her feet and stumbled to the old man's table. Her body could wait. He was glaring back at her, his eyes blackened and bloodshot from lack of sleep. He looked impossibly frail. With her hand open, she marched up to him. A small, thin bottle containing a shimmering silver liquid was placed in her palm. She gave it a shake and watched it swirl.

'This it?' she asked.

'Yes,' said Ulrich, lowering his head. 'Drop it in his eyes when the enlii has control.' He coughed, drew a long wheezing breath and continued. 'It should be driven out, and your friend will return to normal.'

'Excellent,' she said, slipping the potion into her coat. 'Well, Ulrich, I would say it's been a pleasure doing business with you, but it really hasn't. Any regrets?' she added, glancing at his ruined hand.

'No, you'll be the one with the regrets,' he croaked, pushing himself up with the arms of his chair. 'Whoever, or whatever, has the Gramarye will track down that soul within Killian, and then you'll regret all of this.' He went to steady himself on the table, accidentally used his broken hand for support, screamed and slumped back into the chair. 'You'll see I was right.'

Lily pulled her green bandana from her pocket. 'You're lucky I've left you alive to see it.'

CHAPTER
FIFTY-SEVEN

Sasha stood in the barn smoking while waiting for Varo and Quint. The muddy straw-covered floor courted her attention, and she shuddered. She glanced up. Kurt was staring at her from across the shadowy gloom. He sent her a slimy smirk. She knew he was thinking the exact same thing as her: another fight was looming. A spike of rage raced up her spine, and she bunched her fists up. Lightning flickered over her hands in tiny pulses, and then it was gone.

Theo was standing a little way from her, leaning against one of the barn's thick wooden supports. His expression was unreadable; his eyes were vacant, but he looked tired. The urge to go to him rose in Sasha, but she held back. If Kurt knew she cared for Theo, he might exploit that. Delphina and Dorian were sitting on the floor together, resting against a dusty haystack, each nursing a mug of beer. Sasha regretted not bringing herself a mug too.

Shafts of weak light filtered through the open barn doors. The oncoming evening had dyed the sky a deep blue streaked with orange-and-pink clouds. Clusters of jackdaws chattered in the nearby hedges and trees as they prepared to roost. A cool breeze fought its way in, its fresh scent clashing with the aroma of Sasha's tobacco. She took another drag, rocked her head back and blew the smoke up into the lofty rafters of the barn.

A flash of green darted into the barn from outside. Varo was walking across the field with Quint in tow. The shimmering green artefact in her hands cast an ethereal glow out into the grasses around her. It was such a beautiful light, and like no colour Sasha had ever seen before. It was rich and full of life. Deep within all the layers of green, a heart throbbed, sending out waves of blue. Sasha glanced at Theo and then at his hands. The radiant light of his magic had not only lit up his room but also his face. It revealed his human side, the side he thought he'd lost. She could see it now, the connection between him and the Gramarye. This device could set her free and heal his broken soul. She had to believe in it.

The barn rippled with incredible green light as Varo walked in. Even Kurt scrambled to his feet as a sign of respect. Sasha gazed at the wooden walls in awe as they glimmered with emerald luminescence. Thin strands of silver, gold and turquoise swam through the green light, making the interior of the barn come alive. It was truly beautiful. Being around this mysterious artefact and the woman who held it made her feel stronger. She stole a glance at Theo, but he appeared just as deflated as before; perhaps it was merely a placebo she was becoming lost in.

Varo stood in the middle of the barn, her skin taking on a jade hue as her marbled parts shifted to a dark blue. Sasha hadn't got used to her solid unblinking eye. It seemed even Theo couldn't fix that, or perhaps he'd tried and that was the final push too far for him.

'Thank you for gathering here this evening. I have much to tell you, so please make yourselves comfortable,' said Varo. Her voice was clear and strong. Her condition had greatly improved since Sasha had last spoken with her. 'The Gramarye, as most of you already know, will open the way to the Otherside. With this gateway flung wide open, we will all be able to pull from the Otherside. Magic from that world will flow into ours and into our bodies freely. Each of us will be able to summon our raw elements from that beautiful world without the fear of burnout and without the fear of death. The same goes for those of us who already pull light and dark from there.' Her brown eye focused on Theo and then Dorian.

'This won't stop with our group. Once this gateway is open, all the mages of Vermor will be able to touch and harness the power of the Otherside. They will reach their true potential and become strong. No more living in fear. No more running and hiding from cleansers. We can finally fight back against the land that has oppressed our kind for so long. And with this power flowing through us, and the thousands like us in Vermor, our victory is guaranteed. This land will be ours. The Gramarye, however, is locked by a complex seal.'

There was a gentle sigh to Sasha's right; it was Theo. A hollow sensation grew in the pit of her stomach. Against her better judgement, she moved to stand next to him.

'Remember my promise,' she mumbled from the side of her mouth.

'I do,' he replied in barely a whisper.

She moved her fingers dangerously close to his arm, then thought better of it and snatched them back.

'This lock, like all locks, can be broken. It will be broken,' Varo continued. 'Fifteen souls are the keys that will allow us to step through into the Otherside. The Gramarye wants to be whole. I feel it every time I touch it.' She paused and looked about the band of assembled mages. 'Just like us,' she added. 'Capturing these souls, these keys, won't be easy. It will change who we are as people. Each of you needs to ask yourself if you can live with what you must do. I'm willing to allow anyone who doesn't want to take part to leave. I won't come after you. Quint won't come after you. You can go back to your lives. Though, if you breathe a word of this to anyone, I will hunt you down myself. I will murder everyone you ever felt anything for, and finally, I will kill you. Do we understand?'

Sasha's palms grew wet with sweat. She wiped them on her trousers. This was getting serious. What had she gotten herself into? What price would freedom and power cost? She swallowed. Her throat was as dry as the straw in the barn. She glanced with envy at Delphina and Dorian, supping their beers.

Kurt's voice broken the silence. 'What've we gotta do?'

Varo removed her tatty cloak and placed it on the floor. She put the Gramarye on top of it and took a step back.

'First, you must cut yourselves on the Gramarye to allow its essence into your bodies. Allow it to be a part of you, and it will show you what it wants. It will show you where the keys are. Once you've done that, each of you will be tasked with bringing a key back, until we have all fifteen and the Gramarye is whole.'

'That doesn't sound too bad,' said Delphina.

Varo looked to the floor, almost as if she was too ashamed to speak the next part. 'You'll have to kill a person and take their soul in order to get the key.'

Sasha's chest froze over, and her breathing momentarily ceased. Kill somebody? She glanced up. Theo was looking directly at Varo, his face unmoved, no emotion, nothing. He must have detected her movement because he turned to look at her.

'It's fine,' he whispered, shaking his head the tiniest amount. 'Leave.'

The fear and revulsion must have been written all over her face. 'I promised you.' She moved her hand, and her fingertips grazed his arm. He pulled away. 'I don't go back on my promises.'

Varo raised her head, her feathery dark hair framing her face. 'Once you've taken your victim's life, you must bind their soul to you.'

'It has to live in me?' Dorian said, his face etched with shock.

Sasha blinked. Dorian seemed more bothered about soul binding than actually killing somebody. A grotesque sickness washed over her.

'Yes,' replied Varo. 'I know it's an old practice, outlawed much in the same way we are.'

'But for good reason,' Dorian put in. Fear coloured his tone.

Varo turned to him, and the tall muscular man shrivelled under her stony marble stare. 'There's no evidence that anyone went mad with soul binding – mad with grief, maybe, but not insane. There's the small risk of a malevolent lingering spirit trying to possess you, but they tend to reside in graveyards, near their own corpses. The risk is low. A fresh kill will release a fresh spirit. It'll be confused and latch on to the first thing that calls it. But I will give you each a bunch of sage as a precaution. Evil cannot stand it.'

Varo paused and rolled up her sleeve. Around her arm was a leather casing bound with thick cord. She loosened the cord and dropped the casing to the floor. Beneath was a layer of shimmering purple velvet. She pulled it away to reveal a glowing blue mark. There was one long vertical line crossed with three shorter horizontal ones.

Sasha's throat tightened. She'd never seen anything like it before. The soul of someone else was living inside Varo. A quick scan of everybody's faces told her nobody else had known it was there. Even Quint's expression was splashed with shock.

Varo held her arm aloft so all could see. 'I would never ask any of you to do something I haven't done myself. If anyone is uncomfortable with this, you can leave.'

Sasha looked around at the broken and defeated people in the barn. They were all damaged in some way. Even those who kept everything hidden had damage. She looked at Varo. The mage was standing in the middle of the barn. She offered them hope. Her unmoving marble eye and the swirls of marble on her face, down her neck and on her body marked her as a warrior. The shimmering blue symbol on her left arm not only showed her pain, but her resilience, and she'd bared it all for them to see. A spirit lived in her arm. Perhaps it was someone she had loved and lost. She was a magnificent person, tormented by hardships, who was still going. She was still on her feet and searching for a way to make life better, not just for herself, but for all mages. All mages. Sasha's skin grew hot as thoughts of her own dismissive selfishness formed in the back of her mind.

'We're all in agreement?' Varo said.

'I've been betrayed, sold out and backstabbed,' said Dorian. 'I'm with you.'

'My family came here for a better life, but I only found misery,' said Delphina. 'I'm with you.'

'What's fifteen people compared to all mages?' said Kurt.

A murmur of agreement ran through the barn, though Sasha didn't detect Theo's voice present. She turned to him, and he shook his head.

'Don't do it, Lightning. You're not lost yet.'

'I can't keep running. I know what I need, what I want,' she whispered back, 'and let me keep my promise to you.' She turned to Varo and said loud and clear, 'You're the only family I have.'

Varo nodded. 'Then it's settled. Sasha, as you were recruited in my absence, I'd like you to go first.'

CHAPTER
FIFTY-EIGHT

LILY CROUCHED IN THE LONG DAMP GRASS WITH Raven and Blake, watching Killian. He was sprawled on the dais, his head rocked to one side, red eyes glaring at his audience.

'Nice to see you back, woman,' he spat.

'The feeling isn't mutual,' she replied.

Killian cackled. 'Upset I killed your friend?'

Lily averted her attention from him. He was disgusting. It wasn't Killian – not one inch of that *thing* locked away in the tomb was him.

'I'm sorry,' said Raven, his beautiful eyes shining. 'I couldn't save him. I couldn't stop it. He's been like this for days. It's my fault.'

'No, it's not, it's Ulrich's, but what's done is done,' she said, reaching to her first mate to give his arm a squeeze. 'And it's fine because I'm going to save him now.' She got up and marched to the door.

'He's dangerous,' said Raven, grabbing her shoulder.

'It'll be fine.' She knew that was a lie. Somehow, Killian could hurt her and break through the defences of the ring. She pushed Raven's hand off and opened the door. 'Lock it behind me and don't open it until I say so.'

The door closed, and the lock dropped. Sickening nerves crawled all over her as she walked towards Killian's still body. He looked so thin and frail. His chest was rising and falling in the gloom, but that was the only movement his body offered. The bottle of cool silver liquid pressed against her chest from inside her coat. She slipped her hand inside and touched it. There was only half the potion in the bottle. Blake had the other half, just in case she somehow failed. She was a few paces away from Killian when he sat up, swivelled around and faced her, his red eyes aflame in the dark shadows of his face.

'Pirate bitch! Nice of you to visit my temporary cell.'

'Permanent cell,' she ground out through her teeth.

'We'll see.' He slipped off the platform and ran his fingers up and down his shirtless body. 'I'm a little skinny right now, but I'll sort that out when I'm free.'

'You'll never be free.'

He put his hand to his mouth and laughed. 'Yes, I will, silly. First, I'll kill you, then your men out there and then I'll be free. Another life, another chance.'

'You've already had your life,' said Lily, clenching her fists in preparation. 'You've got one more chance to give Killian his back before I take it from you.'

He laughed again. 'No, this is mine now.'

'No, it's not.' Lily jumped towards him, powered by fury and fight.

Taken by surprise, Killian was knocked down by Lily's ferocity. There was a crunch as he hit his side on the thick slabs of the floor, but he rolled once, then sprang back to his feet. Lily hunched over and glared at him, ready to attack again.

Killian rubbed his hip. 'Big mistake.'

He ran at her; she dodged out of the way and pulled herself up onto the dais. He fell into it, winding himself on the sharp edge.

'You made the mistake when you stole that body.'

She dropped low and kicked him hard in the chest. He coughed and staggered back, clutching his body. Lily jumped down from the dais and punched him in the ribs and in the hips, then smashed her knee into his stomach. The ring pulsed with every shade of green in the known universe, but again she held off from using it. What if she lost control and accidentally killed him?

He doubled over, reeled back and slumped to the floor. Seizing her chance, Lily leapt on top of him, pinning him down with her knees. She glared at him, her teeth gritted. He looked up at her and grinned, and then he bucked his hips, throwing her off. She flipped over him, her arms flailing as she crashed to her back. All the air rushed from her lungs. She rolled to her front and crawled along the cold stone floor, gasping for breath. A strong kick found her ribs and sent her into the icy slabs. Burning pain coursed through her body. Why did he hurt her? How could he hurt her?

Laughing, Killian put his boot into her back, pinning her down. 'Come on,' he said, 'up you get. Pathetic little woman, playing at being a hero. Remember, my dear, you're a pirate, a scumbag, filth. You're a parasite, no better than me.'

White-hot rage rushed through Lily, and she couldn't hold back. She glanced at the ring and allowed its strength to flow through her. With a cry of fury and frustration, she threw him off. A scream of surprise rang out as he hurtled through the air. It was cut short with a sickening thump as he collided with his prison wall. Exhausted and aching from the fresh blows Killian had dealt her, Lily lurched to her feet.

Killian picked himself up and grinned. 'That's better.'

He darted forwards, and she dodged to the side. With liquid fluidity, she drove her elbow into his stomach, using just enough of the ring to cause damage but nothing lasting. While he was stunned, she kicked at his legs. He stumbled but quickly regained his balance. Before Lily had a chance to attack again, a fist collided with her face. The blow was so hard her vision exploded with white light. She tripped backwards, holding her jaw, blood dribbling down her chin.

A tremendous blow took her in the abdomen. The air rushed from her body in a crushing gasp. Cruel fingers pressed into her shoulders, and she was shoved against a cold damp wall. The remainder of her breath was forced from her sore lungs.

'You can't win,' he growled, releasing her shoulders to thump her in the stomach.

Lily gasped. She'd never felt this much pain before. Everything hurt. She could hardly breathe. Her lungs were refusing to work, her mouth was full of blood and her head swam. She was losing focus.

With a deep growl, Killian grabbed her by the throat and lifted her up. She struggled in his deathly grip, but it was useless. Her feet dangled and swayed as she choked and rasped. She was going to die in the exact same way as *him.* No, not that way, anything but that. Tears burned her eyes as the horror of the situation throttled her. Then, almost as if Killian had grown bored with her, he tossed her to the floor like a sack of rubbish. Unimaginable pain rinsed through her. Despair settled over her. She tried to move but couldn't. All she could taste was rank metallic blood. He swooped over to her and crouched down, putting his legs on either side of her body.

He nudged her with his foot. 'Still awake?'

She didn't have the energy to speak. He laughed, sat on her chest and slapped her face.

She glared and snarled. 'Fuck you!'

'Listen to you, insolent and vile till the end.'

He adjusted his body and rammed his knee into her stomach. White flashed across her vision. He punched her in the ribs and across the cheek and slapped her mouth, splitting her lip. Blood splattered the stone slabs. There was a heavy rasping sound. It took Lily a second or two to realise it was her.

'Looks like I win,' said Killian.

A strange expression of confusion and fear crossed his face. His grin faded, and he screamed out. He went rigid, then flopped forward like a broken marionette. With a desperate fumble, he attempted to crawl away from Lily. It was as if he feared her. Lily rolled onto her side as he tried to slither to safety. His head rocked back, and he screamed again.

'No,' he shouted, 'no, no, stop!'

Lily staggered to her feet. His voice was changing. He stopped crawling and turned to her. Beautiful blue eyes stared back at her. Bewilderment streaked his sweat-and-blood-covered face.

'Lil?' he gasped.

'Killian?'

'Do it, quickly, before he comes back,' he said.

'What?'

'Kill me, quick. You'll get both of us.'

'Don't be an idiot,' she said. 'I can save you, but I need him back now.'

Before Killian could respond, she kicked him in the stomach. He cried out and collapsed to the floor. Hearing him and seeing him in so much torment hurt her more than any of her wounds ever could. She grabbed him, rolled him onto his back and pinned him down again. Some of the green had faded from her ring, but there was more than enough left for her to keep him trapped. He screamed out and tried to throw her off, but she was like iron, like stone. She would not be moved.

Red eyes glared up at her, brimming with malevolence. 'He helped you,' he snapped, blood oozing from his mouth. 'The weak bastard came through and helped you!'

Lily pressed down harder with her knees and took the bottle of silver liquid from her coat. She punched him in the cheek and grabbed his jaw in a vice-like grip.

'Wha . . .' he croaked.

'Goodbye,' she said. She popped open the bottle and poured the silver potion directly into his baleful eyes.

He screeched and threw her off. She collided with the dais and sank to the floor. Killian lumbered to his feet, still screaming, his hands over his eyes. Bright red light poured through the gaps in his fingers. His body shook and went limp. Lily stopped breathing as she watched him levitate. His head rocked back, and his arms dangled at his sides. Flaming red light raced from his body, desperate to get away. The room lit up like a volcano, crimson, deep orange and blinding gold everywhere. Then it was gone, and the tomb was gloomy once again. Killian's body hovered a second longer, then dropped to the floor like a stone.

Lily was trembling. All she could do was stare at the small heap that was Killian's body. She knew she had to get up, she knew she had to see him, but she was terrified of what she might find. What if it hadn't worked? What if he was still controlled by the enlii? What if he was dead? She shook her head and used the dais to help her stand.

'Killian,' she whispered as she staggered towards him, one hand on her stomach in a vain effort to suppress the pain.

She knelt next to him and laid her hand on his heart. It was just as strong as ever. Exhaustion leached into every aspect of her body, but she couldn't sleep; she had to know he was all right. Grunting, she grabbed his chest and dragged him into her lap. She wrapped her arms around him and hung her head, her hair cascading over her shoulders and onto his body.

'Killian,' she whispered again. A tear trickled out and splashed onto his chest, and she gripped him tighter. 'Killian, please.' Her voice cracked as more tears fell.

She lifted her head and sat back. He looked so peaceful, even through her tear-blurred vision. She traced a wet salty hand over his cheekbones and down to his jaw, then drew her thumb over his lips.

'Lil . . .' he murmured.

Her breath caught in her throat as his eyes fluttered open. Even in the dull light of the tomb, she could see they were blue. They shone like a summer day amid the cold grey of their dismal surroundings. He reached a hand up and touched her face.

'You're real.'

She placed her hand on top of his and held it against her cheek. 'Yes.'

He let out a deep sigh and smiled. 'Thanks.'

'You're welcome.' She couldn't think of what else to say.

'Lil . . . I . . .' But no more words came. His hand dropped, and he passed out in her arms.

CHAPTER FIFTY-NINE

A DARKNESS BLACKER THAN ANY NIGHT AND DEEPER than any ocean wrapped itself around Killian as he fell. He was at peace. His mind and body no longer felt pain; he was free. Responsibility had been lifted; he'd done his duty, and now he was surplus to requirements, cast out alone into the void to fall forever or until his body withered and ceased to function. It was a small price to pay.

POLL crept into view through the trees. Night was already settling across the valley. Smoke curled away from the chimneys in the cool evening breeze. The village lamps were illuminated one by one, their warm orange glow a beacon for the weary traveller.

'We're here, Killian,' whispered Lily.

Killian didn't respond, but she wasn't surprised; he'd not been doing any talking at all lately. Ever since she'd freed him from the grip of the enlii, he'd been unconscious. On the first day, she wasn't too worried – after all, he had slept a lot when he returned from the Drop, and he'd been out of it all day the time he'd collapsed on the beach. She'd figured it would only be natural for him to be sleeping a lot after spending all that time possessed. However, he was now on his second full day, and the worry was beginning to set in.

She put her arms under his thighs and hitched him up her back a little farther. His limp arms hung over her shoulders and down her chest, and his head rested against the back of her neck. The more she carried him, the more shades of green faded from her ring, and it was at least two weeks until the next new moon. She would lose her strength and, because of that, her invulnerability too, but it was a small price to pay for feeling his heartbeat against her back, as was the aching in her body. Bruises littered her torso, making every footstep more painful than the last. Her lip was swollen, and her left eye was surrounded by various shades of grey, purple and yellow. Never before had she taken a beating like this. How and why Killian could hurt her truly was a puzzle – one she desperately needed an answer for.

'Want me to take him?' asked Raven.

She smiled her split lips and turned – Killian's lifeless arm flapped as she moved. 'It's fine, we're almost there.'

With that, she marched down the path towards the bridge.

By the time they arrived in the centre of Poll, the sky was a deep shade of blue and the streets were bathed in a luminescent orange glow. Lily paused outside the tavern and glanced up the quiet streets in the direction of Ulrich's house.

'Blake, go to the tavern. Get us some rooms and order food.' She handed him a coin purse.

'Aye, Captain,' said Blake, breaking away from the group.

Lily and Raven pressed on towards the old husk's house. If he couldn't fix Killian, she didn't know what she'd do. His heart thumped against her back. At least he was alive. But what was wrong with him?

Her footsteps were growing heavy. She glanced at her ring; it had dulled since the morning, but she could still carry him. Exhaustion was setting in rather than the loss of her strength. Footsteps clipped on the stone walkways, and she glanced up as two people came towards her.

'Had too many?' asked the young man, nodding up towards Killian.

'Yeah, something like that,' said Lily.

The man laughed and nudged the woman with him. 'You can do that for me later.'

'I'll leave you to crawl,' she retorted as they walked away.

Lily sighed and headed on up the hill. Despite deliberately dragging her feet for fear of what Ulrich might say, she eventually reached his run-down cottage. She hitched Killian up her back and gave the door three loud raps. Tom's muffled voice worked its way through the thick wooden door. He sounded excited. Finn's gruff tones followed, and the door swung open. The grin melted off Tom's face as fast as butter in a hot skillet. Finn's brow furrowed.

'Cap'n, what happened to you?' Tom gasped. His peridot eyes fixed on her blackened ones.

'Nothing, I'm fine.'

He glanced at her shoulder. 'Is Killian . . .' He paused. 'Dead?'

'No, Tom, he's alive, but I don't know.' She shook her head. 'I need the old codger.'

She pushed past her two crew members and into Ulrich's house. Raven's footsteps echoed down the corridor after her. In the main room stood Ulrich, his wrinkled mouth partially open, his pale eyes full of fear. In his hand was a conical bottle filled with deep red liquid. It slopped about with the viscosity of blood. Poppy sat on her perch and glared at Killian, her fluffy eyebrows down, her hooked beak open.

'You're back,' Ulrich rasped.

'Extremely observant of you,' said Lily. She had no time for pleasantries. 'What's wrong with him?'

'I don't know.' Ulrich took a step backwards.

'Yes, you do. What did I put in his eyes?' Lily kept her voice calm and level. Shouting at him wouldn't help.

'You put the antidote in his eyes,' said Ulrich, a tremor creeping into his voice. 'I promise you, I swear, that's all it was.'

'You sure about that?' said Finn, coming up on Lily's left. She pulled her gun from her belt and levelled it with the old man.

'I'm sure, I promise,' said Ulrich, his tone rising as he took another step back. 'You can check my books. You can check everything I used.' He paused, his chest heaving and his lips trembling. 'D-did the enlii leave?'

'Yes, it did,' said Lily.

'Then it worked. Whatever's happening to him now is nothing to do with me.'

'Fix him.'

'Excuse me?'

'I said,' Lily spat through her teeth, 'fix him.'

'No, he should die.' Ulrich lifted the bottle of red liquid and stared into it.

'Please don't make me kill you,' said Lily, edging closer to the old man.

'I won't,' he said, moving behind the round wooden table so it was between him and her. He put the bottle to his lips and downed the contents. 'You have destroyed this world.' Liquid trickled from the corner of his mouth as he spoke. 'All for your own selfish needs. In saving this one person, you've probably damned millions, you thoughtless scum. The demon with the Gramarye will curse you all. It will hunt you down, take that soul and unleash who knows what onto this doomed world.' His voice wavered, and his breathing grew heavy. He winced and clutched his chest. 'Either you'll kill me now, or I'll live to see the world . . . burn because of your . . . selfish desires.' Red dripped into his beard like a poisonous rainfall. 'I'd rather go on my own terms. I hope he dies . . . and that soul can go with him before it's caught.' He fell onto the table, gasping and wheezing as the poison whittled away his life. 'Get out of . . . my house . . .' He fell to the floor with a heavy thump and didn't move again.

Lily wanted to scream, she wanted to cry, she wanted to burn down his wretched house. She wasn't selfish. This wasn't her fault. The world was not damned because of her. That was speculation from a bitter old man, a husk. He was pinning his crimes on her, that was all. How did he even know that whoever had the Gramarye was up to something nefarious? Heat erupted in her cheeks. He didn't know, but she did. That mask, that voice, Ren's screams. She'd seen and heard it all. Had she cursed the world because of Killian? His breath blew through her hair, and she gripped him tighter.

She turned to her silent crew and drew in a deep breath. 'Grab the book with the Gramarye in it, and let's go.'

Finn nodded and snatched the red-leather-bound book from Ulrich's table.

'Wait,' said Tom, walking over to Ulrich's body. He looked at the owl and held his arm out. 'Come on, Pops, like before.'

The owl hopped from its perch and onto Tom's awaiting forearm.

'Got yourself a pet, eh, Tom?' said Finn.

'Aye, looks like I do.'

CHAPTER SIXTY

SASHA DUMPED HER OVERNIGHT BAG ONTO THE wooden bed in her room at the inn. She'd spent most of the day travelling east to the town of Millenderry, where she'd tracked down her soul, or key. Calling it a key rather than a soul or a person somehow made the job more bearable. All she wanted to do now, though, was flop onto the bed with her belongings and sleep. But she had work to do, gruesome work.

Locating the actual soul had been strangely easy. Varo's guidance, help and reassurance had no doubt aided her. It seemed that the soul closest to her physical location was the first one to shine out. That poor person. She closed her eyes and moved her head. Now that she was in Millenderry, she'd need a more precise location to hunt the key down. A dim blue light flickered in blackness. That was it, that was where she must go. Her stomach roiled, and her head was light and dizzy.

She reached into her bag and pulled out the metal gauntlets Quint had given her before she left. They seemed so unnecessarily brutal and cruel. She put her hand inside one, made a fist, then spread her fingers out one by one. The metal plates clacked softly against each other, and the light of her oil lamp glinted off the sharp edges of the fingertips. She took it off and tossed it onto the bed. With a little bit of concentration, she brought a spark of lightning to her fingers. She'd do it her own way. As quick and as painless as possible. She wrapped her cloak about her shoulders, snatched up her bag and left the inn.

Millenderry was situated on the river Tor, which ran to Torran, the capital of Vermor, no doubt prospering from all the traders who used it as a stop-off point. It was a hive of activity even though it was getting dark. Makeshift stalls littered the town square, with farmers, merchants and traders selling their wares at bargain prices. There were artists with easels set up beneath the street lamps, painting scenes and portraits of the rich. A man with long dark hair was playing a harp, its delicate and magical lament a beautiful backdrop to the hustle and bustle of the square. Sasha spied a trickster at work. A woman with short red hair was sitting at a wooden table, and her gold-ringed hands, skilled in the art of legerdemain, were moving a set of cards about as if they were made of smoke. Someone from the crowd tapped a card, and the woman smirked as she flipped it over. A jovial but disappointed roar burst from her audience, and a gold coin was placed in her outstretched hand.

A voice caught Sasha's ear. 'Excuse me, miss, could I interest you in a new cloak?'

She turned to see a young blond-haired man smiling at her. He was standing beneath the awning of his stall, which housed a rich array of clothes – cloaks, dresses, trousers and bags.

'No, thank you, I—' Theo appeared to her in his tatty clothes. He had a cloak, and it was holey and ripped beyond repair. It was almost like him. She scanned the store and spied a deep maroon one. 'I'll take that one,' she said, pointing.

'Excellent choice,' he said, taking it off a hanger. 'It goes with your eyes.'

'I get that from all the merchants,' she said, giving him a playful wink. 'But it's not for me.'

'A gift,' he exclaimed in that joyful yet overly dramatic tone reserved for most salesmen and merchants, 'even better. I could tell you were a thoughtful soul.'

'Oh, really?' Sasha arched an eyebrow as she reached for her purse. 'How much?'

'For anyone else, ten, but as it's you and a gift, eight. Gift wrapping?'

'No, it's fine as it is,' she said, folding it neatly and slipping it into her bag.

The merchant nodded and took her payment. 'It's your eyes.'

'Excuse me?' said Sasha as she buckled up her bag.

'Your eyes, that deep stormy blue – they show how kind you are. Your hair has the waves of the ocean, which marks you as a strong person, and as for its colour, is it brown, is it gold, is it red? It's all three. It's the colour of nature itself, which shows your deep connection with all life here on Vida.'

Sasha was momentarily stunned by what this person had said – this person who didn't even know her name, this person who didn't know she was on her way to commit a murder.

'Don't worry, I don't charge extra for the reading,' he said with a smile. 'I just wanted you to know – you looked like you needed to hear it.'

'Thank you,' she said.

'Not a problem. Enjoy your evening, miss.'

'You too,' she said with a nod.

Sasha paced away and across the square, keeping her head down to avoid any further interactions. Though, she had to admit, that one had been rather pleasant. Besides Ruby, it had been a long time since she'd spoken to anyone outside the group. It was refreshing to speak to someone innocent of who and what she really was.

She passed a great round ball of a man selling wooden mugs of ale from a keg. She was tempted to stop for one, but she had to keep a clear head so hurried by. A woman in a top hat with a carriage and horses looked as if she was about to offer her services as a ride.

'No, thank you,' Sasha said before she could get any words out.

Once she was across the square and away from the bustle of people, she closed her eyes and focused on the soul. The blue light flickered again; it was closer now, brighter. She opened her eyes, and the light remained locked in her vision like a lighthouse, guiding her. She followed.

She went down various cobbled streets and past narrow two-storey town houses, taverns and inns. Laughter, merriment and smoke poured out of them in buckets. Everyone was social, everyone was having a great time, and she was alone. She grimaced and sped up. She didn't want to get to her destination, but she didn't want to prolong the inevitable.

Could she do it? Could she really do it? Could she murder someone and take their soul? It repulsed and disgusted her, and yet there she was, in Millenderry, on her way to kill someone. It wasn't just for her and her power though. It was for Theo. He needed this, and she had to help him. All mages too, they needed this, didn't they? Kurt was right. What was fifteen people compared to Theo, her and all the mages in Vermor? It was nothing. A teardrop in the ocean.

This person, this soul and key, however, was innocent, born with the wrong soul at the wrong time. Was it fair to take their life? As she walked, her mind strayed to her younger brother, and her heart ached. He'd been innocent too. What would he think of her and what she was doing? He'd hate her more. He could never feel anything for her but hate after what she'd done to him. His sweet, beautiful face ruined in a moment of fury. The poor boy probably grew up blind, if he grew up at all. It was all her fault. She shook her head. Thoughts like that wouldn't help her now; they wouldn't help her ever.

Horse hooves clipped on the cobbles behind her, and wooden wheels creaked. She glanced over her shoulder to see the carriage from earlier. The woman in the top hat was driving the horses while two people who looked as if they'd indulged in too much ale lay sprawled across the back seats. The carriage overtook her, and she followed it a way down the road before turning off to the right.

The buildings and roads gradually changed as she moved out of the town. The cobbles faded away to be replaced by a dirt track, and the buildings changed to one-storey cottages with thatched roofs that sprang up out of the grass like mushrooms. The air was cooler and clearer, and the way was mostly lit by the natural light of the moon. Street lamps were few and far between. The outskirts of Millenderry were more like a small self-contained village. Beyond the cottages were several large barns, and fields of livestock rolled off into the moonlit night.

Sasha wandered through the small village, the blue light growing brighter. She reached the crossroads, and sitting on a bench under a tree was a man. His whole body shimmered with blue light. This was it. He was her target on the cold lonely night. She took a deep breath and approached him.

'Can I sit?' she asked.

'Of course,' he said, looking up, the red glow of a cigarette lighting up his face.

'Nice night,' said Sasha, taking out a cigarette of her own and lighting it, anything to calm down her nerves.

'Sure is,' he agreed. 'I've not seen you before, have I?'

'Nah, I'm passing through on my way to Torran.' She took a long drag. 'Seemed like a nice place, thought I'd stay a night.'

'You ain't wrong. Torran, eh? I couldn't live there – too big, too many people, too noisy,' he said with a dismissive wave of his cigarette.

'Me neither. I'm just visiting.' Sasha thought fast. 'My aunt is ill.'

'Oh, I'm sorry about that.'

A wretched sickness poured through her. She didn't deserve this man's sympathy for her fake story. 'It's fine. So, you live here?'

'Yeah,' he said, a proud edge to his voice. 'I run a livestock farm, and I've finished for the day. I'm just sitting here, waiting for my wife and son to come back from town. Market day – she loves it, so does he,' he added with a grin. 'It's a little ritual of ours. She always brings me a treat, sometimes food, other times clothes. It can be anything, really.'

Sasha's skin grew numb, and she found it hard to even smoke her cigarette. Her vision blurred, and her eyes stung. What was she doing? Why was she doing this? The knife at her hip felt cold even through its leather sheath. She couldn't do this, she couldn't. She should leave and never come back. Never go back to the mages. Leave and run. Her mind flashed to Theo – poor Theo, wasting away before her eyes. He'd saved her twice; she owed him. Then Ruby. She'd promised her no more running. She'd promised they'd be safe in Vermor together, that she could live a normal life without supressing who she was. A dull pain rippled across her ribs; it was like her scar had a mind of its own. She instinctively touched it. That was the night she'd almost died. The night she met Ruby, the night she found someone worth living for.

The man interrupted her thoughts. 'I'm sorry, I didn't mean to drone on and on. Do you have a husband, children?'

'No,' she replied. 'I have someone, but we're not married.'

'Maybe sometime in your future, eh?' he said kindly, giving her a gentle nudge in the ribs.

Sasha finished her cigarette, stubbed it out and tossed it aside. 'Yeah, maybe.'

She balled her fists up underneath her cloak. She had to do it, and soon. It was dark, there was nobody about. It was perfect. The man on the bench was staring wistfully down the darkened lane. Guilt and fear lanced through her. Her brother screamed and cried. The smell of roast pork filled her nostrils. Her stomach lurched. She was dragged away from Ruby screaming and thrown into a cell, chains around her hands and neck, a drum beat as she was led to her execution. Theo faded to nothing, his ruined soul beyond repair. It had to be done.

She would be quick. It would be painless for him.

'I'm so sorry,' she said.

'What?' The man turned to her, still smiling.

His gaze fell on Sasha's flashing white hand, and his smile melted away into a look of confusion. Before he could get another word out, she lunged on him. She pressed her palm firmly to his chest and sent a powerful pulse into his heart. Less than half a second later, a low rumble coursed through the air around them. She let go, and he fell back onto the bench, lifeless.

Despite her fingers' reluctance to work, she managed to roll her sleeve back and pull the knife from her side. The revulsion for what she'd done was creeping up on her, threatening to overwhelm her, but there was one thing left for her to do. She turned her arm over and made the necessary cuts into her skin. It hurt so much. Blood splattered all over her boots. She pulled a small bunch of sage from her pocket and scrunched it up, then grabbed the sprig of rosemary and set it alight.

She put her lips close to the smouldering plant and murmured into the herbal smoke, 'Come to me, join with me, we shall live as one.'

A fierce pain tore through her arm as if it were being ripped apart. She wanted to scream but bit down on her tongue to stop herself. She looked at her bleeding arm through blurred vision. A silvery light hovered over it, then settled into her. An intense burning sensation coursed through the slash in her arm. It was as if someone were pouring molten metal into her skin. Then the pain stopped. It wasn't gradual; it was like it had been switched off instantly.

Sasha's arm glistened with a beautiful spectral turquoise mark, edged with blood. She blew out the burning rosemary, scooped up the sage and pocketed them both. It was bad enough that he was going to be found dead, but for his wife to suspect his soul had been stolen too would be too much pain for one person. She pulled her sleeve down, sheathed her knife and got up. After giving the dead man one last glance, she hurried off into the night, wretchedness, nausea and guilt clawing at her with every step she took.

She was leaving the outskirts when she heard a haunting scream ring out into the night. Sasha's vision misted over as burning tears streaked down her icy cheeks.

CHAPTER SIXTY-ONE

KILLIAN'S RIGHT ARM TWITCHED, FOLLOWED BY HIS left, and his body went rigid. He took a deep gasping breath, and as he blew out, his eyes opened. Darkness filled his vision, endless, cold and lonely. He reached out, but there was nothing to touch, nothing to feel. A black void had welcomed him in, and there wasn't anything he could do about it.

With a twist of his hips, he rolled over to face a different direction. There was nothing there, nothing beneath him, above him or to the side. A never-ending black expanse of emptiness.

He was alone, completely alone. A tremor rattled through his tight chest. Was this his fate? Lost in oblivion forever. Doomed to die alone, with all sensations snatched away from him. In the void, there was nothing – no light, no sound, no feeling.

RAVEN leapt through the treetops in search of Lily's mage camp, his keen eyes scanning every patch of unusual-looking undergrowth, his nimble feet pushing him on. The cool wind whistling past his ears was invigorating after a sweaty morning of trudging through fields. If this group of bandits really did have a powerful healer, maybe Killian would wake up. Raven frowned; he couldn't help but feel this idea was a lost cause – not that he'd ever say that to Lily. She needed to cling to something, however unlikely the outcome. Shattering her hopes now would only break her. They needed their captain strong and full of hope.

The air shifted; it was full of deep pine scents, and the forest morphed. Dense trees clogged the way before him. He leapt down to the mossy, needle-covered ground and tried to peer through the tangle of vegetation. It was impossible to see beyond it. The trees darkened into an impenetrable black mass. Walking through wasn't on his agenda. He considered summoning his wings but dismissed the notion and decided on a more traditional approach.

He tensed and jumped onto the nearest tree trunk. As soon as his foot struck the wood, he pushed forwards, his feet slamming down one after the other as he powered upwards into his vertical run. The trunk tapered as he reached the top. He reached down and pushed himself off the very tip of the tree, flipping himself over in mid-air. With a soft thump, he landed in the clearing, bending his knees at the impact.

The camp was empty. Three dull green canvas tents were secured to the ground with thick ropes. Before them lay what would obviously be a campfire later. The clearing was so quiet, the thick ring of trees muffling most of the noise from the surrounding forest. After another quick glance around the camp, Raven approached one of the tents. He'd only taken a few steps when he was swept off his feet. Fierce winds swirled all around him as he hung suspended in the air before being unceremoniously dumped to the ground.

'Who are you?' snapped a voice.

Raven got to his feet. A half-dressed man with heterochromatic eyes was gliding towards him. This must be Leif. He didn't seem as friendly as Lily had described. Maybe it was because he wasn't a woman, or Lily.

'How'd you get in here?'

Raven opened his mouth to explain but was knocked to the ground in a puff of needles and grass. Without giving him the chance to move, Leif lifted him up. Raven struggled against the violent winds, his arms uselessly scrabbling for something to grab on to. He wriggled and thrashed, but the mage had him trapped. Leif's arms were visibly trembling, but he gritted his teeth with determination. With a click of his fingers, he banished the winds, and Raven fell to the ground again.

'Let's have some fun,' said Leif, smashing his fist into his palm.

Raven smiled as he got onto all fours. He glanced up at Leif through his hair and leapt into the air. He twisted over the startled mage, landed behind him and dealt him a kick to the back. Leif put his hands out, creating a cushion of air to save himself with. Raven darted forwards and kicked Leif's legs from under him. The mage went tumbling to the dirt. He rolled onto his side and staggered to his feet.

'You're not a mage,' he panted, glaring at Raven. His olive-brown skin was slick with sweat.

'No, I'm not, Leif.'

'How d'you know my name?' he demanded. A weak gust of wind blew from his fingertips to tousle Raven's hair.

'I believe you know my captain, Lily Rothbone.'

'Lily, is she all right?'

Raven nodded. 'We need your help.'

LILY used the air tunnel first, holding on to Killian as she went. Her crew followed swiftly behind her. Tom gasped in wonder at the size and structure of the mages' hideout while Finn whistled and rolled a cigarette. Poppy flew over the treeline to land on Tom's shoulder. Blake strutted around like a guide and took them off to explore the camp.

Killian's weight had grown heavy on Lily's back. Her ring was now almost completely grey. Once she put him down, she knew she'd only be able to pick him up once more, and then her enhanced strength would be gone. If that happened, she'd have to remove her ring and lose her invulnerability or face the ring draining her life for its own. Hopefully it wouldn't come to that, and with any luck, by the next new moon he'd be able to pick himself up.

Seeing Leif again, and so soon, filled her with an infuriating amount of nerves. With Killian slung over her back, she approached him. 'On your own, Leif?'

'Yeah,' he said, the sadness in his voice coming through despite his cocksure smile. 'I've not been out with the others since you left. Need a hand with him?' he added, nodding towards Killian.

Guilt lanced through Lily. Something had happened to him, and it was most likely because of her. What was she doing to people? 'No, I'm fine,' she said. 'Can I lay him in a tent?'

'Sure.' Leif paced over to their collection of tents.

Lily followed, noticing that he had a slight limp and that his footsteps were heavy and laden with exertion. What had she done to him? Her own bruised ribs groaned in sympathy, but that didn't matter. She didn't matter. Not now.

He pulled back the tent flap and held it open for her. She ducked under and rolled Killian off her back. She dropped down to her knees and tried to make him comfortable. Leif let go of the canvas, stepped inside and crouched in the doorway.

'You all right?' he asked, tapping his eye, followed by his lip.

'I'm fine. Just a bit of a scuffle, that's all.'

'Seems like you do that a lot. This your friend, the one who was depending on you?' He gestured to Killian.

'Yeah,' she said, pulling a blanket over him. 'He's not too good.'

'I see,' he replied. He wobbled and put his hand down to steady himself.

'I was hoping Arow might be able to help him.'

'He might. Depends what mood he's in.' Leif sat down, resting his back against one of the dark wooden struts that supported the tent.

'I see you've still not taken to wearing shirts,' remarked Lily, trying to keep the atmosphere light.

He smiled weakly. 'I don't sleep in them. Your beautiful man woke me up.' He rocked his head back, and his eyes started to close.

'I broke you, didn't I?'

'A little.' He sighed. 'I burned out. I knew I would. What I did was ridiculous, but I didn't think it would be as bad as it was.'

'Which was?'

'I only know what they told me. Arow had to restart my heart, and he wasn't happy about it; Nedge had to force him. I died. Can you believe that? I actually died for a few minutes. I was out for about three days, and when I came to, I could hardly do anything. I'm pathetic. That little skirmish I had with your pretty man took it out of me. I didn't think I'd be able to make the tunnel. I hope I can let the others back in.'

'If you can't, Raven can get them.'

Leif looked at her and smiled. 'No, that's on me.'

'Not if it's going to hurt you.'

'I'll be all right.'

'You're so annoyingly stubborn,' she muttered. 'Don't blame me if you burn out again.'

'I won't. It was my fault anyway. I thought I could do more than I could. I thought I was more than I am. I've learnt that lesson.'

'Good.' She didn't really know what else to say to that. What he'd said was true – he didn't need her to tell him that.

'So,' said Leif, reaching behind her to drag a shirt out from a pile of clothes, 'which one is your lover, then?'

'My what?' she snapped, keeping her voice low.

'Well, I figured it wasn't Blake – you two didn't seem together in that sense. So, which one is it? Which one is responsible for keeping us apart?' He grinned mischievously, buttoning his shirt halfway.

'None of them,' she whispered.

'I'm to believe you like women, or that you're celibate?'

'Yes,' she said.

'Nedge'll be pleased.'

'What?'

'She likes women too, when it suits her.'

'Good.'

'It's him, isn't it?' said Leif, motioning towards Killian.

'No.'

'It's all right to love somebody, Lily. He's a lucky guy, even if he is . . .' Leif shrugged. 'Half dead?'

Lily looked at Killian, then back to Leif. 'I just . . .' She paused and failed spectacularly in her attempt to keep tears at bay. 'I just want him to wake up.'

Leif leant forwards and pulled her into his arms. She buried her face into his chest and sobbed.

'Don't cry,' he whispered, stroking her hair. 'I'm such an idiot. I'm sorry, I shouldn't have said anything. I didn't mean half dead, I meant something else. Tired. Tired, that's what I meant.'

'It's okay,' Lily choked out.

'I'll put a good word in for you with Arow – it's the least I can do.'

Lily pulled back and wiped away the tears. 'What do you mean, "put a good word in"? Arow knows me. He'll help.'

Leif sat back and ran a hand through his wavy dark hair. 'Arow is complicated – healing mages *are* complicated.'

'Nedge mentioned something last time.'

'Look, Arow's been at it for such a long time, he's not like he was. His grumpy-old-man thing isn't an act; it's what that power has done to him. Nedge had to threaten his life – seriously threaten it – so he'd save me. He was gonna let me die. I credit her for saving me as much as he did.'

'And you're still friends with him?' Lily asked. She wanted to punch him herself. What sort of person would let a member of their crew, their guild, die?

'Of course. It's not his fault. It's a corruption. I can't blame him.'

'So, he might not help?'

'Like I said, it depends on his mood. I'll see what I can do.'

CHAPTER SIXTY-TWO

KILLIAN DRIFTED BACK TO CONSCIOUSNESS. WITH great reluctance, he peeled open his eyes to face the darkness. He gasped and blinked. All around him, pulsing balls of light hovered in the air like minute stars. It was as if someone had poked holes through the blackness while he slept. They were everywhere, as far as he could see, each one giving him a small piece of hope. They passed into his body as he touched them. Each fleck of light he absorbed seemed to increase his strength. He held his arms out and concentrated. The iridescent glow flowed through his body like a lazy river, and his muscles tightened with power. Magical light rippled across his skin in colourful waves. Focusing, he drew the light into his hands, draining it from the rest of his body with his mind. They shone like two stars, and he squinted at their brightness. Was the Gramarye power killing him? Was he already dead?

He flicked his wrists, and the light leapt from his skin. It plummeted into the darkness, leaving a shimmering trail in its wake. Killian watched it go. It sucked in any nearby stars as it fell, like a basking shark filtering for plankton. A strange idea formed in his head, and he pulled more of the glow into his hands. He flexed his fingers and launched down a second blast. It raced off, gathering speed, momentum and stars. There was a tremendous flash of light as the two bolts of iridescent energy collided, forcing Killian to shut his eyes and cover his face with his arm. A thunderous crack echoed all around the starry void. Only when the rumbling had subsided did he dare to look. There was something beneath him, something large and flat. It was dark like it was covered with shadows, but it was definitely solid.

Killian held his arms out and tilted his body so that he was falling feet first. The dark mass beneath him grew closer. He tensed his body and covered it with the glow. He focused and willed himself to slow in his descent, and to his surprise, he did. Bathed in shimmering light, he floated down, and finally, his feet touched something solid.

The ground yielded to his weight; it was soft and springy. A tremor shot through his body, rendering him unable to stand, and he collapsed to his knees. He wanted to weep, but his face was bone dry, his emotions a confusing tangle.

He was surrounded by darkness; the strange land mass was as devoid of life as the space between the stars. It stretched on for miles like an elongated shadow at dusk. He pressed his palms into the cold lifeless ground to push himself up. Without warning, a great surge of power leapt from his body and melted into the ground. His knees buckled, and he slumped down. He shut his eyes and hung his head, his breath deep, even and heavy. His heart pounded violently, like it was trying to force its way through his breastbone and escape. Even though he knew it would have no effect, he put his hand to his chest and held it steady. It took a few minutes, but eventually his body returned to normal. Tentatively, he opened his eyes.

The first thing he saw was his hand in front of him. It was glowing; light pulsed on his skin and flowed out into the ground. He got to his feet once more. The light cascaded from his body and spilt over the dark land. Crystalline blades of grass sprouted where his glow flowed.

He held his palm over the ground, and the light leapt up and into his hand, yet the iridescent patches of grass remained. Killian held on to the intense energy. It felt so good, so warm and powerful. He took a deep breath and threw a pulse of light as far as he could. He gritted his teeth and urged the magic along, to move faster, farther. As it sped away, a whole new world emerged in its wake.

Glistening trees erupted from the shimmering grass. Smooth hills covered with trees and glowing rocks rolled off into the distance. A pathway cut through the hills, revealing the flatlands up ahead. Tall crystal seed-covered grasses shimmied around the shores of a massive silvery lake. The waters were so gentle they barely bothered the glittering sandy shoreline. The flats spread out for miles and miles, so far that Killian couldn't see where they ended and the soaring mountains began. Their gigantic rocky faces were predominantly black with streaks of silver outlining their crags, and atop each one was a thick layer of white.

Killian rubbed his eyes; he couldn't quite believe what he was seeing. A new world had been created. It was amazing, like nothing he'd ever seen in his life. He walked over to the nearest tree and placed his hand on its trunk. It was cool, its surface was tattered and rugged, and it felt real. It felt like a tree. He walked up the small hill behind it, stopped halfway and turned around to look. From there he could see the vast expanse of his world. The lake flashed with brilliant light, the long grasses nodded approvingly and the mountains kept a protective watch. The grasslands rolled and tumbled playfully until they reached the flats, where they sank and became orderly, but without losing any of their sparkling shine.

He sat down, and the soft ground beneath him dipped to accommodate his body comfortably. He wrapped his arms around his head and stared up at the thousands of twinkling stars looking down at him. Steadily, his vision blurred, and the stars began to lose their shape and merge together.

Where was he? Was any of this real? Had he created this place? And how could he leave?

CHAPTER SIXTY-THREE

Lily took the bowl of stew Leif offered with a sharp tug, saying more than words could in one movement. He sat next to her and picked at his own. He glanced in her direction, but he said nothing. The night was rapidly drawing in, and he still hadn't spoken to Arow. Frustration and impatience were building up within her. She took a spoonful of stew and forced herself to keep her emotions from bursting out. She needed Arow to help Killian. She'd already decided they couldn't leave and return to the ship until he was fixed, but from what Leif had said, getting Arow's help could be a delicate process.

She looked up from her bowl at the firelit faces around her. The healing mage's face was etched with a scowl, a scowl she wanted to punch off. She gritted her teeth and drew an angry breath through her nose. Rage and brute force wouldn't help her now. The weakest glimmer of green remained in her ring. But it would be so good to use some brute force. No. She bit back that thought. Not today. Wasting the last vestiges of her power on him wouldn't do. She could slip the ring off, though, and just punch him anyway. She had a mean right hook with or without an enhanced boost of strength. No. Just no. That wouldn't help anyone, and it certainly wouldn't help Killian.

'Get much today?' Leif asked Raynn, breaking the sombre silence.

'Not a lot.' Raynn put down his bowl to loosen his doublet, which appeared to have a hole in it. 'Managed to snare a couple of travelling merchants doing the usual route. One of them got a lucky stab in.' He picked his bowl back up.

Arow grunted with obvious contempt.

'We got a few coins, so it wasn't all bad,' Raynn continued, ignoring Arow's distaste. 'Here, I got you a present,' he added, tossing a jar towards Leif.

Leif caught it with one hand and beamed. It was packed to bursting with marinated olives – green, black and purple.

'I don't know how you can eat those things.' Raynn grimaced. 'They set my teeth on edge.'

Leif unscrewed the jar and popped one into his mouth; his eyes glistened, and a satisfied smile spread across his face. 'You should try them again – they grow on you.'

'No thanks, I wouldn't want to take one away from you,' said Raynn. 'How're you feeling?'

Leif scratched his chest. 'Could be better, could be worse.'

Raynn nodded, then turned his attention to Lily. 'So, Captain Rothbone,' he said in a tone that suggested they were both on the same level, 'how long will we have the pleasure of your company?'

'I haven't decided yet.'

'Oh, really.' He sounded a little flustered, like he'd prepared a play in his head and she'd just read the wrong line. 'Well . . . you're welcome to stay fo—'

'I know, you owe me and my crew.' She turned a cold glare onto Leif, put her bowl down and got to her feet. 'Speaking of which, I'm going to check on Killian.'

Killian was exactly where she'd left him, lying on his back, his arms on either side of him. She knelt next to him and watched his chest rise and fall.

'Come on, Killian,' she said, 'wake up, you cretin.' Her throat tightened as emotion tried to choke her. 'Wake up, you fucking idiot! I hate you. I hate you so much. Wake up so I can tell you.'

Unsurprisingly, he failed to respond. Lily took his arm and rolled it over, staring at the glowing blue light of the orm. Had it been worth it? All this pain and misery just to hide that stupid seal. From the way Ulrich had spoken, it might matter a great deal to the rest of the world, but to her, she didn't care. She just wanted him back. She wanted him to argue with her again, she wanted to see his eyes open, she wanted him to be alive, not just breathing. Did that make her a bad person? Selfish? If Killian died now, it could be better for everyone. But she didn't want that; she just wanted him back. They could figure out what to do when he awoke.

She flipped his arm back over, grabbed a drab green woollen blanket and drew it over him.

'Sleep well,' she murmured, getting up and returning to the others.

Everyone was lying down with their backs propped up by a sloped section of earth that resembled a small theatre. At the bottom of the slope stood Blake, his eyes a dazzling white.

He blew out a great cloud of sweet smoke and set to work. Plumes of colour shot up, and a beautiful female cornelian appeared, all glittering horns and ruby hair. Lily sighed. She wanted to join them, and she knew she should, but she couldn't bring herself to do it. She glanced towards the fire and saw Leif stretched out before it, a blanket wrapped around his body. She bit down on the inside of her lip and, against her better judgement, sloped over to him.

He was fast asleep, his breathing deep and rhythmical. She sat next to him, stole an olive and stared into the fire. The crackling flames were just as strong as when Raynn had lit it; his magic must have been keeping it that way. Cries and shouts came from the group surrounding Blake, and she smiled thinly. It was good that they were having fun. She tapped her fingers on her knees; she was getting restless. She looked at Leif again.

'Not you too,' she muttered, shaking her head.

Leif rolled onto his side and opened his bleary mismatched eyes. 'Not what?' he asked thickly.

'Oh, you are awake,' she said.

He yawned. 'I wasn't, but I am now.' He sluggishly pushed himself up, the blanket falling away to reveal his body.

'Stopped wearing clothes again,' said Lily, eyeing him.

He gathered the coarse blanket up and wrapped it around his shoulders. 'We've been through this – I don't sleep in my shirt. I can put it on if the sight of me repulses you.'

'No, it's all right.'

Leif reached for the jar of olives and offered it to Lily.

'Thanks,' she said, taking one.

'Before you say anything, I've not asked him yet.'

'I wasn't going to,' said Lily. She tossed the olive into the air and caught it in her mouth. It was so tangy, salty and delicious.

'So, you've been stabbing me in the gut all night with your eyes for no reason?'

Lily spat the pit away and grabbed another olive from his jar.

'He's in one of his moods – you can blame Raynn for that.'

'Getting himself stabbed?' Lily asked, looking over at the assembled group.

'Yup. Idiot.'

Lily ran her hands through the thick mossy grass. It was cold and refreshing to the touch, just what she needed. A rich earthy smell rose from the ground as she disturbed it. Tiny orange mushrooms were scattered about the clearing, absorbing the light from the fire. Off in the bushes, a collection of green fireflies shone as they lazily circled one another.

'Why are you slumming it over in reject corner anyway?' he asked, picking up an olive and giving it a gentle squeeze before dropping it into his mouth.

'What d'you mean?' She took another; their juicy salty flavour was addictive.

'You're not mingling with them.' He waved his hand towards the others. 'You're here with the useless mage instead.'

'Don't flatter yourself. I'm not mingling with you, I merely wasn't in the mood for socialising en masse. That and I thought I could intimidate you into speaking with Arow.' She paused and made a fist. 'Before I have to speak to Arow.'

'All right,' he said, 'you've succeeded in intimidating me.'

'Good.' She smirked and stole another olive. 'What's all this about being the useless mage?'

He drew his knees up and rested his arms atop them. 'I don't want to talk about it.'

'Okay,' said Lily, turning towards him. The flickering fire cast dancing shadows over his handsome face. 'What do you want to talk about, then?'

'I . . . I don't know,' he muttered, grabbing an olive and stuffing it into his mouth.

'Leif,' she said, softening her tone. She could tell he was hurting.

'I just feel so useless,' he said. 'I've always been able to wield well. I've only ever burned out a handful of times, and those were when I was young and cocky—'

'As opposed to being old and cocky?'

'Kick me while I'm down, eh?'

'I'm only playing.'

'Well, good,' he said, running his fingers through his wavy black hair. 'I just feel . . . I don't know. I don't know how I feel. I've never felt like this before.' He emptied his lungs and rested his chin on his knees, not breaking eye contact with Lily. 'I feel like I'm not needed anymore. I feel useless. It's hard to explain with you not being a mage.'

'Try.'

'Okay. I've been doing this for so long, and it's always come easy for me. I was lucky because I was one of those who found it naturally easy. But now . . . Now it's so hard. The tunnel should be easy for me to do, but it puts so much strain on my body, I amaze myself every time I manage to do it.' He scratched his jaw, his eyes not leaving hers. 'Put it this way: if I wanted to seduce you tonight – not that I don't want to seduce you tonight, I do, but I know I shouldn't – I wouldn't be able to jump us over the trees for privacy like I did before, especially after making two tunnels and having a little scrape with Mr Pretty Eyes. I wouldn't be able to do it.'

'Why don't you try?' she said.

'I can't. I'm not strong enough.'

'How do you know that?' she said, getting to her feet.

He laughed. 'I just can't, all right? You don't understand.'

'Come on,' she said, holding her hand out. 'Get up, and let's go.'

He laughed again and rubbed his fist into his forehead. 'I really can't do it.'

'Bollocks! You can, and you will.'

'I don't know,' he murmured.

'Exactly, you don't. What happened to that narcissistic cock I knew a few days ago?'

'He died,' said Leif.

'Don't be so dramatic.'

Leif shook his head.

'How are you supposed to stand up to Arow and get me what I want with this self-pitying attitude? Stop being such a defeatist. I've no time for it.'

'All right,' he said, tugging off the blanket and pulling his shirt on, only doing it up halfway. 'But if something happens to me, you've got to get us back.' He took her hand. 'Or we could just sleep out there, huddled next to each other for warmth.'

'You'll be fine.' She yanked him to his feet.

'If you say so.'

'Go on, then,' she said, holding her arms out.

He stepped forward and took her in his arms. He tilted his head, rested his cheek on top of her head and breathed deeply. She put her hands around his back, and her pulse quickened. Earthy scents poured from his silky dark hair.

'Ready?' he said.

'Yes,' she replied, tightening her grip.

He paused for a few seconds. There was a howling rush of wind, and they were lifted above the treetops. Lily clung to his body, pressing her head against his chest, the air rushing through her ears. The winds waned until they were as soft as the falling snow.

'You can look,' he whispered.

He held her arms, turned her around and pulled her close.

She had to catch her breath. They were hovering way above the campsite. Before her lay the forest, glowing silver in the light of the moon. Towering mountains loomed in the distance, snow-capped and gleaming. Snaking silver rivers plummeted over craggy cliff faces, dissolving into fine mists before they had the chance to hit the ground. Rolling fields covered most of the vista, sparkling white and tumbling away out of sight.

Leif's body tensed; she could feel the strain it was putting on him. She looked around from the spectacular scene before her to his face. His eyes were closed and his jaw set. He was deep in concentration.

'I'm going to . . . put us down now . . .' he said.

They began their gentle descent to the other side of the camp. Soft winds buffeted their clothes as they sank. When Leif's feet touched the soft ground, he staggered but maintained his balance. Lily released him from her grip and looked at him, a smirk pulling at her bruised and split lip. It ached, but she didn't care.

'I told you you could do it.'

'You did,' he said. 'Can I seduce you now?'

Lily curled her lip and shook her head.

He held his hands out, palm up. 'Well, it was worth asking.' He lowered himself to the ground and stretched his legs out. With a deep breath, he looked up to the trees.

Lily sat next to him in the same position, enjoying the creaking of the trees, the rustle of animals in the undergrowth and the far-off howl of a razortail.

Leif sighed and turned to her. 'We'd make a good team, wouldn't we?' he asked.

'No.'

He adjusted his body and faced her.

Lily's heart thumped, and warmth crept over her body. She rolled onto her side, propping her head up with her hand, her hair flowing over her shoulders. His shirt gaped open, but she fought with all her will to keep from staring.

He reached forward and laid a hand on her shoulder. 'You love him, don't you?'

'No,' she said. 'I hate him even more than I hate you.'

'Oh, it's like that, is it?' He grinned.

'Yes, it is,' she said. Her hand moved, and she almost placed it on his hip but thought better of it.

He chuckled. 'It looks like I met you too late.'

Lily pursed her lips and sneered.

He laughed again, and it wrapped a sensation of ease around her.

'Perhaps.' It felt strangely good to be almost honest for once – freeing and refreshing, like a weight had been lifted from her shoulders, one she'd carried for so long.

'You're not one to give anything away,' he said, dropping his hand from her shoulder to her arm. He gave her a squeeze. 'He must be pretty special when he's not asleep.'

'He's a crew member . . . He's not even that. He's temporary crew.'

'Nothing special?' he asked.

'No. Nothing.'

A deep sadness washed through her. Would he ever wake up? Was it her fault? Was it his fault? Was the world doomed? Could she ever let go of everything that held her back? The fear and the weakness. Those swinging feet. Her persona. A pirate captain needed nothing but respect and riches. Captain Lily Rothbone did not need or desire Killian O'Shea. But what about Liliana Maggiore, what did she want? What did she need?

Leif picked up on her mood. 'Come on,' he said, opening his arms.

Lily pulled herself along the ground and into his embrace. She breathed in the scent of his skin, fresh pines with a smoky edge. He ran his hand through her hair, then dropped it to her back. They stayed like that, just breathing, comfortable in each other's warmth.

'I think you do love him. And when the time comes, for the sake of my broken heart, make sure you tell him.'

A muffled chuckle escaped from Lily.

'I'm serious,' he said. 'I don't know if I'll ever recover after meeting you.'

She lifted her head and stubbornly held his beguiling gaze, refusing to give in to her desires. 'You'll recover as soon as a pretty girl crosses your path.'

He frowned and pursed his lips. 'Pretty girls are so vacuous and dull.' He sighed, his brown and green eyes shimmering. 'With the exception of you, of course.'

Lily laughed and pressed her hands into his chest. 'You can't make me feel guilty.'

'I would never pull such a cheap trick.' He pressed her against him one last time and inhaled deeply. 'We'd better head back before they notice we're gone. We don't want them assuming something.'

'That would be a scandal.' Lily gasped with mock horror.

Leif let her go, and she sprang to her feet. He shook his head and got to his feet. A flicker of pain ran through Lily's ribs. Why did healing take so long? And why did it hurt?

How had Killian done this to her? Killian of all people. An idea formed in her head, one that needed testing immediately.

'Leif, you can pull from the Otherside?'

'I can – badly, as you saw, but I can.'

'Could you do me a favour before we go back?'

'Sure.'

She slowly placed her hands on her hips and threw him a warm smile. 'I want you to hit me.'

'What? No. Why?'

'It's just a theory I'd like to test,' she said.

He shook his head. 'I don't hit women.'

'Don't give me that. There's something I need to know the answer to, and you can help me find it.'

'By hitting you?'

'Yes. And make sure you give it some oomph. I want to feel it.'

Leif shook his head and pushed his hair from his eyes. 'All right, but you asked for this, remember?'

Lily nodded and turned her upper arm towards him. Leif made a fist and swung, punching her firmly on the bicep. She felt nothing. No sting with the impact. No pain. Nothing.

'Do you have your answer?' asked Leif.

'No.' She paused, knowing she was asking a lot. 'Can you do it again, but this time pull some magic from the Otherside?'

He bit his lip and shook his head. 'Lily.'

'You don't have to hit me with it, just have it summoned and then hit me with your other hand.'

'You don't ask for much, do you?'

'Only the bare minimum.'

'All right,' he said, 'but only because you asked so nice.'

Leif drew in a deep breath and made a fist with his left hand. The air whipped up around his hand, and a soft howl whispered through the night. Colours sparked within the winds, pink, purple, blue. It was wild magic from the Otherside. His thick eyebrows bunched together as the strain of holding on to it grew painfully evident.

'Hit me, now.'

Leif nodded and punched her with his right. A deadening pain surged through Lily's arm; she grunted and reflexively grabbed it.

With a soft strained grunt, Leif banished the colour-flecked winds. His hair was slick with sweat, and his body was shaking. 'Sorry,' he rasped, 'I didn't mean to hu—'

'No, you did great.'

Her arm throbbed with a dull ache. Perhaps it would even bruise. Leif was a mage in touch with the Otherside, and he could hurt her when he called on that magic. That meant Killian was somehow connected to the Otherside too. When he'd returned from the Drop, he *had* hurt her in her cabin. That pain had been real after all. The Killian who fell down the Drop was not the same as the Killian who had returned.

Leif interrupted her thoughts. 'Can I ask what that was about?'

'You can ask.'

CHAPTER

SIXTY-FOUR

KILLIAN AWOKE TO A FIERCE PAIN BURNING IN HIS chest. He sat up immediately and clutched his breast, wincing in pain. It intensified, and he cried out – it was like he was burning from the inside out. All his vital organs were melting and flowing around his body like lava. He gripped at the silver grass with his hand and tore chunks from the ground. Sweat rained from his forehead as his body twisted and convulsed in agony. He rolled onto all fours and kicked wildly at the ground as he dug his hands into the soft, cool soil.

Scorching tears mixed with sweat as he tried to regain control over his trembling body. He closed his eyes and breathed deeply to try to blot out the pain. His arms shook under the pressure, threatening to buckle and leave him face down in the dirt. He took another ragged breath and focused on the dormant power within him, bringing it to the surface. His muscles tightened, and his trembling lessened.

Slowly, he opened his eyes, and the pain was gone. He rocked back onto his knees and breathed a juddering sigh of relief. Tentatively, he released the glow and reverted to normal. When his strength returned, he stood. His body remained tense in expectation of another bout of pain.

What was that?

'Pain,' an ethereal voice whispered in answer from behind him.

Killian whirled around. 'Who's there?'

But his voice was met with silence.

'Please, please say something. Tell me where I am. Tell me what's going on.'

More silence.

'How do I get out? How do I get back?'

Nothing.

'Am I alone?'

'Yes,' the voice hissed.

Killian put his face in his hands in despair. 'You're lying,' he muttered into his palms.

Silence again.

He moved his hands away and smiled. 'You're lying. I just spoke to you.'

'Clever,' the voice said, an underlying sinister edge to its tone. 'But how do you know I'm real?'

'My internal monologues rarely answer me back outside my own body.'

The voice snickered. 'Goodbye, Killian. Thanks for the help.'

There was a deep gasping sound and then no more. Killian shuddered. Weakness invaded his body. His legs gave in, and he crumpled to his knees. The stars hummed within the never-ending darkness, and he tilted his head to face them.

'Ren?'

LILY pushed the flap of the tent up, squinting as the light beamed into the clearing. She rubbed her eyes and ran a hand through her messy hair. Leif had kindly donated his tent to her and the unconscious Killian. Even he wasn't brazen enough to try to sleep next to her again. Instead, he'd squished himself into someone else's tent, and that was fine by her.

Nedge and Finn were sitting next to each other in the sunken hollow. A smouldering roll-up dangled from Finn's mouth as she carefully constructed another and passed it to the mage.

Nedge rocked her head back and shouted, 'Oi! Raynn, get out here and light me up!'

'No!' came the blunt response from Raynn's tent. 'I'm very busy.'

She cackled and let Finn light the roll-up with a match.

Lily smirked to herself and ambled over to the two women.

Finn looked up as Lily approached, screwing her eyes up in the light. 'Mornin', Cap'n,' she said, smoke tumbling from her mouth like a toxic waterfall.

'Morning.' She nodded to them both and sat down in the hollow. It was soft, spongy and slightly damp from the morning dew, but so relaxing. She lay back against it and grunted with satisfaction. 'This is nice,' she murmured through half-closed eyes.

'It's the moss,' said Nedge. She took a drag. 'Arow can talk to it, whisper to it, encourage it to grow. Makes life comfier.'

'I could fall asleep all over again,' said Lily.

'I know that feeling.' Nedge yawned and stretched. 'Hey! Raynn!' she shouted again. 'Get out here and stick a pot on!'

'Do it yourself!' came the flustered response.

Nedge looked over at Finn and Lily and winked slowly. 'But you make it so well.'

'I'm busy!'

'Please, Raynn,' she said, barely suppressing an evil grin. 'You're so good at it.'

'I know, I know.'

'I'll just burn it. You know what I'm like.'

'Yes, I do.'

'And we have guests.'

'True, true.' He paused. 'All right, I'll be out in a second.'

Nedge smirked at the other two. 'Gets him every time.'

'Ain't he in charge?' asked Finn.

'He'd like to think so, and he'd like you to think so.' She took a drag on her cigarette and blew out a great cloud of smoke. 'I guess he is, but don't let him know I said that out loud.'

The words had barely left her lips when Raynn burst from his tent, his blond hair perfectly sculpted, with one side neatly tucked behind his ear. He wore a white shirt and a brown jacket with tails, brown boots laced up over smart dark trousers. He looked like he was on his way to a fancy function, not about to make a pot of coffee for a camp of brigands.

'Do not fret, I am here to save the morning,' he announced with a flourish of his hands, walking over to the pile of camping utensils. He lit a fire with a brush of his fingertips.

'My hero,' Nedge drawled.

'Speaking of, how's shithead this morning?' Finn asked.

Lily loved how tactical she was, just dropping it casually into conversation, almost like she'd forgotten about him.

Lily flashed a lopsided smirk. 'You know him – asleep.'

Finn sucked a breath in through her teeth. 'Typical. He's a lazy bastard.'

'Leif said he was gonna talk to Arow about him today, see if he can find out what's up.'

'Good luck with that,' Nedge put in. She crushed her roll-up out in her palm and didn't so much as flinch. 'Arow isn't exactly accommodating with his talents at the moment.'

Lily sat up. 'Leif told me what happened.'

Nedge pursed her lips. 'Did he now? Well, he was dead at the time, so he's probably a little hazy.' The mage moved closer to Finn and Lily and opened her hand. Purple smoke and black lightning flickered in her palm. 'He'd have let him die. Leif is a sleazy flirt, but he's my mate. I wasn't gonna let him die.' She flashed her dark eyes in the direction of Raynn, who was happily humming to himself while brewing coffee. 'He wasn't gonna do anything – well, he might have set his shirt on fire if pushed, but we needed something a little more convincing.' She made a fist, and the dark magic blew away, harmless as smoke.

'Shit,' Finn muttered under her breath, 'he's that bad?'

'It's not his fault – it's the corruption. If anything, it's our fault for pushing him into healing us all the time. We went with the rule of "one more won't matter." Turns out, sometimes it does matter.'

'Well, our cap'n can be quite . . . persuasive.' Finn glanced in Lily's direction.

'What are you three plotting?' Raynn asked, stepping into their group with a wooden tray of drinks. He crouched down and offered the steaming coffees out.

Lily took a deep swig of the warm bitter liquid. Nedge wasn't joking – Raynn knew how to make decent campfire coffee.

Raynn took the fourth mug for himself and sat amongst them. He ran his hand through the grass, the dewdrops catching the light and sparkling like diamonds. 'I see the flavour of my coffee has stunned you into silence.'

Lily sniggered. 'It's good, but it's not silencing.'

'What were you talking about, then?' he asked, drawing his knees up to his chest. 'I feel left out.'

Lily caught a questioning glance from Nedge and gave her a gentle nod.

'Arow,' said Nedge, curling her lip slightly as she said his name.

'Arow, our lord and saviour,' said Raynn. He took a swig of his coffee. 'Damn, that's good.' He lowered his eyes in a conspiratorial way. 'Leif went off with him early this morning. Woke me up fiddling with his boots and muttering something about a miserable swine. My mystery is solved. Now, why would he be going off with Arow?' Raynn turned to Lily and cocked his head in question.

Lily held his stare with ease. 'Well, obviously, I want him to examine my injured crew member. That's why I'm here. Surely you worked that out?'

'Of course I did.' Raynn huffed. 'So, Leif is trying to talk Arow around for you?'

'He is.' Lily nodded and took another sip of her drink.

'And if he doesn't succeed?'

Lily blew out a long breath and cast her eyes up to the misty morning sky. 'Then I'll just have to crush your miserable mage's throat until I get what I want.'

CHAPTER
SIXTY-FIVE

SASHA ARRIVED BACK AT THE HIDEOUT AT NOON, having spent all morning travelling. She was exhausted, and her eyes were raw. That man's smile had faded in and out of her consciousness all night, and whenever it seemed like she might finally fall asleep, his wife's scream jarred her back to reality. Quint was waiting on the porch when she returned, as if he knew she was on her way.

'Welcome back, kiddo,' he said, cigarette smoke falling from his mouth with each word.

'Thanks,' she said through a yawn. 'Sorry, shattered.'

His cold eyes softened as he looked at her, and the scar on his face sparkled with golden ice crystals in the midday sun. 'You should go and see Varo before you fall asleep standing.'

Sasha nodded and pushed the door open. 'Where is she?'

'Her room.'

Sasha trudged up the stairs. That worn timber smell of the house mixing with the almost-constant aroma of coffee from the kitchen brought with it a comfort. It was familiar. Was it home? She didn't know. She crossed the squeaky landing, giving the flaking white paint a quick glance – the house had definitely seen better days – and knocked on Varo's door.

'Come in, Sasha,' Varo said through the wood.

It was unnerving that the mage knew it was her knocking. She opened the door and went in, closing it behind her. The whole room shimmered and glistened with the emerald light of the Gramarye. The sapphire, gold and silver streams of colour dashed across the walls. It was as if they sensed Sasha's presence, following her as she moved across the room.

Varo was sitting at a tired-looking wooden desk near the window, a book in her hand. She looked up at Sasha and smiled. Even her unmoving eye appeared to smile.

'I'm happy to see you're back,' she said, standing.

'Thanks.' Sasha rolled her sleeve up and bared the underside of her forearm. The mage reached forward and ran her fingers over the glowing mark. Her skin was cold and hard; it made Sasha want to pull away.

'Thank you, Sasha,' she said, her tone quiet yet full of power. 'You've done so much.'

'It's fine.'

'You had no trouble?'

'No. He was easy to find, and the soul binding worked just as you said,' said Sasha, doing her best to keep the emotion from her voice. The more she thought about what was living in her arm, the more disgusted and repulsed she was by herself. She needed it gone. Him gone. It was a constant reminder that she was a murderer. She'd killed someone. And not just someone, not just anyone, someone innocent. Her stomach lurched.

Varo interrupted Sasha's thoughts. 'Killing is hard.'

'It is,' she said, fighting to keep the tremble from her voice. She didn't want to seem weak.

Varo squeezed Sasha's shoulder. 'And by doing this, you have helped us all. All mages. Yourself. Theo.'

Sasha sighed and took a step back. The mark on her arm throbbed with blue light; she ran her finger up and down it. 'It felt so wrong. He was nice. We chatted. He had a wife and a son.' Tears welled up in her eyes, but she blinked them back.

'But if he knew what you were, would he have been so friendly and kind?'

'I don't know.' She shook her head. The truth was, she didn't. If he knew, he may have attacked her first and turned her in for a reward. But not everybody was like that. Ruby knew what she was, and she loved her.

'That's right, you don't know, so it's better to act first before you end up dead.' There was a dark and passionate edge to Varo's voice. 'I'll tell you a story.' She gestured for Sasha to sit at the table, then sat opposite her, her dark hair shining with an inky-blue sheen as she moved. 'My older brother was a mage. Like Theo, he could heal people. He was always secretly healing the cuts and grazes I got on my knees and elbows. I wasn't the most elegant of little girls.' A sad smile formed on her blue lips. 'He was my best friend, the person I told everything to – all my hopes and dreams, my secrets – and he did the same with me. Him being a mage was our biggest secret; we kept it from everyone. Then one day, my parents caught him healing me – I'd tripped over my own shoelaces like a clumsy fool – and that was that. He was dead a few days later, hanged on the village green for everyone to see. I was twelve and he was eighteen. That's no age to see that, and no age to die. So, you see, you can't trust anyone who isn't a mage.'

Sasha looked at the older woman; her one good eye was glistening. 'I'm so sorry.'

'Don't be. We'll make sure his loss – and the loss of others – wasn't in vain. Now, give me your arm. Let's get this out of you. If you don't mind, I'd like to try a little experiment.'

Sasha laid her arm on the table with the glowing soul facing up.

'Removing a soul once it has been bound is difficult. It can be flushed out with a knife tipped with an extract of death angel fungus, but that would be a lot for Theo to contend with, and the hosts rarely survive no matter how good the healer is. You'll be pleased to know killing you outright is out of the question. The soul would remain bound to you in your death, making it impossible to separate the two of you. However, the Gramarye desires to be whole, so it's possible it could extract the soul itself.'

'I'll take that over poison and death.' Sasha rolled her shoulders and tensed her arm.

Varo stood up and crossed the room to the thick wooden trunk where the Gramarye rested. The colours shifted as she picked it up. Sasha gazed at it, transfixed. The hidden teal heart within it pulsed faster the closer the artefact got to her, almost like the artefact itself was alive and excited. The shimmering snakes of colour joined with one another to drift around the Gramarye as one.

Heat was building in the soul in her arm, and the blue grew brighter. The heat turned to burning, then pain, but she bit down on the tip of her tongue to keep from crying out. Varo lowered the Gramarye onto her arm. It was cool, like a soothing balm, snuffing out the flames of pain. Its heart beat harder and faster. It pulsed through Sasha's arm. The coloured snakes swarmed through the artefact together, undulating as if riding up and down on invisible waves.

Then, in a flash, the pain returned. It was raw, burning, as if she were being cut open with a white-hot knife. She gritted her teeth and growled in pain. It felt like the soul was tearing its way out of her skin. She could hear something in the distance. It was horrible, it was haunting, it was grotesque. It was the man screaming as if he were living in a world of pure suffering. She didn't even know his name. It grew louder and louder until he was right next to her, howling into her ears. She glanced at Varo, who seemed unaffected. Perhaps only Sasha could hear his misery. There was a crunching sound, followed by a crack like ice shattering on a frozen lake. It grew louder until it drowned out the screams.

A bolt of pain tore through Sasha, and she cried out, and then everything fell silent. She flopped back in the chair, and her arm slid off the table. There was only blood and smoke where the soul had once been. It hurt so much she could hardly feel it. Her body was slipping into shock.

'Did it work?' she rasped to Varo.

'It did,' Varo replied. 'Sorry I hurt you.'

'Not your fault,' said Sasha, still looking at her smoking arm. Blood was splattering onto the wooden floorboards, and it wasn't stopping.

'Go see Theo,' said Varo.

'No, it's a scratch, I don't wanna be a burden.'

'You'll be more of a burden if you die,' Varo replied. 'You've proven your worth, Sasha. You're important. I need you. We need you. Theo needs you. Now, are you going to see him, or am I dragging you there myself?'

Sasha got to her feet, her body unsteady and threatening to betray her. The pain washed over her again, and for one horrible second, she thought she might vomit. Perhaps it was for the best that she'd skipped breakfast. She grabbed her travel bag from the floor and slung it over her shoulder.

Her head swam as she crossed the dark landing to Theo's room. Nausea and enervation coursed through her. Every exhausted footstep was more draining than the last. The reek of burning flesh forced its way up her nose and into her lungs. She needed help. She rapped on the door and stumbled in without waiting for an answer. Theo was at the window; he turned around. Was there an emotion on his face? He looked pleased to see her, but then whatever it was faded away.

'Theo,' Sasha croaked, 'help.'

Her legs gave up, and she tumbled to the floor. The smack of the hardwood was nothing compared to the agony of the soul having been ripped from her. All she could see was black. All she could feel was pain. Hands grabbed at her, and she was rolled over. Her head flopped back and rested on something soft and warm. She could smell something. Smoke. It was her arm. She was still burning.

'Lightning.' Theo's voice battled through the darkness. 'Lightning.'

Sasha reached for him, grasping into the black for something, anything to hold on to. Something cold grabbed her. His fingers on her arm. She gasped, sat up and opened her eyes. Then all her strength left her, and she wilted back into his lap.

She stared up at him and forced a smile. 'I'm back.'

'I can see that.'

'I got you a gift, it's in my—'

An ethereal turquoise light swam in Theo's hand, and his face changed. A calm serenity poured into his eyes, and the dark circles surrounding them vanished. His mouth curved into a kind and reassuring smile. Even his hair changed – it shone like onyx. He was so beautiful, but that which made him beautiful was killing him.

Sasha wanted to tell him to stop, but she couldn't form the words. He pushed her fringe back, and his skin brushed against hers. He was so warm and alive.

'Can I see your arm?' he said.

Sasha knew there was nothing she could do or say to stop him, yet it ripped her heart in two that he'd asked for permission to see her injury. With all her remaining strength, she turned her arm over. Theo took it in his hands; his touch was so gentle. Every time he'd helped her in the past, she'd not been conscious.

'I won't hurt you.'

'I know,' Sasha murmured in reply.

Turquoise, sapphire, emerald and silver flowed from his hands in calm, soothing waves. Tiny glowing flowers, leaves and vines swirled within the ripples of colour. He was putting life back into her. There was a smell too, fresh herbs, crisp pine needles in the summer sun, hot rocks after a rainfall. Everything fresh, pure and beautiful, and he was giving it all to her. She moved her other hand and touched his arm.

He didn't pull away, he didn't flinch. Instead, he looked at her, his skin awash with iridescent colours, and whispered, 'Thank you.'

She wanted the moment to last forever. She felt so safe and reassured, and Theo looked whole. He looked like the man she knew he would be if he hadn't been used and drained by others. Having his hand in the heavens truly was a blessing and a curse.

But like all precious moments in life, it was fleeting and had to end. The beautiful glow around them faded as Theo slowly closed the gateway within him. There was something cold in Sasha's hand, and she realised with great sorrow that it was Theo's arm. She let go before he could pull away, but she didn't move from his lap. She was too exhausted to even try.

'I'm sorry,' she said. 'I'm so tired.'

'Me too,' he replied. His voice was back to its usual flat and emotionless tone.

Sasha looked up to his face to see he was staring straight ahead. His eyes had dulled, and the darkness beneath them had returned, looking heavier than before. His skin was pale, and there was a thin stream of blood running from the corner of his mouth. She'd done this to him.

'I'm so sorry, Theo,' she whispered as she closed her eyes.

'It's okay, Sasha.'

And she was gone.

CHAPTER SIXTY-SIX

KILLIAN HAD BEEN WALKING FOR WHAT SEEMED like hours. His feet dragged unenthusiastically through the shimmering crystalline grass. His heart was heavy and his soul greatly troubled. Hearing Ren's voice had filled his mind with all sorts of thoughts. Was Ren trapped in this bizarre world with him? Was he trying to hurt him for letting him die? Was Ren dead? It even caused him to doubt whether he was alive himself. He dug his nails into his skin, and it hurt, but was that enough evidence to prove he existed? Killian shook his head; he didn't know.

The glistening lake called to him. It looked more like a pool of melted silver than water. He didn't know why he was heading for it anymore. Earlier he'd had the ridiculous notion that he'd find something there, something that'd give him a clue as to where he was, or maybe even a way out. Staring at the distant silver water now made him feel foolish.

That's it, this is where I stay. May as well make the most of it.

'Don't think things like that,' a gentle voice whispered from behind him. It was different from the other voice, Ren's voice. It was calm, soothing and female.

Killian turned around. 'Who's there?'

A soft breeze blew through him in answer. He closed his eyes and breathed deeply. Something felt familiar. Was this someone he knew?

'Please,' he said.

'You have to keep going,' the voice murmured.

'Where?'

'Go to the shore.'

'Will I get out?' he asked.

There was silence. Killian looked towards the lake, and his vision misted with tears. A hand pressed into his shoulder. It was a touch he knew and had longed for. One from a distant memory. He didn't turn around for fear of scaring away the strange entity.

'Please don't cry, Killy,' she said in his ear. 'Please don't.'

The hand moved from his shoulder to his chest. Another hand came to join it, and the ghostly spectre held him tight in her embrace. She kissed him on the back of the head, her nose brushing through his hair. His body jolted, and tears flowed down his cheeks. A pale slender hand moved up to his face and wiped the tears away.

'Don't cry, Killy.'

He opened his mouth to say something, but no words would come. All he could do was silently cry. Only two people had ever been allowed to call him Killy. It was all too much.

'Shh.'

He placed a trembling hand on top of hers and closed his eyes. 'Mum?' he managed to choke out.

'Yes,' she whispered back.

Was it really her? Could it be possible? There was so much he wanted to say, but the words clogged in his throat. A swell of hope built in his chest only to be replaced by fear. What could he say? How could he make things right? He'd killed her. Silence enveloped him and her spirit.

'I'm sorry,' he eventually said through trembling lips.

'Whatever for, my love?'

'Letting you die. I'm so sorry.'

'Oh, Killy,' she said, gripping him tighter. 'There wasn't anything you could do.'

'I could have—'

'No, do not blame yourself. The man you've grown into, who you are now – you make me so proud. I love you.'

'I'm useless. I've let friends die. I've watched them die.' Burning tears streaked down his cheeks.

'Some things will always be out of your control.'

'I—'

'Shh.'

His breath shuddered, and more tears fell. Her grip tightened around him, and he relaxed back into it. How long they stayed like this, he couldn't say. Minutes, hours, days – he didn't know. Time seemed inconsequential in a world where there was no day or night, no dawn or dusk.

'You must go to the lake,' she said.

'Please don't leave me, Mum.'

'You must catch a star for all your dreams to come true.'

Emotion smothered him into silence.

This time, she sang to him.

'*You must catch a star for your dreams to come true,*
One will fall, and it's meant only for you.'

Killian closed his eyes and was transported back over twenty years. He was in a dimly lit room. It was small and slightly fusty, and the milky light of a pale moon filtered through the thin rags that masqueraded as curtains. Another nightmare had woken him, and his mother cradled him in her arms while she sang songs about stars, hopes and dreams to him. Her sweet, gentle voice lulled him back to a deep peaceful sleep. It never failed to work.

'Don't go.'

'I must, my love. I can't stay here, and neither can you. The lake will help you.'

As he opened his eyes, a tear slid out. 'Okay, I'll do what you say. Before you leave, can I look at you? I need to see you again.'

In answer, she released her grip on him, placed a ghostly hand on his shoulder and encouraged him to turn around. She was wearing the same skirt and blouse he'd last seen her in, though they were clean and intact. Three silver bangles dangled from her right wrist, while her left one was wrapped in a silver cuff. Her long brown hair tumbled down her back and rolled over her shoulders in thick waves. Large blue eyes shone like precious stones plucked straight from the heart of a burning star. She smiled at him, that same crooked smile he knew he used so often. He couldn't speak. She reached forward and took his hands in hers.

'I'll always love you, Killy.'

'I'll always love you too, Mum.'

Her image shifted, and she began to disintegrate into twinkling stardust before his eyes. Wisps of silver glitter blew from her body and swirled into the breeze.

'Don't ever forget that,' she said.

'I won't,' he said, holding her hands tight to try to keep her with him.

As she looked at him, a tiny tear streaked down her ghostly face, like a liquid diamond. 'You're such a beautiful man.'

She smiled, let go and jumped forward into his arms. He held her for a second before she disappeared completely, and he was left holding himself as a cloud of silver dust floated up towards the stars.

CHAPTER
SIXTY-SEVEN

SILVER, GREEN AND BLUE LIGHT BURST FROM KILLIAN'S back. Arow's irritated eyes followed the diagonal line of the savage scar that ran from his shoulder to the base of his spine. He brushed the sweat from his forehead and rolled his patient's body over. The scent of a crisp spring morning – fresh, sweet and full of life – swirled throughout the tent.

Lily had been watching Arow examine Killian for about half an hour, in silence. The testy mage had returned from his talk with Leif oddly compliant. Due to the nature of his moods, Leif had discreetly advised her to make the most of it. She'd wasted no time in dragging Arow to the tent to see Killian – she didn't want to use the last ounce of her enhanced strength to crush his throat if she could help it.

Arow straightened up, felt Killian's pulse and checked his breathing for what must have been the hundredth time. His eyebrows knitted together in a scowl as he turned Killian's forearm over and stared at the mark where the orm resided. It was a part of his skin, like a tattoo. The edges glowed with a soft silver shine while the blue light at the centre shimmered and shifted.

He rocked back on his heels and turned to face Lily. 'Nothing wrong with him,' the mage grunted at her.

A numbness seeped over her body, and her skin turned to stone. She tried to speak but couldn't; her mouth was dry and her tongue a cold, hard slab. Arow was saying something to her, but she couldn't hear a word. It was like she was underwater – everything was muffled and confused. She balled her fist up. She wanted to punch something. Arow, she could punch him. Break his nose, shatter his cheekbones.

'Rothbone! Are you listening to me?'

Arow's stern voice snapped her back into the moment. She narrowed her eyes and levelled them with his.

'No, I wasn't.'

'There's nothing wrong with him. I scanned his body, and besides bruises, cuts and slight malnourishment, he's in perfect working order.' He glared at Killian's body. 'His heart and breathing are fine; there're no breaks. There's nothing for me to fix.'

'There must be something wrong, surely?' She leant forward, and Arow slunk back. 'People don't just . . .' She gritted her teeth, and her nostrils flared. 'People don't just lie there, asleep, if they're fine. If you're holding out on me, I'll make you pay.'

Arow rubbed his hand over his face. 'And I don't doubt that,' he mumbled into his palm. 'The issue is mental, so there's nothing I can do.'

'What d'you mean?' Lily snapped back. A tingle coursed through her arm, and the desire to reach over and shatter Arow's teeth with one punch took hold of her.

'You say he was possessed by an enlii? That would have taken its toll on his mind.' He looked from Lily to Killian. 'I believe his mind has shut down because of immense stress. There's no reason, physically, why he shouldn't be awake.'

Sorrow and regret waltzed in her stomach. 'Will he ever wake up?'

Arow turned his palms up and flicked out his fingers. 'I don't know. Perhaps. All you can do is wait. His body is strong.'

Lily made a fist and curled her lip. 'Can't I wake him up? Give him a shake or a slap?'

Arow closed his eyes and shook his head. 'I see you're used to using violence to get what you want.'

'It helps to speed things up.'

They sat in silence, the tent softly flapping in the breeze, the rise and fall of Killian's breathing in time with it. Lily glanced at him. He looked so peaceful, so relaxed. His forearm was resting on top of the blankets. The sun beamed through the fabric of the tent, and the bright warming light mixed with the cool blue of Killian's glowing scar. She took his arm and tucked it underneath the coarse dark green blanket Leif had donated, snuffing out the light. Gently, she stroked his forehead, brushing the stray locks of hair from his face.

'Is there really nothing?' she murmured, part to herself, part to Arow and part to Killian.

'The only person who can wake him is him. You should be grateful. There're limits to what we can do. There's nasty disease out there, there's rot that festers inside. I've been asked to cure the incurable. I've told people there's nothing I can do for their loved ones and that they'll have to watch them waste away. But him – it's all on him. Though you should stay here for a few days, to be safe.'

Lily's chest fluttered, and she looked towards the mage. His eyes refused to meet hers.

'I'll check on him,' Arow muttered as if the words were trying to stay in his mouth, 'every day, look for changes and improvements you might not see. That's all I can do,' he added, 'no more.'

'Thank you,' said Lily.

Arow nodded tersely and left.

RAVEN lay back on the mossy grass, gazing up at the blue sky above. Fat lumpy clouds bustled by in the high winds, and the tops of the pine trees danced. He drew in a deep breath and wrapped his arms around his head. There was a distinctive itching in his back; it ran over his shoulder blades, and he so badly wanted to scratch it. It wasn't really there, of course. It was merely his desire to be with the clouds, swooping through the landscape and basking in the freedom it brought. But now was not the time for such thoughts. His friend was gravely ill. Could he have done more to help? He'd tried so hard to help him, to pull him back from the brink, but in the end, it wasn't enough. He'd failed. Did that make him less of a being than he already was?

Leif's tent flapped dramatically in the quiet of the clearing, and Raven looked over his shoulder to see Arow stride out. Lily didn't follow. Raven leant back against his elbows and looked at the treetops once more. Tiny orange birds flitted in and out of the branches, chirping to one another. As much as he wanted to go to his captain and hear what had been said, he knew she would come to him if she wanted to talk.

A yellow butterfly with black-tipped wings and blue spots swooped low over Raven and came to rest on his bent knee. He pushed his hair back and watched it as it slowly opened and closed its wings. He and Lily had been a team for such a long time now. He smiled to himself as he recalled their first meeting – in a street fight for money, of all things. She was fighting for the eastern district of Torran, and he fought for the west. There was such surprise on her face when he punched her and it actually hurt, but that was nothing compared to his surprise when she overpowered him and took the victory. It had never happened to him before.

His district abandoned him that night, disgusted not only that had he lost to her, but he'd lost them a lot of money and power too. Their champion was no more. But Liliana Maggiore didn't abandon him. She'd dragged his bloody broken body away from the filthy outdoor fighting pit – unaware that it was slowly healing itself – all the way to an inn. She'd used some of her winnings to pay for his room for the night. And she'd put him to bed, looking after him and caring for him, all without uttering a word. Then she was gone.

He'd awoken the next morning to find a note next to his bed; the handwriting was curly, dramatic and somewhat beautiful. It bore instructions to meet its author in the bar as soon as he was able. A few minutes later he'd walked into the bar to see Lily pouring rum, butter and brown sugar into a bowl of porridge. She'd looked up and ordered him the same, and they'd been allies ever since.

The tent flapped once more, and Lily's shadow fell over Raven. She sat down next to him and hugged her knees into her chest.

'New friend?' she asked.

Raven followed her gaze to the butterfly still sitting on his knee. Its wings unfurled as it basked in the warmth of the sun pouring in through the circular skylight.

He nodded. 'I needed a replacement for Killian.'

Lily chuckled softly. 'Arow can't find anything wrong with him,' she said, her emerald eyes focused on the butterfly.

'I'm sorry.' Guilt lanced through Raven as he spoke.

'He thinks it's all mental, all in his head,' Lily continued. She leaned forwards and approached the butterfly on Raven's knee, holding her hand out, the silver band of her ring flashing in the sunbeams. The green of the moon was almost grey. 'We'll stay for a few days so Arow can check on him.'

The butterfly flapped its wings and fluttered away, taking a detour past Raven's head. Lily watched it go.

'I'm sorry this happened.'

'It's not your fault,' said Lily, shaking her head.

'I tried to keep him here for as long as I could, but it wasn't long enough. I wasn't good enough.'

Lily's warm hand gripped Raven's bicep, and her fingers curled around him and squeezed. He didn't deserve such warmth. Her face was still marred with cuts and bruises from her fight with Killian. Could the mysterious glow that lived within Killian's body break through her defences? She hadn't said anything about it, and Raven was never one to press an issue. She'd open up to him when she was ready.

'I know you'd have tried everything you could,' she said. 'And whatever happened wasn't your fault. I was the one who put that thing in him, and I'm not here beating myself up over it. Things happen, Raven. We did everything right, and somehow it all went wrong. Sometimes I can't help but think that maybe this is for the best.'

'What do you mean?'

Lily took off her bandana and scrunched it up in her hands. 'Ulrich said that if he dies, that soul will go with him, and the Gramarye will never be unlocked. We can all go back to our normal lives, and no one outside of us will be any the wiser.'

'Ulrich, he really got to you.'

'It makes sense though. If Killian dies, all our problems die with him.'

'Does it say anything about that in the book?'

'No. That book's been useless if you ask me. Dead weight. We should have burned it.'

'And did you ever consider that the old man was wrong?'

Lily shook her head; all her focus was on the balled-up green rag in her hands.

'The soul in Killian's arm is bound to him and the Gramarye,' Raven continued. 'Perhaps if Killian dies, the soul will go with him and everything will sort itself out, or maybe it will stay here in our world, waiting for the Gramarye.'

'You think?'

'I do. Who knows how long it sat in that graveyard, waiting.'

'You have a point.'

'I know.'

CHAPTER SIXTY-EIGHT

KILLIAN WALKED IN THE DIRECTION OF THE SILVER lake with a purposeful step. Since his encounter with the apparition of his mother, there had been a sense of hope in his heart. Maybe the lake was the key to his escape. Allowing this thought to dominate his mind felt like the only way to remain sane; after all, he'd just had a conversation with his dead mother.

With a painful stab to his gut, the memories came flooding back. She screamed for him to run, and his pulse leapt. He instinctively put his hand to his cheek to try to wipe away her hot blood. She screamed again, and this time, he ran. Despite his best efforts, the memories still haunted him, and what happened with Ren had brought it all back. The pain, the suffering, the misery, the death. Yet another person had died because of his inability to help.

The glistening ground levelled off as he approached the lake. The grasses encircling it grew tall, blocking his view of the lake entirely. He pushed the gently swaying plants aside and stepped into their domain. They chimed as Killian moved through them, some losing their seeds at his touch. The tiny silvery seeds hovered around him like a swarm of gnats. He brushed them aside, and they raced away towards the starry sky. Just as he was beginning to wonder when he'd reach the shore, a strange noise pierced the silence.

He froze and listened. He shushed the chiming grasses, and they obeyed. The noise rang out again. It sounded like a muffled cry, and it was close. Crouching low, he moved through the undergrowth towards the sound. As he drew nearer to the source, it became apparent that it was sobbing. Deep mournful sobs, full of torment and grief. The grasses murmured to him as he pushed then apart.

Kneeling on the ground with his back to Killian was Ren, his shoulders hunched up and his face buried in his hands. Hoarse painful breaths burst from his lips as he gasped out wretched sobs. Killian opened his mouth to say something, but what could he say? Nothing would make it better, and nothing could bring him back. He could say he was sorry a thousand times, but it wouldn't change anything. He closed his mouth, took a step back and turned to leave.

'Don't go,' Ren whimpered.

Killian collapsed to his knees, gripped once again by that ferocious pain.

'Stay,' said Ren, his voice low and guttural.

'Ren, I—'

'Shut up,' Ren spat. 'I don't want to hear it.'

The pain intensified with Ren's mood, forcing Killian down onto his hands. Splinters dug into his eyeballs, and hundreds of needles scratched at his skin, while his insides erupted into a blazing furnace. He pointlessly gripped his chest in a feeble attempt to placate the searing agony. He cried out and crumpled to the boggy ground.

Ren stood and paced around Killian as he shuddered and convulsed at his feet.

'It doesn't feel good to feel helpless, does it?'

Killian rolled onto his back and tried to focus on Ren, but his vision was hazy and twisted.

'Ren, please.'

'Didn't I tell you to shut up?' Ren kicked him in the stomach with his heel.

Killian groaned and rolled onto his side. He'd take his punishment – he deserved it – but that didn't stop him willing it to be over. He shut his eyes, wrapped his arms around himself and lay trembling as the pain grew. Ren stomped around him and kicked him again, then grabbed him by the shoulders and forced him onto his back. He stepped forward and crouched over him.

'Look at me.'

Killian didn't respond.

'Look at me.'

Killian's eyes flickered open, and he immediately wanted to close them again. Ren's face was as white as bone, and his eyes were black. No pupils, no irises, just empty emotionless voids surrounded by spidery blackened cracks in his skin. Black veins lined his lips, which were pulled over his teeth in a hateful sneer. The curly blond hair was all that remained of the old Ren.

'See what you've done?'

'I'm sorry, I didn't mean t—'

'You're sorry, you're sorry,' snapped Ren, his deformed face plastered with a sadistic grin. He grabbed Killian by the shoulder – his sharp grey nails dug into his skin – and held him still. Three hard punches landed in Killian's stomach. 'I'm sorry, I'm sorry, I'm sorry!'

Killian coughed as the foul taste of blood filled his mouth. 'Ren,' he croaked. 'There was nothing I could do.'

'You're lying. You could have helped me. You could have saved me.' He punched him again.

Killian wheezed. 'I couldn't.'

'But you promised.' Ren's voice was low again. 'You promised you'd get me out alive. You promised I'd survive. I didn't. You showed me how to take your gun. You taught me that, and it got me killed. You killed me!'

'I'm so sorry.'

'You broke your promise,' said Ren, his voice trembling, 'and now I'm dead, dead, dead because of you.' Great tears flowed out of Ren's black eyes and splashed all over Killian. 'I'm dead! I'm dead!' he bawled over and over, raining blows down on Killian with each word. 'I want you to know how much it hurt!'

Ren screamed, and the pain deepened, burning Killian right to his core.

Killian's breathing was ragged and uneven, and his body was racked with pain. His back arched. He dug his fingers into the soft marshy earth as he bit down on his bottom lip, stubbornly refusing to scream.

Ren's midnight eyes glowered. 'I hate you,' he spat, driving his elbow into Killian's ribs.

'Ren . . .'

'You let me die! You let me die!' He drove his knee into Killian's stomach.

All the breath rushed out of Killian, and he gasped desperately for air. A grin cracked on Ren's darkened lips, and he reeled back onto his heels. His hands twisted, and his fingers became cruel and rigid, like the branches of a bare winter oak. A sinister laugh bubbled in his throat, and he brought his fingers down towards Killian's eyes. But his hand didn't reach its target. Killian grabbed it and squeezed. Ren's dark eyes widened, and tears formed in their corners.

'Going for the eyes is so dirty. I taught you better than that,' said Killian.

He yanked Ren down towards him, grabbed him by the shoulders and kicked him over his head. The spectre of Ren hit the ground with a thump and lay in an undignified heap. Somehow, despite searing pain still ripping through his body, Killian staggered to his feet. He looked down at Ren, who lay sprawled in the silver grasses.

'Ren?'

'No,' he whispered, 'I don't want to hear it.'

Ren flicked his wrist, and Killian fell to one knee. Fresh pain surged through his body, raw and unbearable. He clutched his chest with one trembling hand and put the other on the ground to steady himself.

'Ren, please,' he gasped out. 'Listen.'

'You let me die,' Ren growled, sitting up and wrapping his arms about his knees.

'I didn't mean to.' Killian gritted his teeth and somehow summoned the strength to stand. 'I didn't do this.'

'Enough!'

Killian stumbled down to one knee, his body awash with agony. Tremors ripped through his body. Burning tears fell down his cheeks. It had to stop. He had to make it stop.

'Ren,' he croaked. 'Please stop hurting me.'

'No,' said Ren, though his voice wavered. 'You need to be taught a lesson.'

'I couldn't help. I wanted to so bad. But I couldn't.' The pain lessened, and he could lift his head. With a soft groan and a tremendous effort, he pushed himself to his feet. 'I'm so sorry.'

'You're sorry?'

'I really am,' said Killian. He managed to shuffle one of his feet forward.

'You *are* sorry?'

'Yes,' he said. Haze clouded his mind as the soft embrace of sleep tried to claim him. He drew in a deep breath and pushed it away.

'Killian?' Ren's blank gaze was turned to the stars.

Killian, almost bent double with pain, took another unsteady step towards Ren. 'Yes?'

'I know,' said Ren, his tone soft. 'I know you're sorry.'

At this, the pain lessened again. 'I wish I could have done something. I think about it every day, every night. What I could have done.'

'I know you do,' said Ren, getting to his feet, 'and the answer is *nothing*.' He took a shaky step towards Killian and stopped a few feet in front of him. 'You need to know that too. You're creating all this pain for yourself. All this is you.'

Killian raised his head. The blank voids in Ren's face had been replaced with his gentle chocolate-brown eyes, and the blackened cracks in his skin started to fade. He smiled nervously as his body crumbled into flecks of silver. Killian took a deep breath as the last of the pain left his body. All that lingered were the throbbing bruises.

'It's time you were at the lake.'

'Will I get out?' Killian asked.

'That depends on you,' said Ren, walking towards Killian and leaving a trail of silver particles in his wake. He reached out and took his hand. 'Good luck.'

'Thanks,' was all Killian could say. He placed his free hand on Ren's forearm and gripped it tight.

'Goodbye, Killian,' said Ren.

He closed his eyes, and with the whisper of a soft summer breeze, his body exploded into a cloud of silver dust that wended its way to the stars.

'Bye, Thorny,' said Killian, his empty hand extended before him.

CHAPTER SIXTY-NINE

SASHA SCRUTINISED HER FOREARM IN THE MIDDAY sun. It had completely healed – not even a mark, let alone a scar. What Theo had done for her was incredible, yet part of her wished a scar had remained, something to permanently brand her with shame. Even though the soul was gone, she still felt the presence of the man; she could still hear his wife screaming and feel her blood turn to ice. Both her nightmares and daydreams were haunted by that sound, that scream and that poor man's smile. She'd murdered him, and it was something she'd have to learn to live with.

Delphina had left the house early that morning. She'd been chosen to capture the next soul. Assuming Quint would also take a soul, as well as Kurt and Dorian, it would be some time before Sasha was sent out again. Theo wouldn't go. For one thing, his magic wasn't offensive, and for another, they'd need him to heal those who returned. She shuddered as she thought about all he'd be put through. It wasn't fair. It wasn't right.

She drew in a deep breath and headed across the field towards the barn. She wanted to be alone with her thoughts, and Quint had a habit of appearing on the porch to smoke with her. Usually she didn't mind – there was an almost familial comfort in his company – but right now she had to be alone. The only person in the group she felt she could spend time with at the moment was Theo, and she didn't want to burden him with her problems anymore. Every time she thought of him, she felt guilty. Pain clawed at her chest. He'd helped her again, and once again at a cost to himself. She hadn't seen him since he'd healed her. She'd passed out in his room, but this morning she'd woken in her own bed.

Her vision had clouded over by the time she reached the barn. She pushed the door open, stalked in and sat at the foot of a haystack, leaning her back against it. Theo was so pure; she'd seen it with her own eyes, had even smelt it. He was nature itself. Everyone had taken advantage of him. All he'd ever done with his life was give and get nothing in return – unless she counted the cloak that she'd left outside his door that morning. She brushed the tears from her eyes. She had to carry on, she had to get more souls, she had to help him. He wasn't completely lost; she'd seen the man he could and should be.

A fresh determination rippled through Sasha. She would do whatever it took to make him whole again. It wasn't just that – she would be helping mages everywhere, would be helping herself. No more running. Ever. If Varo's parents had turned in their own son, what hope did mages have living side by side with normal people? She'd got lucky with Ruby, but how many more people were like that? Not many, in her experience.

She was groping in her pocket for a cigarette when the barn door opened. As soon as she saw who it was, she halted her search.

'Saw you slither over here,' Kurt said, his slimy grin running from ear to ear. 'Recovered from your little adventure now? I saw Mr Pasty dragging you to your room last night.' He paused to light a cigarette with his fingertip. 'You two are as pathetic as each other. Shame we actually *need* to use him, or I'd roast him up just to amuse myself. Don't need you though.'

Sasha bristled and stood up. 'What is your problem? Why are you like this?' She took a step forward.

Kurt shrugged and smoked. He radiated arrogance, and it was driving her mad. She held her hand in front of her chest and summoned lightning to her skin.

'I asked you a question,' she said. 'What is your problem?'

'I hate people like you,' he said, smoke bursting from his mouth in waves. 'You can't look after yourself, you depend on others. It's pathetic. He's not as bad, he has a use, but you.' Kurt chuckled, but it sounded forced and fake.

'You need him to look after you. Doesn't that make you as pathetic as me?'

'Don't twist my words, bitch,' he snarled, 'or I'll do it again.'

'Do what again?' she asked.

He smirked, winked, then covered his fist in fire. 'You know what.'

Sasha's heart pounded, though not from fear. Pure adrenaline surged through her. She wanted this. She needed this.

'Come on, then, little man.' She beckoned him.

Kurt sucked the remains of his cigarette and tossed it aside. 'You really wanna do this again?'

'I do, but on one condition.'

'Name it.'

'You don't go crying to Theo after I've annihilated you.'

'Done,' he snapped.

Kurt rushed towards Sasha, his hands ablaze. Heat swarmed all around her, but she kept her cool. She waited until he was close enough, then threw a bolt of lightning into the ground, using its energy to propel herself over the top of him. Burnt earth and scorched hay leapt up with her. She neatly flipped over and landed behind him. Without waiting for him to realise what had happened, she dived forward, grabbed him from behind and smashed his face into the dirt.

She stood above him, hands on hips, waiting for him to get to his feet. He lifted his head and glared at her, eyes glowing with pure hatred, blood dribbling down his chin.

'Lucky shot,' he hissed, jumping to his feet and launching a wave of fire at her.

Sasha dodged aside. Kurt curled his lip and threw another at her. She blasted it back with her own force of nature. Kurt's fire faded into nothing, while her lightning sizzled with power.

'What is wrong with you?' Kurt yelled. Sasha wasn't sure if it was intended for her or himself.

She threw a fork at his feet, and he stumbled back. She threw another and another. Panic rose in his eyes, and she drew great satisfaction from it. He tried to draw, to pull his fire from somewhere, but the Fear was clearly making it hard for him to concentrate and focus. Sasha relentlessly shot at his feet until he fell backwards; then she pounced.

She drove her knees into his arms and sat back on his chest. There was a great crackle of energy as she pulled her lightning into her veins, relishing the power and strength it gave her. Beneath her, Kurt squirmed, but his attempts at escape were futile. She knew it, and he knew it too.

'I could stop your heart now if I wanted.' She pressed her hand on his chest and leant towards him. 'One little pulse, and it's all over for you. If you think about it, why do we even *need* you? What have you done for this cause?'

'Don't. Please,' he whispered. His eyes were staring at her, but he wasn't looking at her. They were glazed over and full of terror. 'Don't.'

Pure horror was etched into Kurt's face. His mouth was open, but no more words came. There was something there, something deep and damaged. Sasha got up and stood over him. He was trembling. A tear seeped from the corner of his eye and dripped to the dirt. After all he'd put her through, mentally and physically, now that she stood over him, her hand pulsing with power, she felt sorry for him. He was lost and alone too, but he kept himself isolated by lashing out and picking on those he deemed weaker. A bully. But now, she'd exposed his true core. Words of comfort sped through her mind, but she couldn't bring them to her lips.

She narrowed her eyes. 'If you ask Theo to help you with any of your little bumps and bruises, I will find out.' She made a fist and sent her lightning cracking all over it. 'And I will hunt you down and stop that rotten heart of yours. Do you understand?'

Kurt nodded numbly.

'Good. We won't speak of this again.' And with that, Sasha left him alone, broken and weeping in the barn.

CHAPTER
SEVENTY

Tom feasted his eyes upon the rolling fields around him. They were littered with patches of dark mysterious forest land. A winding dusty path cut through the landscape that connected the towns. The mages had certainly picked a great spot to steal from any travellers. They could see for miles around and vanish without a trace. A wide river ran alongside the path, looking like a giant golden ribbon. Off in the far distance, lofty purple-blue mountains framed the horizon.

Poppy circled above him. Secretly, Tom had always wanted some sort of pet – he'd always been envious of Seth and Rangi – but he hadn't known how to get one or whether the captain would allow it. It seemed, however, that Poppy had chosen him. Did that make him her pet?

Tom and Finn had gone beyond the circle of trees to bask in the views. Blake, Lily and Raven had stayed behind, which was fine by him. Sometimes he enjoyed a bit of peace and quiet. A soft hiss came from his right. Finn was lighting her second roll-up.

The sun was setting, bathing everything around him in a warm peachy light. Grasses swayed in the low evening breeze, their ends tipped with orange sunlight. Above, a new moon grinned in the ever-darkening sky as pale stars glistened through the blue. A murder of crows cawed in the distance as they settled in for the night, allowing the low hoot of the owls to take over. Poppy excitedly joined in.

Finn took a final drag on her roll-up before stubbing it out on her jacket and flicking it away. She opened her mouth and let the smoke tumble from it with her breathing. Tom looked at her and wished he could be as relaxed. Maybe he could if he had a bottle of rum. He could drink all his thoughts away, but that wasn't possible. There was a feeling nagging at him, and he had to say something.

'Reckon we're ever going back?'

Finn jumped and scowled. 'You really know how to ruin an evenin'. I was starting to unwind.'

'Sorry,' said Tom without a shred of sincerity. 'I was curious. What d'you reckon?'

'Ain't up to me, 's up to the cap'n. I get the feeling that we're here till shithead gets up.'

'We've been here ages,' Tom grumbled, running his hand along the edge of Killian's gun as he spoke. The metal was icy on his skin. Deathly cold. Was that Killian's ghost? Was he haunting him? No, that was silly. Killian wasn't dead. Or was he? He hadn't moved in days.

'Aye.'

'We could carry him back – it's no big deal.'

'Tom, in case it escaped your notice, they got a mage here who heals. This is the best place for him right now, so cut your yammering.'

'I thought he was free of that thing . . .' He paused, not wanting to say the word in case it cursed him somehow. 'The enlii.'

' 'Course he is, but he ain't here, is he?'

'Nope.' He sank to the ground, took off his red bandana and fiddled with it. Heat was building in his chest, and his forehead ached. He had to say it, get the words out and be done with it. 'Maybe it's for the best,' he said without daring to look at Finn.

'What?' she grunted.

'You saw what he was like,' he said to the grass.

'That weren't him,' said Finn, crouching down. 'You know that.'

Tom sighed and put his head in his hands. 'I know, I know, it's just that . . .'

'That what?'

'At the time, I was too amazed to let it bother me, but now, looking back, it was really weird.'

'What was?' said Finn. 'Stop dancing about and spit it out. Did I ever tell you I hate it when you do this?'

'He killed those razors. I don't even know how he did it. I was too busy cowering.' Even though he did know – he'd seen *that* glow and *those* horns – he couldn't betray Killian's trust and tell her. What if he found out? He'd do to him what he'd done to those razors, what he'd done to the captain. The captain's face . . . It was such a mess. Red, blue, purple, black.

'Tom, you—'

'He killed them all, Finn!' He lifted his head. 'You didn't see them – they were massive things, fast too. He shouldn't have been able to kill them, not all of them.'

'What you're saying is he should have left you to die?' asked Finn, her eyes wide with disbelief.

'No, no, not that,' mumbled Tom. 'I'm grateful, I am, it's

just . . .' He paused and looked down at his feet. 'It's just what he did shouldn't have been possible.'

'And because of that, you don't want him to wake up?' Finn frowned. 'Tom, you've said some stupid things in your time, but this?'

'He scares me, Finn.' He got to his feet and dusted down his trousers, all while avoiding eye contact. 'He fucking terrifies me. I kept thinking he's gonna wake up and kill us all.'

Finn stood up her mouth twisted with disbelief. 'Are you listening to yourself?'

'Yeah, I know.'

'I just don't understand.'

'Remember how you felt when I brought Blake back?' Tom asked.

'Aye.'

'Well, it's kinda like that.'

'Tom, I didn't want Blake to die.'

Tom sighed and fastened his bandana back about his head. 'I don't want Killian to die, I don't. I'm just . . . I don't know what he'll be like if he wakes up. What if he's not himself?'

'He is. The cap'n saw – you know that. You're talking rubbish.'

'Wouldn't it be better if he didn't wake up though? The orm is in him. He can just stay like this until it all blows over.'

Finn scrunched her fists up and glared at Tom, her eyes as cold and unfeeling as slate. 'Tom, if you don't stop talkin' shit, I'll leave you out here.'

'But, Finn, you saw what he did to the captain.'

'Aye, I did.'

'I ain't never see her all beaten-up like that before, bruised and bleeding. It's not right, it's not her. He shouldn't have done it. No one can do that.'

'He weren't himself then – it was the enlii. You can't blame him for it. You're chatting shit.'

'I suppose.'

Finn nodded solemnly and placed a firm hand on Tom's shoulder. She kept her face blank and unreadable as she stared at him. It was as if she were looking into him. 'But there's always the chance that he could murder us in our sleep. He's our black wave, Tommy lad, an' he's comin' for us. He'll chase us around the afterlife, just so he can catch us to kill us again. Never-ending torment. It'll be like we're drownin' again and again and again.'

Tom grimaced and brushed Finn's hand away. 'Be serious, Finlay!'

'I'm bein' as serious and as believable as you.'

'You were talking bollocks.'

'Exactly,' said Finn, flashing a self-satisfied smirk. 'And so were you.' She slung a friendly arm around him. 'Killian's your mate, Tom. A good mate. He's the same man who saved you and the same crazy shithead who went down the Drop – don't ever forget that.'

'You could be right.' Tom frowned. It all sounded like words to him, words covering up the truth.

'I am, but tell ya what, if he does go crazy, I'll shoot him for you, dead between the eyes. That make you feel better?'

'A little.'

'C'mon, let's get back in the hideout. I'm starvin'.'

Tom glanced up to the feathery white belly of Pops swooping overhead. He clicked his tongue, and the owl gracefully dived down into the mage's camp. Tom smiled. He knew where he was with animals.

BLAKE lay back against the mossy hollow. He was surrounded by mages and pirates alike. His eyes were ghostly white as he made various creatures leap from the smoke of the smouldering fire before them. Colourful glittering cornelians danced around the group, leaving rainbow trails of smoke. The endlessly intriguing and beautiful Big Blue swam about the campsite. Green-and-blue waters swirled all around as the ocean spirit's long kelp-like hair floated on an invisible current.

Lily watched the display, though her mind was elsewhere. Crickets trilled, rodents snuffled and the fire crackled, yet it was hard to find comfort in those sounds. Blake had just finished telling the mages the tale of the Demon's Drop, and now they were all drinking stolen wine while he entertained them with various creatures and scenes from their travels and his imagination. The Demon's Drop, Ren Thorncliffe, the Gramarye – it all felt so long ago. And Killian . . . It had been so long since she'd spoken to him. She missed him deeply, but was that love? Was that what it felt like? She couldn't. She didn't love. She knew what came with that. Her father's feet swung, and her chest ached. It was her birthday. Why did he have to do it on that day? Why did he leave her all alone? It was all because of disgusting love.

'You sea rats have seen a lot.' Leif's smooth voice got Lily's attention, as did the bottle of wine he offered her.

She gratefully took it and had a long swig to chase away her thoughts. It was white – not her usual choice, but it would do. Any booze in a storm, even if it did taste like tangy water. She took a second draught and handed it back.

'We have.'

'Did he really fall down that Drop thing, or is it a tall pirate tale?' Leif asked.

Lily turned to him and stared into his mismatched eyes as the firelight played on his features. 'He dived down, it's all true.'

'That's impressive.' Leif glanced over his shoulder to the tent where Killian lay.

'I know,' said Lily.

'I bet you didn't tell him that.'

'I did, actually.' Lily cocked her head as she spoke. 'So that shows how much you know about me, Mr Leif.'

Leif handed her back the wine like it was a peace offering and made a point of slowly backing away. Lily chuckled.

'I'll miss you when you're gone, Rothbone.'

'Don't cry too much.' She wiped her lips with her thumb and took another sip. It certainly wasn't good wine, but it did soothe the ache in her heart, so at least it was doing its job.

Leif rolled his eyes. 'See, that's why I'll miss you. You're terrifying, yet beautiful. You're funny, and I can have a good conversation with you.'

'Which makes me the exact opposite of you.'

'And sometimes you're just plain mean.' Leif huffed and folded his arms.

'I know.'

The Big Blue swam between Lily and Leif, a smooth muscular body gleaming with silver stars. Lily smiled sadly, knowing this was the only way she'd ever see Blue again. She reached forward, putting her hand into the image's smoky ethereal hair. The sea spirit turned, and for a heartbeat, a pair of soulful green eyes focused on her. Had she done the right thing in summoning this being? What if she needed help again and she'd squandered her request on Killian? The Big Blue blinked once, slowly, as if this illusion of the sea spirit were reading her mind, then swam back to the others, leaving behind a shimmering trail of waves and stars. Blues and greens swirled in the air and then faded to nothing. Neon fireflies hovered in the bushes, and the moon smiled overhead, yet everything seemed darker without the Big Blue. Lily glanced at her ring; once again, it was swirling with multiple shades of green. It was a relief to have it back. She was almost whole again. Almost.

'You didn't tell me how you talked Arow around,' said Lily, eyeing up the jar of olives at Leif's side. He took the hint and tossed them to her.

'I used my natural charm and charisma,' he said, running a hand through his messy hair and winking with his green eye. 'It never fails. Well, almost never.'

'Ah, the famous charm,' said Lily as she plucked an olive from the jar. 'Is that why he was gonna leave you for dead last time?'

Leif slapped his hand across his chest and widened his eyes. 'No. I think you'll find I was very much unconscious then and therefore unable to use my charm and charisma. I'm sure if I'd been awake, Nedge wouldn't have had to use her charm.'

Lily smiled. She and Nedge had a similar idea of charm, it seemed. She popped the olive into her mouth and delighted at the salty tang that danced on her tongue. 'So, tell me, how did you charm him?'

Leif puffed out his chest. 'It wasn't too hard. I . . . Okay, it was sort of hard.' His body deflated, and he looked at Lily in a sly conspiratorial way. 'I reminded him of who he was, what he does, his place in the team. I also gave him a pass for almost letting me die, because it wasn't really his fault. I showed understanding of his situation, and he came around.'

'You manipulated him?'

'Saying it like that makes it sound so dirty.' Leif scowled and reached for the jar. 'Give me one of those.'

Grinning, Lily relinquished the jar. 'I'm right though, aren't I?'

'Give me that wine too,' he said, holding out his hand.

Lily held the bottle out but grasped it tight as he tried to take it. She smirked as Leif struggled against her powerful grip. 'I could swing the bottle and pop your pretty head like an olive if I wanted to.'

Leif rubbed his stubbly beard and glanced to the treetops. 'All right, I used a little bit of manipulation and a little bit of honesty – a good mix. Aren't you glad I did?'

Lily let go of the bottle, and Leif tumbled backwards, spilling some of the wine over his chest as he went.

'I am, thank you.'

Leif sat up and squeezed the wine out of his shirt. 'I get the feeling you don't say "thank you" very often.'

'Correct, so enjoy that one.' Lily pushed her hair over her shoulders. 'Maybe write it down so you don't forget it. You can read it back in years to come and fondly remember that time I most sincerely said "thank you." '

'I'm going to miss you, Captain Rothbone.'

'I know.'

CHAPTER SEVENTY-ONE

KILLIAN HAD SPENT HOURS – OR WAS IT DAYS, MAYBE even weeks – wading through the grasses; there was no time in this darkened world. Eventually they thinned, and he came out to the glittering shore of the silver lake. He sank down onto its shimmering sands and decided to rest. He ached all over. Ren had done him some serious damage. He was utterly drained. His body and mind had taken an equal beating. First his mother and then Ren – it was so hard to cope with. He pulled his knees to his chest and put his arms around them. Someone was missing. Someone else was out to get him.

An icy wind blew in from the lake, reminding him it was there and waiting for him. He looked out across it; it didn't seem like a way out, but what would that look like anyway? A simple door to take him back to his friends was too much to ask for. Where were they anyway? The last thing he could remember was being somewhere cold and damp. What had happened to him? He closed his eyes and shook his head. Lily was the last thing he could remember. She was holding him, smiling, and then the darkness came and took him. Drowning him. He had to get back, he had to get out.

With some effort, he got to his feet, his muscles groaning in protest, and he trudged to the water's edge. Tiny silver waves lapped at the sands, and all around him, the air was silent. He took a step forward and stood in the silver water; it was cool and welcoming. The water soothed his aching body as he waded in farther.

Killian paused and scooped up handfuls of the silver water and poured it over his face. He tilted his head back and allowed the water to run down his neck and over his chest. He ran his wet hands through his hair, gripped the back of his neck and closed his eyes. After a few heartbeats, he released his grip and opened his eyes. He was still there, still up to his knees in the silver lake. Would he have to dive under? Perhaps swim out? Visions of the labyrinth seeped into his mind.

'Hey, Killy,' said Clem.

Killian's chest constricted. He turned around, and there stood Clem. The missing person. The last one to punish him. There was a red hole in his chest. A stream of blood constantly trickled out and dripped into the water. Apart from that haunting void, he looked just how Killian remembered: his dark brown hair a tangled mess, as usual, his stormy blue eyes deep and alert. Even his skin was a healthy complexion with a dusting of freckles across his nose and cheekbones. He was wearing the same dyed-blue trousers and long brown duster coat Killian had last seen him in.

'After all this time, you're not even gonna say hello?' Clem asked. As he spoke, a thin dribble of blood oozed from the corner of his mouth and ran down his chin.

Killian took a wary step back. After what he'd been through with Ren, he wasn't sure he could take on Clem as well. His body hurt so much. He had nothing left.

'Killy?' Clem held out his hand.

'You're . . . You're gonna hurt me,' Killian rasped out.

Clem's brow furrowed. 'Are you asking or telling?'

'I don't know.' Killian's heart pounded. Blood rushed through his head, wrapping him up in a wave of dizziness. 'I don't know.'

Clem sloshed forwards as Killian retreated. 'Why would I hurt you?'

'B-because . . .' Killian paused. His breath was coming out in sharp heavy bursts, making it impossible to form words. Scalding tears streaked down his icy skin. He opened his mouth again but was choked into silence.

Clem stopped walking and held both hands out. 'Killian.' His voice was low and soft, just like he remembered. 'Relax, breathe. It's just me.'

Killian looked up towards the shifting night sky. Silver stars glistened against a dark background, while swirling sweeps of deep greens and purples gently shimmered in and out of view. It truly was beautiful, peaceful. A soft breeze blew across the lake, and the grasses chimed as if they were made of crystal.

He clenched his fists. Clem was here with him, wherever here was. Was it a dream? Was it real? He didn't know.

Clem's voice interrupted his thoughts. 'Killian, it's okay.'

Killian brushed his hair from his eyes. Besides his mother, Estelle, and possibly a pirate queen, Clem was the only person he'd ever loved. It was too much.

'You're dead,' Killian finally said.

Clem pressed a hand against his bloody chest and grinned. 'Am I?' he asked.

'It was my fault.' Killian's eyes welled up again, and his pulse raced just saying those words.

Clem shook his head. 'No, it wasn't,' he said, the blood still flowing from his mouth.

'If I hadn't got so blinded by a hot tip . . . If I hadn't taken you along . . . I should have been more careful.' He blinked, and tears rolled down his cheeks once more. His eyes were burning and raw.

'I still came along, didn't I?'

'You did.' He dragged his hand over his face. 'But it should have been me.'

Clem shook his head slowly. 'But it was me.'

'It was my fault. I should have paid the price.'

Clem closed the gap between them and laid his warm hands on Killian's shoulders. It wasn't a forceful, painful grip, but firm and reassuring.

'Don't you think you've paid the price?' he asked.

'What do you mean? I'm alive – I think – and you're not.'

'And you've been beating yourself up every day since it happened. If that's not "paying a price," I don't know what is.'

Killian stared into Clem's eyes, the eyes of the man he was going to rule the world with. Their grand plans to run off to Venario together, to thieve, swindle and drink until they dropped, had been cruelly crushed out one night. The night Killian sat in an alleyway holding Clem's body until he gasped out his last blood-choked breath was the night all his hopes came crashing down. The night he realised everything was his fault. The night he knew he was worthless.

In trying to help Ren, he'd hoped he would be able to put his ghosts to rest, but that had ended in disaster too. Perhaps he should never leave this strange haunted place. Then no one else would suffer because of his mistakes. Who would die next? Tom, Finn, Raven, Blake . . . Lily?

'Killy,' Clem continued, 'I chose to go with you, I chose to help. I'm as much to blame as you. You can't control everything, and you can't control what people do and choose to do.'

'I should be the dead one though,' Killian murmured.

'Maybe,' said Clem, 'but you're not, and nothing will ever change that. I don't blame you for what happened to me.' He chuckled. 'I did at first, I won't lie, but I'm beyond that. You shouldn't blame yourself either. You need to move on, or you'll be trapped by it forever.'

'I don't know how.'

'Live your life, Killian. Be who you want to be, be with who you want to. Enjoy life because you have it. To squander it like this is a waste – now that would annoy me.'

Clem took a step back and fished about in his trouser pockets.

'I still don't know how I can do that.'

Clem held up a gold coin. It had a band of octopus tentacles around the edge, and in the centre was a squid wrapped around a cowry shell. It was a coin from Venario.

'Remember when we found this on Bracky Beach?' he asked.

At this, Killian cracked a smile; it felt like his first in a very long time. 'Of course. We'd been drinking in the Swan all night, and we staggered down to the beach to "sober up in the moonlight." '

Clem laughed. ' "Sober up in the moonlight," how ridiculous.'

'We actually thought it'd work,' said Killian with a grin. 'I think it made me more drunk, to be honest.'

'And then I found this in the sand.' Clem rolled the coin between his thumb and forefinger. 'I never could roll them along my fingers like you.'

'You've just gotta practice.'

'I've had plenty of time for that – it must be a natural talent.' As Clem held the coin up, the pocked tentacles absorbed the starlight and throbbed with an other-worldly glow. 'Do you remember what we said?'

Killian took a deep breath to steady his emotions. 'That one day we'd go to Venario and spend that exact coin on the most expensive bottle of wine in the first bar we came to.'

'One more stipulation,' said Clem, pointing a finger.

'Ah, yes, the wine *had* to be local. We wanted to be able to smell the vineyard it was squeezed from on the breeze, the warm sea breeze. Posh, expensive local wine.'

'That's exactly it!' Clem smirked and nodded approvingly. 'Hold out your hand.'

He did as he was told, and Clem placed the coin in his palm. Clem delicately took his fingers and wrapped them over the coin, then enveloped Killian's fist with his own hand.

The coin was cold and solid, like real metal. Clem's hand was warm and comforting, like a real human. Killian looked into his dark eyes. Was he real? Did it matter? He just wanted to . . . He needed to enjoy the moment. He put his free hand on top of Clem's and held it firm. Seconds passed by, minutes ticked on, and all Killian could do was stare at him. He needed to think of something to say, something witty, something meaningful, but words abandoned him like the morning dew in a spiderweb.

'Buy the wine, enjoy it,' said Clem. 'And live your life.'

'Clem,' Killian murmured, 'I'm so sorry.'

'Shh.' Clem hushed him and pulled him into a warm embrace. 'I'll be sorrier if you don't use that bloody coin.'

Killian chuckled as he stooped to bury his head in his friend's chest, not caring about the blood that still flowed from his smouldering wound. He closed his eyes and listened to his heart beating. He wanted to stay like this for as long as possible.

Clem's arms held him tight. 'You need to get out of here, Killy,' he whispered into his hair.

'Where is here? Are you real?'

'I'm talking to you, aren't I?'

'Yes.'

'So that answers that. As for here, it's not so simple.' Clem sighed and pushed Killian back but kept his hands on his shoulders. 'This place is a world between worlds, between life and death, and you shouldn't be here. You've trapped yourself, and you need to fight your way out.'

'How do I do that?'

'You need to face what's in the lake. It's your greatest fear made flesh, and it'll kill you if you let it. It wants to kill you.'

Killian's remaining strength drained from him. 'Can you help?'

Clem burst out laughing and took a moment to compose himself. 'Sorry, Killian, sorry,' he said on receipt of an icy glare. 'I can't help you.'

'I kinda guessed that, what with all the laughing.'

Clem flicked his hair back. 'You'll be fine. I promise.'

'Will I ever see you again?'

'Hopefully not in this lifetime. Maybe in your dreams, if you're lucky,' he added with a playful smirk.

'Nightmares more like.' Killian rolled his eyes.

'You don't mean that.'

Killian cocked an eyebrow in response.

'Fine,' said Clem with a shrug and a grin. 'So, this is how we part, on an insult.'

'Would you have it any other way?'

'No, I guess not, but . . .' Clem held his arms out.

Killian needed no further encouragement. He stepped forward and wrapped his friend in his arms. Was he a ghost? Some form of apparition? Was he even real? Killian didn't care; he was real enough, and that was all that mattered.

'By the way, Killy,' Clem whispered, 'I know.'

'What d'you know?'

'I know what you're too stubborn to admit, so get out of here, admit it and live your life.'

He knew exactly what he was too stubborn to admit, and yet he was still too stubborn to admit it. Or afraid of losing her, just like all the others. Killian pulled back, and he and Clem grasped each other tightly on the forearms, something they always did when saying goodbye in the past – a throwback to the time when they were both alive.

'You'll get outta here.' Clem's body shimmered with a silver glow. It was as if thousands of tiny compressed stars were lighting up beneath his skin.

Killian's hands sank into him as his friend became intangible. He knew he couldn't hold him or make him stay, so he resigned himself to losing him once again.

'See you around, Clem.'

'You will.'

Then he burst apart in a cloud of glittering stardust. Blues and purples rippled through it, casting iridescent waves that glistened and twinkled amid the silver. It was truly beautiful. The tiny stars swept around Killian as if giving him one final hug before they drifted up to the sky above.

Killian opened his fist and traced his thumb over the Venarian coin. He rolled it over his fingers and slipped it into his pocket. An intrusive breeze whipped through his hair.

The long grasses of the shore chimed like tiny bells. He rolled his shoulders back and waded in.

Tiny silver waves lapped at his hips, and he stopped to look up. The stars were shining brighter than they ever had – surely that was a good thing? They looked to be wandering amid the black sky. He filled his lungs with cold fresh air; it was revitalising. A flicker of confidence dashed through him. Maybe he could get out. Maybe he could escape. Clem believed in him; all he had to do was believe Clem.

He glanced at the water's surface and froze. A sickening feeling coursed through his gut, and his heart lurched into his throat.

Beneath him floated his reflection, but it wasn't corresponding with his actions. It lay flat on its back, its hands open, palms facing up, its eyes closed. Killian shuddered. It was a haunting image. Slowly, it started to move in a grotesquely creeping manner. It gave off the aura of a fast-growing fungus, sliming and choking. Its hands curled like withered spider legs. Thin black veins scrawled themselves over its pale skin; its mouth twisted into a smile, and its eyes opened.

Killian barely had time to register the black eye sockets and white pupils. A cold hand flashed out of the water and grabbed his forearm. It held him tight and pulled itself out using his weight. Killian was unable to move, let alone attempt to throw the monster off. All his breath left his body in a petrified gasp.

It stood opposite him, a cruel smile on its disturbing face, its black hair plastered to its head.

'Hello, Killian,' it said. Its voice was a horrifying clamour of repulsively recognisable tones.

And then it stabbed him.

CHAPTER
SEVENTY-TWO

Lily jolted awake. Her chest ached, her heart thumped and there was a dull pain in her forehead. She told herself it was a hangover even though she knew it was stress. She looked at Killian, tossed her blankets back and crawled towards him.

There was a peaceful serenity about his face. All his features were relaxed, and his expression was neutral. His hair fell about his shoulders like autumnal leaves. If he weren't so pale, he'd merely look like he was sleeping. His chest was barely moving, his breathing a weak whisper. A blue glow leaked out from under his forearm. Lily reached forward and grabbed his arm. He was so cold. Maybe even colder than yesterday. She turned it over to reveal the pulsing symbol etched into him. She drew her fingers across the line of eerie blue.

Was it worth it? Was any of it worth it? She'd lost the Big Blue and Killian, and for what? To stop some strange floating mask, some insane demon from doing something. She wasn't sure if she cared anymore. Perhaps she should have ignored it all.

After Ren had died and the Gramarye was lost, she should have gotten on with her life. She was a pirate – why should she care about setting right the wrongs? Maybe the world could be saved, but what about her world? She'd used her only chance to summon the Big Blue, and she may as well have not bothered. Killian was trapped, lost, gone forever.

The glow on his skin distorted as tears swamped her vision. She released his arm and wiped away the tears with the back of her hand. She needed to get out of the tent and away from him. In a desperate flurry to escape, she threw on her clothes and darted out into the clearing.

The mage bandits were there – it looked like Raynn was making a pot of coffee. Nedge sat at his feet laughing while Finn smoked next to her. Leif leant over Raynn's shoulder, casting a critical look into the pot. He smirked and then laughed. Raynn screwed his face up and threw his hat to the floor.

'If you think you can do any better, be my guest,' Raynn shouted.

Finn's and Nedge's cackles rose up from the ground. Tom emerged from behind one of the tents, clearly drawn by the commotion. Poppy flew low over his head. He clicked his tongue, and the owl obediently landed on his outstretched arm. It hooted with delight as he affectionately rubbed its belly. Blake pulled back a tent flap and staggered out into the clearing, blinking in the sunlight with heavy rings around his eyes.

'Oh, looks like someone overindulged last night,' said Tom. Poppy hooted in agreement.

Blake grabbed his forehead and shut his eyes. 'Please don't.'

'Whoever is making the campfire brew, you best make it extra strong for Blakey boy. He is a mess,' Tom crowed to the others.

'I thought pirates could handle their booze?' asked Nedge.

'Please don't,' Blake repeated.

Tom burst into peals of laughter.

Lightness surged through Lily's chest at the scene before her. This was what she was doing it for. Not for her, not for Killian and not for her own happiness, but for others and their lives. She couldn't let what had happened to Ren happen to other innocent people. It wasn't right, and it wasn't fair. She was partly to blame, as was Killian, as was poor Ren. Even though they were oblivious to the true intentions of the being within Ren's father, they were still responsible for handing it an object of immense power and then losing it. Other people shouldn't suffer because of their mistake.

'Morning, Lily,' said Leif. 'Any good at making coffee?'

Lily strolled towards him. 'Lovely, Leif. Some people *make* coffee, some are *made* coffee. I think you know which one I am.'

This elicited more chuckles from Finn and Nedge.

'I'm going out for the day.'

'Out?' Leif raised a quizzical eyebrow.

'Beyond your ring of trees.'

'Want any company, Cap'n?' asked Finn.

Lily shook her head. 'I'm fine, thanks. I need to have a think.'

'You can do that here,' Leif put in.

'I can, but you're here disturbing the peace.'

'That's fair enough,' he agreed.

'Now, make me a way out.'

Leif huffed. 'People make you coffee, they make you ways out. Do they do everything for you?'

'Yeah, it's called being in charge. I could punch my way out. I could even use you as a meaty battering ram if I wanted. I'm just being polite.'

'Well, now you've put it like that, one way out coming up.'

CHAPTER SEVENTY-THREE

Killian's eyes fluttered open. Somehow, he'd made it to the sparkling shores, but he could barely move. Pain roared in his shoulder. He put his hand to it, and it came away covered in blood. Above him, the stars twinkled as they looked down on the fallen man from on high. They had it easy. A few feet away, squatting down with its white pupils fixed upon him, was his spectre. It cocked its head to the left as it made eye contact and curled its lip in revulsion.

'How weak you have become,' it said in its haunting layered voice.

Killian said nothing and turned back to the stars. It was right though, there was no denying the truth: he was weak, he couldn't fight it. It was too strong. He had nothing left to give. It may as well just all end here. Lock him up in the darkness forever. At least he'd do no more damage here.

'I knew this was coming,' it continued, but its voice had changed.

A deep pain shot through Killian's chest. Raw burning erupted in his back, like someone was reopening that great scar across it and filling it with salt. He didn't want to look, he didn't want to see, but he had to. Slowly, he sat up and stared into the face of the man who'd murdered his mum. The spectre's skin was still pallid and scribbled with black veins, but the face had morphed into a horrific vision of his past. A wedge of a nose, a pointed chin and long blond hair.

'You've been heading down this path for a long time.' The voice, it was his own, and one from his childhood. One he'd never wanted to hear again.

'Ever since you let your friend die. What was his name?' it pondered. It stood up and rolled its shoulders, and its face changed again. The man who'd killed Clem glared down at him. A cruel handsome face, rich clothes and a gold tooth that glistened when he smiled. 'You ain't been the same. Withdrawn. You ain't got no confidence. It's pitiful. You live afraid of your next fuck-up. You're a shell of a person. You ain't even a person. I told ya, kid, I told ya back then. Wha'd I say? "You're gonna have to live with this," that was it. But you ain't. You ain't even tried. You're nothing.'

It was right.

The man who'd murdered Clem swaggered over to him, starlight winking off his twinkling tooth. 'As if that wasn't enough to fuel me, you're afraid of your own body. Now that is pathetic.'

The glow.

'I'm all you think about, all you consume, all you fear,' it said, stepping towards him. 'If you weren't so scared, you might've escaped. But you're gonna die here, cold and alone.'

It paused and glared at him; its white pupils blazed with malevolence. Its muscles tensed beneath its damp shirt, and a blue-black mist began to wrap itself around its body. A grin spread across its horrific face, and it screwed up its hands. The mist raced towards them, coating them in darkness. A horrific high-pitched scratching sound, as if a rusty knife were being dragged across a pane of glass, emanated from the spectre as long blackened blades formed from each of its balled-up fists and culminated in vicious points. With a shake of its head, Clem's murderer became the mask. That hollow, soulless mask. Taunting him. Smirking at him.

'This is how it ends for you,' the horrendous guttural voice rasped.

But it couldn't end here, not like this. He had to get out, didn't he? He'd unleashed something awful into the world, and he had to make sure it couldn't hurt anyone else. Curling up and dying in this strange world wouldn't help anyone. And his friends – didn't he want to see them again? Lily, last time he'd seen her, had been bruised and bloody, and there had been tears in her eyes. He had to make sure everyone was all right.

Killian got to his feet and, using everything he had left, harnessed the glow. Bright iridescent blades erupted from his fists.

'Not here,' said Killian, 'not by you.'

The masked spectre lunged for him, but he neatly dodged aside. With one swift move, he slashed his demon across the chest. It screamed out and banished a blade to put a pale hand over the oozing black wound. The thick blood welled up between its fingers and dribbled down its white skin like dark slime.

'Perhaps I underestimated you.' It shook its head, and once more it bore Killian's own twisted face.

Killian wiped his lips with the back of his glowing hand. 'Shall we find out?'

'My pleasure.' A dark blade reformed.

Their blades clashed. Black and iridescent sparks flew and crackled like lightning. Shocks raced down Killian's arms. He bit his lip and tried to ignore the sensation. He blocked, stabbed, dodged and ducked as the creature relentlessly attacked. He didn't want to die here, cold and alone. His heart thumped. Heat smothered his skin. The monster's face blurred and changed. His mum's killer was coming for him. He pulled up his glowing blades and parried the creature's attack. It jumped back into a defensive stance.

'Do you think you can win?'

That voice, that smug repulsive voice. Anger and exhaustion fought inside Killian.

'I'll take that as a no.'

Hate and fury flowed through Killian. He hissed through his teeth and attacked. The monster parried, riposted, was parried in return; its footwork was faster than Killian's. It danced about him, making him work harder, sapping his already-fading energy. It wasn't even trying to strike him. It was draining him. Heaviness draped itself over Killian's body, his movements becoming sluggish. The spectre grinned sadistically. It knew. That face, how he hated that face. White-hot rage blinded him. Searing pain awakened him and brought him tumbling back into the present. It burned. He was burning.

He gasped out and staggered back in shock. His legs shook; they wanted to give up, but he stubbornly refused to let them. A thin slash ran from his shoulder to his hip. Black flames danced around the edge of the wound. He slapped his arm across it to staunch the malignant fire. When he moved his arm away, the blood came. Tributaries of crimson flowed down his body. Each breath became a titanic effort, rasping and wheezing in his throat. His body was awash with pain. Blood dripped and spattered onto the glistening sands like liquid rubies.

The monster growled deep in its throat and thrust towards him. Killian defended against its attacks but was forced back. Jabs and slashes rained down. Blood trickled from his chest. So much pain. Cool water lapped at his feet as he was pressed into the silver lake. Sweat stung his eyes. Every movement made him leak more blood. The lake sloshed and surged around him. He was pushed farther and farther in, the water creeping up his calves. He couldn't keep going, he couldn't keep fighting. Exhaustion gripped him. Every movement he made was more listless than the last.

The monster was relentless with its attacks, its haunting pupils always searching for a fracture in Killian's defence. Its face morphed with each thrust of its blades: his mum's killer, Clem's killer, Ren's killer, Killian himself. It was disorientating. Numbness seeped over his body. His lungs were burning. His heart raced. His end was coming. A soft chime filled the air, and the demon pushed Killian. He staggered backwards and rested a hand on his thigh. That thing wasn't fighting, it was staring up at the sky.

Killian followed his monster's gaze. Above, the stars were shifting. They floated through the dark sky like jellyfish in the waves. They trembled to the sound of tinkling glass. One became dislodged, and it fell, leaving a long, thin trail of silver in its wake. It chimed as it hit the surface of the lake. It skimmed across the water four times – each ding a higher pitch than the last – and then sank below the surface. Another fell to replace it.

'*You must catch a star . . .*'

'This is the end,' the demon rasped in all four voices.

Knowing he could collapse at any moment, Killian flung himself into a desperate attack. They fought toe to toe in the water, stars falling, red and black blood dripping all around them. The monster took a dirty swipe at his leg. Killian defended, knocking it back, slicing deep into its left arm and catching it hard in the jaw as he swung round. It staggered, snarled and spat a lump of blood into the lake.

There was so much power surging through Killian's blades. The multitude of colours swirled together amid a silvery haze. He opened his fists and allowed the light to flow over his hands. It crawled up his arms and poured over his battered body. A wave of power rippled through him. The growling demon dashed at him, but he sidestepped with ease and dealt it a deep slash to its back. It screamed but remained standing.

Blades clashed. Stars fell, filling the air with their ethereal sounds. Killian fought on. The spectre fought on. Each was determined to survive. They pushed each other backwards and forwards, blood splattering everywhere. Despite the bleeding gash across its back, the monster didn't give up, not for a second. Blow after blow rained down in Killian's direction. He parried well and even cut another bloody slash into its arm, but he was tiring fast. The blades were becoming heavier and his arms weaker. He knocked back every thrust, blow and swipe, but he was entirely on the defensive now. If he continued to defend, maybe the creature would tire, and maybe he'd be able to use the glow properly.

A harrowing scream rang out into the quiet air. It was full of anguish and misery. The sound of someone reaching their end. Begging for their end. A dark blade had sunk deep into Killian's upper left chest. He cried out again as the blade grated against his bones. He'd failed. He was going to die here, cold and alone, never to see his friends again, never to feel warmth again, never to set right the wrongs he'd started. The light faded from his body, and he slumped against the blade. The sickening sound of metal on bone jarred in his head. Cold skin grasped at his chin, and his head was tilted up to face his nightmare.

'This is how it was always going to end,' it said, brushing his hair out of his face and lightly tracing his cheekbones. 'Now you won't be able to hurt anyone else.'

Killian put a tremulous hand on its shoulder to steady himself. He opened his mouth, but no words came, only a dribble of blood.

It wiped the blood from his lips. 'This is for the best.'

Its face became the mask once more, and it yanked its blade from his body in a shower of dark flames, sparks and blood.

It patted out the crown of flames that had bloomed on his chest. 'Are you ready?'

Killian closed his eyes and listened to the stars crash into the lake. Was it his fault that Ren, Clem and his mum had died? Was anyone else going to die because of him? Was that all he did, breeze through people's lives, leaving nothing behind but a trail of corpses? If he was gone, would everyone else be safe? The truth was, he didn't know. He couldn't change the past, and he couldn't predict the future. There was a chance, a slim one, that everything he thought about himself was wrong. Wasn't that chance worth fighting for? Wasn't it worth seeing his friends again and carrying on?

The moment he sensed the creature move, he ducked. The blade ripped through nothing but air. Killian clenched his fist and summoned the glow with all that he had, and as he stood, he buried it deep into his demon's stomach. He reached up and grabbed its shoulder with his feeble left hand to help him stand. Its mouth dropped open, and a rivulet of black blood oozed from the corner.

'You . . . weren't meant to,' it choked out. 'You don't . . . want to go back. You'll kill them. You'll kill them all.'

Killian pulled the blade up a little, and it hissed with pain. 'Are *you* ready?' he asked.

The demon drew a ragged, tortured breath. With the remains of its strength, it gripped his wrist. 'End it.'

In a shower of black blood, Killian pulled his blade from its stomach. It howled with pain, and its body grew rigid with agony, twisted hands clawing at the stars above. With a choking rasp, it fell limp and flopped into Killian's shaking arms. It raised its head and looked at him. The visage of the man who'd killed his mum appeared, then faded into the man who'd killed Clem; that face merged into the haunting mask, and finally the spectre changed back into Killian.

Killian drew his blade back and thrust it deep into the monster's heart, his own dark heart.

A star dropped from the sky. It chimed as it skimmed the lake, a beautiful haunting melody like a ghost singing a mournful lament to the moon. Silver light flashed momentarily, then was extinguished as the water drowned the star. Killian's breath hung heavy in the air. The spectre gurgled and rasped, its face changing as Killian's tormentors flashed over its features again in endless waves. Unable to look upon it anymore, he dragged his weapon out of the demon's chest, and it lolled forward, gasping a last juddering breath into its blood-filled lungs. Thick black blood pumped from its ruined body and all over Killian's bleeding chest. Then his strength failed, and he collapsed into the shallow water. He held the spectre's shuddering body against his and sobbed. Salty tears and red blood dripped from his chin and trickled down his dying opponent's back. Too weak to even contemplate moving, he just clung to the demonic shadow. Holding it somehow made him feel alive.

Killian didn't know whether he'd succumbed to unconsciousness while holding his demon, but when he opened his eyes, it was gone, and his arm was wrapped around his own body. His left arm hung limp and useless. He sat still, listening to the sound of the silver lake teasing the glittery sands and the high chime of the stars as they skimmed the lake's surface. Heat and pain rose in him; he was a mess of red-and-black smears. With a blood-covered hand, he scooped up some water and poured it over his chest, mesmerised by the blood and the silver mixing together. Tiredness nudged him, and his eyes threatened to close again. He shook his head and took a long breath – he had to get out.

Slowly, painfully, he staggered to his feet, blood dripping into the water. Stars skimmed the surface of the lake. He walked until he was waist-deep and then stopped. Did he have the strength to escape? With a jolt, a blade appeared from his right hand. He took a deep breath and uncurled his fist. The iridescent light raced up his arm and over his bloody, bruised body. The glow soaked into him, soothing all that pain.

A star fell.

'*It's meant only for you . . .*'

It streaked the darkened sky with its silver tail, hit the surface and bounced, skimming towards Killian as if it were being pulled to him. Its light filled his vision as it drew closer – it was so pure. It bounced once, twice before striking him square in the chest. He was engulfed by light and the piercing sound of shattering glass. He breathed out as he fell backwards.

The silver water bent around him as he fell, and the whole world curved inwards. Great silver walls of trees, grasses and rocks built up around him as he plunged through the twisted chaos of the world. The melodic tinkle of broken glass and the chime of the falling stars filled the air. It was as if they were cheering him on. He'd won. His body didn't feel like it had, and he was sure he didn't look like he had, but he'd won.

His descent slowed as his body reached some resistance. Slower and slower he fell until he floated onto a cold flat surface. He got to his feet and looked up. The whole world was stretching down towards him. The trees, the grasses and even the mountains were looking down at him from the edges of what had once been the lake. Beneath his feet was a thin sheet of partially transparent silver, below it only darkness.

He tightened his fist and thrust the blade into the floor. With a splintering snap, a series of gigantic cracks raced from beneath him and tore upwards through the silver landscape, shattering everything in their wake. The ground crumbled to dust, and he tumbled into the black. Above, his world was ripped apart in seconds, leaving nothing behind but shards of glinting silver.

He lay back and watched the silver for as long as his body would allow him to. His whole world had been utterly destroyed by him. There was nothing left but a faint scattering of stardust. He opened his right hand, and the glow drained from him. Exhaustion pulled at his eyelids, but he didn't want to sleep. What if he didn't wake up again? He'd lost a lot of blood. If he fell asleep, that would be the end; he'd bleed out his last in the dark nothingness, powerless to stop it.

He tried to move his body, but nothing responded; his arms and legs hung limp behind him as he drifted down.

Never in his life had he felt so weak. Unconsciousness swooped down towards him, seducing him with thoughts of painless, comfortable sleep. Unable to resist, he closed his eyes and yielded to its charms.

CHAPTER SEVENTY-FOUR

Lily sat on the edge of a grassy knoll and looked down the valley at the river, her back to the mages' hideout. She ran her hands through the grass, and its soft spikes tickled her fingers. The air tasted so fresh. The scents of pine, grasses and morning dew combined around her. She stretched her legs out and rested back against her elbows.

It was such a beautiful, peaceful place. Brilliant emerald meadows interwoven with pink, blue, yellow and white flowers tumbled before her. The grass moved in waves as the breeze raced across the fields. It was so calming to watch. Lily smiled sadly to herself. The flowers danced a joyful jig, and she longed for her troubles to be taken away with the winds. She closed her eyes and imagined what it would be like if that were possible. Life would be so much easier if all you had to do to make your troubles vanish was stand in a field and wait for the wind to take them away. She opened her eyes and chuckled to herself. Leif was an air mage, and he'd given her nothing but trouble.

She pulled a leg up to her chest and flicked the buckle on her boot. Her body still ached from her fight with Killian. Somehow, he was connected to the Otherside, but how? That was a puzzle. Ugly yellow bruises littered her ribs and stomach, and her face hurt. Whenever she smiled, her lip split and she could taste blood again. It had been so long since she'd had to deal with her own physical pain, she'd forgotten what it was like. It hurt, and it was annoying. It was a hindrance. And was it even worth it? Killian was still asleep, and this morning he looked worse than ever. If Arow didn't have some sort of breakthrough soon, they'd have to leave. She had to get back to the *Tempest* and slide into the skin of a pirate queen.

She gazed over her knee and continued to robotically flick at the buckle. Metal smacked against leather. The great snow-capped mountains loomed in the distance, the morning sun painting their craggy peaks with gold. A pirate queen had no need for Killian or the confusing feelings he tried to give her. Besides, she knew all too well what happened when two people cared about each other too much: swinging feet, death and loneliness. The bitter stench of despair and desperation. No, she wouldn't allow herself to get like that; she wouldn't take after *him*. A pirate captain was stronger than that. Stronger than *him*.

A rustling came from the trees behind her, but she didn't turn around – it would only be Raven checking up on her. He liked to do that, and it didn't displease her.

With a heavy thump, he dropped to the ground. It was strangely graceless of him. She could make out the outline of his body in her peripheral vision. He was mimicking her pose, one leg drawn up to his chest and his arm draped around it.

The sounds of nature wrapped around the pirate captain and her first mate – tweeting birds, the shimmying of the grasses, the distant rush of the river. Raven always knew when to speak and when to enjoy the silence; it was one of the many things she loved about him. He merely stared at the landscape with her. The winds ruffled his hair and flapped his shirt.

'Did you miss me?' a painfully familiar voice asked.

Lily caught her buckle in her hand and squeezed it hard. Heat flashed through her skin, and her chest tightened. There was a swelling in her throat, and her mouth went dry.

She needed a drink. A good drink. Not that tangy water back at the camp. Seth's rum. Venarian red wine. Anything. Get drunk, pass out and wake up somewhere else, with someone else.

She released the buckle and turned. Blue eyes. Stubbly beard. Chestnut hair rippling in the breeze. She wanted to touch him, needed to know he was real. She wanted to grab him, hold him, feel him. Emotion mushroomed inside her, threatening to burst through her defensive dam.

No. She was a pirate queen. No. Love led to ruin.

'No. Did you miss me?' she replied.

'Nah,' said Killian with a wolfish grin.

'Sleep well?' What a ridiculous thing to ask.

'I could do with a few more days, to be honest.' He yawned and stretched.

'Do that again and I'll leave you here.' A pain shot through her chest. She couldn't leave him, not ever. Captain Rothbone could though. Leave him like spoiled cargo. Cut off the millstone. Drop him down a blue hole.

He twisted to face her, and his supporting hand moved dangerously close to hers. He glanced about the forests and valley. 'Where is here?'

'Somewhere between Poll and Scherben.'

'Doesn't it have a name?'

'It's a wood, Killian. A wood made by a bunch of highway mages. I doubt it has a name.'

'I'll name it.'

'Please don't.' She smiled, and her lip throbbed.

'No, no, I can do things like this. I shall name it the Whispering Woods.'

'Why that?'

'It rolls off the tongue nicely, and it's better than the Shitty Sticks, which was my second choice. Quick, go and get your map, and I'll mark it on.'

Even though she really tried not to, Lily couldn't help but laugh. Having him back was like a blessing and a curse. A vile metallic taste filled her mouth. She fumbled to try to hide her bleeding lip, but it was too late.

'Lil, you're bleeding.'

He moved as if he was about to touch her, and she quickly swiped his hand away. She didn't need his touch or sympathy.

'I know,' she huffed, wiping it away with her thumb.

'I didn't wanna say, but your eye . . .'

'Is bruised, I know, but thank you for pointing it out.'

He looked her up and down and frowned. 'Did I miss something?'

At this, Lily cracked another smile. 'Yes is the answer to that.'

He patted her hand and smirked. 'How about you tell me all about it?'

Her pulse raced at his touch. He was real. He was awake. His skin was warm. Gone was that deathly cool that had haunted him for so long. Feelings tangled up within her. Rothbone and Maggiore were at war with each other. Rothbone was stronger though; she could crush Maggiore, destroy her with a single punch.

'How about "Captain Lily Rothbone came out here for some peace and quiet." It's not "story time for Killian." '

'Fair enough.' He stretched out his legs and lay down in the grass.

Lily released her knee and rolled onto her side. She looked him up and down. Were his eyes closing, or was he just squinting into the sun?

'Killian?'

'Yeah.'

'Don't you dare fall asleep.'

CHAPTER SEVENTY-FIVE

KILLIAN ATE HIS WAY THROUGH A DISH OF HEARTY stew. It was full of vegetables and beans, all held together in a thick gravy that had a slight undertone of cider. He had to admit, Leif, the handsome one, was a good cook. He'd been sitting with him, but as soon as the mage had finished eating, he'd wandered off to one of the tents. He was a nice-enough guy and at one point seemed to be flirting with him. Killian glanced about the group of mages in the flickering firelight.

Finn was sitting with Nedge, both cackling about something and chain-smoking. Nedge looked like she could throw a mean punch, and he'd been told she could summon powerful dark magic. It was no wonder she and Finn had formed a bond. Raven was sitting with Blake and Tom, the latter with Poppy, Ulrich's pet owl, sitting on his knee. It seemed the young pirate had adopted himself a feathered friend. Next to them was Arow, who had a sour look on his face. It seemed odd to Killian that someone with the power to heal could be so miserable. Raynn, the leader of the group and the one who'd got the fire going with a click of his fingers, was talking to Lily.

Killian set his bowl down and slipped his hand into his coat pocket. Something cold brushed his skin. Circular, metal. And something else. A piece of paper. He pulled them out.

In his hand lay a small discoloured piece of parchment with the words *spend it* written on it in agonisingly familiar handwriting. The other item was a golden coin. Clem's golden Venarian coin. He turned it over, and there was the squid wrapped around a cowry. Puckered octopus tentacles grazed his finger as he traced its edge. Tears prickled his eyes, and his chest tightened. How was this possible? Where had it come from? Why hadn't he found it earlier? It didn't matter. He squeezed the coin and silently vowed to spend it one day on the best wine Venario had to offer. After taking it on a journey across his knuckles twice, he dropped it and the note back into his pocket. Safely stowed.

Leif reappeared and slumped next to Killian with a clink. He had four open wine bottles with him. This was exactly what he needed.

'It's not a celebration without wine, is it?' The mage grinned.

'Nope.' Leif was definitely all right by him.

'Don't worry,' said Leif as he cast the bottles out around the group, 'there's more in the tent. I know what you sea rats are like.' He handed a bottle to Killian.

Killian took a deep swig. It was white. Tart and tangy. He was no wine expert, but he preferred red. Though this would certainly do, and at least it wouldn't turn his brain into mush like red had a habit of doing. He took another sip and handed it back to Leif.

'I'm not a sea rat,' he said.

'No?' Leif raised his eyebrows.

'Nah. I'm just along for the ride and to make everyone's lives difficult.'

Leif smirked, then knocked back some wine. He passed the bottle back to Killian. 'I reckon you're good at that.'

Killian chuckled and took another deep draught. He turned to pass it over to Blake, but Leif caught his arm and pulled it back.

'Let's keep this one between us.' He winked with his green eye. 'I'd like to get to know you.'

'Sure,' said Killian.

For the next hour, Killian and Leif chatted. Killian told him the heavily edited version of his life story, leaving out most of the painful moments and focusing on the adventure and good times. He told him about the Demon's Drop and the world beneath it and briefly outlined the tasks, mostly to make himself look heroic. When they ran out of wine, Leif staggered off to fetch a fresh bottle, and they carried on chatting.

Leif was an interesting man, born in Venario to a winemaker. He'd spent his childhood learning about and tending to vineyards, as well as being self-conscious about his eyes. He was supposed to take on the family business, but the winds took him. No one else in his family had learnt to be any class of mage because they'd always put their hearts and skills into farming, but he felt different. Magic came to him easily, and by the time he was a teenager, he was trying his father's patience, so he left his home in search of something new and fresh. One day while out on the road, Raynn tried to rob him, and that was that. They'd been honourable thieves ever since.

'So, let me get this straight,' Killian said with a slight drawl. The wine was going to his head nicely. 'You steal from people for some of the year, spend the rest of the year spending what you stole, then do it all again the next year?'

'Yup. It's a bit of a vicious cycle.'

'You don't say.' Killian laughed. 'But you enjoy it?'

Leif ran his thumb along his bottom lip. 'I do.'

'Then it doesn't matter.'

Leif burst out laughing. 'I like your thinking.'

They stayed with each other, drinking, chatting and joking for most of the night. Leif was a really good guy, and for better or worse, he reminded Killian of Clem. He was easy-going and a fellow thief, and he enjoyed a drink and an adventure. Given the way he spoke of his gang, he sounded loyal, like a true friend, someone who could be depended on. Talking to him was simultaneously uplifting and saddening. Leif was a living, breathing reminder of all that he'd lost but was also tangible proof that, in a way, Clem could live on.

Killian was very drunk.

'You all right?' Leif asked, breaking into his thoughts.

Killian snapped to attention. 'Oh, yeah, sorry.'

'It's fine,' said Leif with a twinkle in his eyes. 'You were just looking at me like you wanted a hug or something.'

Killian shook his head and pushed his hair back. His gaze roved to Lily, still sitting with Raynn. 'Sorry, I was thinking of someone.' He took a swig from the half-empty bottle of wine in his hand.

'I was sure she loved you.'

Killian spat the bottle and, wastefully, some wine from his mouth. 'I certainly wasn't thinking of her.'

'I'm not normally wrong about things like this, but I don't know – tonight, she seems cold. I don't know why she's sitting with Raynn.'

'I don't know where you got that idea from. I'm temporary crew. The captain has a duty to look after her crew. That's probably carved into some stone tablet of pirate law somewhere.'

Leif chuckled. 'I reckon so. Pirates, they're a strange lot.'

'Aye.'

Killian leant back and stared up through the circle of wavering treetops. The sky was a dark blue with a dusty sprinkling of stars. Thin clouds edged in white rolled on the breeze. He drew in a deep breath. The air was full of woodsmoke; it was cosy and relaxing and made him drowsy, or perhaps that was the wine. The fire crackled as the pine trees rustled. He ran his fingers through the grass, pausing to flick the head off a tiny orange mushroom.

'She's quite a woman,' said Leif. 'I tried my moves on her, but she didn't want to know.'

Well, that was a ridiculous mistake on Lily's part. Killian looked at Leif, drinking from the bottle of wine, his lips full, his eyes closed. This man was gorgeous; he was fun and easy to talk to and drink with. He wasn't sure if he'd be able to turn Leif down if he was propositioned. Lily was a fool.

Leif set the bottle down in his lap and stared at Killian. 'When she brought you here, the way she acted, I was convinced she loved you. What do I know, eh?'

'It's what she's like with all her crew.'

Leif shrugged. 'Maybe she is celibate or does prefer women.'

'Maybe.' Killian tipped the bottle to his mouth, only to drink a few dribs.

Leif smacked him on the back. 'I'll get us another bottle. I may as well send you on your way tomorrow with a hangover. It'll make the trip more interesting.'

'Ah, the old "am I gonna throw up, pass out or sweat myself to death" game. I enjoy that.'

With a chuckle, Leif left to raid his stash. Killian glanced across the fire at Lily. Orange light pooled on her skin, and she was laughing at something with Nedge. Almost as if she sensed him looking, she turned her head in his direction. A brief half smile flickered over her lips, and she turned back to the mage. Something smooth and hard pressed against Killian's neck. He reached behind and seized the bottle from Leif.

He slumped down next to him. 'Let's get disgraceful.'

Killian swigged the wine. That sounded like a fine idea.

CHAPTER SEVENTY-SIX

Sasha sat on the porch with a coffee in one hand and a cigarette in the other, watching Kurt slope off down the path and out onto the lane. It was his turn to support the group. She wasn't sorry to see him go, but she hoped he could handle what lay ahead of him.

Delphina had returned the previous night. Her wretched screams had blasted through the walls as Varo ripped the soul from her arm. It was a sound that froze Sasha's blood, but she knew it was for the future and for the protection of mages. And it was the key to making Theo whole again. It had to hurt if it was to heal.

She took a drag on her cigarette and blew a curl of smoke out into the afternoon breeze. The next kill would be easier, or so she told herself. She'd even considered volunteering herself instead of Kurt. After she'd broken him down in the barn, she wasn't entirely convinced he was up to the job. But she knew she should rest. Going through the soul binding and removal rituals so soon after the first time wouldn't be good for her physically or mentally. She didn't want to be a burden on Theo so soon either. She'd yet to see him today. No doubt he was still recovering from healing Delphina's bleeding, smoking arm.

Dark grey clouds gathered overhead, blocking out the blue of the sky. Sasha shuddered and pulled her cloak closer. She took a sip of her coffee and winced. It was so bitter. She never could get the coffee-to-water ratio right. The grasses in the field before her rustled and trembled as the winds picked up. The horses were at the far end of the field. They stood shoulder to shoulder, their large sad eyes gazing out down the track and away from the house. There was a soft pattering on the sloped shelter above her as rain started to fall. She tossed the dregs of her poorly made coffee over the porch and pulled her legs in to her chest.

The front door opened, and the sound of claws clacking on wood followed it. Sasha glanced over her shoulder to see Red trotting towards her. The sweet fox nuzzled her thigh and then scampered down the porch steps to frolic in the rain and tall grass. Theo's footsteps were slow and heavy. A swell of fear rose in Sasha. Even his steps sounded more drained than usual. She kept her eyes firmly on the happy fox as it danced and twirled through nature. It was a beautiful sight, full of life and innocence. Her vision blurred, and she neatly wiped away the tears. There was a heavy thump as Theo sat down next to her.

'I got you this,' he said, handing her a mug.

She took it from him and peered in. Honey-coloured liquid sloshed around inside. She had a deep sniff, and her shoulders relaxed.

'How did you know I felt like a beer?' she asked.

'Lucky guess.'

'Very,' she agreed, then took a swig. She allowed herself to look at him.

A bolt of white-hot pain raced up her nose, and her heart squeezed against her breastbone. His skin was so pale he could melt away with the snow and not be missed. Beneath his eyes lay dark and shadowy crevasses. The whites of his eyes were scrawled with tiny red bolts of lightning. He was holding a mug himself, but it looked like it was an effort. Around his shoulders he wore the cloak she'd bought him, its deep, rich colour a stark contrast to his faded complexion.

'What's wrong?' he asked, his haunted brown eyes not leaving her face.

'Nothing.' She took a final drag on her cigarette, stubbed it out on the side of her boot and flicked it away.

'Good.' He tugged on his cloak and pulled it around his body. 'Thanks for this. It's warmer than my old one, and it doesn't have any holes.'

'It's okay,' said Sasha, a deep pain pressing against her heart.

'I think I've only had one other gift before.' He stared at the raindrops as they smashed and exploded on the wooden porch steps. 'I can't remember what it was or who gave it to me.'

Sasha took a deep draught from her mug, anything to keep the threatening tears away. How could he have only ever been given two gifts? His whole life he'd been used and then cast aside when he wasn't needed anymore, without a thought for him or his well-being. How could nobody care about him? Use him, drain him, toss him aside like a piece of rubbish. It made her so angry she wanted to scream. She finished her drink and put the mug down. Strangely, the wash of alcohol gave her more clarity.

'Theo, how have you lived like this?'

He turned to her. A flicker of emotion and a flicker of a soul danced in his deep eyes, and then it was gone. It was as fleeting and fragile as a snowflake. 'What do you mean?'

'So many people must have used you and tossed you aside, or you wouldn't be—' What was she going to say? How could she say it? She didn't want to hurt him more, if indeed he could be hurt emotionally.

'I wouldn't be blank, devoid of humanity, emotionless.' Theo finished the sentence for her. 'If I hadn't been used so many times, I'd know what a smile felt like, I'd take pleasure in things like the warm sun, birdsong, a winding river, waves breaking on a beach. I'd know what food and drink tasted like. I'd enjoy them rather than consuming them out of necessity. I'd know what love feels like. I'd want to touch someone, and not just to heal their pain, but to feel them, physically and emotionally. I'd know what loss and pain feel like. I'd argue with people, I'd kiss people, I'd enjoy getting drunk, I'd dance. I'd walk in the moonlight and bask in its glow. I'd write, paint, and play an instrument. But I can't do any of that because I'm not a person, not a real one.'

Sasha reached forward and touched his arm. Theo looked from her hand to her face and didn't pull away. She wrapped her fingers around him and gently pulled at him, encouraging him to move towards her.

'Come here,' she said.

He moved.

'Let me hold you,' she said.

'I don't know what to do,' he said, his voice low.

Sasha almost laughed at the absurdity of the situation. How could someone not know how to be held, not know how to take comfort from another person?

'Put your head on my shoulder, here. Now, put your arm

across me.' When he didn't move, she took his hand in hers and put it about her waist. She put her arm around his shoulder and pulled him close. 'There, that's all there is to it.'

They stayed like that for some time, the rain growing heavier and the wind getting wilder. There was a comfort to be had with Theo, and Sasha hoped he felt the same about her. The sky was dark, and the thick grey clouds clogged out the light. Red didn't seem bothered though. He continued to leap and pounce amidst the grass. Sasha tightened her grip on Theo, and she felt him do the same. She wasn't sure if he was merely mimicking her or if he was feeling some sort of emotion.

'I'm going to help you, Theo,' she murmured, 'and I don't care what it takes. You've done so much for others, now let someone do something for you. I'll make sure you get to where you need to be. I'll bring back all the souls by myself if I have to. I'll unlock the Gramarye myself if I must. I'm going to protect you. I will look after you, and I'll make you whole. I promise.'

'Sasha, I'm not worth it.' His voice was faint and weak.

She ran her hand through his thick dark hair. 'You're worth so much more than you know, and I'll prove it to you.'

Theo's head moved slightly, perhaps nodding, but knowing him, he was shaking it in disagreement. No more words came from him. His breathing grew heavier, as did his weight. The arm framing Sasha's waist went limp and slid into her lap. She held him tighter and pulled his cloak about them both as he slept.

CHAPTER SEVENTY-SEVEN

After days of solid and uneventful hiking, the weary group of travellers finally arrived in Scherben, which meant real beds, decent sleep and fresh food. Delighted by this, Killian threw his pack down at the foot of his bed and paced towards the glass doors. A gust of cold air blasted into the room when he flung them open.

Taking a deep breath, he stepped outside. The cool invigorating air ruffled his hair, and the cathedral rose before him, all spikes, black stonework and wonder. Its spires seemed to scrape at the clouds as if looking for a way out. The streets flowed out beneath him, large and cobbled. People traipsed up and down. Horses and carts trundled down the wide roads. Tall, narrow black-and-white buildings lined the streets and were flanked by metal street lamps. The sound of distant guitar music floated on the breeze; no doubt some entertainers had set up in the square. Killian's fingers tapped on the railing in time. Despite the view and the distractions, frustration gnawed at him.

During their cross-country journey, Tom had barely uttered a word to him. And in all honesty, it hurt. They were friends, drinking buddies, he'd saved his life, and yet the young pirate was pushing him away. It didn't help that Pops, his new pet, kept her unnerving amber eyes fixed on Killian at all times. Suspicion and fear radiated from that fluffy ball of feathers, and it seeped into Tom. There had to be some way of making it right, some way to gain his trust again. He didn't want him to be afraid. But he had to admit, witnessing him possessed by the enlii, while knowing about the glow, would be a frightening combination for anyone to cope with.

Lily was also an issue, but when wasn't she? She'd not allowed him to take a turn on watch for the whole trip. The party were exhausted, and it was all his fault. She'd said it was because he'd been through so much and needed rest more than anyone, but he knew it was because she didn't trust him. It was pathetic. If she knew all he'd been through, all the fighting he'd done just to wake up, she'd soon change her tune. If she knew about the glow, she'd certainly have a different view of him.

He wasn't useless. He closed his eyes and rocked his head back. The wind caressed his cheeks. The magnetic pull of the glow whispered to his body, and he embraced it. An incredible rush of strength coursed through him, and his muscles hardened in response. He sucked in a deep breath and focused on the power; he wanted to hold on to it for as long as possible. He had to learn to control it. Iridescence flashed in his eyes, and his skin crawled with glowing pastel colours. The melodic chime of crystals resonated in the air around him. He lifted his arms and, for the first time, looked at the spectacle on his skin without fear or concern.

A glowing silver made up the base of the light, but other colours frequently flittered about the surface – shimmering greens, yellows, purples, pinks, blues and that shade of pale orange that scatters the sky at the start of a beautiful sunrise. He tensed his arm, and the colours swirled together. They shifted and twisted like the surface of a soap bubble. He moved his arm, and long wisps of light drifted on the breeze, never quite detaching from him.

Slowly, he unbuttoned his shirt. His chest was glowing too. His body was awash with surging power. It was intense. It was raw and powerful. A hot sweat broke out over him, and he trembled as his strength wavered. The glow was sucking out his life; he had to let it go.

'You have to go,' he whispered, closing his eyes. He muttered the mantra over and over again, and eventually, the glow complied. All his breath rushed from his body with it, and he crumpled to his knees.

His breathing was laboured, and he was drenched and drained, but that didn't keep a crooked smile from his face. He'd held on to the light without fear, he'd embraced it, and he was still conscious for his efforts. Using the railing, he hauled himself to his feet and clung to it. He thought back to Raven leaping from the same balcony, darting from spire to spire, and yearned to do the same, but his exhausted muscles warned him against such recklessness.

He stepped away from the balcony and staggered slightly but managed to grab the door for support. He steadied himself and ambled towards his bed. The heavy wooden door on the right opened, and Raven stepped from the bathroom, towel about his waist, his hair wet and dripping. He glanced from the open balcony door to Killian.

'Admiring the view?' he asked.

Killian nodded. 'She does have an eye for a view.'

'She does,' agreed Raven. 'Are you going to bathe so we can get some food?'

'Yup, I need to get this road stink off me,' said Killian, walking towards the bathroom. He bit his lip, hoping he didn't look too frail. 'Are you going out tonight?' he asked. Raven would pick up on the veiled meaning.

'I should think so. There's an even better view from up there,' he said, nodding towards the cathedral.

'Good,' said Killian. 'I'll join you.'

TOM tightened Nima's ribbon around his fingers, weaving it between his collection of golden rings. Tonight, he was going to give it back to her; it only seemed right, after all. He'd made sure that the party of pirates hadn't gone to her tavern. This was something he had to do without being seen. Everyone thought he was lying about her anyway, so they were only too happy to visit somewhere else. Killian had made some sort of excuse and left early, which Tom was glad about, if he was perfectly honest. It was hard to look at the man now without seeing those blazing red eyes and thinking about his crystalline horns. He made him nervous. And tonight, he could do without that.

Finn was smoking and chattering to Lily while they drank hot spicy wine. Raven and Blake were doing the same but with less chatter. Tom's heart pounded in his ears. He reached for his mug of wine and downed it in an attempt to shut out the noise. It didn't work. He glanced to the bar; it was rammed with patrons while the staff hurried up and down. He needed another drink, but perhaps now was the perfect time to slip away.

'Ya being shifty, Tom.' Finn's voice broke into his head.

'Wh-what?'

'You're being shifty,' she repeated, a thick cloud of smoke accompanying her words.

'Nah, I'm . . . I don't know. I feel a bit warm. I don't think the food agreed with me. I'm gonna get some air.'

Before he even knew what he was doing, Tom was outside. His palms were sweating, so he loosened his shirt to let the cold Scherben air caress his skin. He was very warm, but it wasn't anything to do with the food or the booze.

The streets were a hive of late-night activity. Horses and carts trundled up and down, vendors were selling street food and groups of people rolled from tavern to stall and back again. He glanced up the cobbled street. Nima's tavern was only a few minutes' walk away. Without putting another shred of thought into it, he put his head down and paced in its direction.

He had to see her again, just once. She was his first, after all, his only. He'd swagger in, and she'd smile, tears brimming in her eyes. She'd lean over the bar and kiss him. She'd call him silly and tell him to keep the ribbon to remember her by. He'd give her the ring from his little finger, and she'd squeal with delight. It would be a perfect reunion.

Tom stood outside the tavern and glanced up. The Lost Lobster. He hadn't noticed the name before. If a lobster had come this far up the river, it certainly was lost. He chuckled to himself. Nima had probably come up with that name – she was unique and creative like that. He pushed the door open.

A thick draught of tobacco and woodsmoke rushed out and assaulted him. Tom embraced it like an old friend and stepped inside. The tavern was heaving. All the tables were full of punters surrounded by mugs of beer, piles of coins and decks of cards. The potent scent of the sweet, spicy local wine hung in the air. Several lamps accompanied a roaring fireplace to bathe the building in a toasty orange light. A piano had residence next to the bar. A woman with short curly blonde hair and dressed in a black suit was playing a jaunty melody while two of her friends sang along.

Tom scanned the sea of faces, searched the bar and then saw her. Nima. Her long red hair was piled high on her head, stray strands twisted and curled around her face. A pair of large blue eyes shone with sensual warmth, and an easy, relaxed smile adorned her strawberry lips. He squeezed the ribbon once more for luck and approached the bar.

'Good evening,' she said, tucking a piece of fiery hair behind her ear. 'What can I get you?'

'Nima?' said Tom. His voice was dry and cracked; he should have had another drink to loosen himself up.

She frowned. 'Yes, do we know each other?'

'We, erm, we met a few weeks ago.' Tom wanted to leave, he wanted to leave and never return.

She put her elbow on the bar and leant forward, giving him an eyeful of her ample assets. 'Are you sure?' she asked with a touch of playful laughter.

'Yes, I . . .' Why was the ground not swallowing him up? Why was he still alive and talking? He unwound the ribbon from his fingers and dangled it over the bar with trembling hands. 'Th-th-this is yours.'

She snatched it from him. 'I was wondering where that old rag had got to.'

'You really don't remember me, do you?'

'Listen, sweetie, a lot of folks breeze in and out of here. You can't expect me to remember you all, now, can you?' She smiled as she spoke, but it was sickly sweet, like she was talking down to a wounded animal that was beneath her notice. 'Are you ordering a drink, darling?'

'No, no, I'm fine. I'm leaving.'

Tom stumbled out into the night. He felt tiny, pathetic and used. Humiliation sat on his shoulder and roared with laughter. He blinked away the burning tears and decided to head back to his room at the inn. Poppy would be waiting for him there; at least she cared about him.

THE half-moon was surrounded by thin streaks of clouds, its eerie glow highlighting their edges. A scattering of pale stars peered through the gaps between the clouds, and Killian glanced up and wondered whether they were waiting to see him fall again. He shook his head. He shouldn't think like that. Cold air whipped around him, and he pulled his long brown coat close. With soul-crushing trepidation, he reached for one of his swords. He gripped the hilt tight and waited. Nothing. He felt nothing. They were lifeless. Their bond had truly been severed.

He released the sword and groped around in his inside pocket for the coin. Slowly, he traced his thumb up and down the edge, feeling the lumpy metal octopus tentacles against his skin. A calm serenity fell over him. The coin was something real. Something tangible. Something that proved what'd happened to him, had really happened. He scanned the city as his fingers rubbed the coin.

The gigantic cathedral towered above the city, black against the silvery grey of the night. Its four spires pointed towards the sky like long spindly fingers, far from Killian's reach. Lamps flickered at the base of the building, bathing the lower walls in a wavering orange light. People wandered up and down the streets, some in groups, others alone. It seemed there was always somebody somewhere. Killian pulled himself up onto the railing and crouched down for balance.

The door creaked open behind him. Raven had returned.

'How was it?' Killian asked without turning.

'All right,' said Raven, joining him on the balcony, his shirt absent. 'You should have stayed. They're all still out there, drinking and smoking the night away.'

'I'm not in the mood.'

Raven leapt nimbly onto the railing and stood. Killian, still crouching, looked up at him. His mouth moved as if he were muttering something, but Killian heard nothing. Great black-purple wings materialised in a swirl of smoke. The first mate unfurled them to their full span, twitched them and folded them behind his back.

'Are you up for this?' he asked, his tone as soft and charming as ever.

'Yeah.' He wasn't sure, but he had to know.

Raven folded his arms and stood perfectly still, the breeze ruffling his feathers and dark hair. He looked down at Killian, a purple glow radiating from his irises. 'When you're ready.'

Killian relaxed his muscles and allowed the glow to surface. It flowed over his body, covering him with swirling colours. Crystals shattered and faded into a soft ghostly chime. He got to his feet and stood next to Raven. He closed his eyes and took a deep breath. Power washed through him. It coiled around his muscles, tightening them. It felt so good to have such strength flowing within his body, a strength he was beginning to control. After a moment, he blew all the air from his lungs and turned to Raven, whose eyes widened at the sight of his shimmering companion.

'Stay close,' said Raven, 'then if you ne—'

'All right.'

'Ready?'

Killian nodded, his heart pounding with determination.

Raven spread his wings and leapt from the balcony. Killian watched him glide silently towards the cathedral. His body tensed, and a pang of doubt shook his nerves. *I don't have any wings.* Before he could think himself out of the situation, he leapt.

A jolt of power burst from his legs as his body was launched across the carriageway and towards the massive building before him. He flipped over in mid-air and planted his feet on the blackened brickwork. He pushed off and powered forward. Long tendrils of light hung from him as he ran vertically. The strong beat of his heart pounded in his ears. The more he ran, the more energy he seemed to have. He glanced to his left, then to his right, but he could see no sign of Raven. A gentle flap came from behind him. Whatever happened, he was safe.

A window ledge jutted into his path; not wanting to sway from his route, he aimed for it. His foot stretched for the ledge. As soon as it made contact, he bent his knee and pushed off, vaulting himself over the gigantic stained glass window. Red, blue and green glittered beneath him. He landed on the edge of the window arch and sprinted forwards as soon as he was on solid ground. The narrow walkway that encircled the main spire drew closer. He pushed off the wall, clearing the walkway to land on the tiled spire.

It was more difficult to keep his pace on this surface, but he refused to give in. To fall now would undo everything he'd achieved this night. He focused on the great black oak tree jutting from the apex of the spire; its thick branches were calling to him. Everything around him melted like a waxwork in the sun. All he saw was the dark metal tree. He threw his arms back, and dropping all his power into his legs, he leapt forward.

His body easily reached the top of the spire, and he flung his arms out. Cold metal brushed against his fingers as he grasped for the trunk. He dropped his focus to his arms. They pulsed with power as he pulled himself towards it. His body slammed gracelessly against it, and for one horrible moment, he thought he might fall. The light was fading from his skin and taking all his strength with it. With everything he had left, he hauled himself up the metal trunk, his shoulders burning. Five twisted metal branches loomed above him, and he reached for the closest, pulling himself up to sit on it. Relief descended upon him, and he blew out a heavy sigh as he leant his head against the icy metal. His eyes threatened to close, but he stubbornly refused to let them have their way.

'Over there,' said Raven, nodding towards a high walkway that ran around the edge of the spire to their left, 'is more comfortable, and it has a better view of the city.'

'I can't get over there.'

'I can.'

Killian grabbed Raven's arms and allowed himself to be flown to the next spire. He staggered when his feet touched solid ground. Raven grabbed him and aided him in sitting down. He dangled one leg over the edge into the abyss and drew his other up to his chest. Raven sat next to him, heat radiating from him.

Scherben was so far away from up there, it didn't feel like they were in the city anymore. The river that cut the city in two was clear and white in the milky light of the moon. The long, narrow houses of the city sprawled off before Killian's eyes, meeting the dark shadows of the meadowland, which was swallowed up into the night. Lamps lit up the carriageways, creating a warming orange path that was visible from the cathedral, twisting and trailing through the city.

'It's amazing up here,' Killian whispered.

'Glad you came?'

'Yeah.' Killian's eyes welled up as he followed the course of the snowy river.

'Good. Oh, I forgot to give you this back.'

Raven delved into his trouser pocket and produced Ren's blunt potato knife. The blade was dull and the wooden handle tired. He passed it to Killian, and it rattled as it moved between their hands. Killian squeezed it tight. It was such a precious treasure.

'Thanks for keeping it safe.'

'Of course. You might want to get that blade sharpened.'

Emotion swelled up within him. 'It was Ren's,' he said, twirling it in his fingers. 'Seth gave it to me. I'll sharpen it, make it useful. Then maybe it'll be like he's almost with us – in the form of a tatty kitchen knife.'

Raven chuckled. 'I don't think he'd have it any other way.'

'It . . . wasn't my fault, you know,' said Killian.

Raven put one hand on the stone ledge as he looked in Killian's direction.

'Ren's death,' Killian continued. 'It wasn't my fault. There wasn't anything I could do, and I can't change what happened.' The words tumbled from his mouth like they had a life of their own.

Raven stayed silent.

Killian kept his focus on the city below him; it was easier to talk that way. The chilly wind breezed through his hair, and he gripped the ledge. 'Things have haunted me for some time.' Pain gnawed at his soul, but he continued to speak. 'When I was a boy, my mum was killed in front of me. She screamed and begged for me to run, so I did. There was nothing I could do, but it didn't stop me blaming myself. If I'd stayed, maybe I could have saved her. If I hadn't opened the front door and let a cleanser into our house, maybe she'd have been fine.' He screwed his eyes up and forced back the tears. 'When I was a teenager, Clem, my best friend, my closest friend, was murdered in front of me. I can still feel his blood on my chest, and I still hear his gurgling last breaths. I caused the mess we got into, and it should have been me who died for it. But it was him, and there was nothing I could do. I couldn't control the situation. I'd created it, but it spiralled beyond me.

'Having Ren die in front of me brought everything back. It made me feel useless, worthless, cursed. I was trying to save his dad to wipe away the pain of losing my mum and Clem, but instead, I got Ren killed.' He rubbed his eyes with the heels of his hands. 'I was so scared that one of you would die on this mission and that it'd all be my fault.' He planted his elbow into his thigh, sighed and fell silent.

Raven drew his legs up and rested his chin on his knee. There was a soft rustling sound as he relaxed his wings behind him.

'After you guys ripped the enlii out of me, I got trapped in some place between life and death. I wasn't asleep – I was in another world. It doesn't make sense saying it out loud, but it was real, this other place. All my doubts, feelings of inadequacy and fears came back to haunt me.' He paused to flick away an escaped tear. 'I saw Ren, I saw my mum, I saw Clem. I spoke to them all.'

He put his arms behind him, spreading his hands out over the cool stone, and leant against them. 'I had to fight to get out. There was a monster. It was everything wrong and bad in my life. I was so tired. I almost let it win. It seemed easier that way. Then I thought about everything that'd happened – all the death, misery and loss – and I realised that maybe it wasn't my fault. Sometimes things happen and we can't do anything about them. Letting myself die wouldn't achieve anything, it wouldn't bring anyone back.' He paused to compose himself. 'So, I fought my way out because there's a slim chance, a very slim chance, that I won't kill you all by accident.'

Killian pulled his knees into his chest and wrapped his arms around them. He blew all the breath from his lungs and tightened his resolve, determined not to cry. 'Pretty messed up, eh?' he said, and the corner of his mouth twitched up into a lopsided smile.

Raven nodded. 'You should have said something. You should have told me about your mum and Clem. You should have told me what happened to you in that place. And you should have told me about this glow of yours as soon as you found it.'

'I don't like to make a fuss,' said Killian.

Raven shook his head and laughed.

'What?' asked Killian.

'I can't believe I just lectured you on keeping secrets.' He looked at Killian and grinned.

Killian laughed and turned to look back out over the city. They sat together enjoying the silence as the clouds raced across the starry sky and obscured the silvery moon. Killian's eyes followed the dark slate rooftops. It was as if the whole of Vida had opened before him and revealed another world for him to explore. He wanted it all, wanted to run through that world, feel the wind on his face, see things he'd never seen before. It would take time, dedication and practice. His body was useless and drained, yet a determination welled up inside him. He smiled to himself. Perhaps the Gramarye wouldn't kill him after all. Maybe cutting his hand on it was the best thing he'd ever done. Only time would tell.

Raven got to his feet and fanned his wings out. They flapped like the sails on a ship. 'Ready to go back?' he asked.

Killian nodded and stood. The last thing he remembered was the creeping darkness invading his vision as he fell forward.

CHAPTER
SEVENTY-EIGHT

ORANGE FADED INTO RED AS THE FIRE DIED down to glowing embers. The sky above had shifted to a deep shade of blue signalling the oncoming dawn. Lily dusted her hands off and got to her feet. It was time to wake Killian for the last watch. Since leaving Scherben, she'd allowed him on watch – it was only fair to the rest of her crew – but this was the first time she would have to wake him herself.

She stood over him. He looked so peaceful. His mouth was slightly open, his hair a messy tangle and his breathing deep and heavy. An eerie blue glow caught her attention as he shifted in his sleep, and she crouched down. Had she done the right thing? Should she have just left him to die? But what if Raven was right? What he'd said had made sense: the soul was tied to the Gramarye and had been for years. Killian's death, more than likely, wouldn't fix anything. A warm red glow cast itself over his skin, emphasising his roguishly rugged features. He was handsome, and truth be told, she found him painfully attractive. But it wasn't just skin-deep with him like it had been with so many others. Her lip curled as she briefly mused over Raphael d'Roué.

With Killian, she unlocked another part of herself, a part she kept hidden from everyone. She felt like she could truly be herself with him. She could let go of her pirate-queen persona and have fun, let him know her secrets and wants. The shimmering green-and-blue lights in the ocean, the stars from her cabin window, two or three bottles of good Venarian red – she could share them all with him and feel so comfortable. Be herself without judgement. Was she selfish for wanting to keep that part of her alive? He rolled over and grunted in his sleep.

But where did he fit into her life? She was a pirate queen; she had a ship, a crew and a duty to them. Killian did not fit into that life with her. He couldn't. It was impossible. A pirate queen sailing with her lover was no pirate queen. He made her weak, irrational and selfish. And what if she let him into her life, truly and completely, and then lost him? She'd seen what that could do to someone. After she'd slaughtered her own mother in childbirth, her father had to bring her up alone. He had tried to live with his beloved wife's murderer for five long years until he couldn't take it anymore.

Heat exploded in her chest. It wouldn't do. Being with Killian couldn't work; she'd already made too many mistakes because of him. She'd keep him around until the mess with the Gramarye was fixed, then erase him from her life. Keeping him at arm's length until then was the best way forward. That way she couldn't get hurt or make any more mistakes.

With her resolve hardened, she grabbed his shoulder and roughly shook him awake.

'Your watch,' she said when he looked at her with bleary eyes.

'Surprised you bothered to wake me,' he said, his voice gruff from sleep.

'And why is that?' said Lily, turning away from him to pick up her blanket.

'I didn't think I was good enough for a watch.'

'Well, you are now.'

He stood as she turned around, and they glared at each other in the dim morning light, like a pair of cats sizing one another up. Hot curls of breath peeled away from them, dissolving into the air. A thin layer of morning fog swirled at their feet.

'I was fine before Scherben.'

Lily's heart ached when she saw the sadness in his eyes, but she bit back the urge to be kind. 'I wasn't prepared to risk everyone so that you might feel better about yourself.'

'You mean you didn't trust me.'

'No, I didn't, and is there any reason as to why I should? You,' she seethed, pointing her finger at him, 'are the biggest calamity going. We wasted days with those mages waiting for you to wake up. If not for you, I'd be on the *Tempest* and away by now.'

Killian folded his arms. 'You could have dragged me back to the ship.' His voice was low and controlled.

'Number one, Arow could have helped, and number two, I would not allow my crew to see me carrying you. That would show weakness in me and my leadership. Show your crew you care too much and you lose all respect.' She dug her heel into the dirt as if to emphasise the point. 'I was lucky they didn't turn on me for looking after you last time.'

'I didn't ask you to look after me,' he whispered.

'You certainly weren't capable of looking after yourself,' she retorted, a cruel sneer perfectly arranged on her face. 'That much was obvious. Left alone, you'd have bled to death.'

Killian dropped his arms to his sides but remained silent.

Lily scowled at him. She wanted to stop, she wanted to go to him. Guilt rippled through her, but she tightened her muscles and fought it off. 'How're the nightmares?' she asked with a grin.

Killian's eyes widened as if he'd been punched in the stomach. 'I don't have them anymore.'

'Well done, Killian, you can sleep without help. What an achievement that must be for you.'

He sighed and shook his head. 'You should have left me in the fucking tomb.'

The blue light of the orm glimmered on his skin. 'With that?' she growled, closing the distance between them in an instant and slapping his arm. 'The whole reason we came out here.'

He grabbed her forearm and held her steady. 'Why is that so important to you?'

'It is of importance to the world, and therefore it is important to me.' She made no effort to break his grip. 'If something happens to you and that is lost, who knows what will happen.'

'Nothing is going to happen to me,' said Killian, narrowing his eyes.

Lily slipped from his grip and laughed. 'Of course, Killian,' she said, 'you'd do well to remember which one of us saved the other. I'm beginning to forget how many times I've had to drag you to safety. You really are quite pathetic.'

He looked so wounded, like he'd been slapped across the face for no reason.

'If that's how you feel about me, you black-hearted bitch,' he said as he swiped the blanket from her arms, 'then I'm obviously not good enough for the watch.'

Lily felt the smile fade from her lips as he stalked away and flopped to the ground by the fire. He shuffled about under the blanket, then fell still. She sighed and sat down, drawing her legs to her chest. Warm tears flooded her eyes. She tried to keep them back, but one blink sent them cascading down her face. Misery racked her very core, but it was done. She'd finally severed her ties with him. At least she hadn't had to play the Ren's-death-was-your-fault card, but she'd been willing to. Anything to snuff out the flicker of a relationship that was threatening to tear her life apart. She would not end up like her father, choked and swinging, stinking and dead. Pathetic and weak, all for love. It was disgusting. She was a pirate queen; she cared for her crew and, most of all, herself. No one else fit into that equation. And yet, despite these glaring truths, she wept bitterly until the mists faded.

CHAPTER SEVENTY-NINE

SASHA WAS STANDING ALONE ON THE PORCH WITH her fingers curled around a steaming mug of coffee. She took a sip, and it wasn't too bad for a cup she'd made herself. It would never be as good as Delphina's, but it was almost a close second. The pale lazy sun was rising and casting the world in a watery yellow light. These quiet moments, with nature and the morning light, were what she'd come to cherish. A warm bitter drink while wrapped in loneliness as the early birds chattered to one another in the bushes always soothed her after a night of turbulent sleep.

Every night in every dream, the man – her victim – came to her. He'd smile and tell her about his wife and child in great detail. Sasha knew what they did with their free time and how they celebrated their birthdays. His son was learning how to handle the farm himself. He told her his hopes and dreams for the future, of his eventual retirement, of his grandchildren playing in the fields and tending to his livestock. He'd smile, and then he'd scream. It was a horrific sound, and it seeped deep into her skin, filling her with unimaginable agony. Blue light poured from her. It flashed white, blinding her. The screaming grew louder as the man drew closer. He was in her. He was living in her every pore and filling her with his pain and misery. Her pain and misery.

Clattering jackdaws swooped low over the farmhouse in a rustle of feathers. She swallowed the remains of her coffee and set the mug down. The skin on her arm was so pure and fresh, it was hard to believe it had once housed a screaming tormented soul. Next time she'd ask Theo to leave a scar. Those souls deserved to leave their mark on her forever. She idly traced her finger up and down where that poor man had once been.

It wasn't right. Murder was not right. But neither were the outdated laws of Vermor, and with the Gramarye whole, she could help bring about a change. She chewed the inside of her cheek. Did that make her kills justified?

Something in the distance caught her eye. A slender human shape was tottering down the drive. She put her hand up to keep the sun from her eyes and squinted. The person was swaying and seemed to be in pain as they staggered this way and that. They lurched to the left and collapsed in a heap in the mud. Without a second thought, Sasha vaulted over the porch rail and raced up the dirt track, her cloak flapping behind her.

The wind whistled through her hair, and foggy clouds of dust kicked up from the muddy track as she ran. Someone needed her help, and she would give it. As she drew closer, the person came into focus. Pain twisted in her stomach. It was Kurt.

'Kurt,' she panted as her heart hammered in her ears.

He lay face up on the ground, his eyes closed and his chest rising and falling rapidly. Blood smeared his face and trickled into the mud, turning it a dark treacle-like colour. His clothing was ripped and torn. Maroon splatters covered his brown trousers. Sasha crouched down and lifted his ragged shirt to reveal a deep stab wound to his gut. She popped the remaining buttons and pushed the rest of his shirt away from his body. A tightness coiled around her throat, and she staggered back. A huge pink scar spread across his chest and reached down to his stomach. It looked like a complex tangle of tree branches, all clawed and vicious and scratching at his skin for eternity. It was old – she could tell by how much it had healed – but it was a shock to see. She knew exactly what had caused it.

'Now you know why,' Kurt rasped.

His cold icy eyes were open and staring at Sasha. The white of his left eye was filled with red. He blinked, and a bead of blood oozed out and down his cheek.

She whipped her cloak off and pressed it into the deep gash in his gut. 'What happened to you?'

'Cleansers got me. They're following me. I know it.' He blinked, and tears joined the blood. He grunted and turned his forearm over. A shimmering blue light pulsed within his arm. 'I got it. I did it. Then I messed up. They're coming for me. I'm going to die.'

'No, you're not,' said Sasha. She grabbed his hand and pressed it on top of her cloak. 'Hold this and wait for me.'

'What're you . . . ?'

Sasha didn't respond. She rolled her shoulders and strode out beyond the boundary of the farmhouse. Two shadowy figures loomed part way down the winding path to the right. They moved with a swift and purposeful step. Arrogance. A spike of pain tore through her own scar on her ribs. Varo's brother dangled before her, all the life choked from his body. All he ever did was heal and help. Kurt lay prone in the dirt, covered in blood and clinging to life. Theo would save him – she knew he would – but at what cost to his own life?

The figures drew closer. One was a man, the other a woman. Dark metal pistols swung from their hips. Death. The man had a sword strapped to his back, and the woman had two long, thin daggers stuffed in her belt and a crossbow slung over her shoulder. Sasha's hand trembled, but not from the Fear. She sucked in a deep breath. Lightning flickered across her hands and sank into her skin. It rippled through her body. It felt incredible, powerful, sensual, like a lover's kiss.

'Good morning, miss,' said the woman as she approached. There were several gold chains around her neck, and her hands were adorned with jewelled rings that glinted in the morning sun. She was a successful cleanser and clearly wanted everyone to know about it.

'Morning,' said Sasha.

'Have you seen a man scamper by recently?' she asked. She was young, perhaps in her early twenties. Too young to be covered in so much blood.

Sasha shook her head and clenched her fist behind her back. 'Why?'

'No reason,' said the man. He was older, possibly in his forties. An obscene medallion swung like a pendulum over his chest.

The woman spat on the ground and hissed through her teeth. 'I can't believe we've lost him. No body, no cash.'

'What did he do?' Sasha asked. Lightning flickered over her shaking fist.

'He's just a filthy mage,' said the woman, turning back to Sasha. 'We saw him light a fire in the woods last night, and we've been tracking him since. We managed to get a few stabs in, but he somehow squirmed away. I prefer to stab them – that way you get to see the light go out in their eyes. I suppose in this case I should have used the crossbow. I won't make that mistake again.' She turned and surveyed the rolling countryside. 'He can't be far. But don't you worry, miss, we'll keep you safe.'

Sasha set her dark-tinted goggles over her eyes. These people weren't innocent like the poor man in Millenderry. They were vile, hateful things, grotesque creatures who murdered for pleasure and gold. Sickening. 'I don't need you to keep me safe,' she growled. The voice didn't feel or sound like her own. It was the voice of her rage and of all the dead mages who hung around this woman's neck.

The woman spun back around, her brown eyes wide. She reached for her dagger, but it was too late. Sasha hurled a web of white lightning into her chest. The woman barely had time to scream as she fell back. The man managed to tug his pistol from its holster, took aim and fired. Sasha darted to the side and pulled her element into her body; she drew her hand back and launched a powerful volley of crackling energy directly into his face. An agonising shriek rang out, followed by a rumbling thunderclap that echoed around the hills and through the valley. Then silence.

Lightning crawled over Sasha's body. She felt so alive, so energised, though she knew that when she let it go, it'd take part of her strength as payment. She closed her eyes and mused over what it would be like to pull lightning from the Otherside, the wild and magical Otherside. Never before had she been able to hold such magic or even entertain the idea, but with a few more souls and the Gramarye unlocked, it was possible. No more burnout ever again. And with power like that, the Fear would become a thing of the past. It would be glorious. All those hidden mages in Vermor would be able to come out and bask in their power. They wouldn't need to run from people like this ever again. The hunters would become hunted.

A thick blood-coated rasp and a guttural breath pulled Sasha back to the present. Her eyes snapped open, and the stench of burnt meat engulfed her. It smelt just like her brother.

The two cleansers lay at the side of the road, their bodies smoking, and yet, somehow, their chests were still rising and falling. The man's face was almost completely gone. His eyes had melted away, and his nose had been burned to a cinder. His mouth gaped open, drawing in quick shallow breaths in a futile attempt to keep him alive. For what reason, Sasha did not know. The woman stared up at Sasha, her eyes filled with tears and her face etched with shock. Her chest was charred, her coat and shirt burned away, and her gold chains had melted into her body to become a part of her.

'Why?' she gasped.

Sasha's shadow fell over the woman. 'Why? Because you're just a pair of filthy cleansers.'

She pulled her lightning back into her hands and turned both of their bodies into ash.

CHAPTER **EIGHTY**

It was early in the afternoon, and the sky was as dull and grey as Lily's mood. They'd long since passed by Morell, and despite Tom's desperate pleas, Blake flat out refused to return to the town to terrorise the residents with another smoke demon. Killian kept as far to the back as possible, which in Lily's opinion was the best place for him. Out of sight, out of mind. They hadn't spoken since the night in the woods, and it would be best for everyone if it stayed that way.

She kept a steady pace with her head down and a grimace on her face that refused to be moved on. Up ahead, a misty pine forest loomed. Once they were through that, they'd be back in Rinden and to her ship. She pulled in a lungful of chilly air. It tickled her throat and awakened her senses.

They'd spend one night in the harbour, then leave first thing in the morning. They'd be back on her island in a week, less if she was lucky. It was an excellent plan. She sighed.

What was she going to do with Killian? He couldn't stay on her island with them – not now, not ever. Somehow, she'd have to keep watch over him while she worked out what to do with the Gramarye situation. First, she'd have to track down the soul-sucking demon that stole it, then destroy them both. It sounded so easy in her head. Grab, smash, kill, done.

The dark forest opened its branches and welcomed her inside. Most of the light was smothered by the thick pines, and the scent of the damp vegetation filled the atmosphere. The ground was soft and spongy under layers upon layers of fallen needles. Lily wrapped her arms about her chest and picked up her pace.

She couldn't watch Killian, not all the time. One day she'd see something she didn't want to. Her stomach tightened at the thought of him with another woman. Quickly, she scolded herself for such feelings. She'd cut him off. He was free to do as he pleased; she shouldn't care about it. She didn't care about it.

She was a pirate queen – she cared about herself and her crew, that was all. Once they got back, she'd let him go. Raven could keep an eye on him – he was good at that sort of thing. That way she wouldn't have to see anything. Feel anything. Just focus on the task at hand.

How Killian was in touch with the Otherside was another conundrum that irked her. He, of all people, could hurt her. She wasn't sure if he knew he could. They hadn't discussed their fight in the tomb. It had become a strange unspoken thing. It was as if saying he could hurt her out loud would make it so. But she already knew it was so – she just couldn't bring herself to say it.

A soft thump came from behind her as Raven leapt to the forest floor. He sidled up next to her, matching her footsteps.

She glanced over her shoulder at the rest of the party, who were a good distance behind them thanks to her rapid pace.

'You're in a hurry.'

'I want to get back to my damn ship,' she said. She gritted her teeth and rubbed her forehead through her sweaty bandana. 'I've been away too long.'

'Understandable.'

Lily puffed and shook her head. 'Sorry, I didn't mean to snap.'

'That's fine,' said Raven, his tone as comforting as ever. He looked behind them. 'It seems you're not the only one in a black mood today.'

She grunted in response.

He placed a warm hand on her shoulder. 'Something you want to tell me?'

'No,' she said, brushing his hand off.

They remained side by side, walking in silence. The soft patter of rain filtered through the forest. The temperature dropped, and Lily pulled her coat tight to her body. For the most part, she remained dry, the thick canopy providing shelter. Raven swam into her peripheral vision. She needed to speak to someone, and Raven had always been that someone. She focused ahead, not daring to even flick the slightest glance in his direction.

'I ended it before it started. I don't care about anyone but my crew and myself,' she said. Her face tightened, and she banished the threatening tears. 'I'm a pirate queen. I have feelings for no one.'

'That's not true though, is it?' said Raven.

Lily choked on her words, unable to respond.

'Is it?' Raven pressed.

'Yes, it is.'

He groaned and shook his head. 'It's not.'

'I can't have feelings,' she said. 'I'm a pirate queen – my loyalty is to my crew. I cannot allow my mind to be clouded by feelings. Feelings equal weakness, I've seen it happen. I know it happens.'

'You're not your father.'

She chose to ignore his statement. 'What if I've doomed the world by saving him? I can't keep making mistakes.'

'Lily, please listen to yourself – you can't live like this.'

'I'll be fine,' she said blankly.

'Do you care about him?'

'I . . .' She sighed and remained silent.

'Answer me.'

'I give the orders around here. Remember your place, Raven.'

'Of course,' he said.

'Don't,' she whispered, 'please. I'm sorry.'

'I shouldn't have pressed you. I'm the one who should be sorry.'

'I do care about him,' she murmured. 'I feel it inside me when I'm with him, when I look at him. It's like part of me goes away, and I feel different. He makes me feel free. When I'm with him, I have no responsibility – it's just him and me. I've never felt this for anyone before, ever. I need to make it go away.'

'Why?'

'I have a crew to think of. I have a life that he doesn't fit into. I've already neglected my duties to the crew enough as it is because of him. It can't and won't happen again.'

'You're only serving to make yourself miserable. Think about what you're doing, what you're giving up.'

'It doesn't matter now,' she said. 'I ended it a few nights ago. Now I doubt we'll even be friends.'

'What did you do?' asked Raven, turning to look at her.

She shied away from his gaze. 'Let's just say I'm a black-hearted bitch and leave it at that.'

The rain eased off to a drizzle as Lily and her party stepped into Rinden. The briny smell of the sea wandered down all the streets. Her pulse quickened; she was almost back at her ship. This would be it. They'd sail back to Brackmouth, and more likely than not, Killian would leave – she certainly wouldn't have to push him. She couldn't blame him after the way she'd treated him. A cluster of seabirds on a nearby house chattered at her as if they agreed with her thoughts.

He would go, and she'd never see him again. Raven would keep an eye on him while she sorted out the Gramarye and demon problem. Everything would be fine.

Her boots clipped on the dark grey cobbles of Rinden. She didn't want to be there, not so soon. She wished they were still with the bandits or in Scherben; she'd even take Morell over this. If she had a little more time with him, maybe she'd be able to explain herself in a rational way. He'd understand her if she explained. Maybe they could even be friends.

She screwed up her fists and upped her pace. It was too late for that now; what was done was done. She dodged in and out of the locals, determined to reach the docks and retire to her comforting cabin as soon as possible. The ocean waves grew louder and the gulls more frantic; she'd arrived at the docks.

She scanned the harbour. Vessels great and small creaked and strained as they bobbed on the gentle currents. Sails flapped in the weak winds. Taut ropes refused to flex an inch. Fishermen ambled back and forth, stray cats stalking their shadows. The stench of salt and sea creatures filled the air. A crab scuttled to the edge of the harbour and dropped back into the sea.

Something was wrong.

She squinted and took another look. The *Tempest* – she couldn't see it. It wasn't where she'd left it. Her heart lurched into her throat, and sickness twisted in her stomach. Fire blasted her hollow chest. She looked up and down for a dock-worker, anyone would do. Surely it must have been moved. *There must be a reasonable explanation.*

She spied a short man with an armful of documents pacing along the quay. She dashed over to him, grabbing him roughly by the shoulder and spinning him around.

'Excuse me, miss,' he gasped in shock.

'There was a ship, over there, the *Tempest*.' She pointed to the last place she'd seen her beloved vessel. 'Where is it?'

'I'm not at liberty to give out such information. Were you acquainted with the ship in some way?'

'Yes,' said Lily, fighting to keep the politeness in her tone. 'I'm its captain.'

The man's pupils dilated, and a layer of sweat formed on his top lip. 'The captain, you say,' he said, flicking through his papers.

'Yes. Lily Rothbone.'

'I'm sorry, there must have been an administration error.'

'What do you mean?' She tensed her fists, ready to strike the cap from his head.

'I have it here that one Morton Roberts is the captain of the *Tempest*. And it left two days ago.'

'What?' Lily held her hand out, and the man passed her a paper. She scanned it. It did indeed say Morton Roberts was the captain. This wasn't real. It was fake, a forgery. 'How much did he pay you to do this?' she growled.

'Nothing, never. I promise. Never.'

Lily wanted nothing more than to snap his scrawny neck, but that wouldn't get her anywhere. Not everything could be resolved with force alone. 'Okay,' she said.

She paced away from him to the edge of the quay and slumped down, dangling her legs over the hungry water below. Numbness pulled at her. How could this have happened? The drizzle grew heavier, fatter, drenching her hair and making it hang around her face in thick tendrils. They'd gone, they'd left her. She'd given her life to those ungrateful bastards, and this was how they repaid her. Burning tears streamed down her face, mingling with the cool rain. She wasn't a pirate queen; she was nothing. Voices swam all around her, but she couldn't hear words. The utter disbelief of the situation had left her feeling drunk, but without any of the joy. Gradually, the voices glided away, leaving her alone with her misery.

A hand pressed on her back. It was warm. Someone had remained and was sitting on the quay with her. The hand moved across her back and onto her shoulder. With a little encouragement, she was pulled towards the person. She turned her head.

'Killian . . .' she whispered hoarsely, shifting her body around.

'Shh,' he breathed as he wrapped his arms around her.

She collapsed against his chest, sobbing. Her arms gripped him tight, and her body shook as she cried. She didn't care what any of the others thought of her. She'd lost her crew, her ship and her life. Everything was gone. Everything was meaningless. What was a pirate queen without a ship?

Not only that, but she'd lost Killian. How could he forgive her for the things she'd said? How could she forgive herself? She grabbed hold of his shoulders, tremors shooting through her body as all her emotions flooded from her. He'd never forgive her; he was gone too. She pressed her head against his chest. He was all she wanted, all she needed, but she'd ruined everything. With him, she could be free, she could finally be herself. It was all in tatters now.

'Here,' he said, peeling her off him.

She was too shocked and cold to feel anything. He took his coat off and helped her put it on. The arms were much too big and completely drowned her hands. But it was warm and smelt so delicious. It was hot rocks after a rainstorm. It was his scent.

'Better?' he said, rain already soaking his shirt.

'Thank you,' she managed to say through trembling lips.

'It's okay,' he said, getting to his feet. He held out his hand and pulled her up.

'Killian,' she murmured. 'I don't deserve this . . . You shouldn't.'

He put his hand under her chin and encouraged her to look at him. Despite the cold, the wind and the driving rain, he smiled. 'I know you don't,' he said, 'but I can't stand to see you cry.'

At this, fresh tears ran down Lily's cheeks, and she threw her arms around him, burying her face into his chest. 'I'm sorry, Killian,' she whispered, 'so sorry.'

He held her tight, stooping to rest his chin on her shoulder. She clung to him, not wanting to let go, ever.

'Come on,' he said, 'we should find somewhere to stay in town.'

Lily detached herself from him and turned to look out to the sea; the waves were dark, aggressive and choppy. She drew in a deep clarifying breath and reined her emotions back in. The tears stopped. The shaking subsided, and her muscles bunched up. She gritted her teeth as images of shattering

Morton's jaw to dust played in her mind's eye. She was *still* a pirate queen. That ship was hers, and she would get it back one way or another.

'I'll have to call in a favour to help fix this.'

'You have friends?'

Despite the situation, Lily couldn't help but smile. It was funny, and she did deserve it. 'There's someone in Venario who'll be at Bluefin Rock by now. He owes me.'

'Venario, eh? I've always wanted to go there. Looks like you're stuck with me for a little longer,' he added with a shrug.

'Were you going to leave?'

Killian chuckled. 'Would you have missed me?'

'No,' she replied. 'Would you have missed me?'

'No.'

LEARN MORE ABOUT THE AUTHOR

WWW.JODELANCEY.COM

ACKNOWLEDGEMENTS

The image of the writer, lonely and isolated in their tower of imagination, can be true to an extent, but for a book to really shine, it needs more than one person. I couldn't ask for a better crew to help me on my writing journey:

Lesley Jones, my wonderful editor. Thank you so much for helping me wrestle this beast of a book to the ground and lock it in the 1-2-3 pin. Your notes and comments were invaluable in helping me to shape the plot and my characters' stories.

Natalia Leigh, my fabulous editor. You helped polish my prose until it glittered just as much as the ruby Lily Rothbone keeps in her bedside drawer.

Thea Magerand, my incredible cover and character artist. Your art is stunning, it always blows me away. And you definitely made the right decision with regards to Raven's shirt.

Luke Harrison, for helping to fill my book with the magical cornelian glyphs.

Greg Rupel, for hammering this monster together and making it sparkle.

Chris Howker, for putting a logo in the foam. For being such a supporter of my work and letting me waffle on about pirates and stuff. I hope you enjoyed this Raphael-free book!

I want to give a special shout-out to:

Josie Sexton, not only has she decorated my walls with paintings of my characters, but she is also tattooing her own design, based on my books, onto my leg and ribs. That means she has to spend a lot of time in my company. So, thank you!

Liam Sellars, for creating me an amazing light-up 3D version of Brackmouth for my writing cave. It goes so well with your Cylus.

Agata Żebrowska, for the beautiful character commissions and the art you've created for my YouTube channel.

Also, Tess Serrano, Michela Bottin and Hana Oni. Your character commissions still decorate my writing cave and keep me going.

I would also like to thank the below swashbuckling heroes, for helping me get through all this:

Meg Rouncefield, you are strong and always cool! You're such a wonderful person; I love how freely I can talk to you. Your love and support mean the world to me. Never change.

Bibi Omar Zajtai, thanks so much for reading several drafts of this monster. Your thoughts and notes on it helped me so much. I really hope you like the finished version.

Rachel Willoughby, thanks a lot for trawling through a pretty naff draft of this and for pulling me up on various things. I hope you enjoy this version . . . now with real place names!

Dave May, for reading more drafts than any sane person should and for always being honest with me, even if it hurts.

Mum and Dad, for allowing me to be the sword-swinging, Spider-man-suited, Sonic-loving child I was.

Justine, for always being kind and gentle. You're the best sister I could have, and we are going to Cinque Terre!

Dan, you're not here, but you're always with me and inspiring me. I hope you're proud of your little sister.

Finally, I'd like to thank you, the reader. I cannot express how much it means to me to take another person on this journey with Killian, Lily and the crew, and now Sasha and Varo and the mages too. It's quite overwhelming for me. I hope you enjoyed this book and that you'll return for the next adventure.

JO DE-LANCEY

is a fantasy author from the UK. Even though she currently lives in a landlocked county, her Cornish blood always calls her back to the sea, so sailing away with Killian on his adventure was the most natural thing in the world for her.

She draws influences from many places, including books, movies, life experiences, her crazy dreams, and the early Final Fantasy games – IX is the best, fight her. Fun facts time: Captain Lily Rothbone's backstory came to her in a dream and Thomas Gainsborough's appeared to her during a gong meditation session in a disused mine. If you're intrigued, pop along to her website and ask. She'll happily tell you about the gongs.

In her free time, she likes reading, hiking, watching old Italian films, petting her bearded dragon like a Bond villain, spoiling her cat, exploring red wines and playing video games with her fiancé.

For more information, please visit: www.jodelancey.com

Sign up to her mailing list via her website for an exclusive art bonus. She sends out a newsletter on the last Sunday of the month, and this is where everything happens first: cover reveals, character art, blurb reveals, book previews and release dates. You also get a monthly picture of her cat, Billy, and a bunch of other fun stuff.

You can stay connected on Instagram at @jodelanceyauthor

If you would like to explore her magical world for yourself, follow her YouTube channel at @temperedsleep